BLACK MASK STUDIOS
PRESENTS

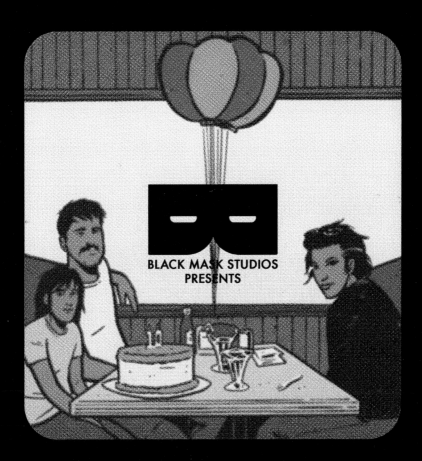

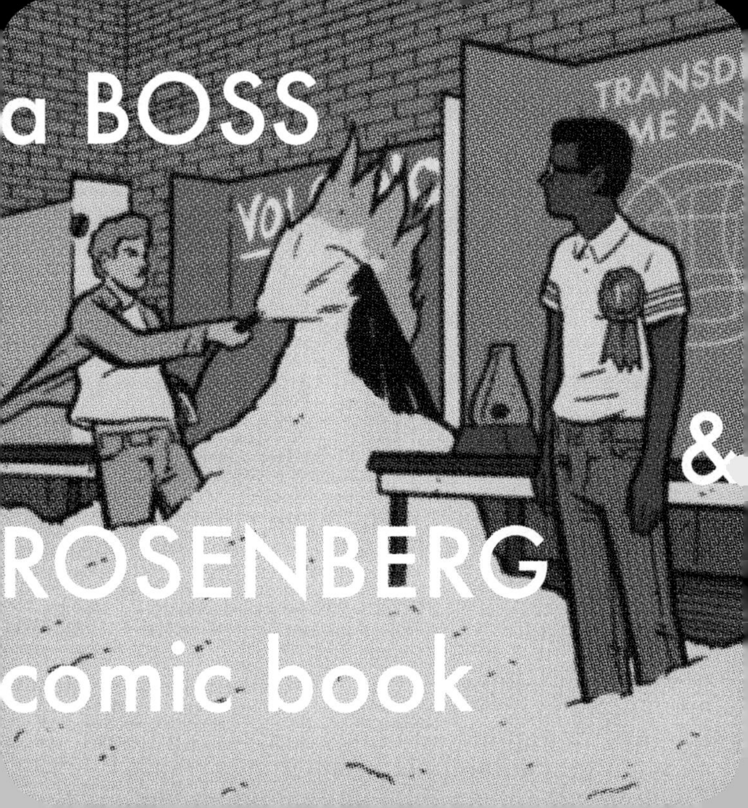
a BOSS
&
ROSENBERG
comic book

with

THOMAS
MAUER

4KIDS WALK INTO A BANK

Art/Design .... TYLER BOSS
Flatting .... CLARE DEZUTTI
Lettering .... THOMAS MAUER
Wallpaper Design .... COURTNEY MENARD
Writing .... MATTHEW ROSENBERG

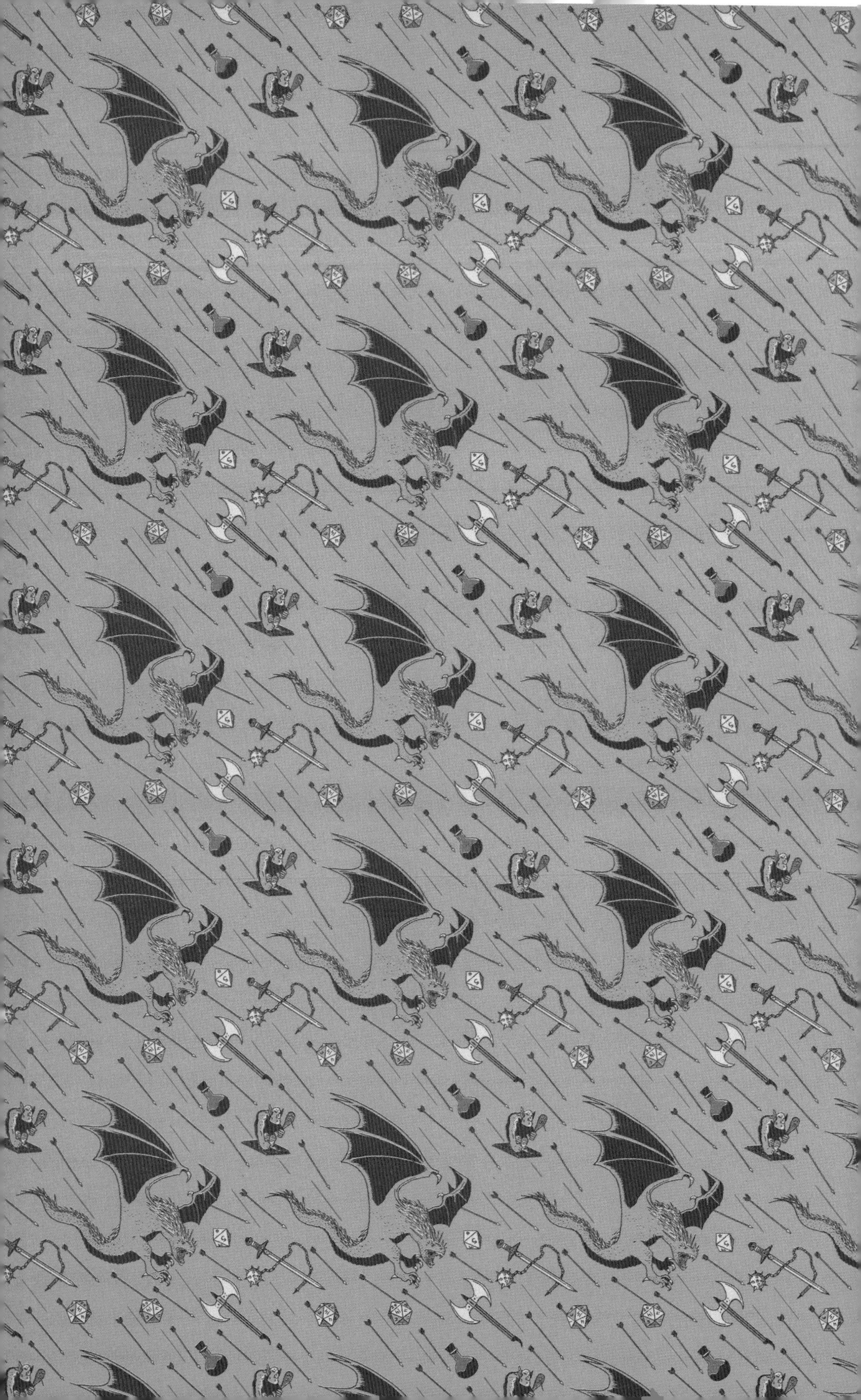

CHAPTER ONE

As far back as lunchtime
I always wanted to be a Gangster.

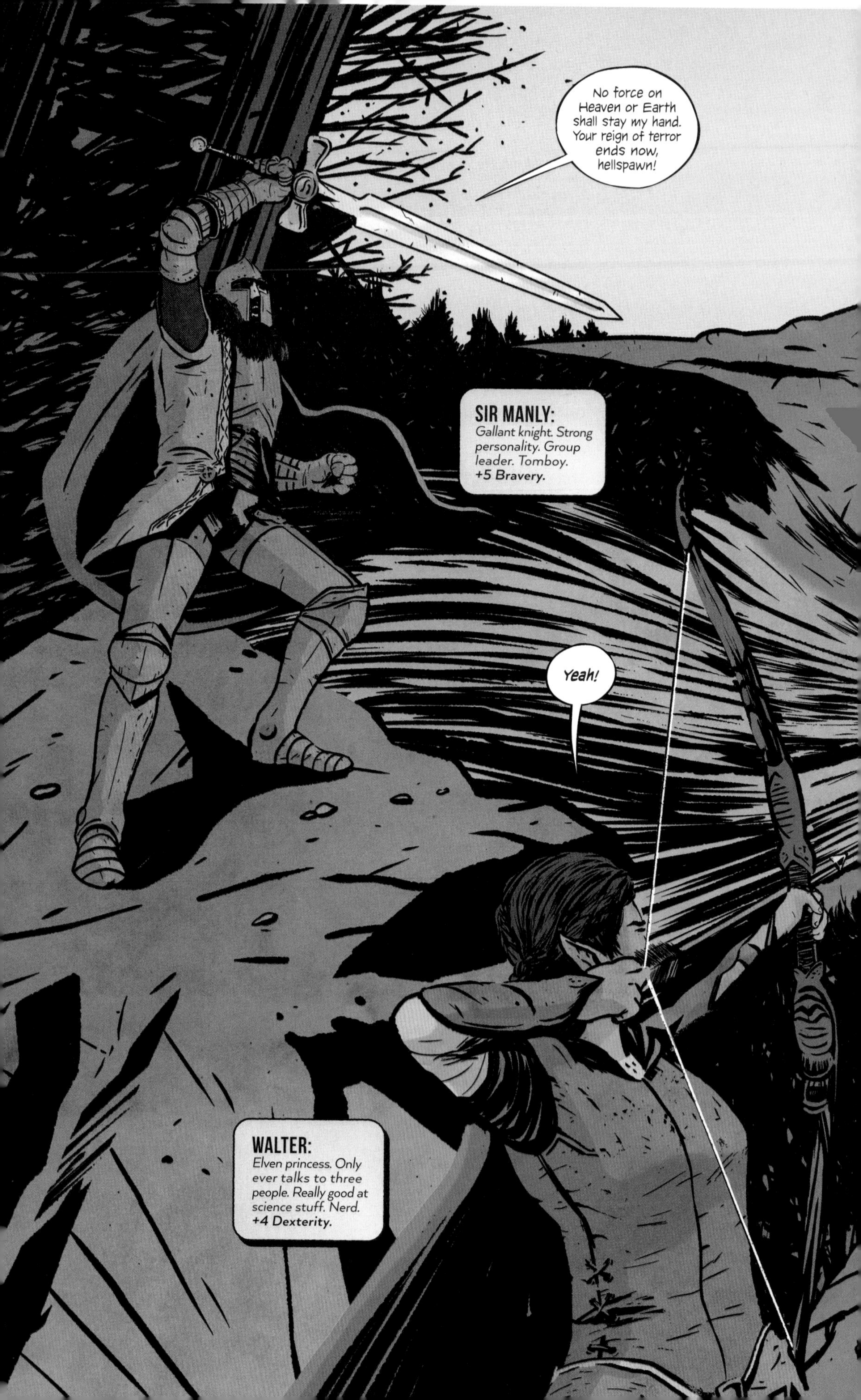
No force on Heaven or Earth shall stay my hand. Your reign of terror ends now, hellspawn!
SIR MANLY:
Gallant knight. Strong personality. Group leader. Tomboy.
+5 Bravery.
Yeah!
WALTER:
Elven princess. Only ever talks to three people. Really good at science stuff. Nerd.
+4 Dexterity.

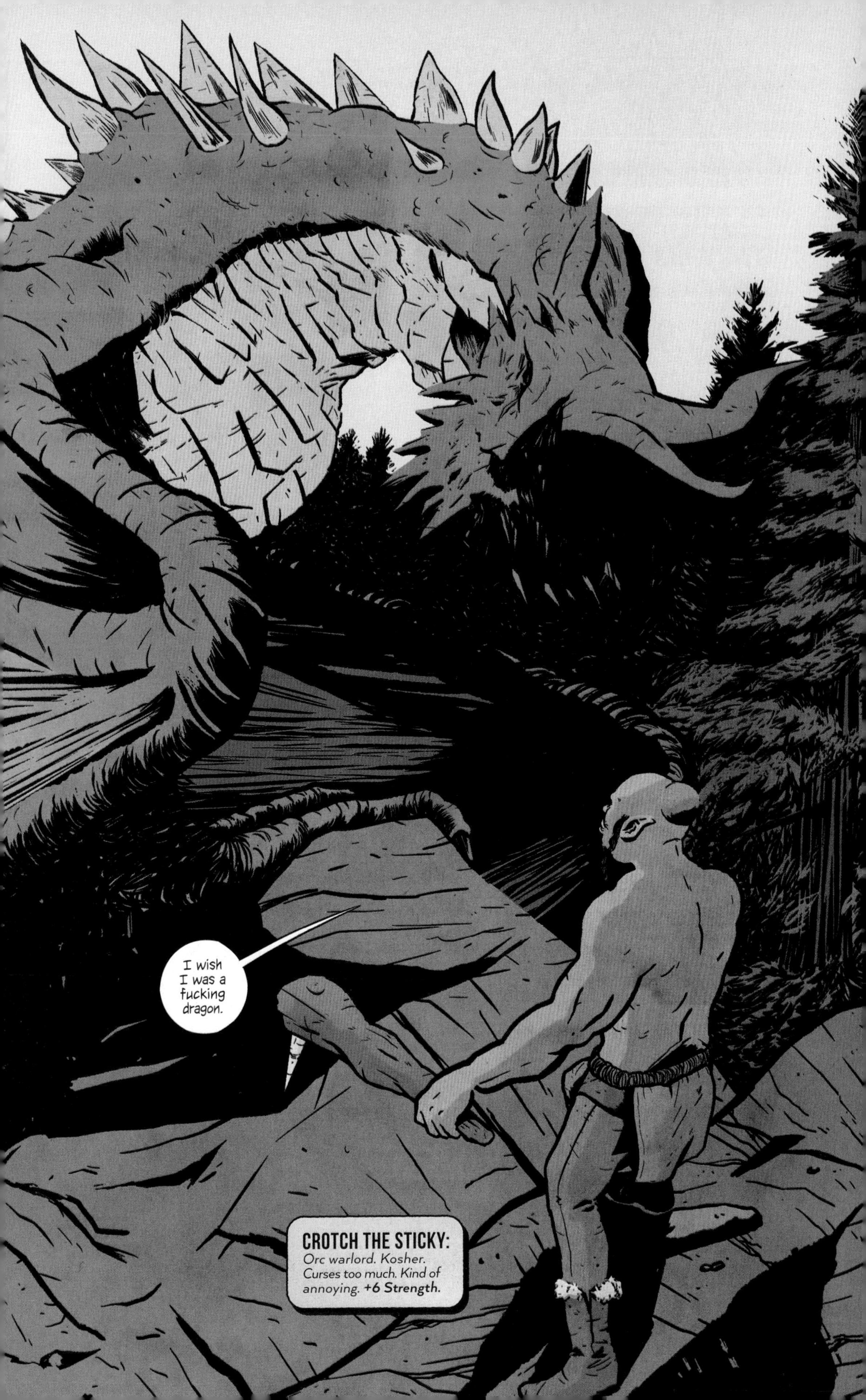
I wish I was a fucking dragon.
CROTCH THE STICKY:
Orc warlord. Kosher. Curses too much. Kind of annoying. +6 Strength.

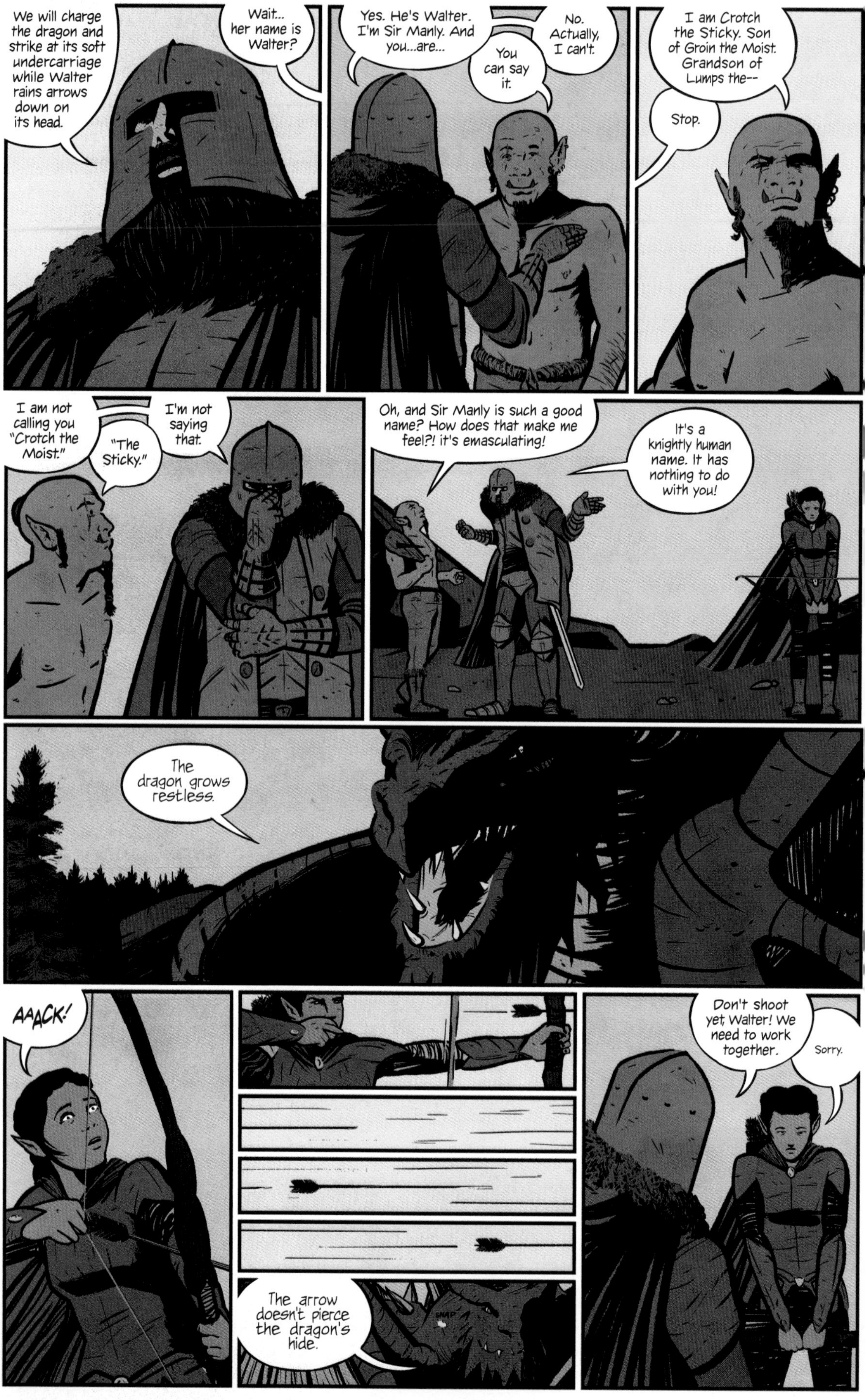
We will charge the dragon and strike at its soft undercarriage while Walter rains arrows down on its head.
Wait... her name is Walter?
Yes. He's Walter. I'm Sir Manly. And you...are...
You can say it.
No. Actually, I can't.
I am Crotch the Sticky. Son of Groin the Moist. Grandson of Lumps the--
Stop.
I am not calling you "Crotch the Moist."
"The Sticky."
I'm not saying that.
Oh, and Sir Manly is such a good name? How does that make me feel!?! it's emasculating!
It's a knightly human name. It has nothing to do with you!
The dragon grows restless.
AAACK!
The arrow doesn't pierce the dragon's hide.
Don't shoot yet, Walter! We need to work together.
Sorry.

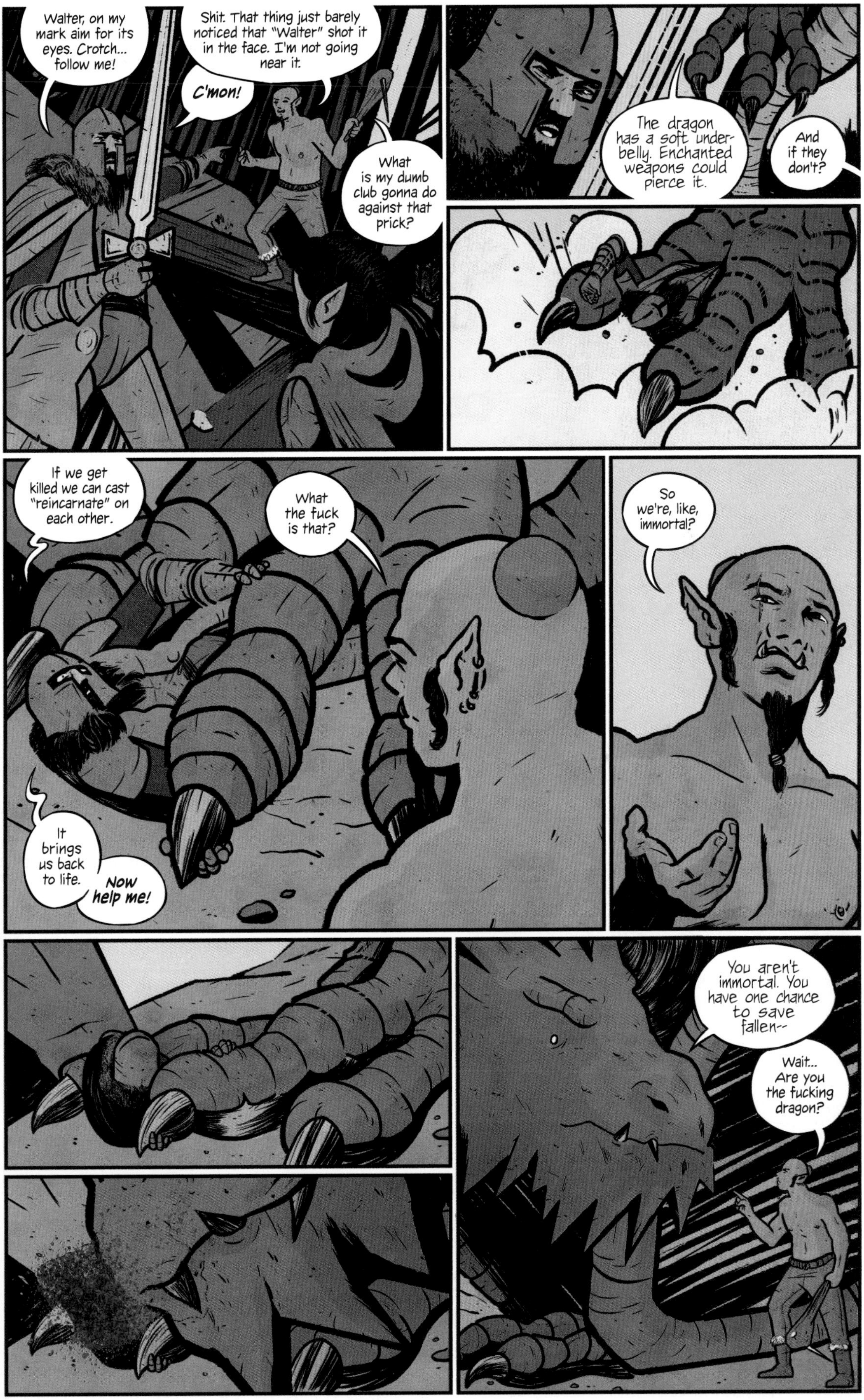
Walter, on my mark aim for its eyes. Crotch... follow me!
Shit. That thing just barely noticed that "Walter" shot it in the face. I'm not going near it.
C'mon!
What is my dumb club gonna do against that prick?
The dragon has a soft underbelly. Enchanted weapons could pierce it.
And if they don't?
If we get killed we can cast "reincarnate" on each other.
What the fuck is that?
It brings us back to life.
Now help me!
So we're, like, immortal?
You aren't immortal. You have one chance to save fallen--
Wait... Are you the fucking dragon?

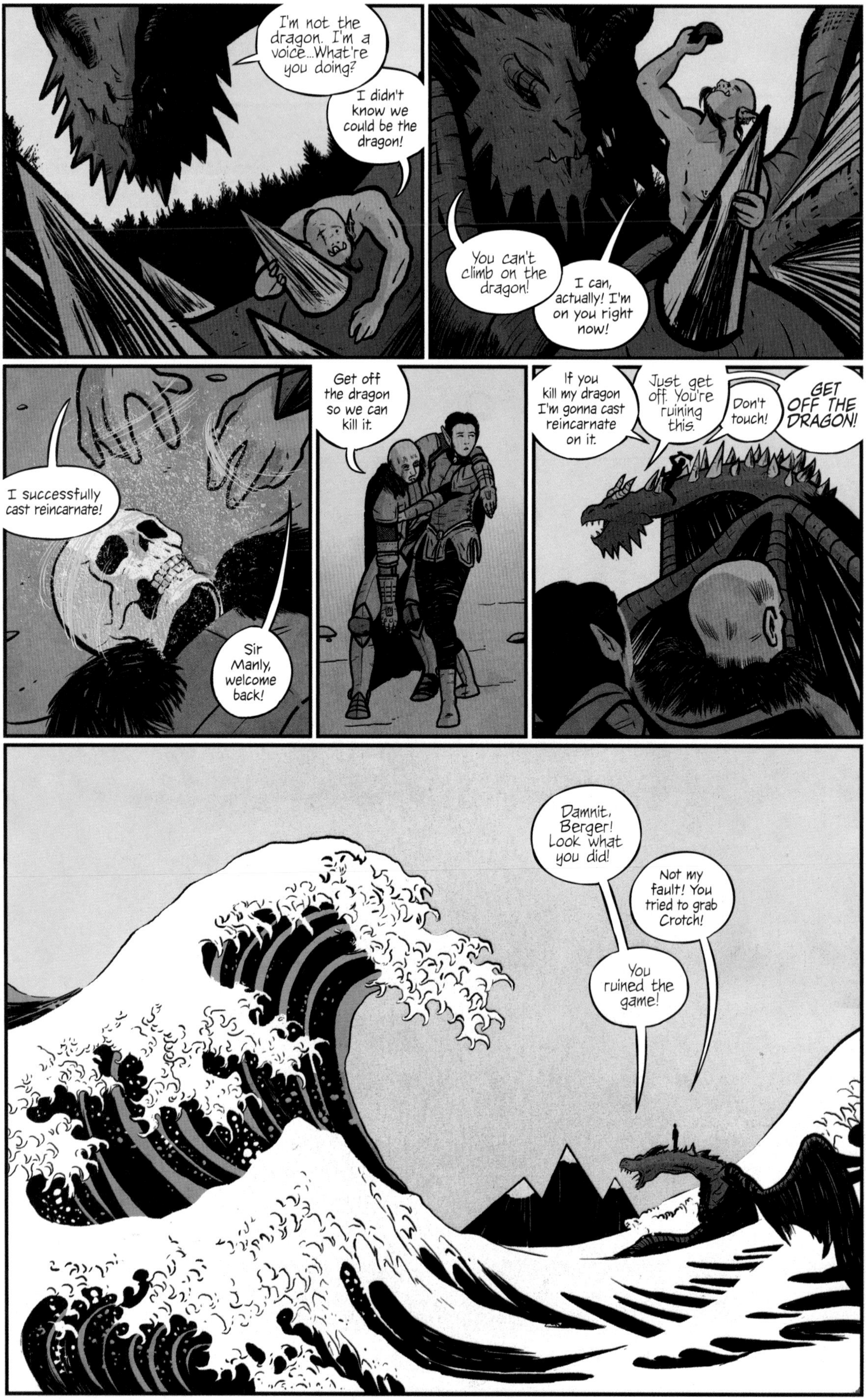

I'm not the dragon. I'm a voice...What're you doing?
I didn't know we could be the dragon!
You can't climb on the dragon!
I can, actually! I'm on you right now!
I successfully cast reincarnate!
Sir Manly, welcome back!
Get off the dragon so we can kill it.
If you kill my dragon I'm gonna cast reincarnate on it.
Just get off. You're ruining this.
Don't touch!
GET OFF THE DRAGON!
Damnit, Berger! Look what you did!
Not my fault! You tried to grab Crotch!
You ruined the game!

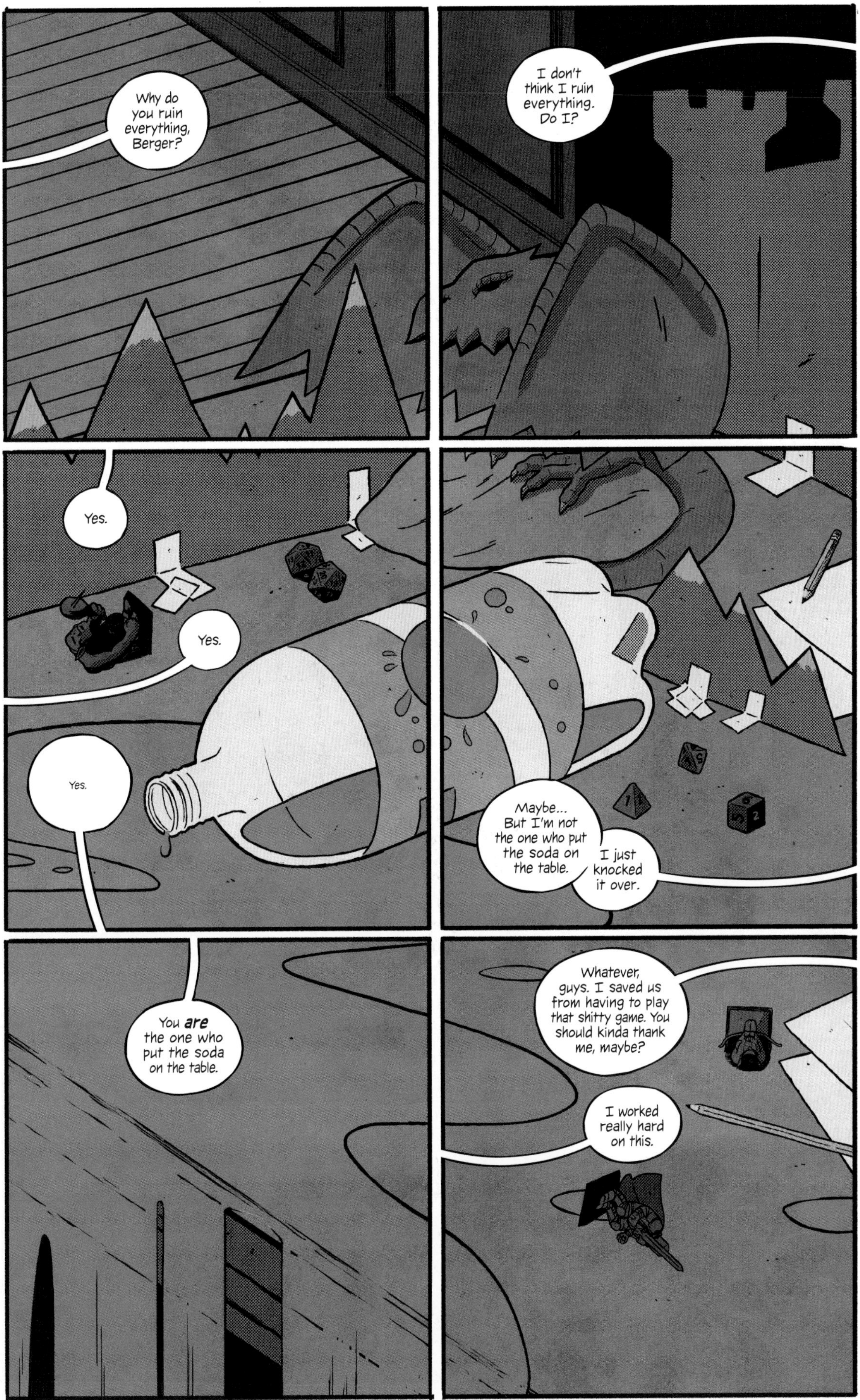
Why do you ruin everything, Berger?
I don't think I ruin everything. Do I?
Yes.
Yes.
Yes.
Maybe... But I'm not the one who put the soda on the table.
I just knocked it over.
You **are** the one who put the soda on the table.
Whatever, guys. I saved us from having to play that shitty game. You should kinda thank me, maybe?
I worked really hard on this.

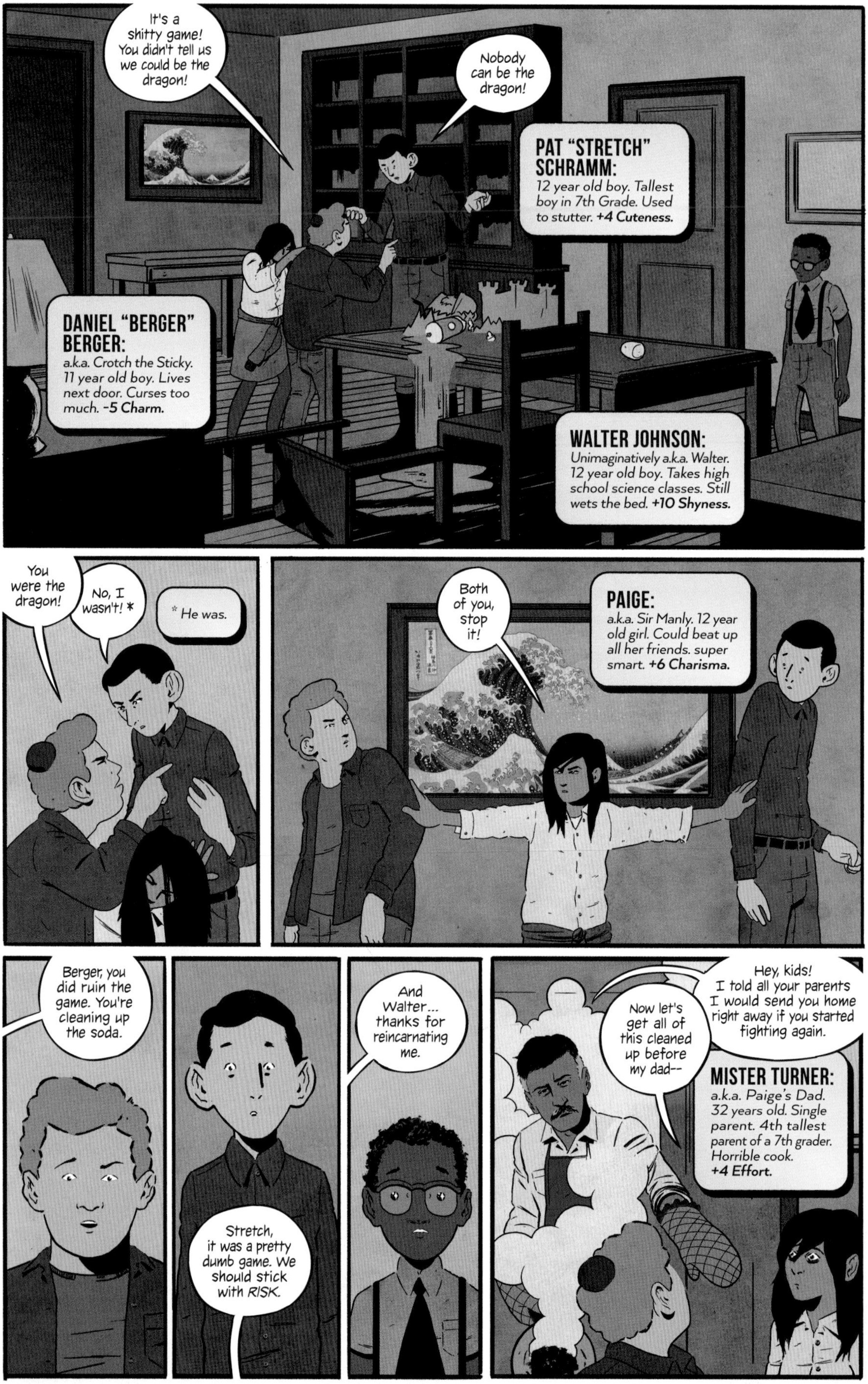
It's a shitty game! You didn't tell us we could be the dragon!
Nobody can be the dragon!
PAT "STRETCH" SCHRAMM: 12 year old boy. Tallest boy in 7th Grade. Used to stutter. +4 Cuteness.
DANIEL "BERGER" BERGER: a.k.a. Crotch the Sticky. 11 year old boy. Lives next door. Curses too much. -5 Charm.
WALTER JOHNSON: Unimaginatively a.k.a. Walter. 12 year old boy. Takes high school science classes. Still wets the bed. +10 Shyness.
You were the dragon!
No, I wasn't! *
* He was.
Both of you, stop it!
PAIGE: a.k.a. Sir Manly. 12 year old girl. Could beat up all her friends. super smart. +6 Charisma.
Berger, you did ruin the game. You're cleaning up the soda.
Stretch, it was a pretty dumb game. We should stick with RISK.
And Walter... thanks for reincarnating me.
Now let's get all of this cleaned up before my dad--
Hey, kids! I told all your parents I would send you home right away if you started fighting again.
MISTER TURNER: a.k.a. Paige's Dad. 32 years old. Single parent. 4th tallest parent of a 7th grader. Horrible cook. +4 Effort.

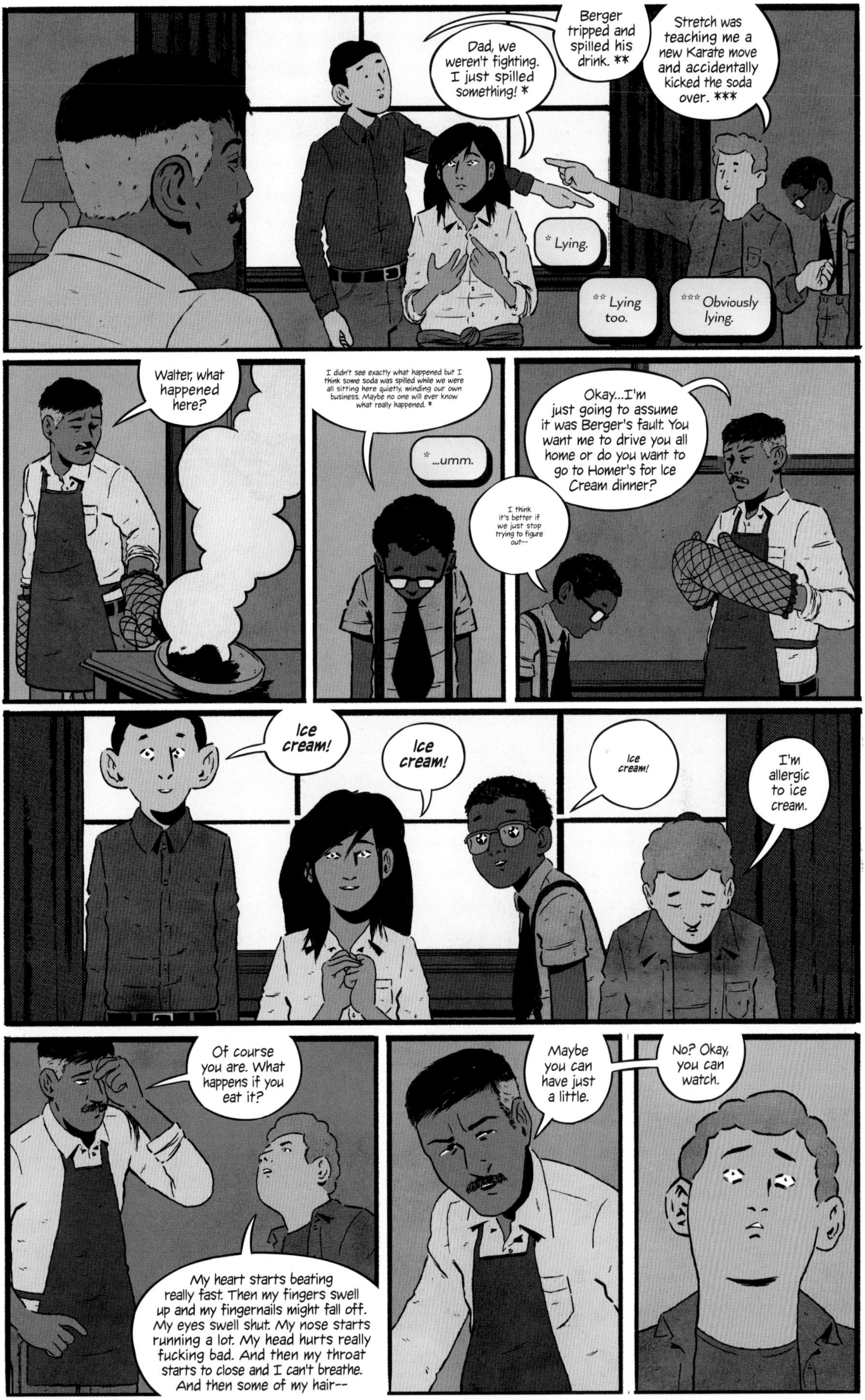
Dad, we weren't fighting. I just spilled something! *
Berger tripped and spilled his drink. **
Stretch was teaching me a new Karate move and accidentally kicked the soda over. ***
* Lying.
** Lying too.
*** Obviously lying.
Walter, what happened here?
I didn't see exactly what happened but I think some soda was spilled while we were all sitting here quietly, minding our own business. Maybe no one will ever know what really happened. *
* ...umm.
Okay...I'm just going to assume it was Berger's fault. You want me to drive you all home or do you want to go to Homer's for Ice Cream dinner?
I think it's better if we just stop trying to figure out--
Ice cream!
Ice cream!
Ice cream!
I'm allergic to ice cream.
Of course you are. What happens if you eat it?
My heart starts beating really fast. Then my fingers swell up and my fingernails might fall off. My eyes swell shut. My nose starts running a lot. My head hurts really fucking bad. And then my throat starts to close and I can't breathe. And then some of my hair--
Maybe you can have just a little.
No? Okay, you can watch.

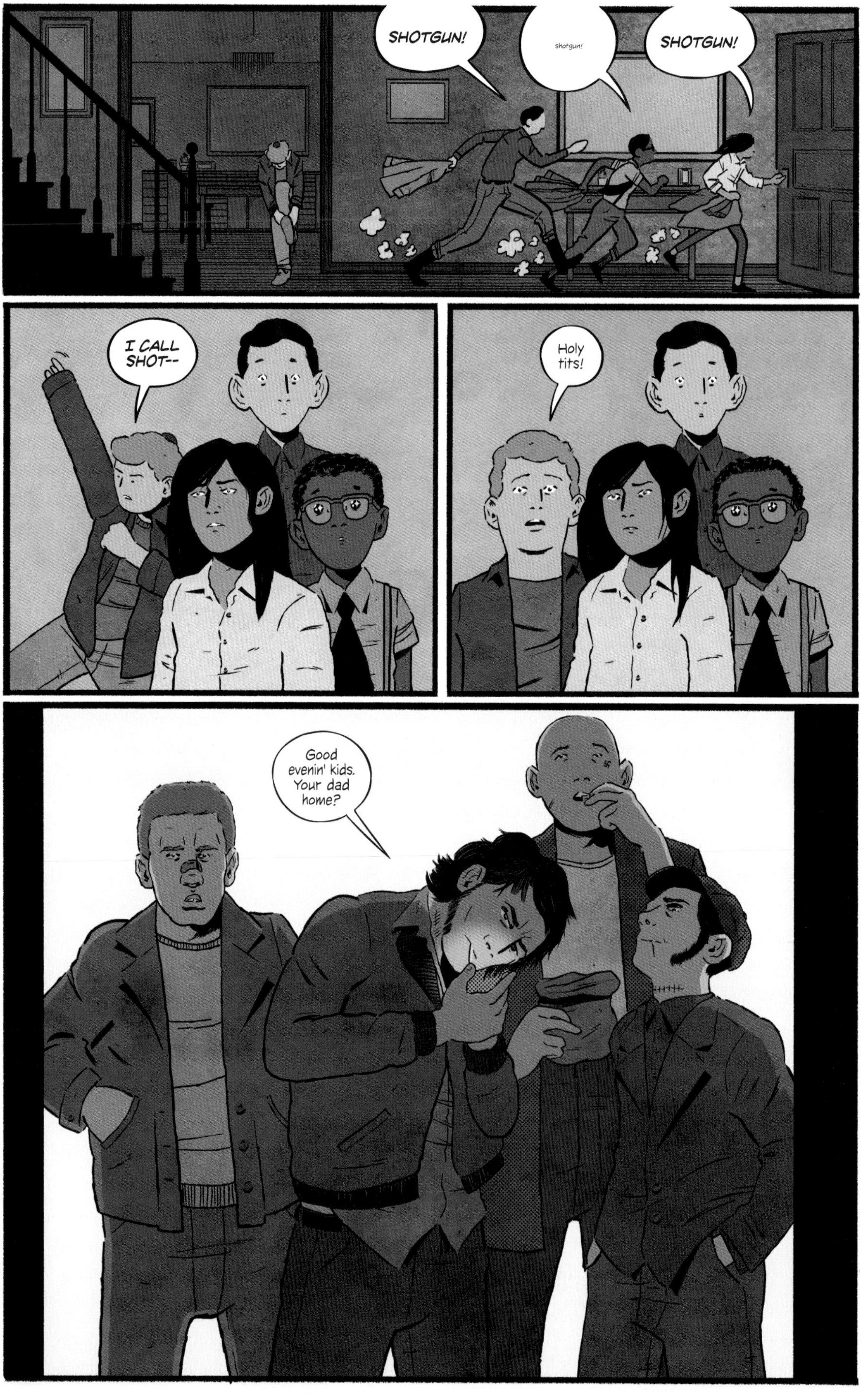
SHOTGUN!
shotgun!
SHOTGUN!
I CALL SHOT--
Holy tits!
Good evenin' kids. Your dad home?

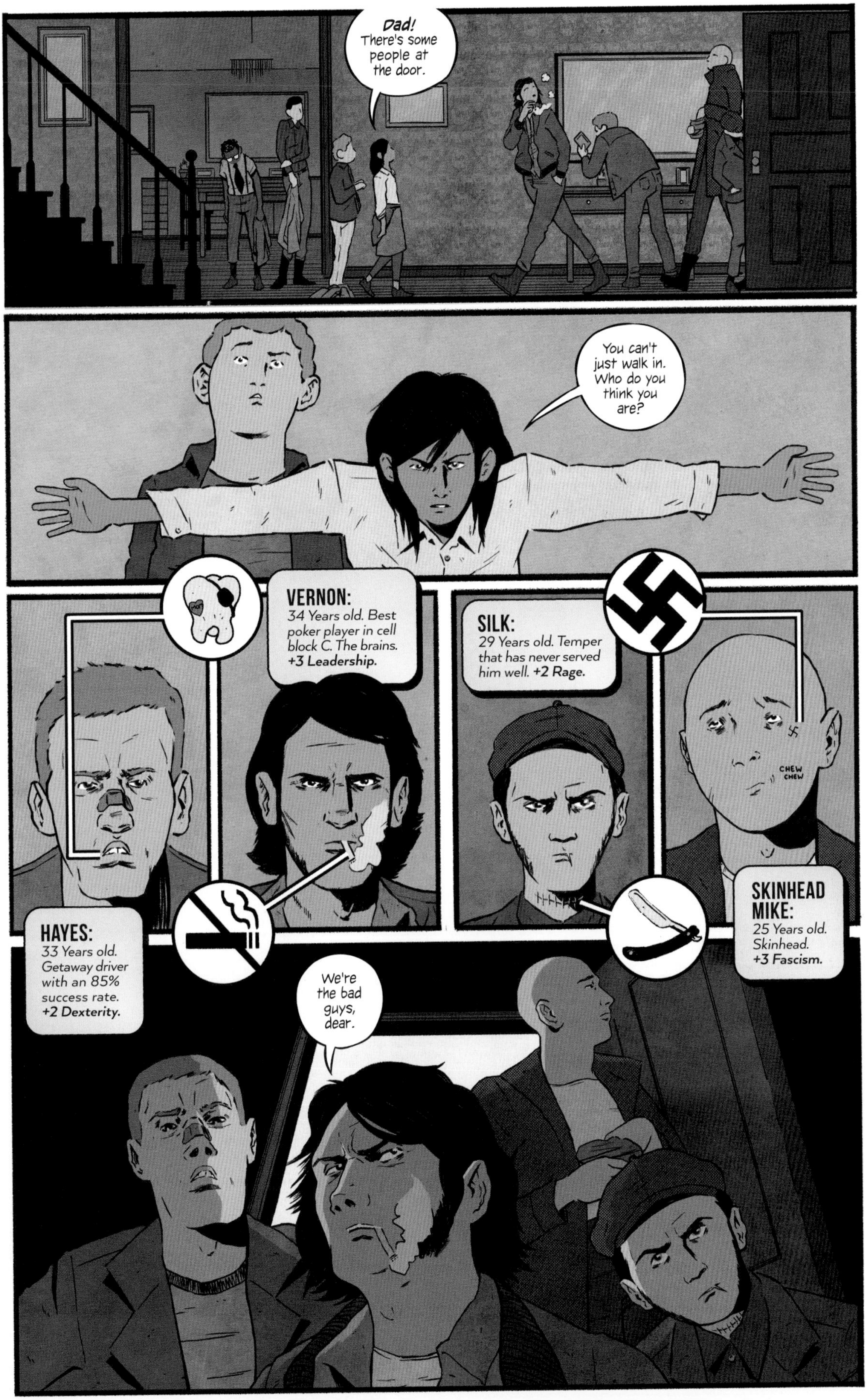
Dad! There's some people at the door.
You can't just walk in. Who do you think you are?
VERNON: 34 Years old. Best poker player in cell block C. The brains. +3 Leadership.
SILK: 29 Years old. Temper that has never served him well. +2 Rage.
CHEW CHEW
HAYES: 33 Years old. Getaway driver with an 85% success rate. +2 Dexterity.
SKINHEAD MIKE: 25 Years old. Skinhead. +3 Fascism.
We're the bad guys, dear.

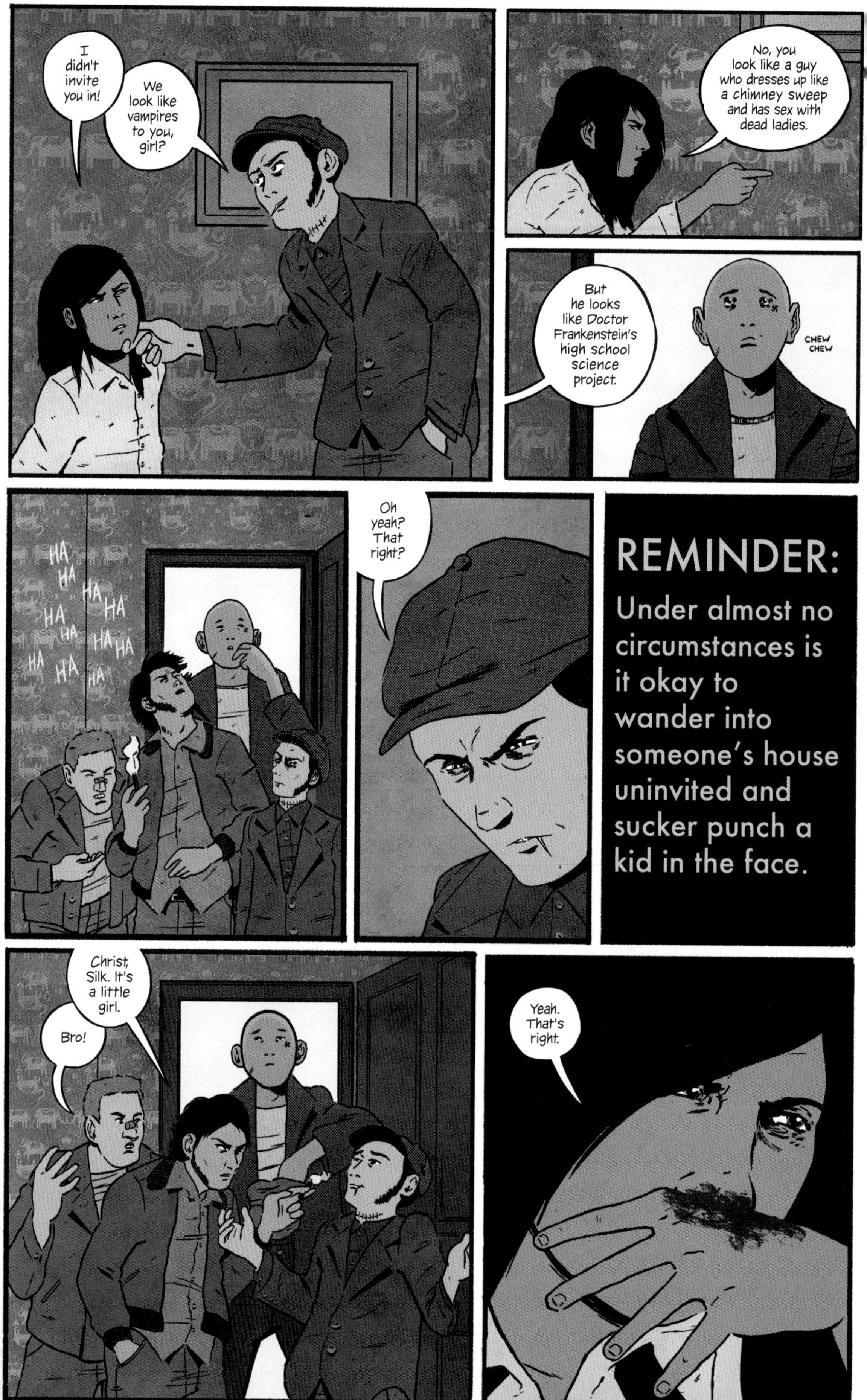

I didn't invite you in!
We look like vampires to you, girl?
No, you look like a guy who dresses up like a chimney sweep and has sex with dead ladies.
But he looks like Doctor Frankenstein's high school science project.
CHEW CHEW
HA HA HA HA HA HA HA HA HA HA HA HA
Oh yeah? That right?
REMINDER:
Under almost no circumstances is it okay to wander into someone's house uninvited and sucker punch a kid in the face.
Christ, Silk. It's a little girl.
Bro!
Yeah. That's right.

I'm sorry I did that. You shouldn't talk to strangers like that though.

Strangers shouldn't barge into my house.

Look Girly, I didn't come here--

Now, Berger.

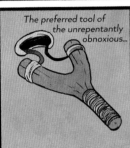

The preferred tool of the unrepentantly obnoxious...

...the son of Groin the Moist.

The eye of a grown-ass man who punches little girls.

GAH!

Goddamnit!

Goddamnit!

Alright kids, playtime's over.

Owww.

And that means you have to leave so we can have our ice cream.

Did you just shoot a fucking troll into my eye?

He's an Orc Warlord.

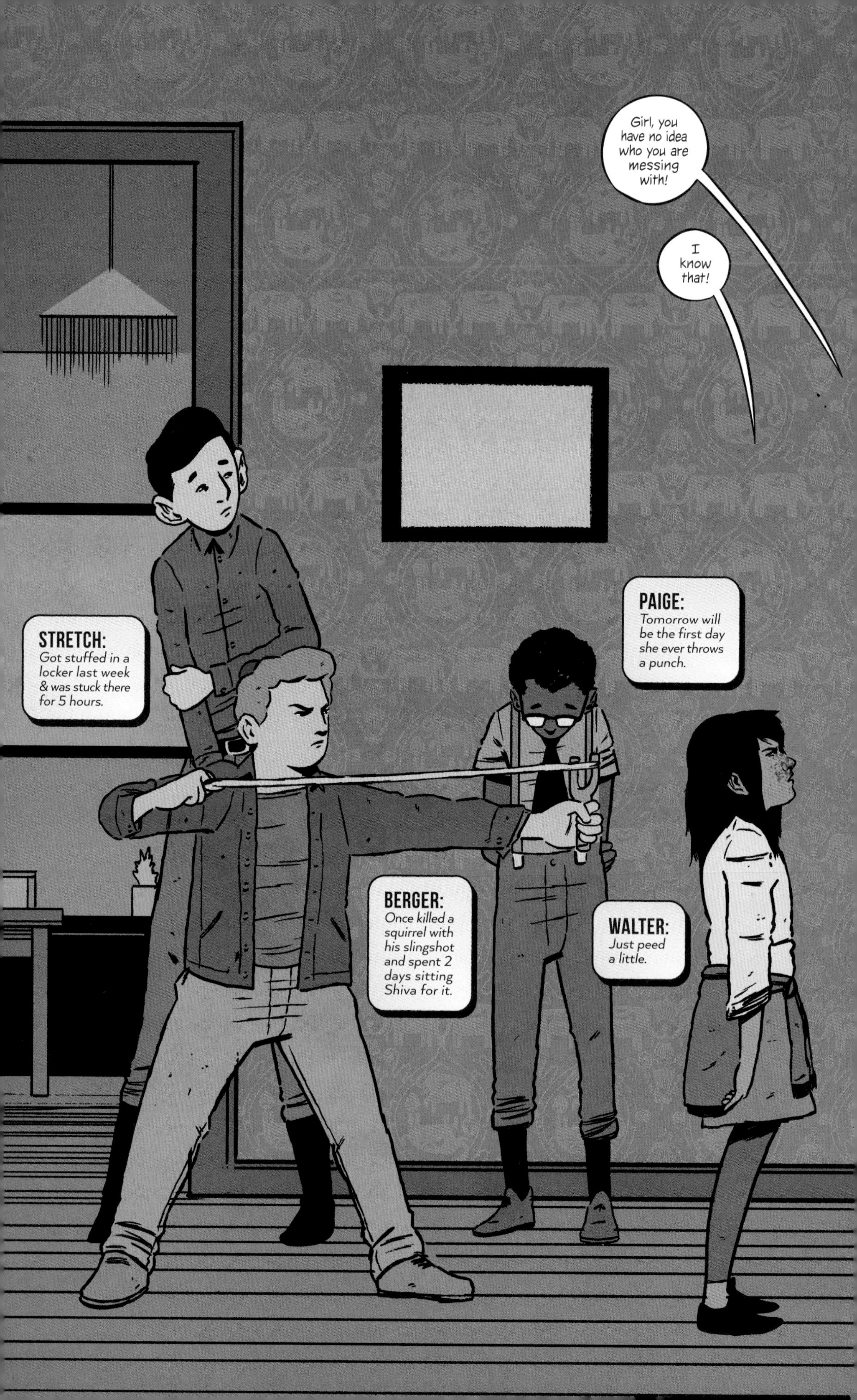
Girl, you have no idea who you are messing with!
I know that!
STRETCH: Got stuffed in a locker last week & was stuck there for 5 hours.
BERGER: Once killed a squirrel with his slingshot and spent 2 days sitting Shiva for it.
PAIGE: Tomorrow will be the first day she ever throws a punch.
WALTER: Just peed a little.

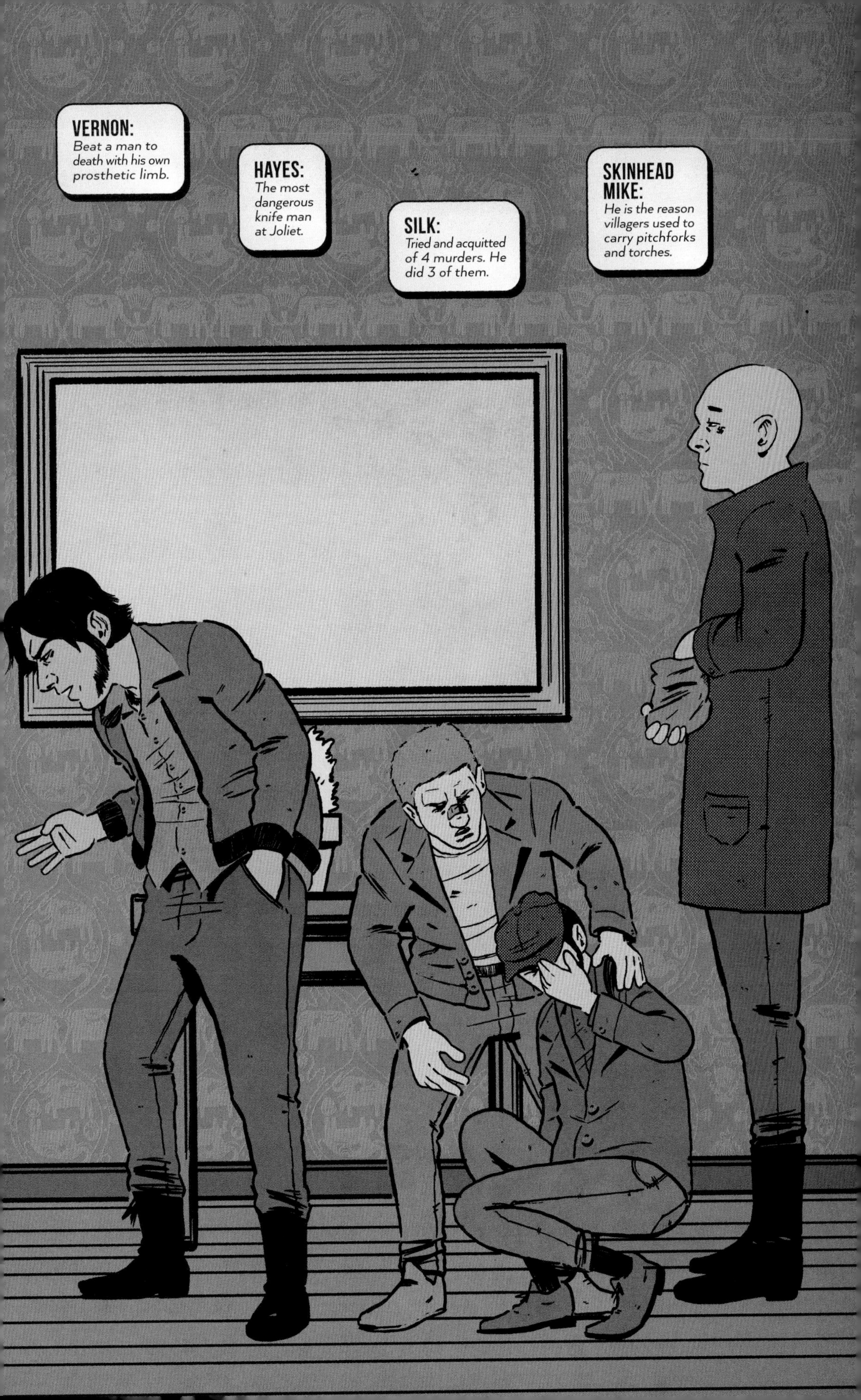
VERNON:
Beat a man to death with his own prosthetic limb.
HAYES:
The most dangerous knife man at Joliet.
SILK:
Tried and acquitted of 4 murders. He did 3 of them.
SKINHEAD MIKE:
He is the reason villagers used to carry pitchforks and torches.

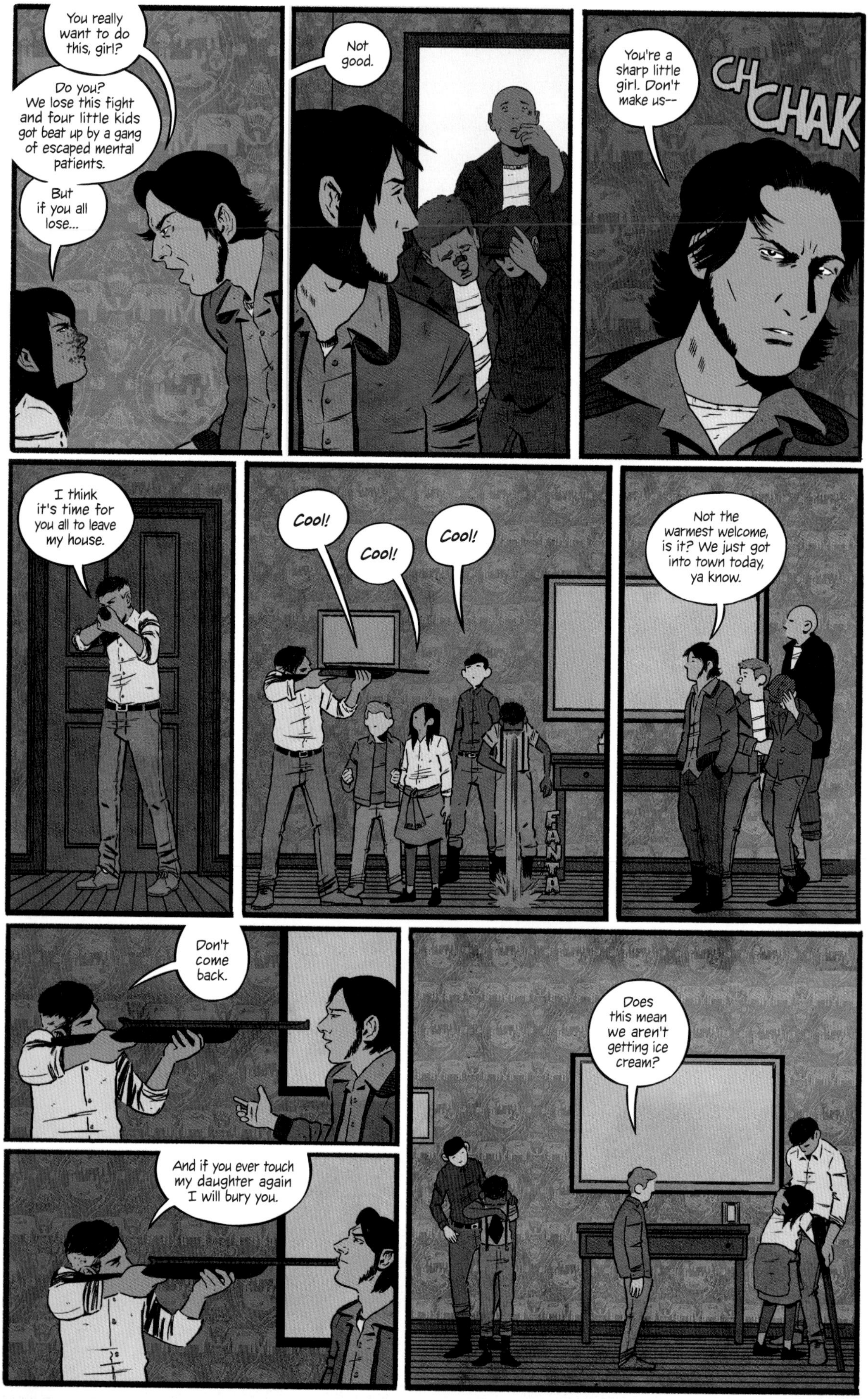

You really want to do this, girl?
Do you? We lose this fight and four little kids got beat up by a gang of escaped mental patients.
But if you all lose...
Not good.
You're a sharp little girl. Don't make us--
CHCHAK
I think it's time for you all to leave my house.
Cool!
Cool!
Cool!
FANTA
Not the warmest welcome, is it? We just got into town today, ya know.
Don't come back.
And if you ever touch my daughter again I will bury you.
Does this mean we aren't getting ice cream?

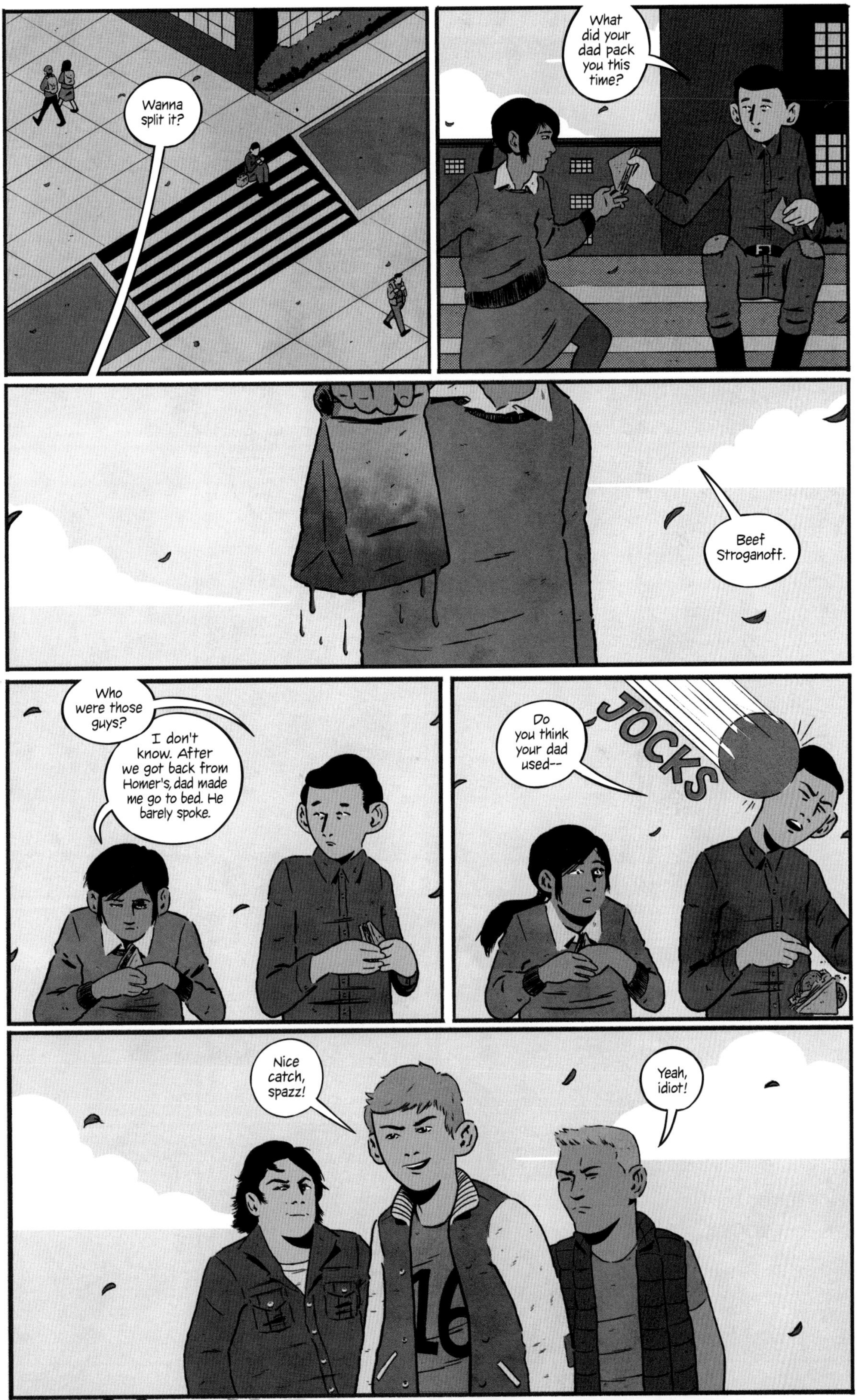
Wanna split it?
What did your dad pack you this time?
Beef Stroganoff.
Who were those guys?
I don't know. After we got back from Homer's, dad made me go to bed. He barely spoke.
Do you think your dad used--
JOCKS
Nice catch, spazz!
Yeah, idiot!

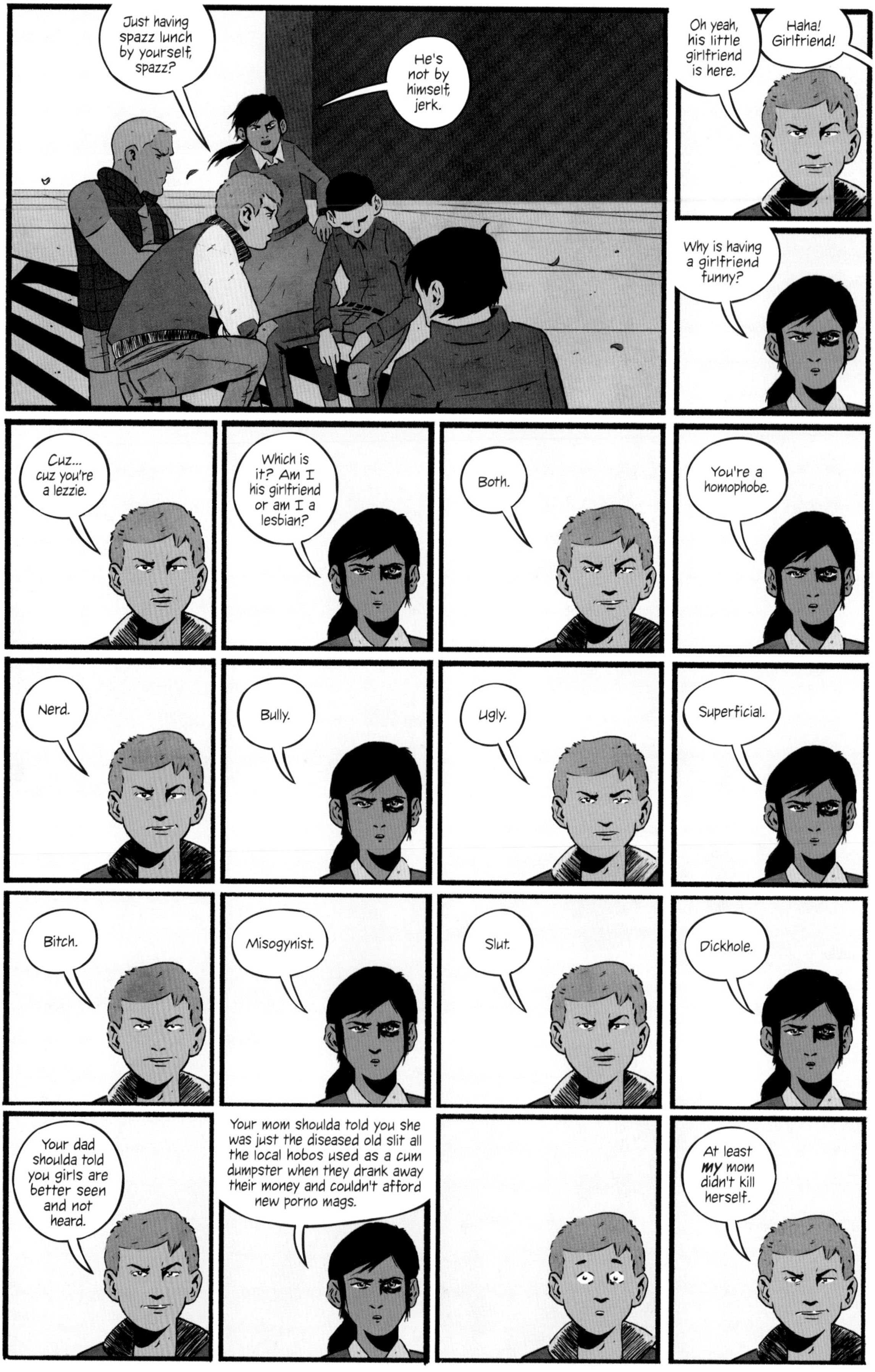
Just having spazz lunch by yourself, spazz?
He's not by himself, jerk.
Oh yeah, his little girlfriend is here.
Haha! Girlfriend!
Why is having a girlfriend funny?
Cuz... cuz you're a lezzie.
Which is it? Am I his girlfriend or am I a lesbian?
Both.
You're a homophobe.
Nerd.
Bully.
Ugly.
Superficial.
Bitch.
Misogynist.
Slut.
Dickhole.
Your dad shoulda told you girls are better seen and not heard.
Your mom shoulda told you she was just the diseased old slit all the local hobos used as a cum dumpster when they drank away their money and couldn't afford new porno mags.
At least **my** mom didn't kill herself.

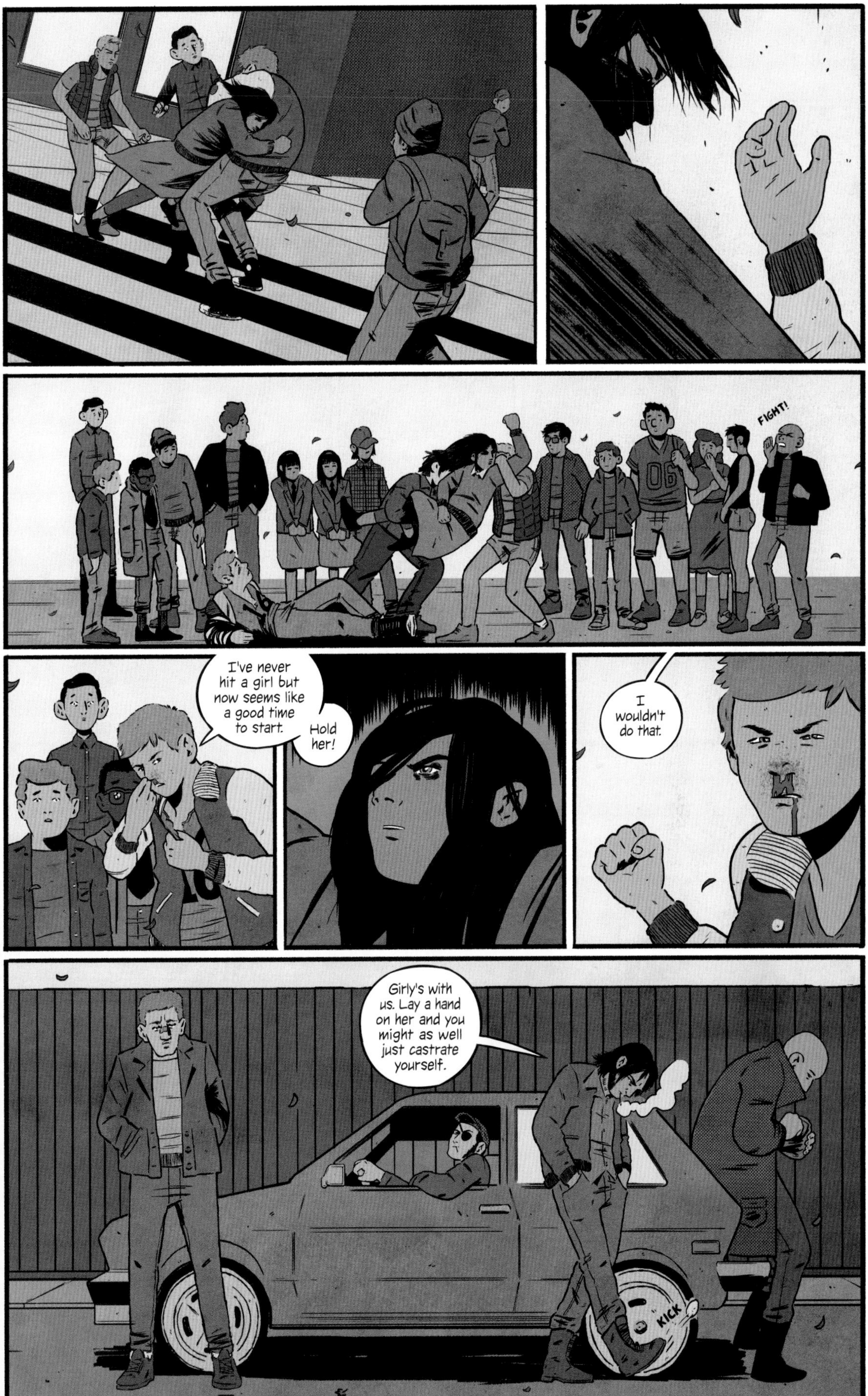
FIGHT!
I've never hit a girl but now seems like a good time to start.
Hold her!
I wouldn't do that.
Girly's with us. Lay a hand on her and you might as well just castrate yourself.
KICK

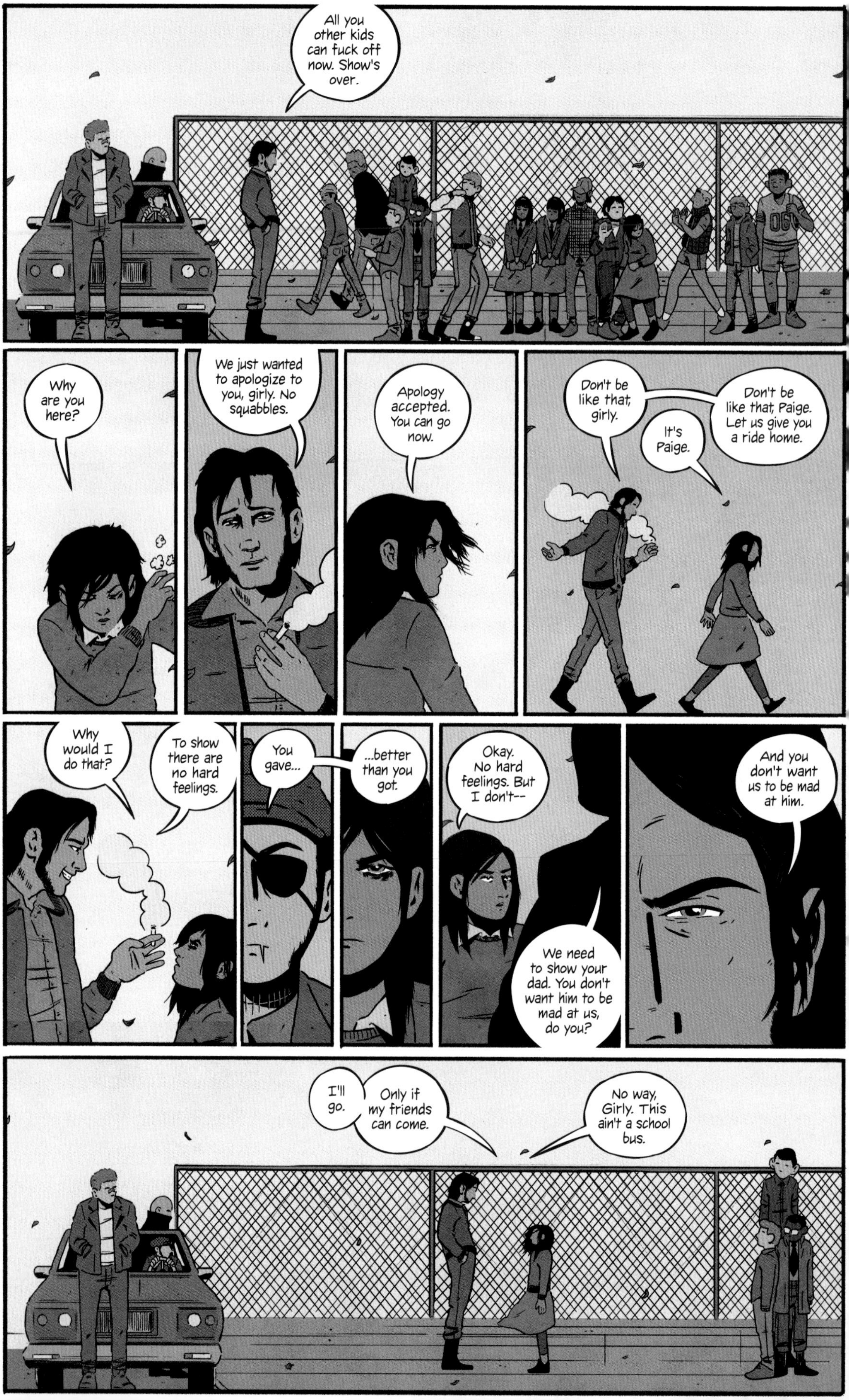
All you other kids can fuck off now. Show's over.
Why are you here?
We just wanted to apologize to you, girly. No squabbles.
Apology accepted. You can go now.
Don't be like that, girly.
It's Paige.
Don't be like that, Paige. Let us give you a ride home.
Why would I do that?
To show there are no hard feelings.
You gave...
...better than you got.
Okay. No hard feelings. But I don't--
We need to show your dad. You don't want him to be mad at us, do you?
And you don't want us to be mad at him.
I'll go.
Only if my friends can come.
No way, Girly. This ain't a school bus.

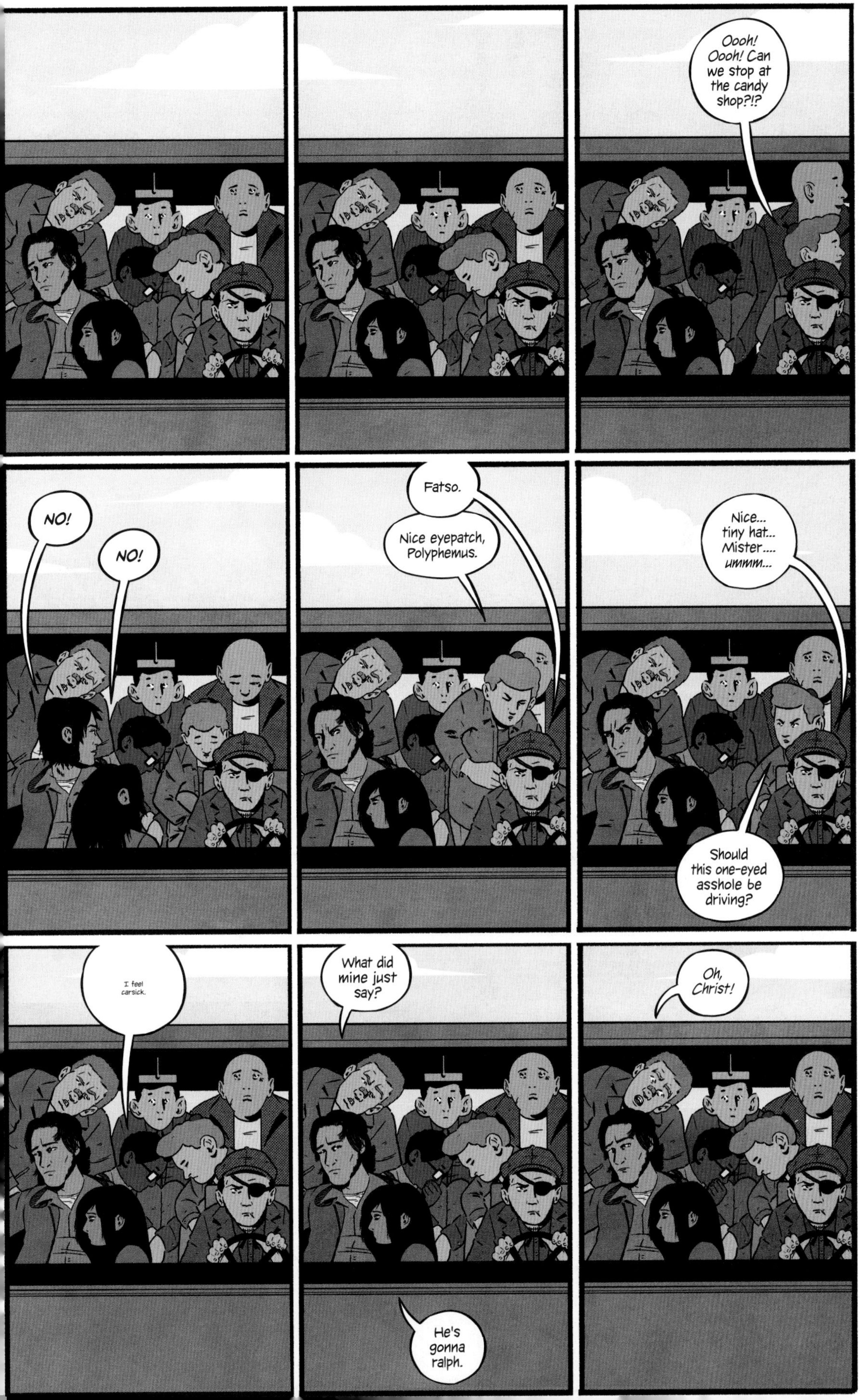
Oooh! Oooh! Can we stop at the candy shop?!?
NO!
NO!
Fatso.
Nice eyepatch, Polyphemus.
Nice... tiny hat... Mister.... ummm...
Should this one-eyed asshole be driving?
I feel carsick.
What did mine just say?
He's gonna ralph.
Oh, Christ!

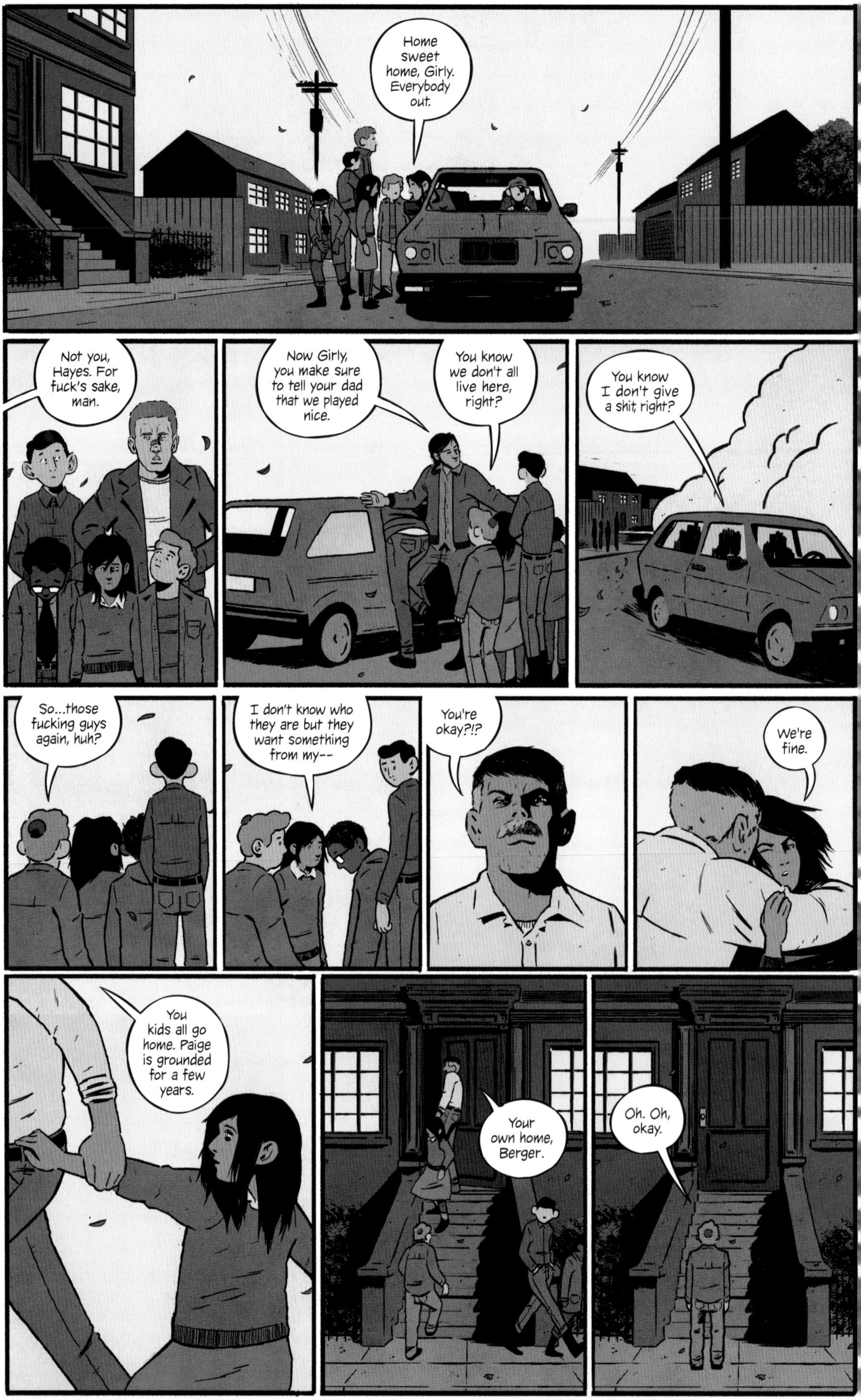

Home sweet home, Girly. Everybody out.
Not you, Hayes. For fuck's sake, man.
Now Girly, you make sure to tell your dad that we played nice.
You know we don't all live here, right?
You know I don't give a shit, right?
So...those fucking guys again, huh?
I don't know who they are but they want something from my--
You're okay?!?
We're fine.
You kids all go home. Paige is grounded for a few years.
Your own home, Berger.
Oh. Oh, okay.

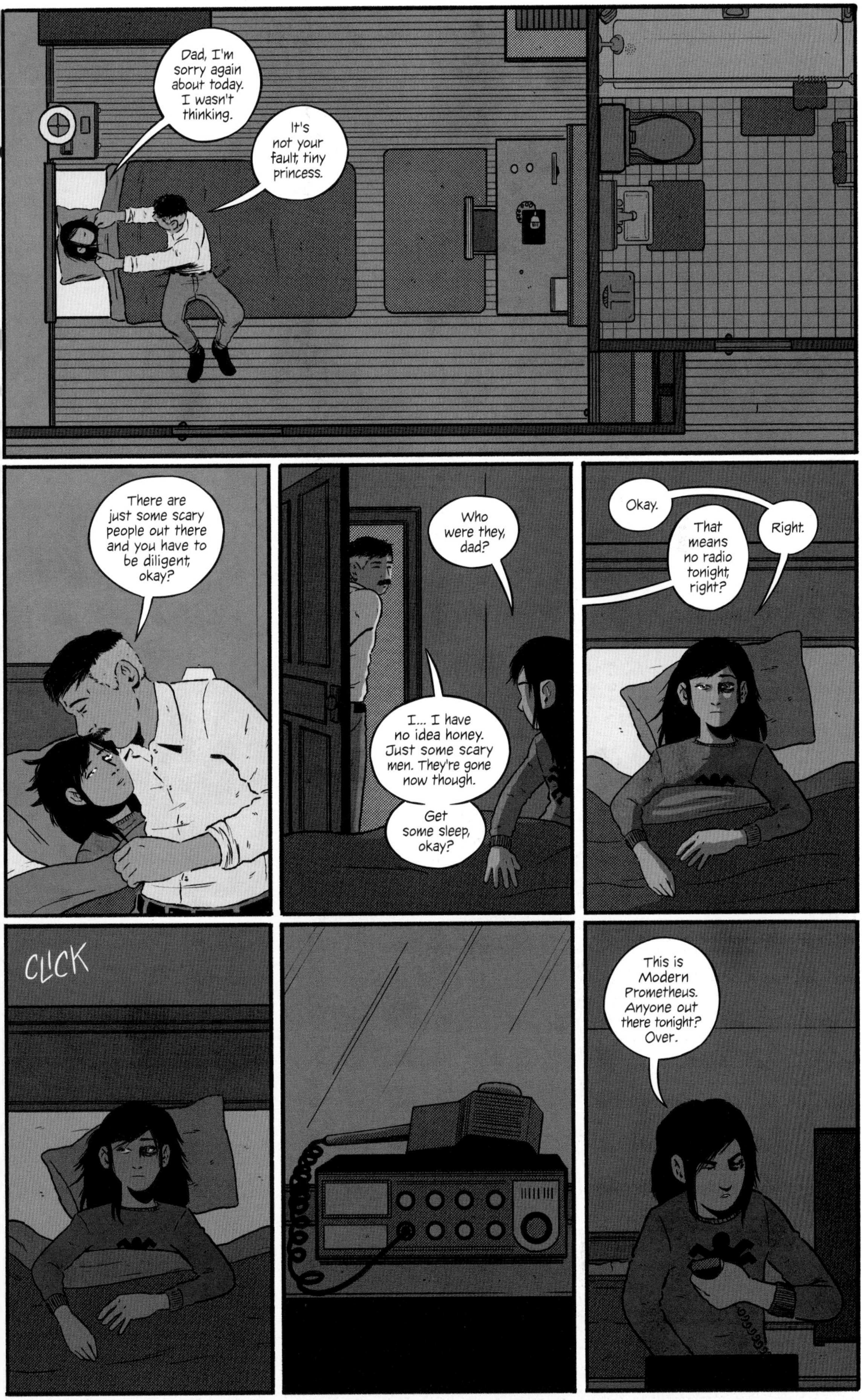
Dad, I'm sorry again about today. I wasn't thinking.
It's not your fault, tiny princess.
There are just some scary people out there and you have to be diligent, okay?
Who were they, dad?
I... I have no idea honey. Just some scary men. They're gone now though.
Get some sleep, okay?
Okay.
That means no radio tonight, right?
Right.
CLICK
This is Modern Prometheus. Anyone out there tonight? Over.

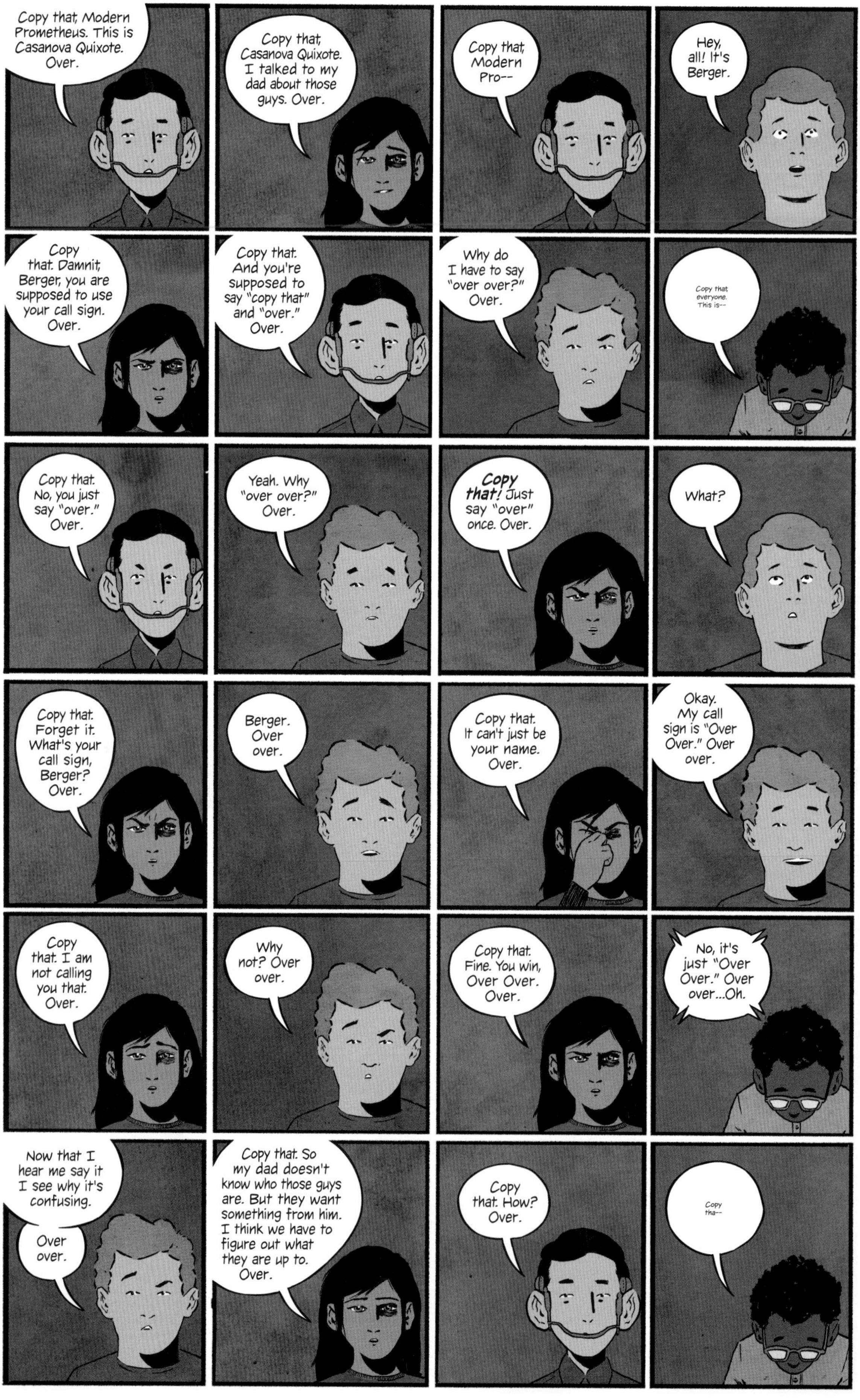
Copy that, Modern Prometheus. This is Casanova Quixote. Over.
Copy that, Casanova Quixote. I talked to my dad about those guys. Over.
Copy that, Modern Pro--
Hey, all! It's Berger.
Copy that. Damnit, Berger, you are supposed to use your call sign. Over.
Copy that. And you're supposed to say "copy that" and "over." Over.
Why do I have to say "over over?" Over.
Copy that, everyone. This is--
Copy that. No, you just say "over." Over.
Yeah. Why "over over?" Over.
Copy that! Just say "over" once. Over.
What?
Copy that. Forget it. What's your call sign, Berger? Over.
Berger. Over over.
Copy that. It can't just be your name. Over.
Okay. My call sign is "Over Over." Over over.
Copy that. I am not calling you that. Over.
Why not? Over over.
Copy that. Fine. You win, Over Over. Over.
No, it's just "Over Over." Over over...Oh.
Now that I hear me say it I see why it's confusing.
Over over.
Copy that. So my dad doesn't know who those guys are. But they want something from him. I think we have to figure out what they are up to. Over.
Copy that. How? Over.
Copy tha--

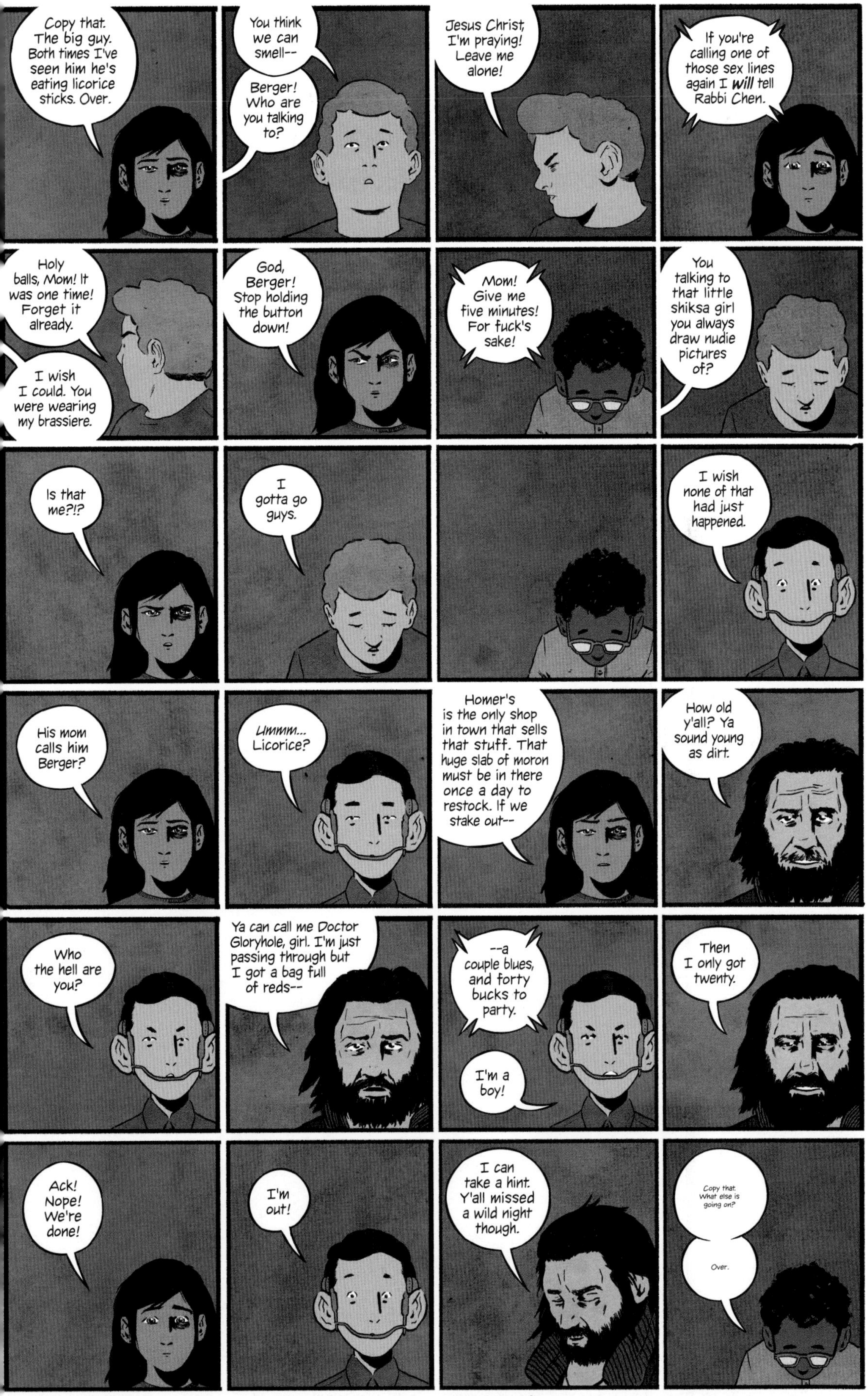
Copy that. The big guy. Both times I've seen him he's eating licorice sticks. Over.
You think we can smell--
Berger! Who are you talking to?
Jesus Christ, I'm praying! Leave me alone!
If you're calling one of those sex lines again I *will* tell Rabbi Chen.
Holy balls, Mom! It was one time! Forget it already.
I wish I could. You were wearing my brassiere.
God, Berger! Stop holding the button down!
Mom! Give me five minutes! For fuck's sake!
You talking to that little shiksa girl you always draw nudie pictures of?
Is that me?!?
I gotta go guys.
I wish none of that had just happened.
His mom calls him Berger?
Ummm... Licorice?
Homer's is the only shop in town that sells that stuff. That huge slab of moron must be in there once a day to restock. If we stake out--
How old y'all? Ya sound young as dirt.
Who the hell are you?
Ya can call me Doctor Gloryhole, girl. I'm just passing through but I got a bag full of reds--
--a couple blues, and forty bucks to party.
I'm a boy!
Then I only got twenty.
Ack! Nope! We're done!
I'm out!
I can take a hint. Y'all missed a wild night though.
Copy that. What else is going on?
Over.

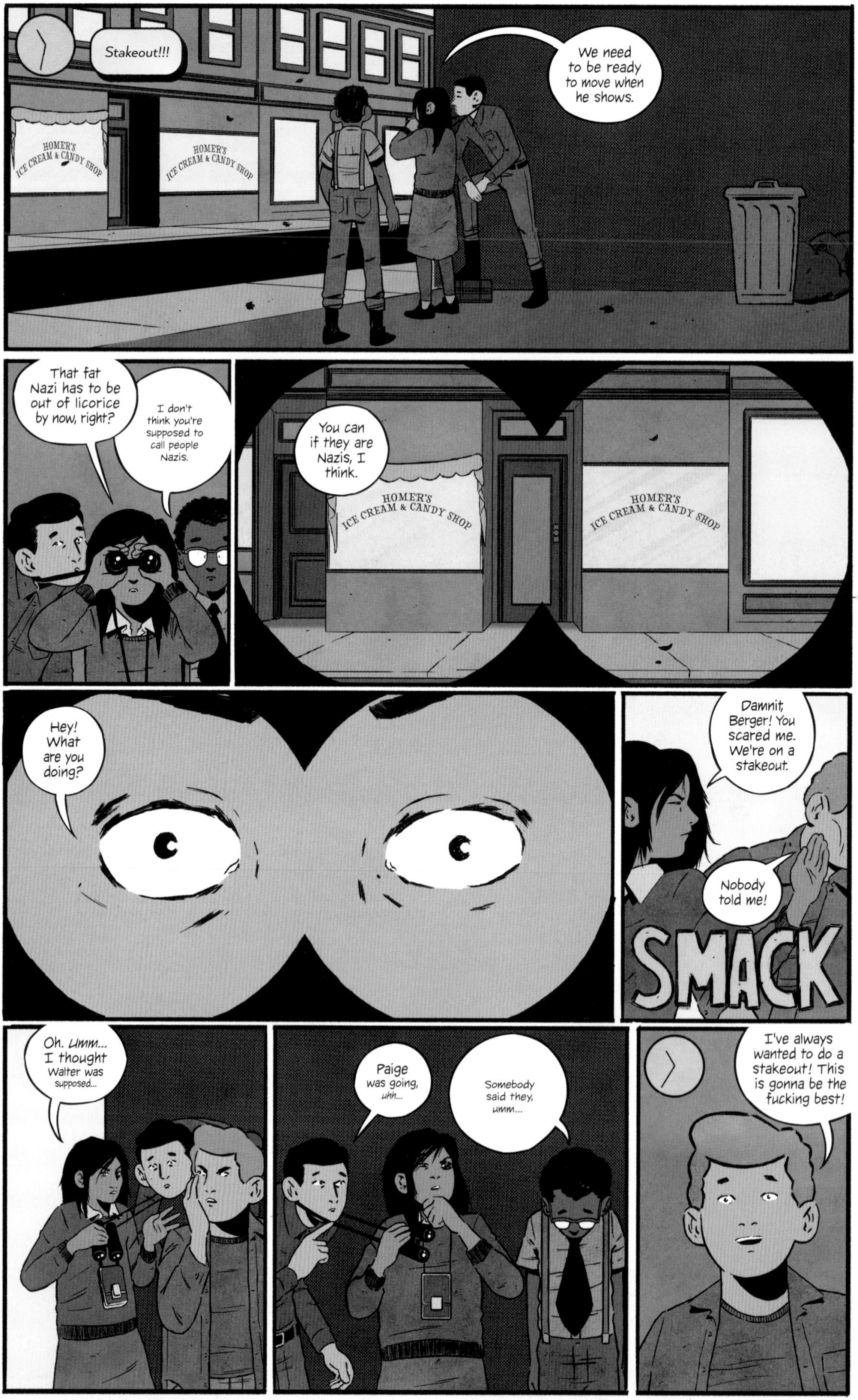
Stakeout!!!
We need to be ready to move when he shows.
HOMER'S ICE CREAM & CANDY SHOP
HOMER'S ICE CREAM & CANDY SHOP
That fat Nazi has to be out of licorice by now, right?
I don't think you're supposed to call people Nazis.
You can if they are Nazis, I think.
HOMER'S ICE CREAM & CANDY SHOP
HOMER'S ICE CREAM & CANDY SHOP
Hey! What are you doing?
Damnit, Berger! You scared me. We're on a stakeout.
Nobody told me!
SMACK
Oh. Umm... I thought Walter was supposed...
Paige was going, uhh...
Somebody said they, umm...
I've always wanted to do a stakeout! This is gonna be the fucking best!

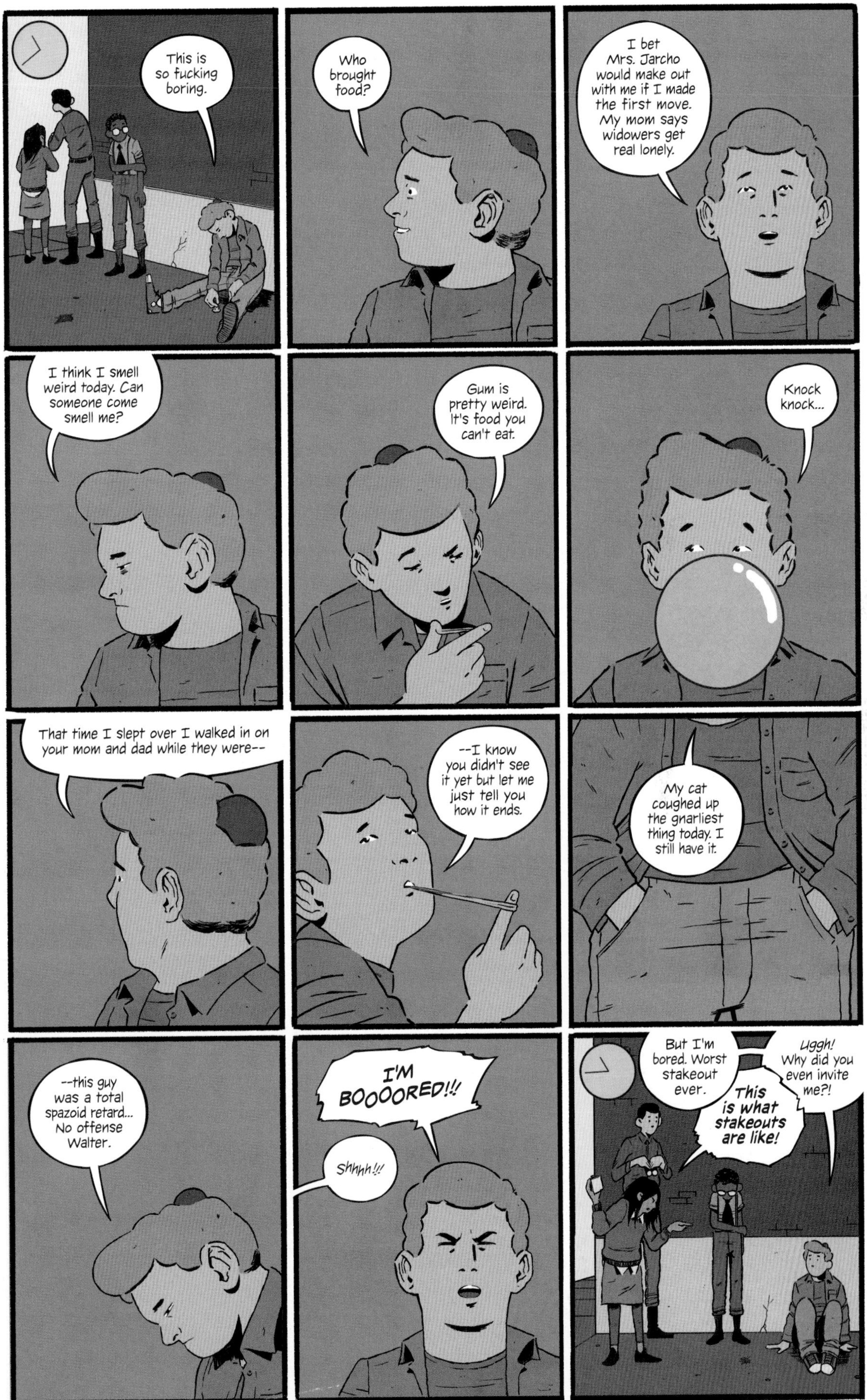
This is so fucking boring.
Who brought food?
I bet Mrs. Jarcho would make out with me if I made the first move. My mom says widowers get real lonely.
I think I smell weird today. Can someone come smell me?
Gum is pretty weird. It's food you can't eat.
Knock knock...
That time I slept over I walked in on your mom and dad while they were--
--I know you didn't see it yet but let me just tell you how it ends.
My cat coughed up the gnarliest thing today. I still have it.
--this guy was a total spazoid retard... No offense Walter.
I'M BOOOORED!!!
Shhhh!!!
But I'm bored. Worst stakeout ever.
Uggh! Why did you even invite me?!
This is what stakeouts are like!

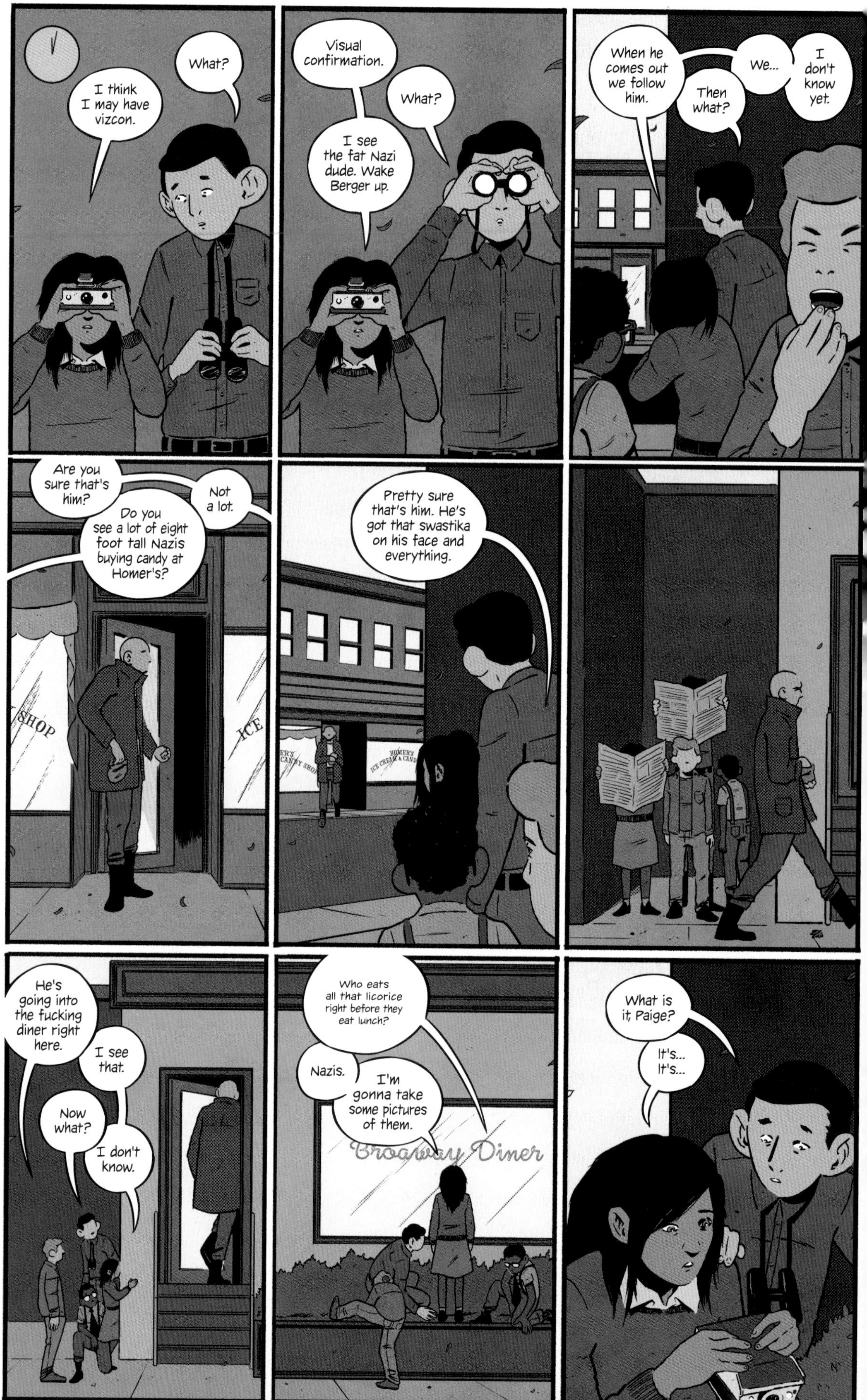

I think I may have vizcon.
What?
Visual confirmation.
What?
I see the fat Nazi dude. Wake Berger up.
When he comes out we follow him.
Then what?
We...
I don't know yet.
Are you sure that's him?
Not a lot.
Do you see a lot of eight foot tall Nazis buying candy at Homer's?
SHOP
ICE
Pretty sure that's him. He's got that swastika on his face and everything.
He's going into the fucking diner right here.
I see that.
Now what?
I don't know.
Who eats all that licorice right before they eat lunch?
Nazis.
I'm gonna take some pictures of them.
Broadway Diner
What is it, Paige?
It's... It's...

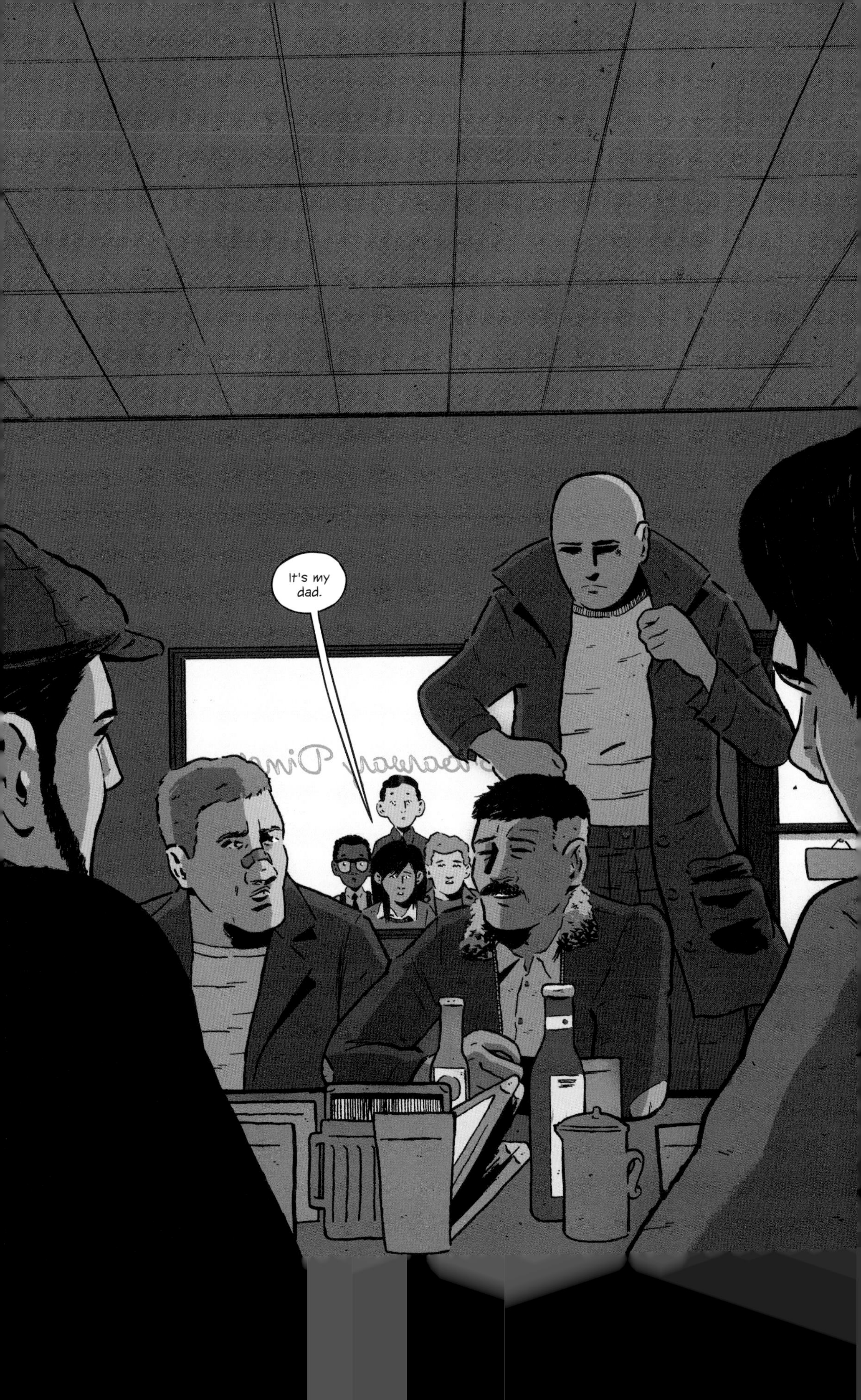
It's my dad.

CHAPTER TWO

You don't make up for your sins in school.
You do it at the arcade.
You do it at the candy store.
The rest is bullshit and you know it.

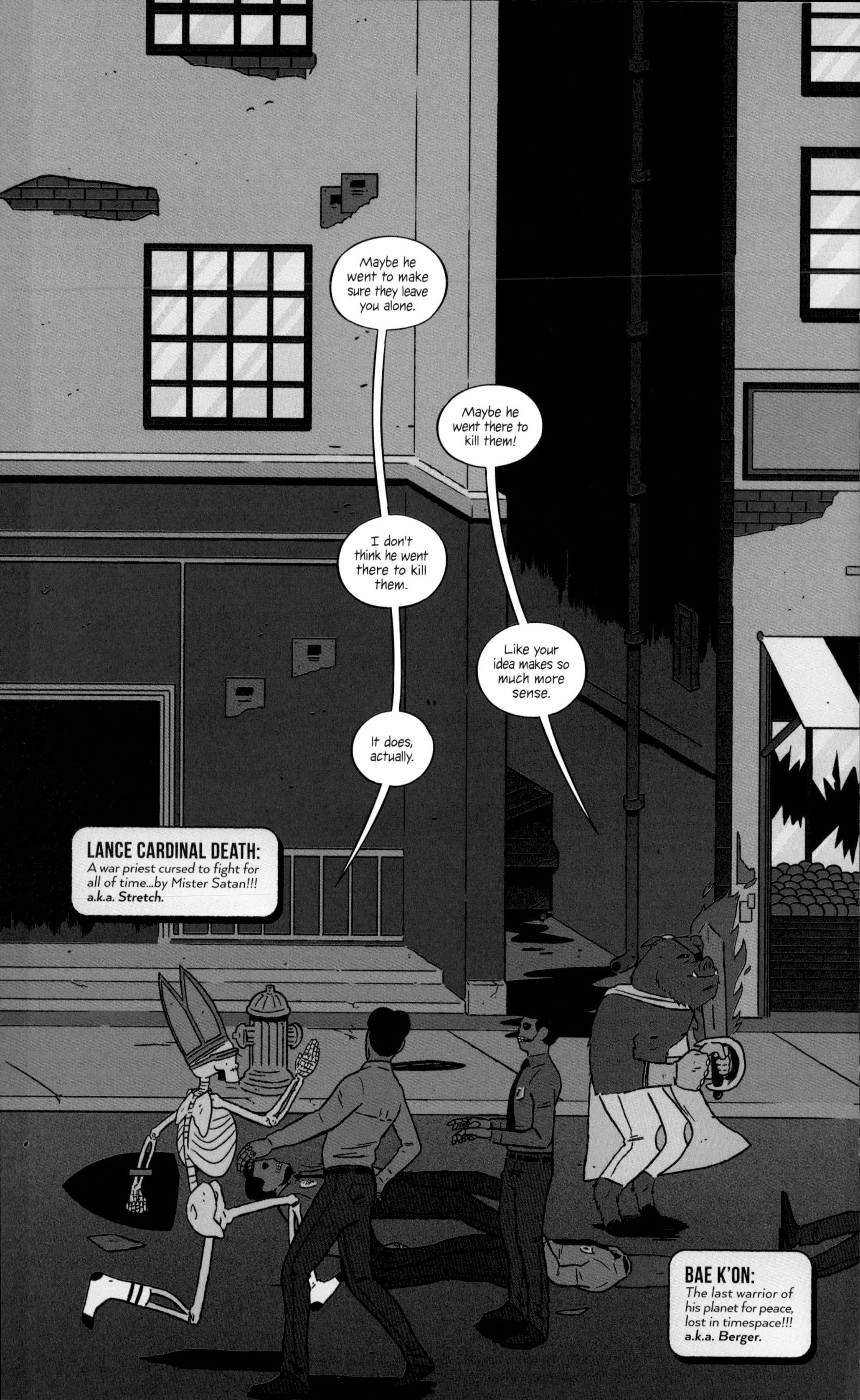
Maybe he went to make sure they leave you alone.
Maybe he went there to kill them!
I don't think he went there to kill them.
Like your idea makes so much more sense.
It does, actually.
LANCE CARDINAL DEATH: A war priest cursed to fight for all of time...by Mister Satan!!! a.k.a. Stretch.
BAE K'ON: The last warrior of his planet for peace, lost in timespace!!! a.k.a. Berger.

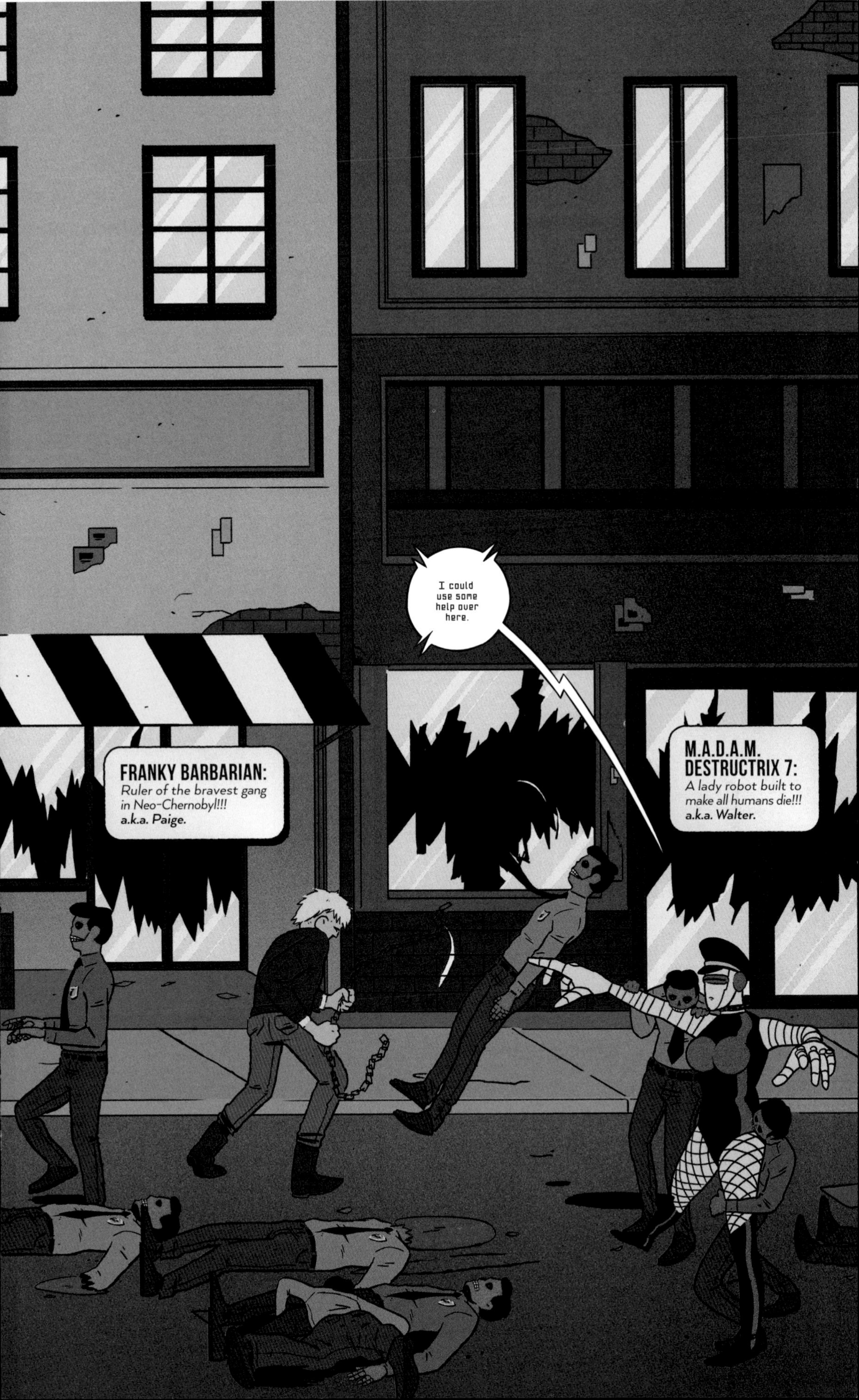

I could use some help over here.
FRANKY BARBARIAN:
Ruler of the bravest gang in Neo-Chernobyl!!!
a.k.a. Paige.
M.A.D.A.M. DESTRUCTRIX 7:
A lady robot built to make all humans die!!!
a.k.a. Walter.

Can we stop talking about this?

Maybe your dad just happened to be eating in the same place as the Nazis and invited them to eat with him.

A little help?

Why would he do that, Berger?

It's, like, the Christian thing to do. Right?

My dad's an atheist. Can we please change the subject?

What do *YOU* want to talk about, Paige?

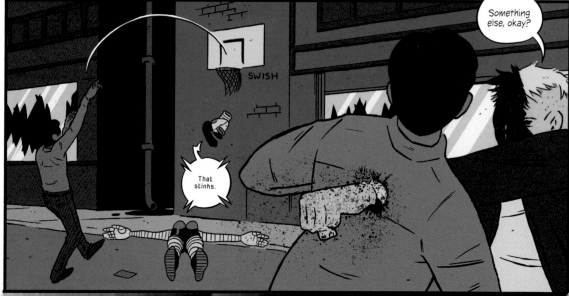

SWISH

That stinks.

Something else, okay?

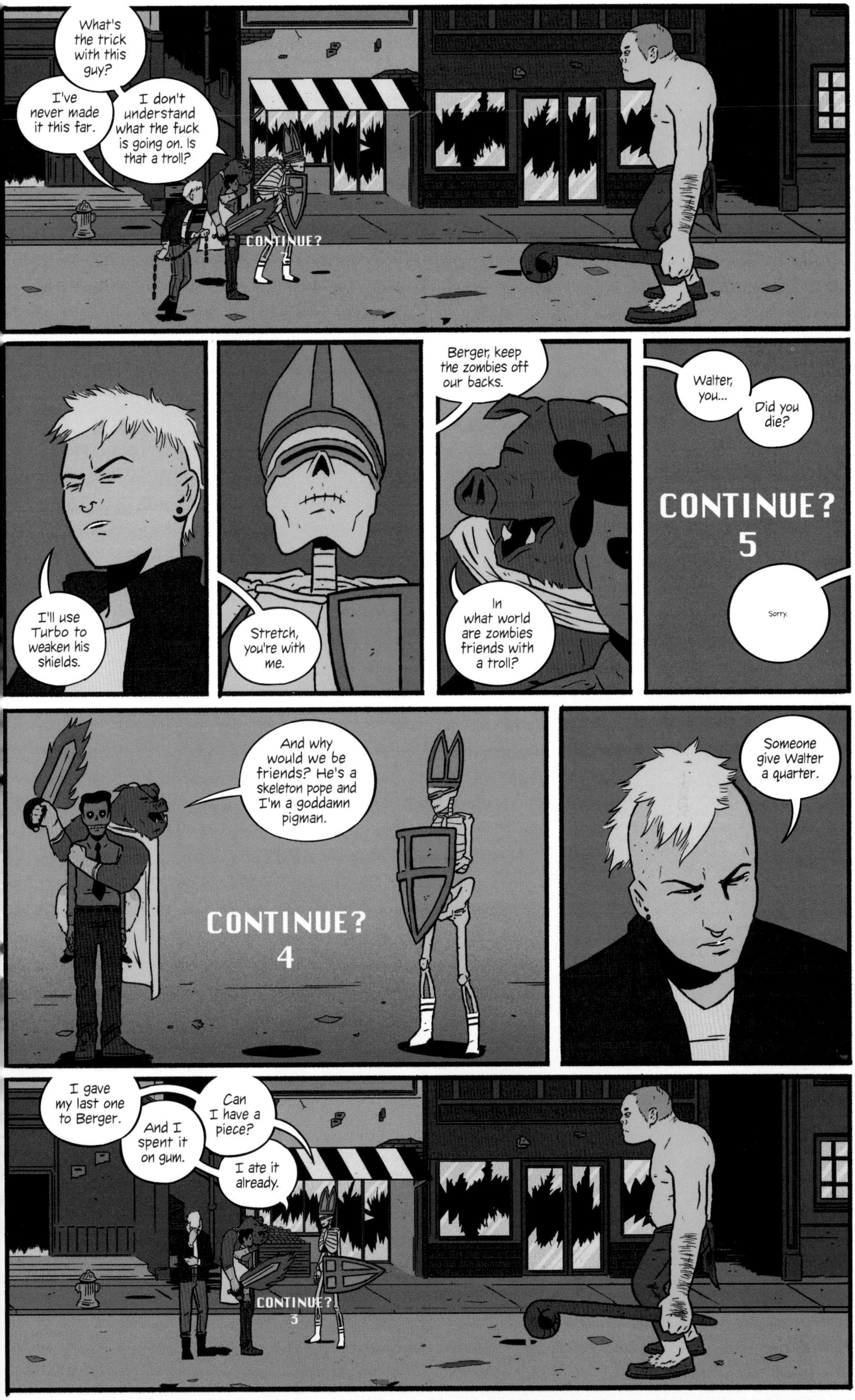

What's the trick with this guy?
I've never made it this far.
I don't understand what the fuck is going on. Is that a troll?
CONTINUE?
I'll use Turbo to weaken his shields.
Stretch, you're with me.
Berger, keep the zombies off our backs.
In what world are zombies friends with a troll?
Walter, you...
Did you die?
CONTINUE?
5
Sorry.
And why would we be friends? He's a skeleton pope and I'm a goddamn pigman.
CONTINUE?
4
Someone give Walter a quarter.
I gave my last one to Berger.
And I spent it on gum.
Can I have a piece?
I ate it already.
CONTINUE?
3

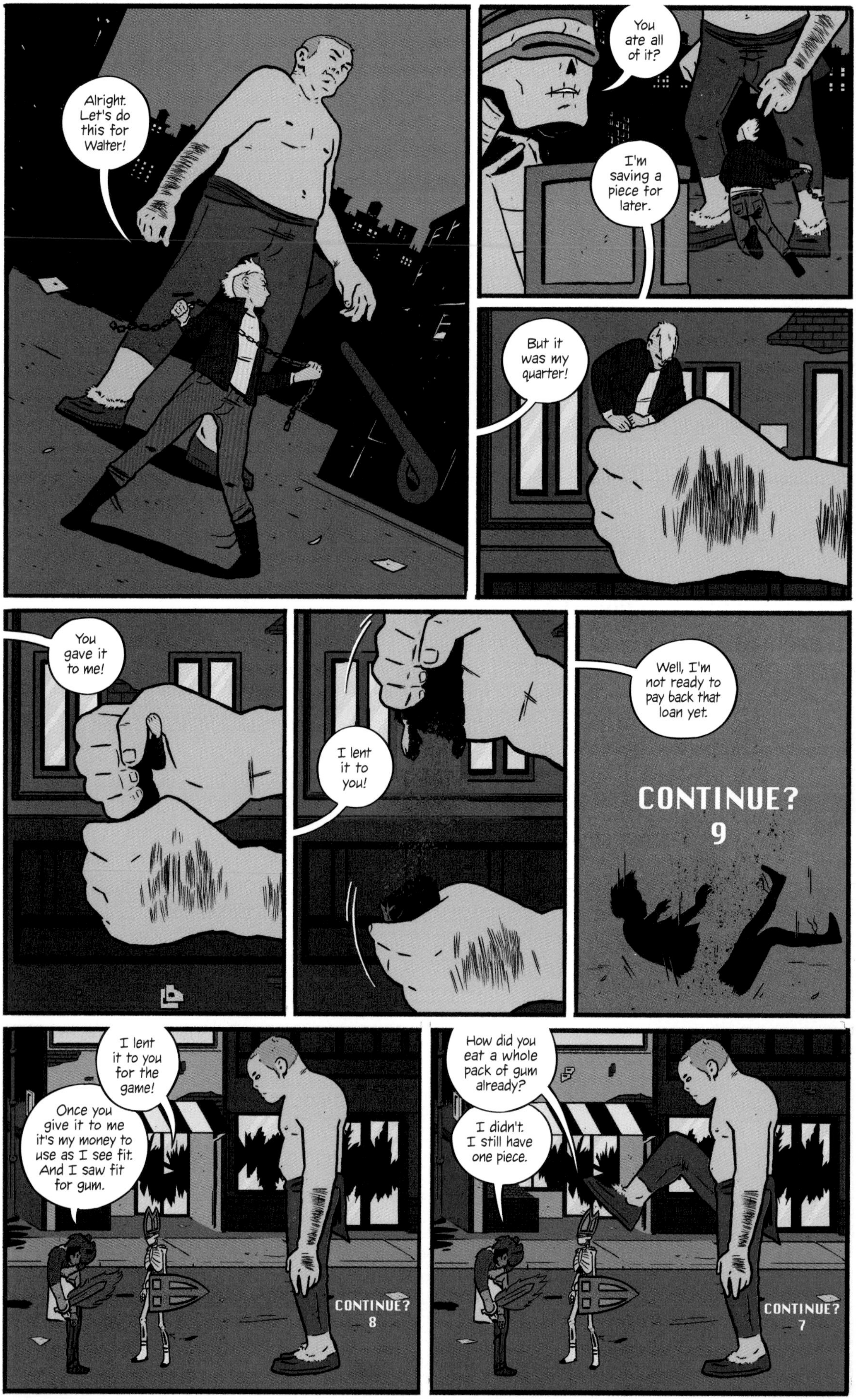

Alright. Let's do this for Walter!
You ate all of it?
I'm saving a piece for later.
But it was my quarter!
You gave it to me!
I lent it to you!
Well, I'm not ready to pay back that loan yet.
CONTINUE?
9
I lent it to you for the game!
Once you give it to me it's my money to use as I see fit. And I saw fit for gum.
CONTINUE?
8
How did you eat a whole pack of gum already?
I didn't. I still have one piece.
CONTINUE?
7

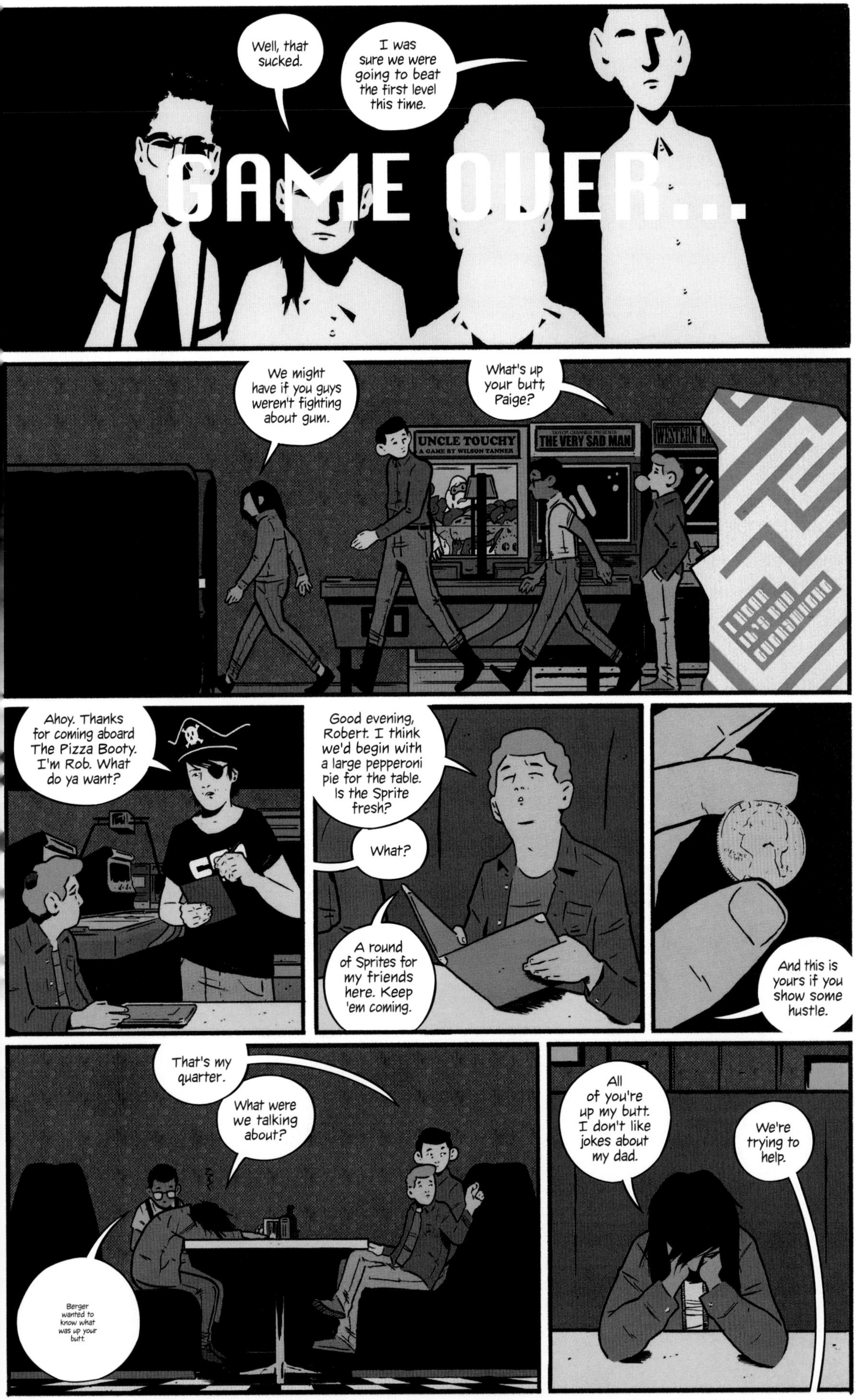
Well, that sucked.
I was sure we were going to beat the first level this time.
GAME OVER...
We might have if you guys weren't fighting about gum.
What's up your butt, Paige?
UNCLE TOUCHY
A GAME BY WILSON TANNER
TAYLOR CABANISS PRESENTS
THE VERY SAD MAN
Ahoy. Thanks for coming aboard The Pizza Booty. I'm Rob. What do ya want?
Good evening, Robert. I think we'd begin with a large pepperoni pie for the table. Is the Sprite fresh?
What?
A round of Sprites for my friends here. Keep 'em coming.
And this is yours if you show some hustle.
That's my quarter.
What were we talking about?
Berger wanted to know what was up your butt.
All of you're up my butt. I don't like jokes about my dad.
We're trying to help.

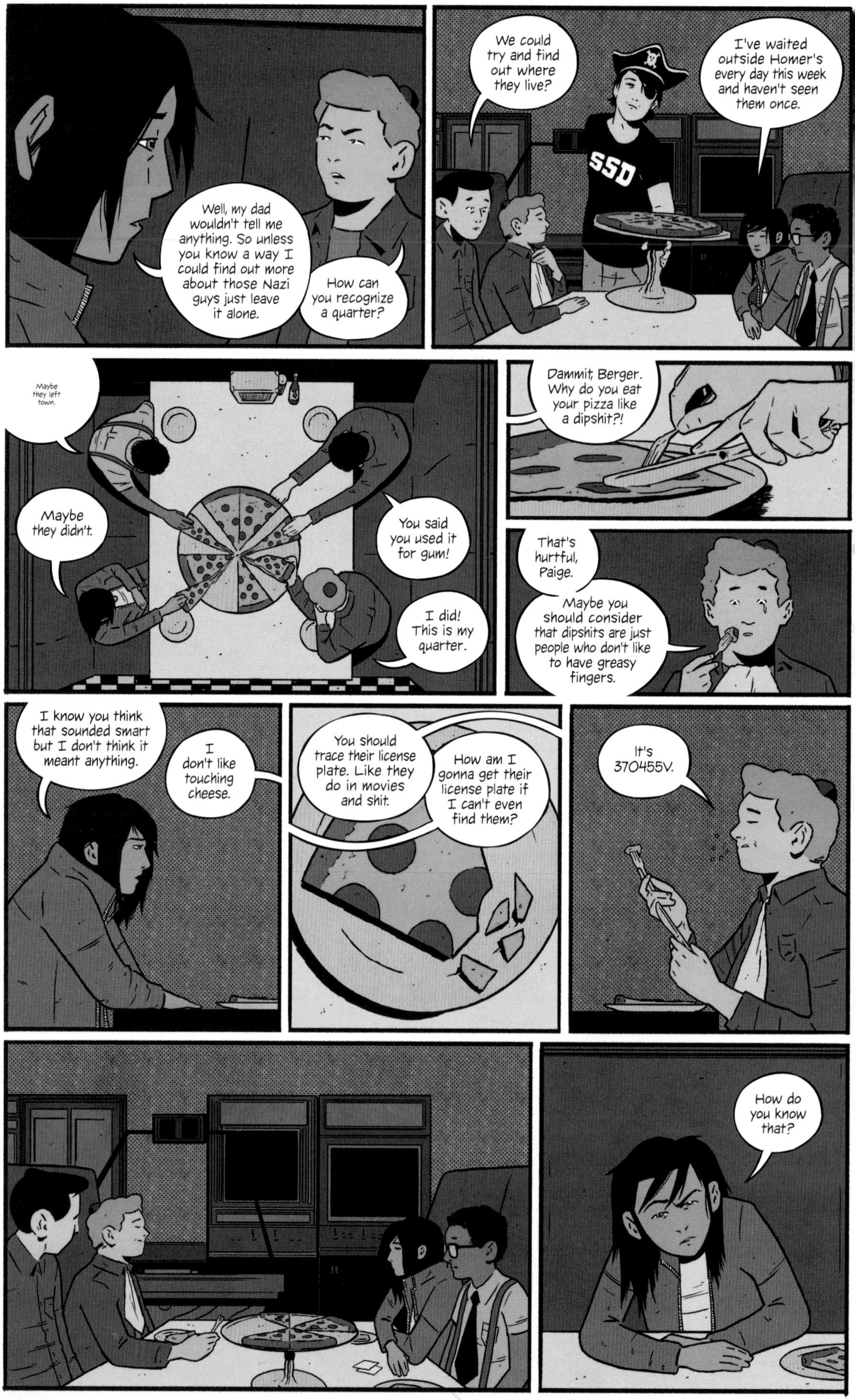
Well, my dad wouldn't tell me anything. So unless you know a way I could find out more about those Nazi guys just leave it alone.
How can you recognize a quarter?
We could try and find out where they live?
I've waited outside Homer's every day this week and haven't seen them once.
SSD
Maybe they left town.
Maybe they didn't.
You said you used it for gum!
I did! This is my quarter.
Dammit, Berger. Why do you eat your pizza like a dipshit?!
That's hurtful, Paige.
Maybe you should consider that dipshits are just people who don't like to have greasy fingers.
I know you think that sounded smart but I don't think it meant anything.
I don't like touching cheese.
You should trace their license plate. Like they do in movies and shit.
How am I gonna get their license plate if I can't even find them?
It's 370455V.
How do you know that?

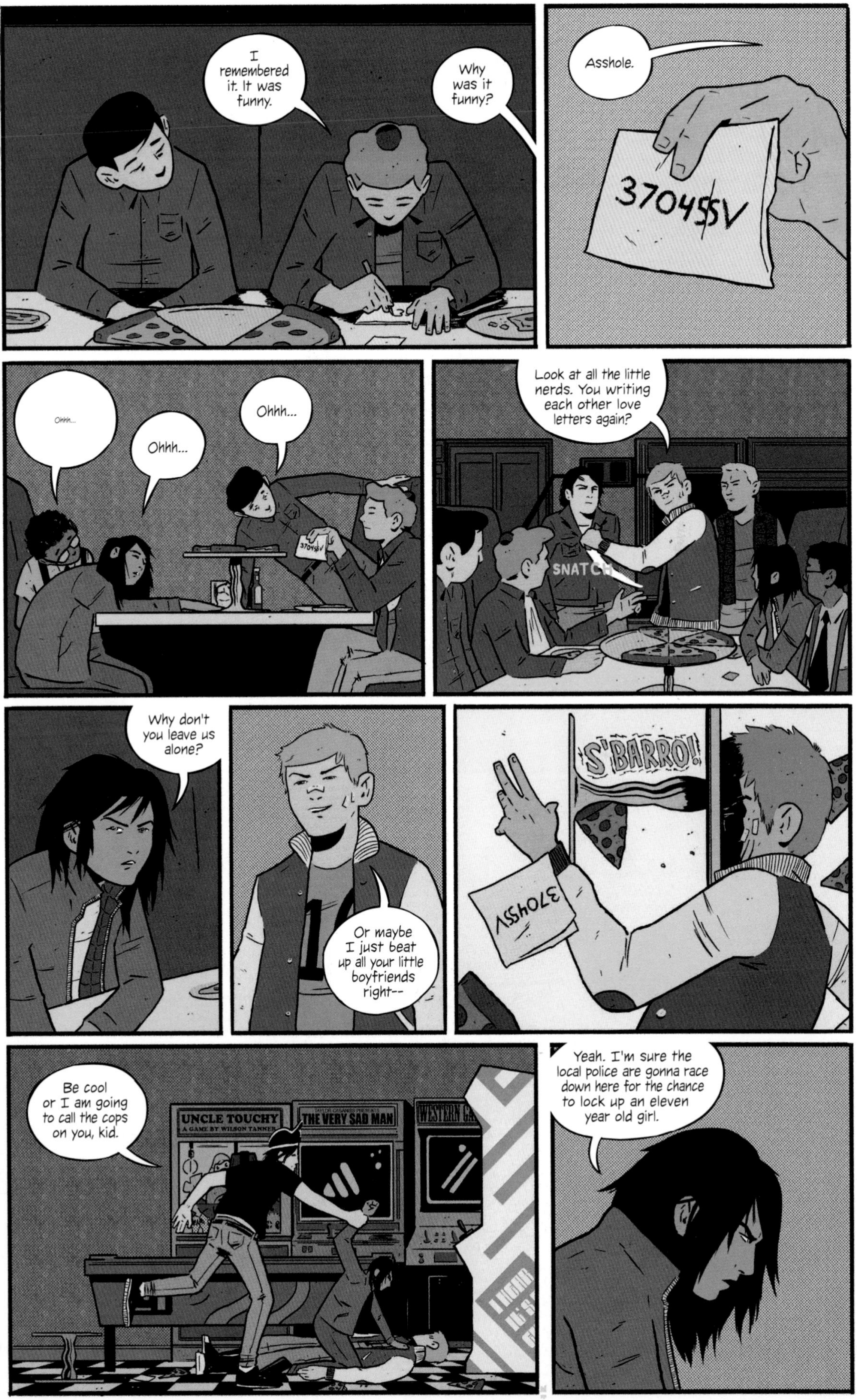

I remembered it. It was funny.
Why was it funny?
Asshole.
37045SV
Ohhh...
Ohhh...
Ohhh...
Look at all the little nerds. You writing each other love letters again?
SNATCH
Why don't you leave us alone?
Or maybe I just beat up all your little boyfriends right--
S'BARRO!
Be cool or I am going to call the cops on you, kid.
UNCLE TOUCHY
A GAME BY WILSON TANNER
THE VERY SAD MAN
Yeah. I'm sure the local police are gonna race down here for the chance to lock up an eleven year old girl.

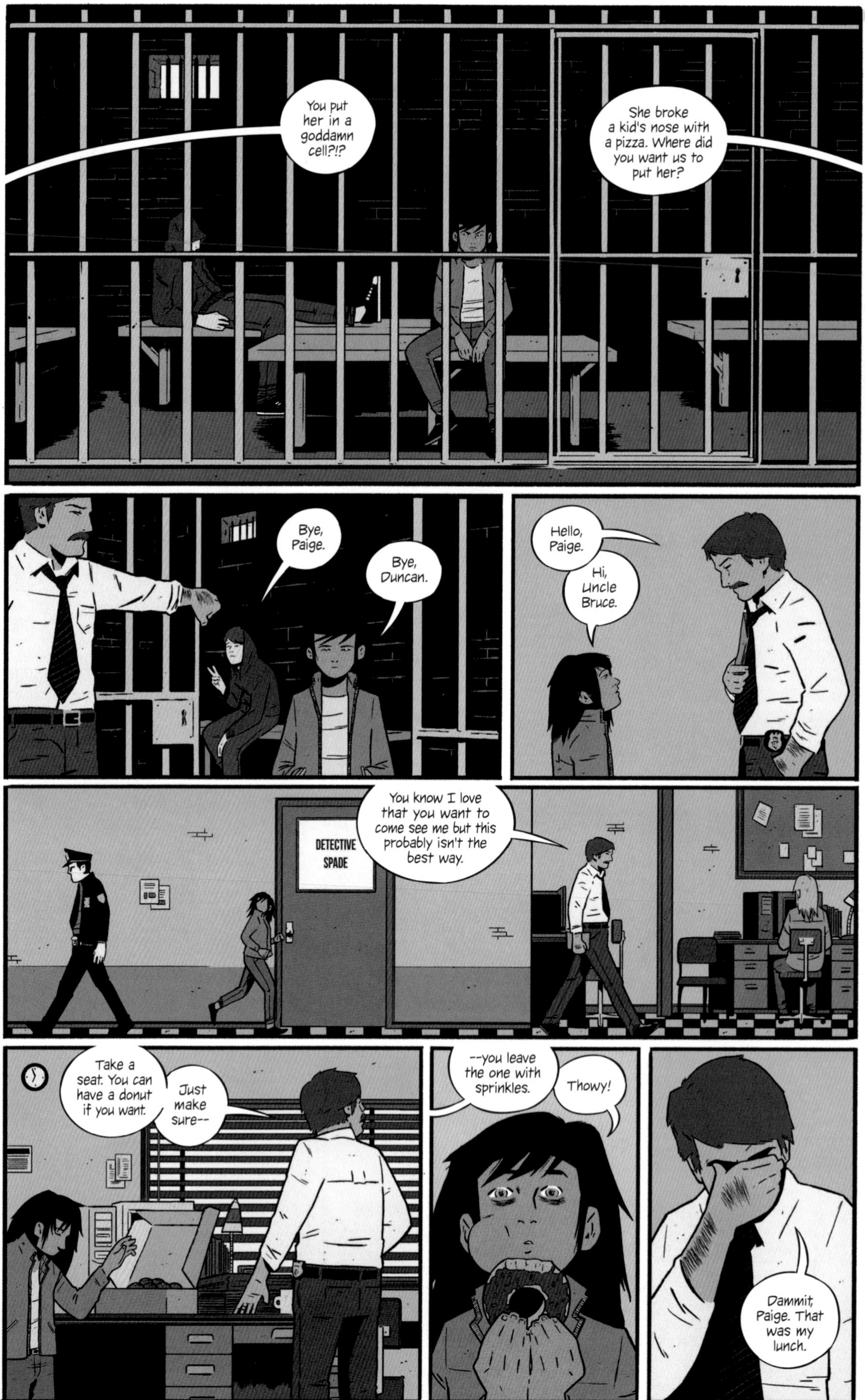
You put her in a goddamn cell?!?
She broke a kid's nose with a pizza. Where did you want us to put her?
Bye, Paige.
Bye, Duncan.
Hello, Paige.
Hi, Uncle Bruce.
You know I love that you want to come see me but this probably isn't the best way.
DETECTIVE SPADE
Take a seat. You can have a donut if you want.
Just make sure--
--you leave the one with sprinkles.
Thowy!
Dammit, Paige. That was my lunch.

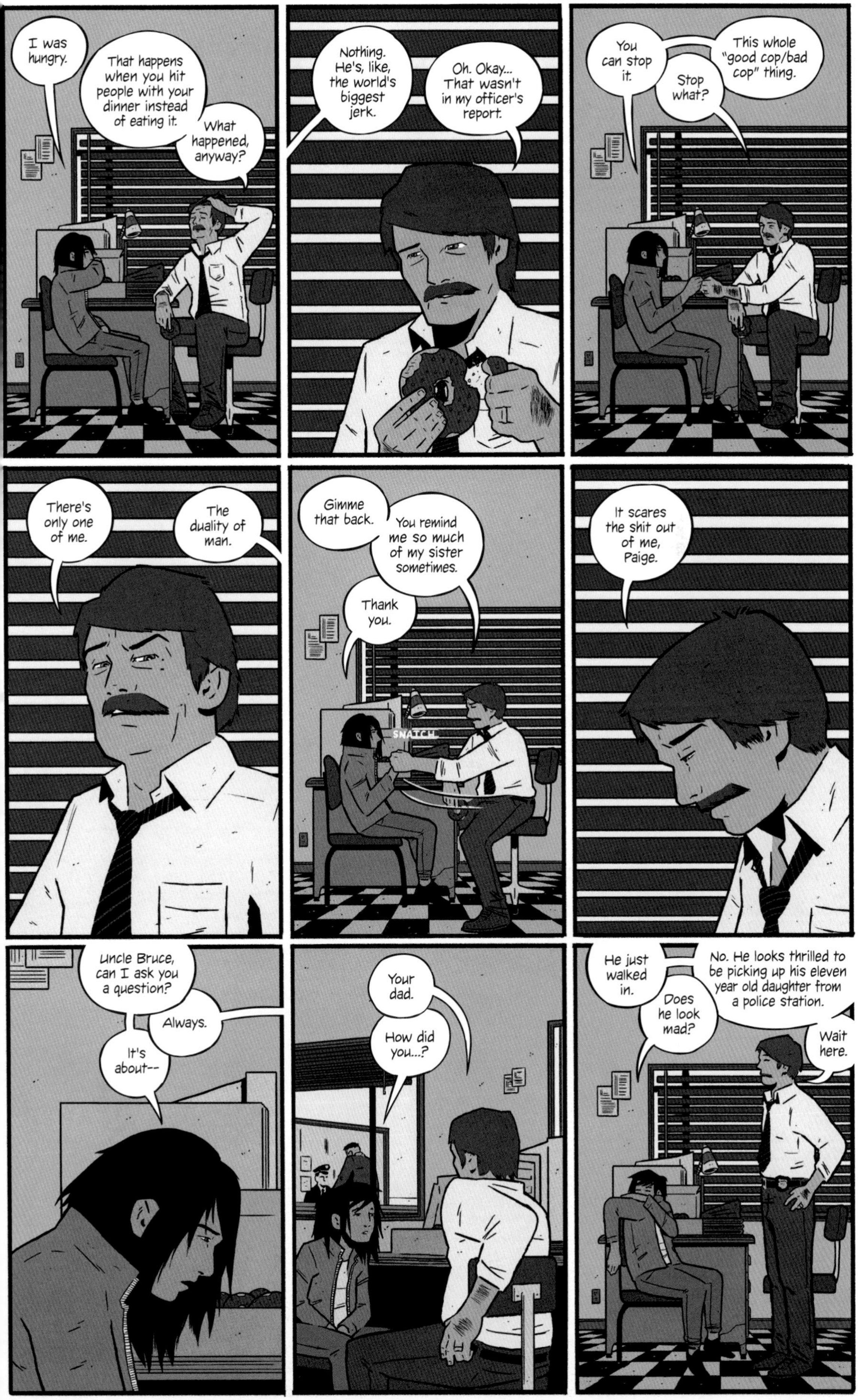
I was hungry.
That happens when you hit people with your dinner instead of eating it.
What happened, anyway?
Nothing. He's, like, the world's biggest jerk.
Oh. Okay... That wasn't in my officer's report.
You can stop it.
Stop what?
This whole "good cop/bad cop" thing.
There's only one of me.
The duality of man.
Gimme that back.
You remind me so much of my sister sometimes.
Thank you.
SNATCH
It scares the shit out of me, Paige.
Uncle Bruce, can I ask you a question?
Always.
It's about--
Your dad.
How did you...?
He just walked in.
Does he look mad?
No. He looks thrilled to be picking up his eleven year old daughter from a police station.
Wait here.

3704$V
Vehicle Search: 37045
ENTER
ENTER
HOMER'S
Felton's Computer
File Edit View Favorites Tools Help
ASSOC. MATTHEW HAYES
Police
Local Disk [D.]
Local Disk
Capacity: 34.2 GB
Used: 1.32 GB
KNOWN ASSOCIATES:
MATTHEW HAYES
ARRESTS: 6
CONVICTIONS: 3
Felton's Computer
File Edit View Favorites Tools Help
ASSOC. DANIEL SILK
Police
Local Disk [D.]
Local Disk
Capacity: 34.2 GB
Used: 1.32 GB
KNOWN ASSOCIATES:
DANIEL SILK
ARRESTS: 5
CONVICTIONS: 3
Felton's Computer
File Edit View Favorites Tools Help
ASSOC. EDWARD TURNER
Police
Local Disk [D.]
Local Disk
Capacity: 34.2 GB
Used: 1.32 GB
KNOWN ASSOCIATES:
EDWARD TUNER
ARRESTS: 1
CONVICTIONS: 0
Felton's Computer
File Edit View Favorites Tools Help
ASSOC. EDWARD TURNER
Police
Local Disk [D.]
Local Disk
Capacity: 34.2 GB
Used: 1.32 GB
KNOWN ASSOCIATES:
EDWARD TURNER
ARRESTS: 1
CONVICTIONS: 0
MORE INFO

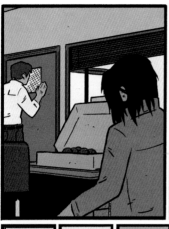

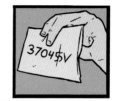

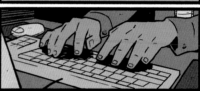

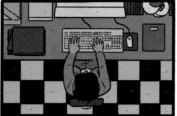

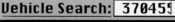

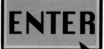

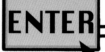

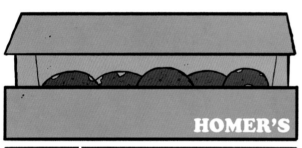

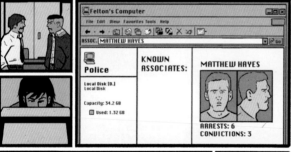

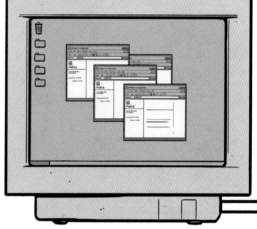

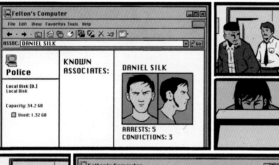

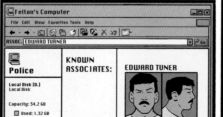

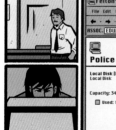

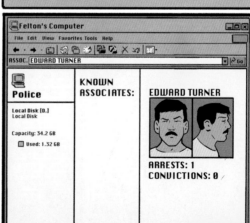

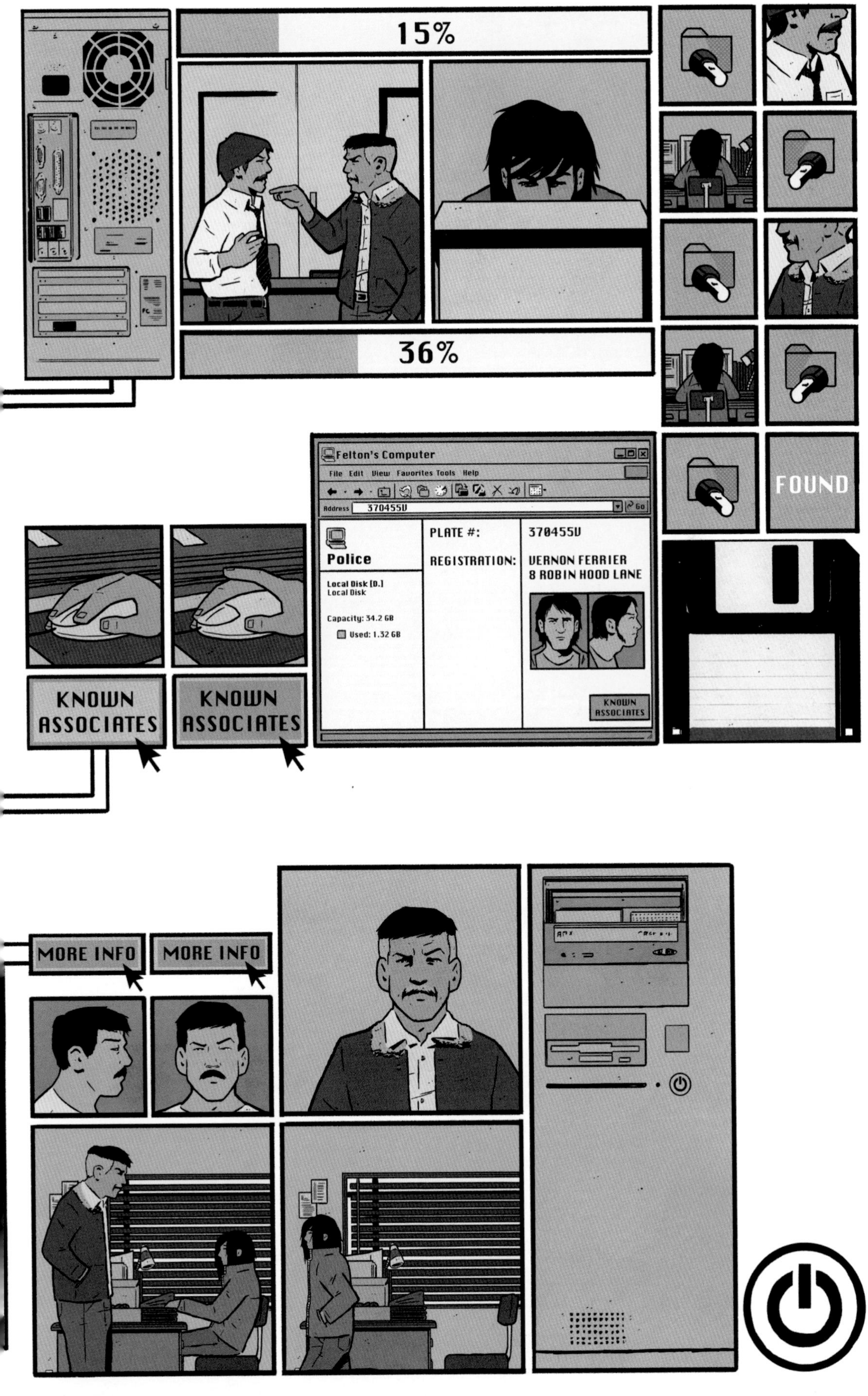
15%
36%
FOUND
Felton's Computer
File Edit View Favorites Tools Help
Address 370455V
Police
Local Disk [D.]
Local Disk
Capacity: 34.2 GB
Used: 1.32 GB
PLATE #:
370455V
REGISTRATION:
VERNON FERRIER
8 ROBIN HOOD LANE
KNOWN ASSOCIATES
KNOWN ASSOCIATES
KNOWN ASSOCIATES
MORE INFO
MORE INFO

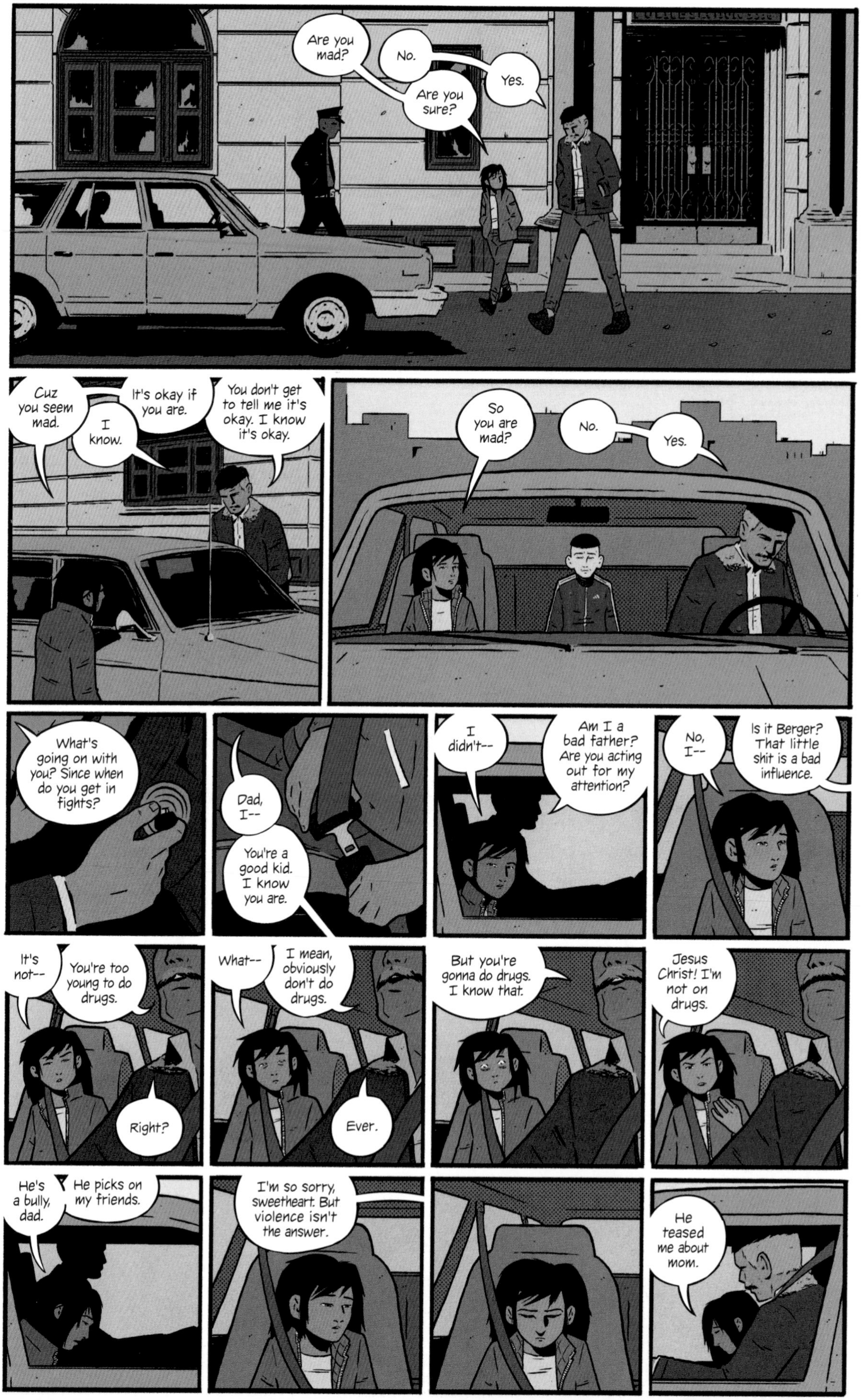
Are you mad?
No.
Yes.
Are you sure?
Cuz you seem mad.
It's okay if you are.
I know.
You don't get to tell me it's okay. I know it's okay.
So you are mad?
No.
Yes.
What's going on with you? Since when do you get in fights?
Dad, I--
You're a good kid. I know you are.
I didn't--
Am I a bad father? Are you acting out for my attention?
No, I--
Is it Berger? That little shit is a bad influence.
It's not--
You're too young to do drugs.
Right?
What--
I mean, obviously don't do drugs.
Ever.
But you're gonna do drugs. I know that.
Jesus Christ! I'm not on drugs.
He's a bully, dad.
He picks on my friends.
I'm so sorry, sweetheart. But violence isn't the answer.
He teased me about mom.

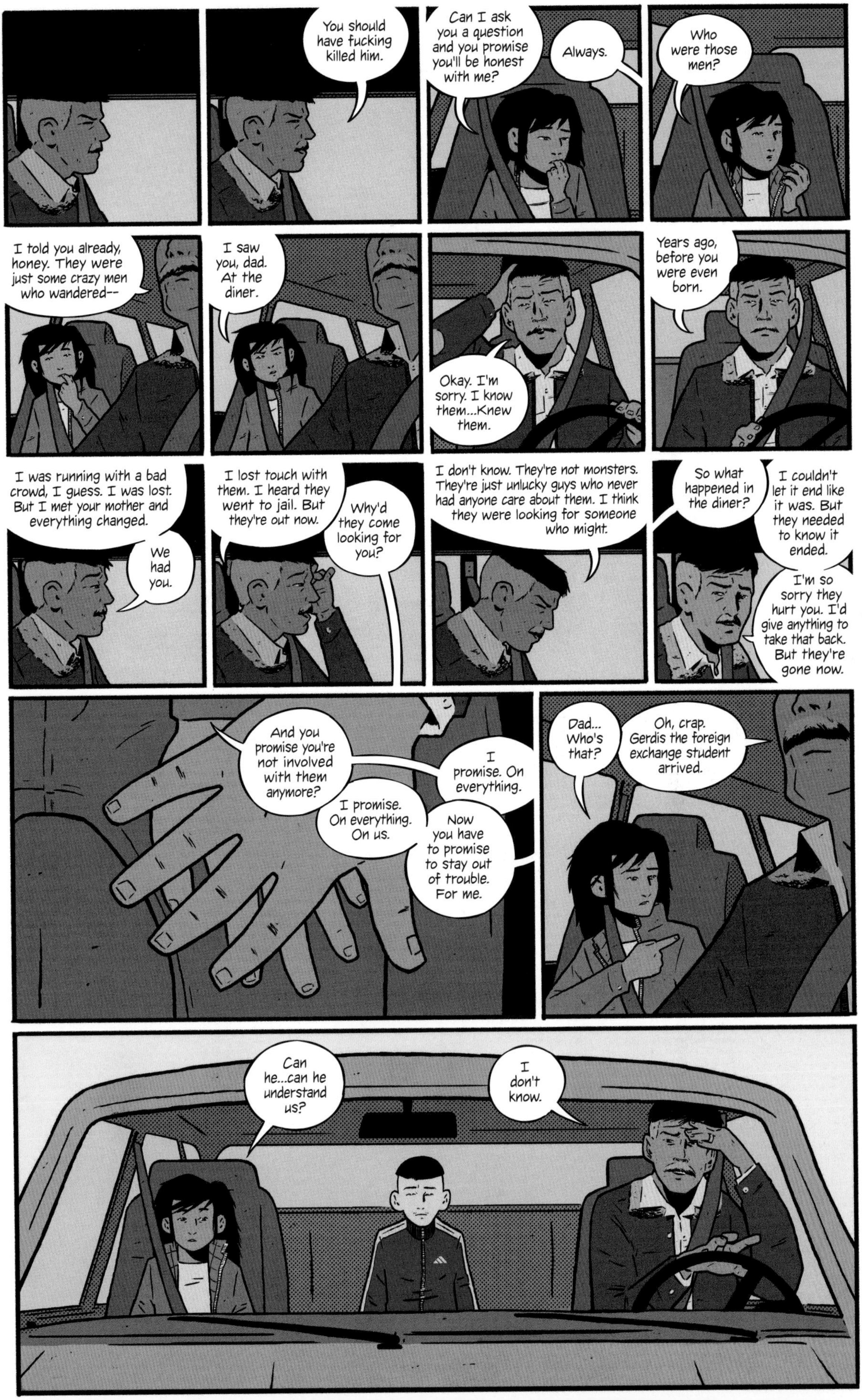
You should have fucking killed him.
Can I ask you a question and you promise you'll be honest with me?
Always.
Who were those men?
I told you already, honey. They were just some crazy men who wandered--
I saw you, dad. At the diner.
Okay. I'm sorry. I know them...Knew them.
Years ago, before you were even born.
I was running with a bad crowd, I guess. I was lost. But I met your mother and everything changed.
We had you.
I lost touch with them. I heard they went to jail. But they're out now.
Why'd they come looking for you?
I don't know. They're not monsters. They're just unlucky guys who never had anyone care about them. I think they were looking for someone who might.
So what happened in the diner?
I couldn't let it end like it was. But they needed to know it ended.
I'm so sorry they hurt you. I'd give anything to take that back. But they're gone now.
And you promise you're not involved with them anymore?
I promise. On everything.
I promise. On everything. On us.
Now you have to promise to stay out of trouble. For me.
Dad... Who's that?
Oh, crap. Gerdis the foreign exchange student arrived.
Can he...can he understand us?
I don't know.

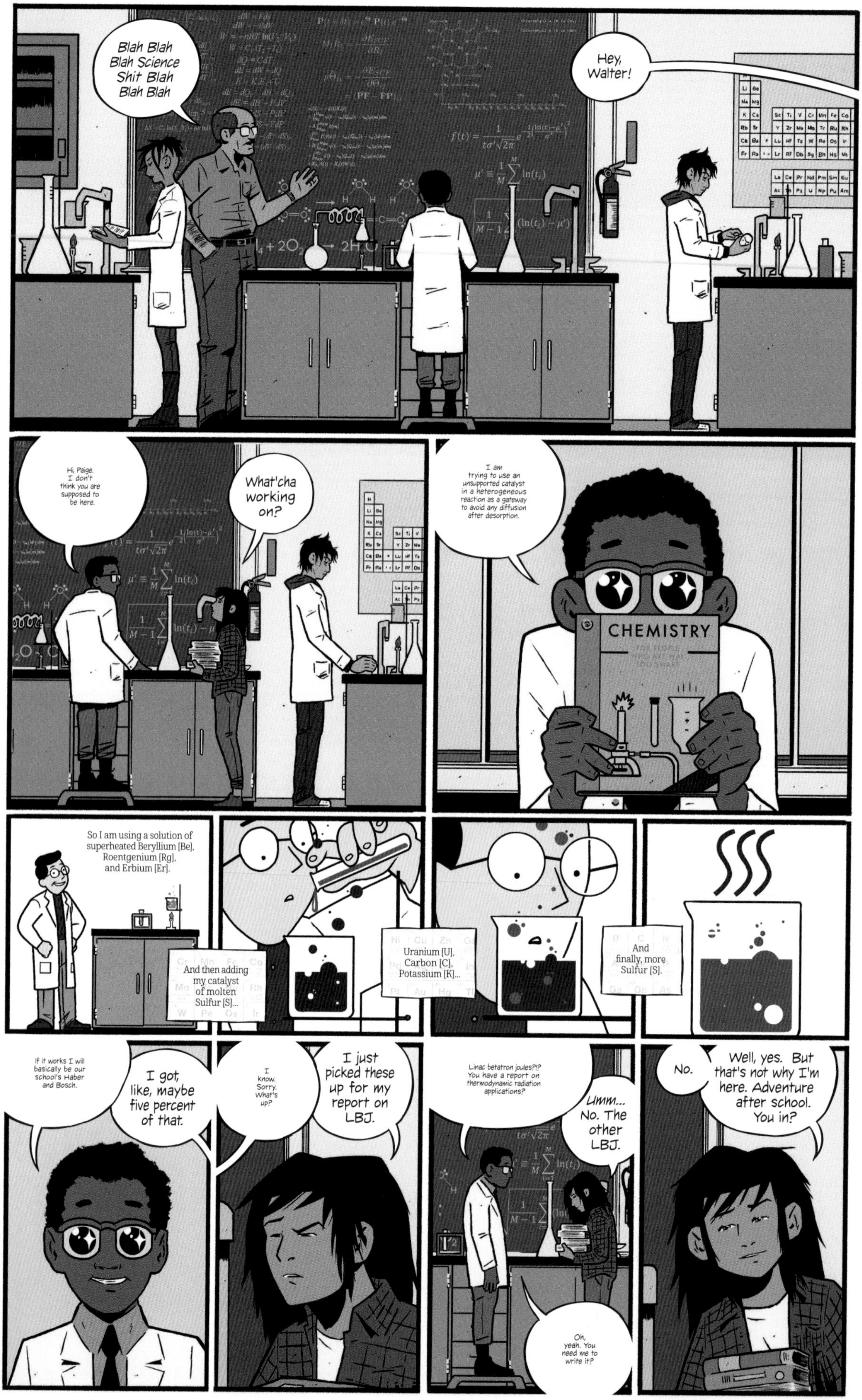
Blah Blah Blah Science Shit Blah Blah Blah
Hey, Walter!
Hi, Paige. I don't think you are supposed to be here.
What'cha working on?
I am trying to use an unsupported catalyst in a heterogeneous reaction as a gateway to avoid any diffusion after desorption.
CHEMISTRY
So I am using a solution of superheated Beryllium [Be], Roentgenium [Rg], and Erbium [Er].
And then adding my catalyst of molten Sulfur [S]...
Uranium [U], Carbon [C], Potassium [K]...
And finally, more Sulfur [S].
If it works I will basically be our school's Haber and Bosch.
I got, like, maybe five percent of that.
I know. Sorry. What's up?
I just picked these up for my report on LBJ.
Linac betatron joules?!? You have a report on thermodynamic radiation applications?
Umm... No. The other LBJ.
Oh, yeah. You need me to write it?
No.
Well, yes. But that's not why I'm here. Adventure after school. You in?

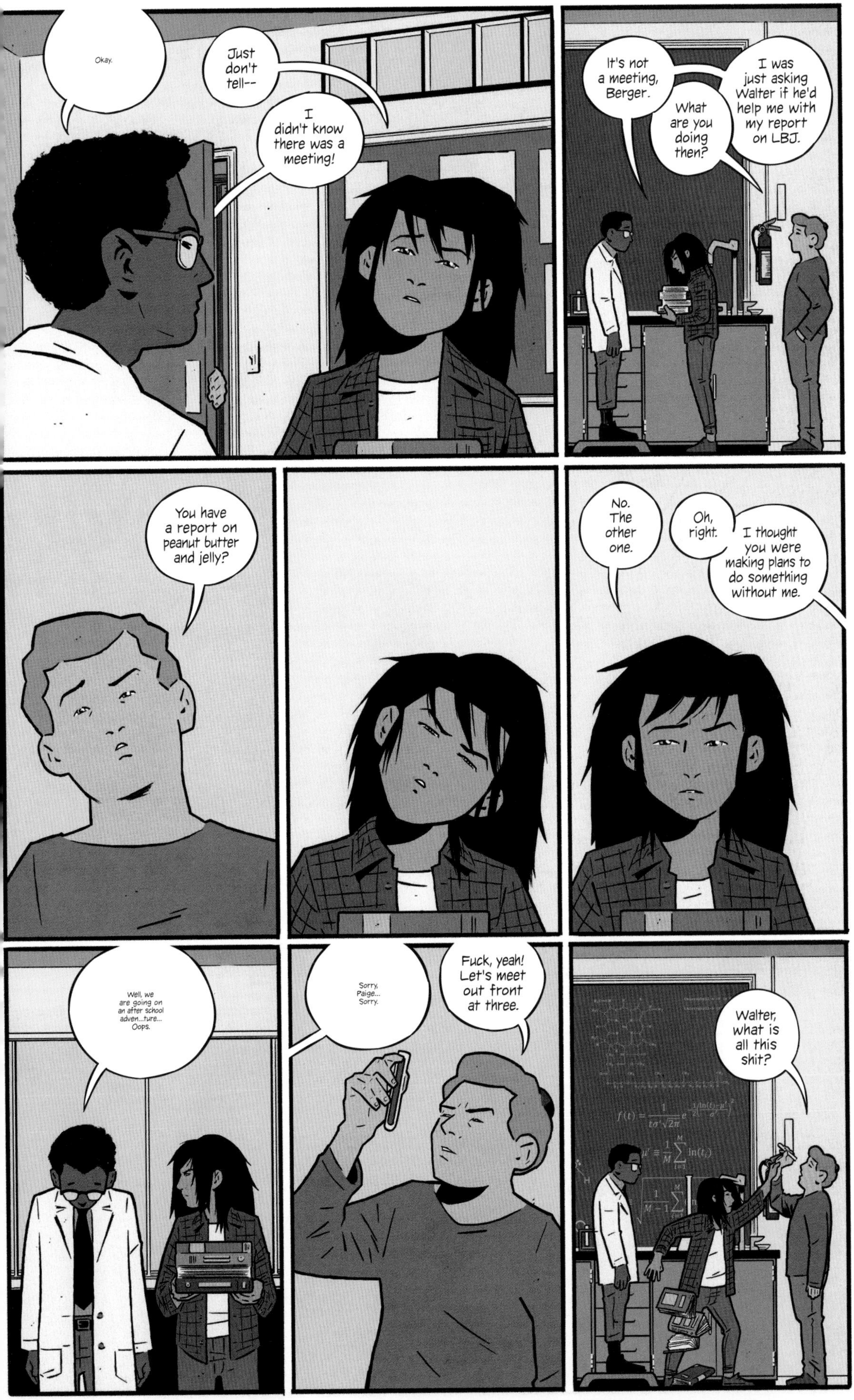
Okay.
Just don't tell--
I didn't know there was a meeting!
It's not a meeting, Berger.
What are you doing then?
I was just asking Walter if he'd help me with my report on LBJ.
You have a report on peanut butter and jelly?
No. The other one.
Oh, right.
I thought you were making plans to do something without me.
Well, we are going on an after school adven...ture... Oops.
Sorry, Paige... Sorry.
Fuck, yeah! Let's meet out front at three.
Walter, what is all this shit?

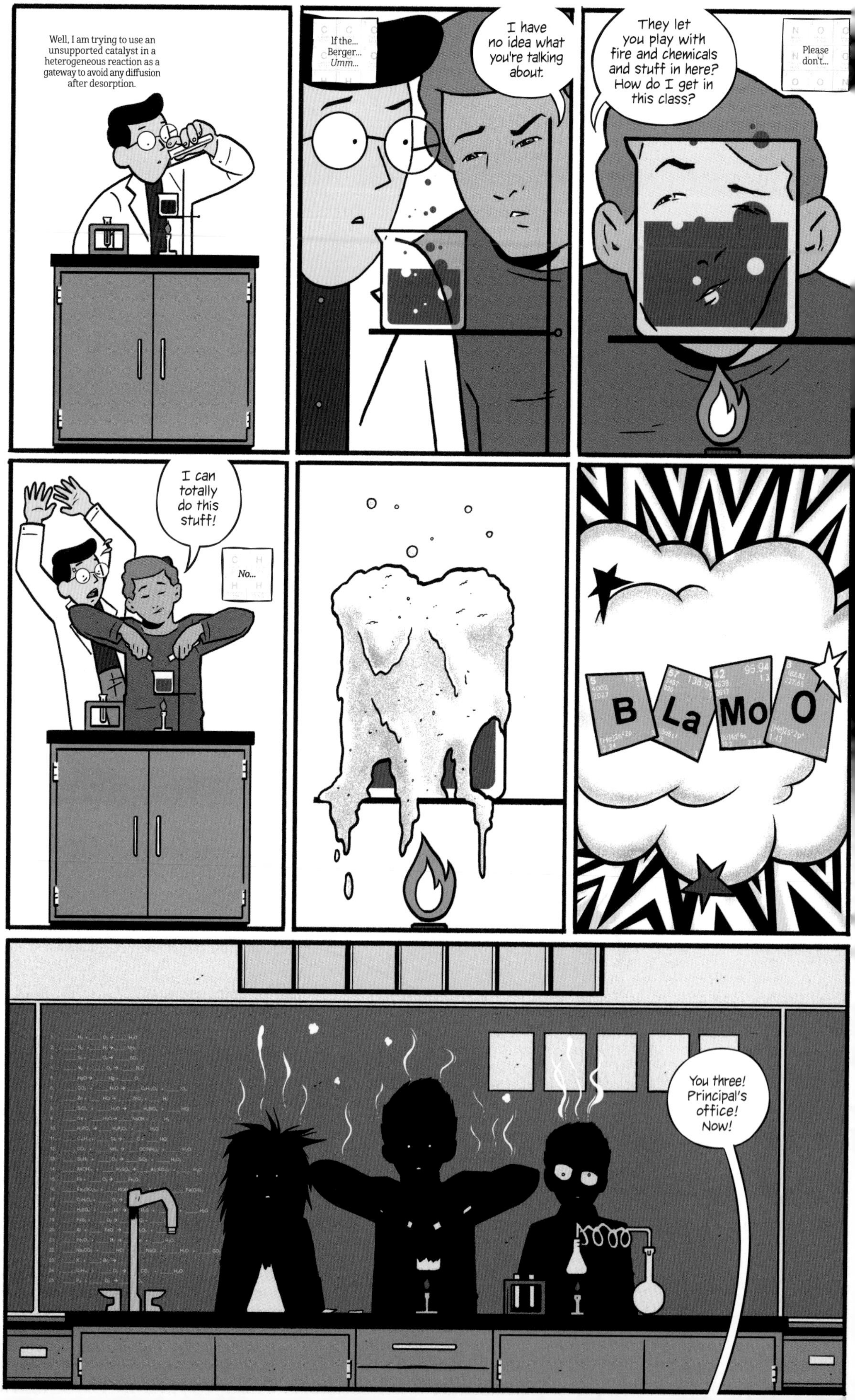

Well, I am trying to use an unsupported catalyst in a heterogeneous reaction as a gateway to avoid any diffusion after desorption.
If the... Berger... *Umm...*
I have no idea what you're talking about.
They let you play with fire and chemicals and stuff in here? How do I get in this class?
Please don't...
I can totally do this stuff!
No...
B La Mo O
You three! Principal's office! Now!

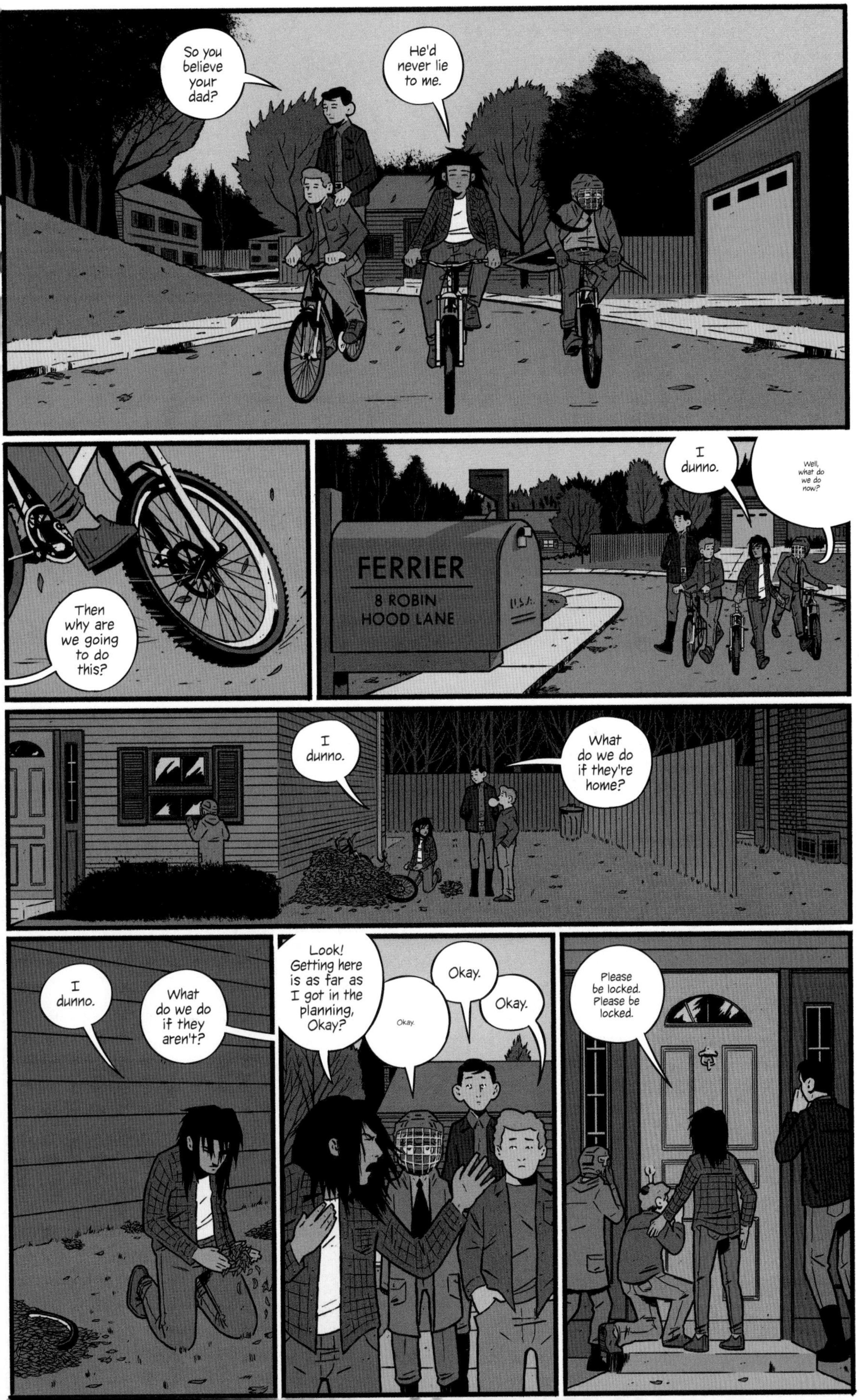
So you believe your dad?
He'd never lie to me.
Then why are we going to do this?
FERRIER
8 ROBIN HOOD LANE
U.S.A.
I dunno.
Well, what do we do now?
I dunno.
What do we do if they're home?
I dunno.
What do we do if they aren't?
Look! Getting here is as far as I got in the planning, Okay?
Okay.
Okay.
Okay.
Please be locked. Please be locked.

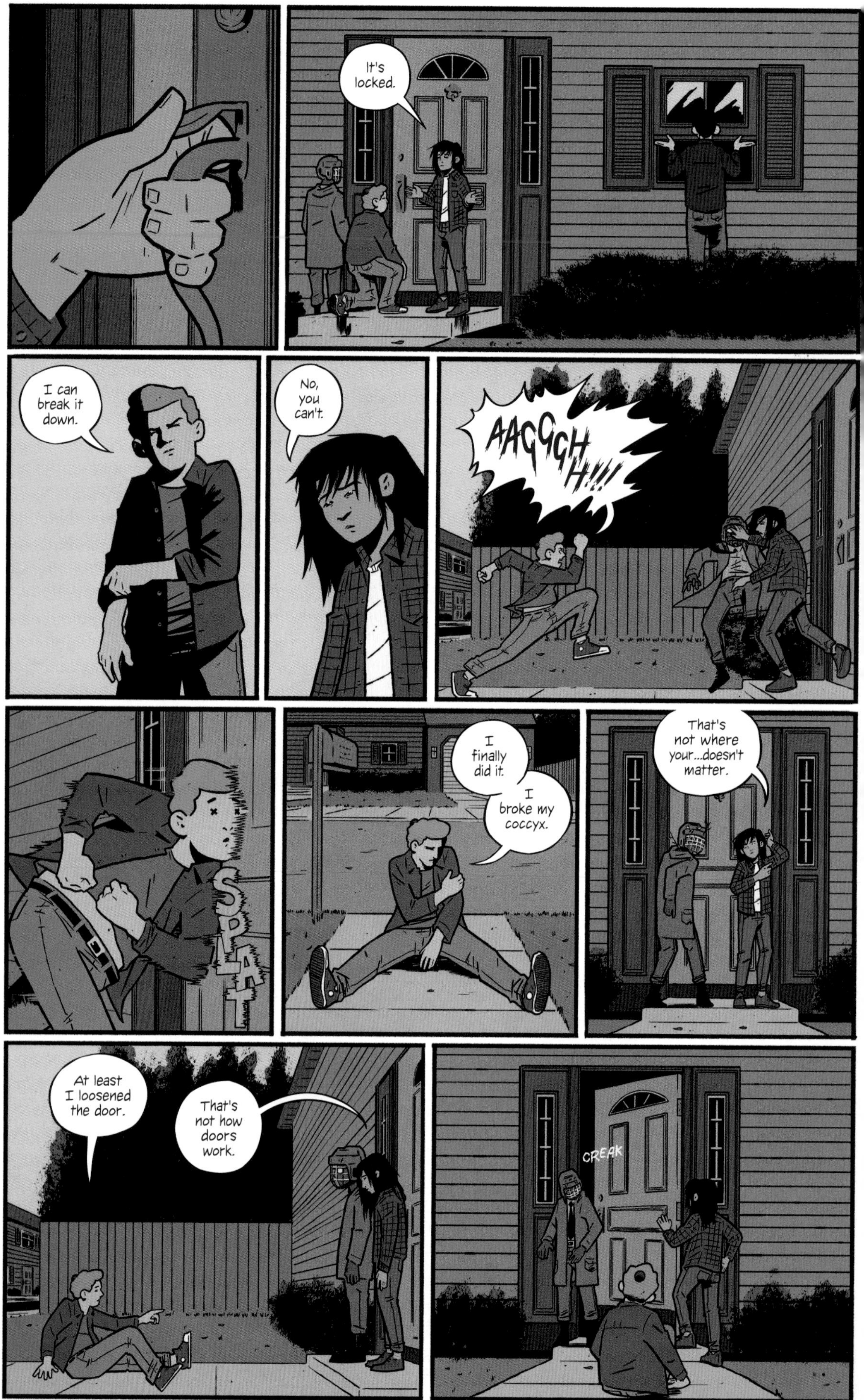

It's locked.
I can break it down.
No, you can't.
AAGGGHH!!!
SPLAT
I finally did it.
I broke my coccyx.
That's not where your...doesn't matter.
At least I loosened the door.
That's not how doors work.
CREAK

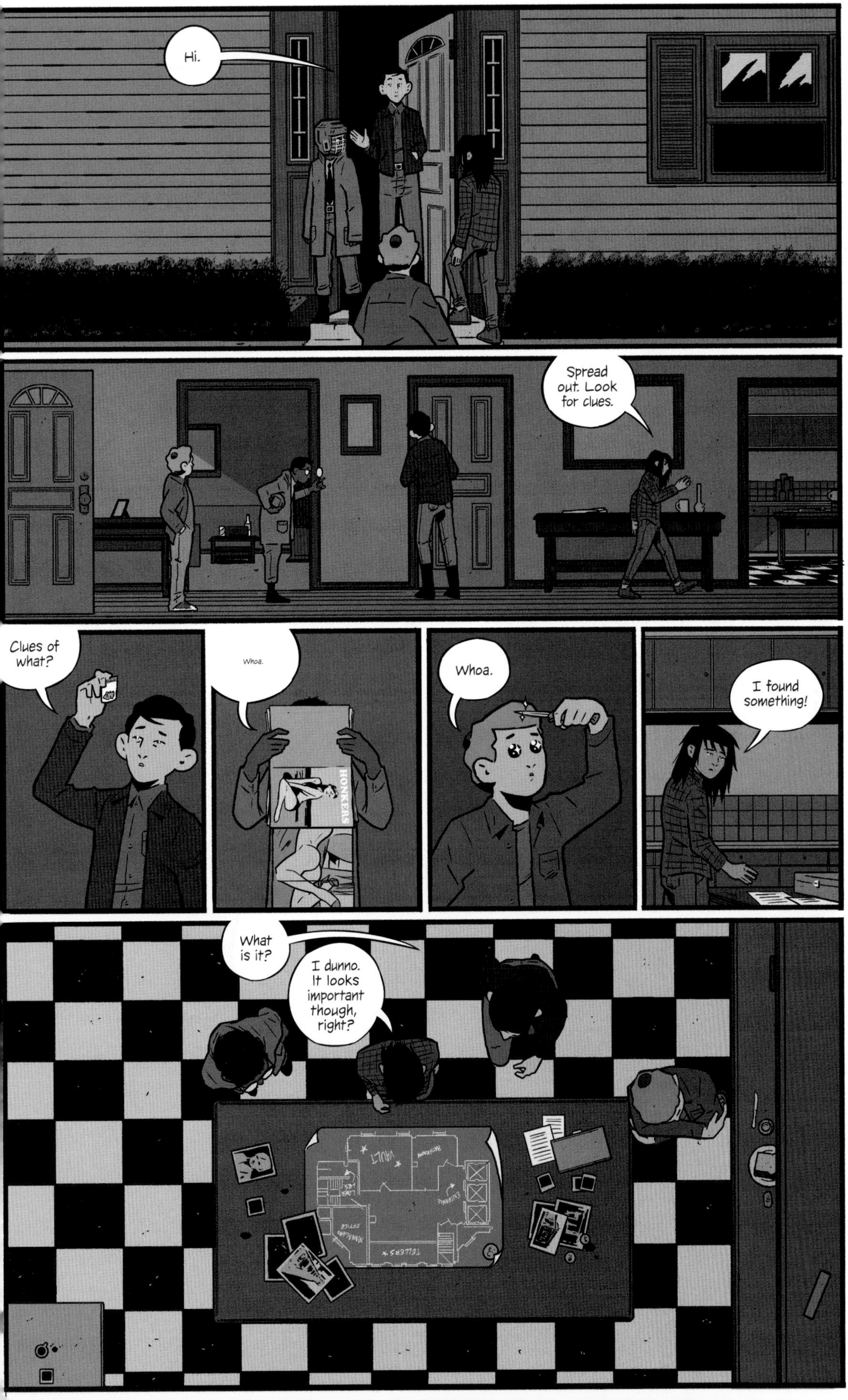
Hi.
Spread out. Look for clues.
Clues of what?
Whoa.
HONKERS
Whoa.
I found something!
What is it?
I dunno. It looks important though, right?
VAULT
TELLERS

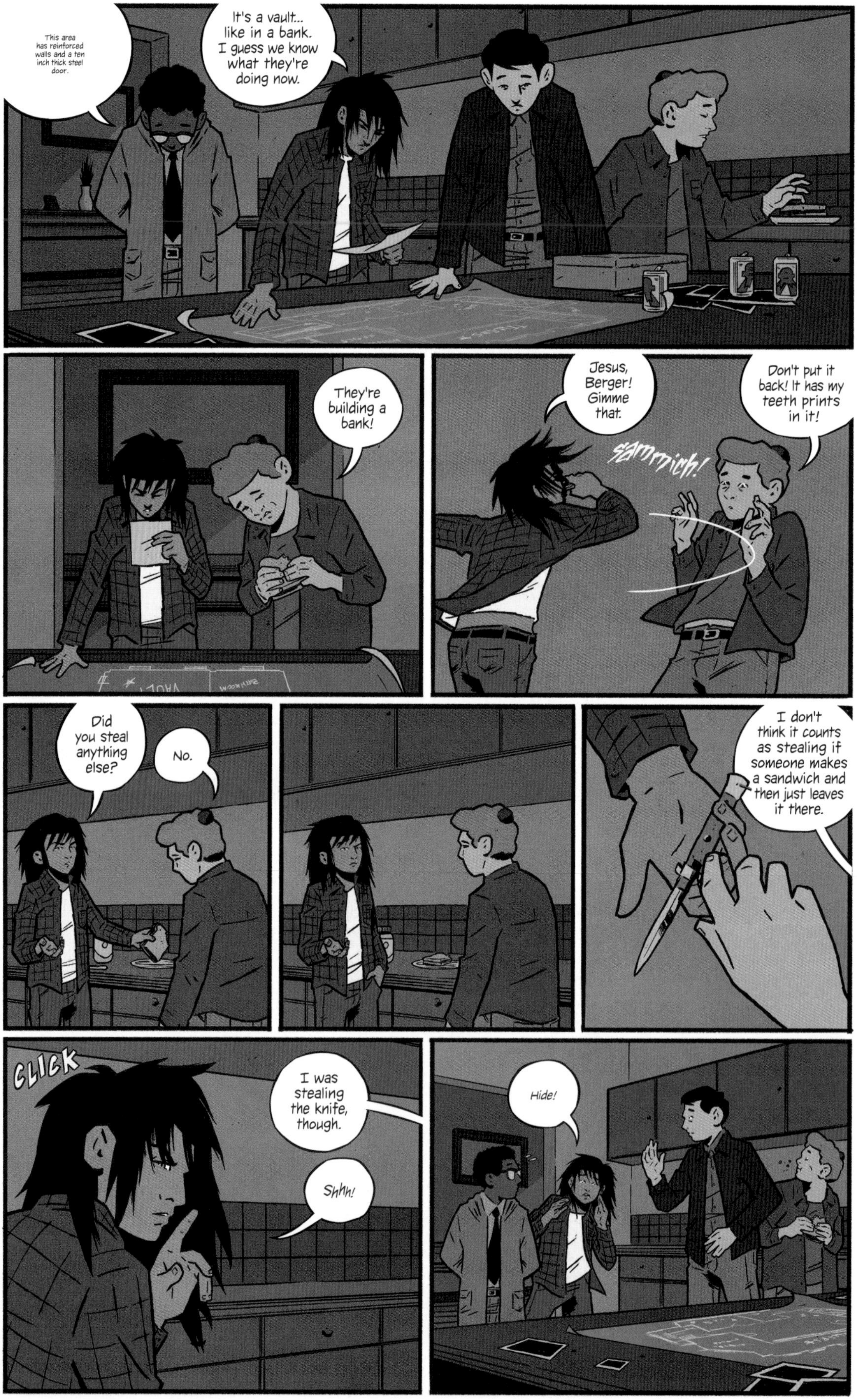
This area has reinforced walls and a ten inch thick steel door.
It's a vault... like in a bank. I guess we know what they're doing now.
They're building a bank!
Jesus, Berger! Gimme that.
SAMMICH!
Don't put it back! It has my teeth prints in it!
Did you steal anything else?
No.
I don't think it counts as stealing if someone makes a sandwich and then just leaves it there.
CLICK
I was stealing the knife, though.
Shhh!
Hide!

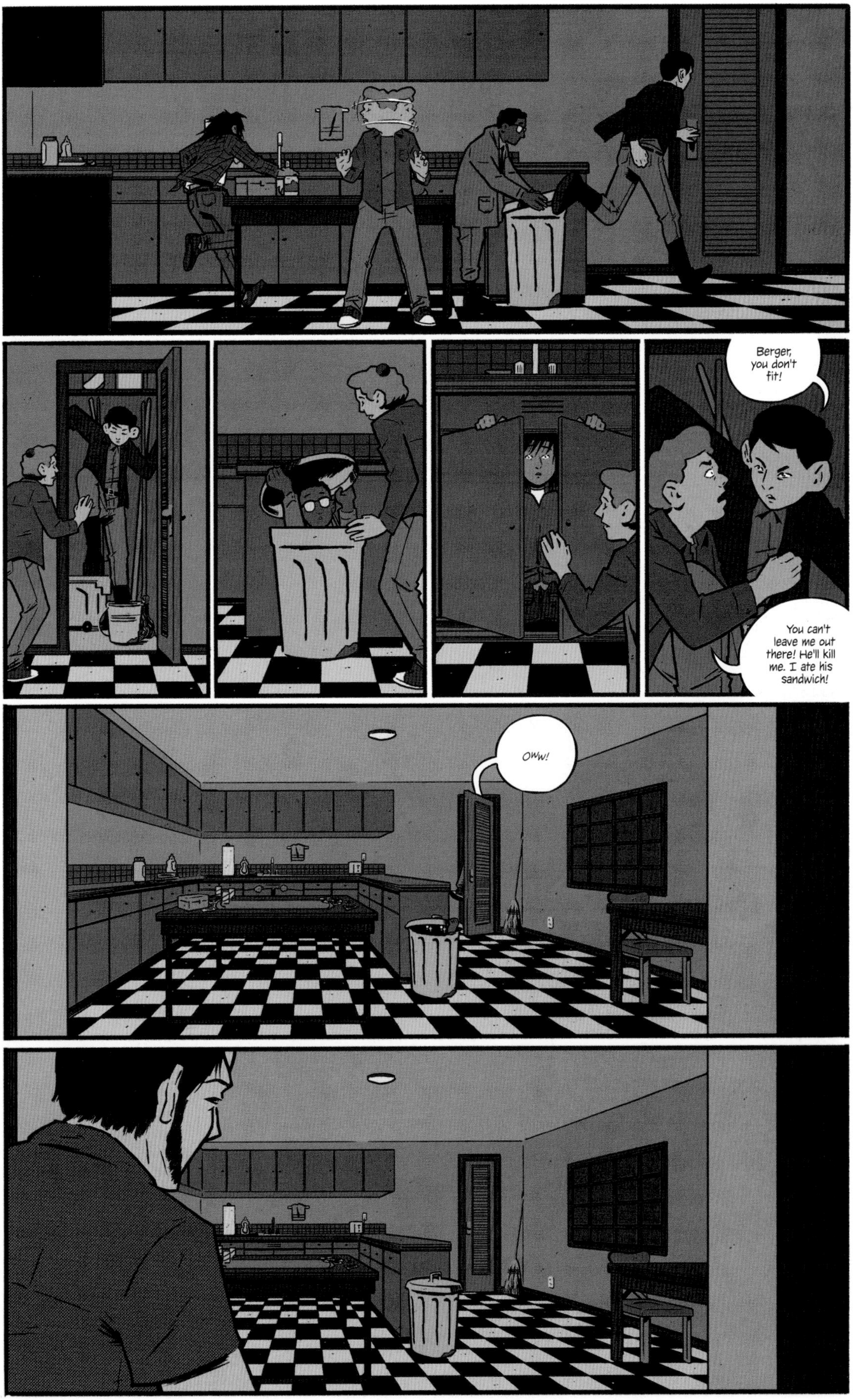
Berger, you don't fit!
You can't leave me out there! He'll kill me. I ate his sandwich!
OWW!

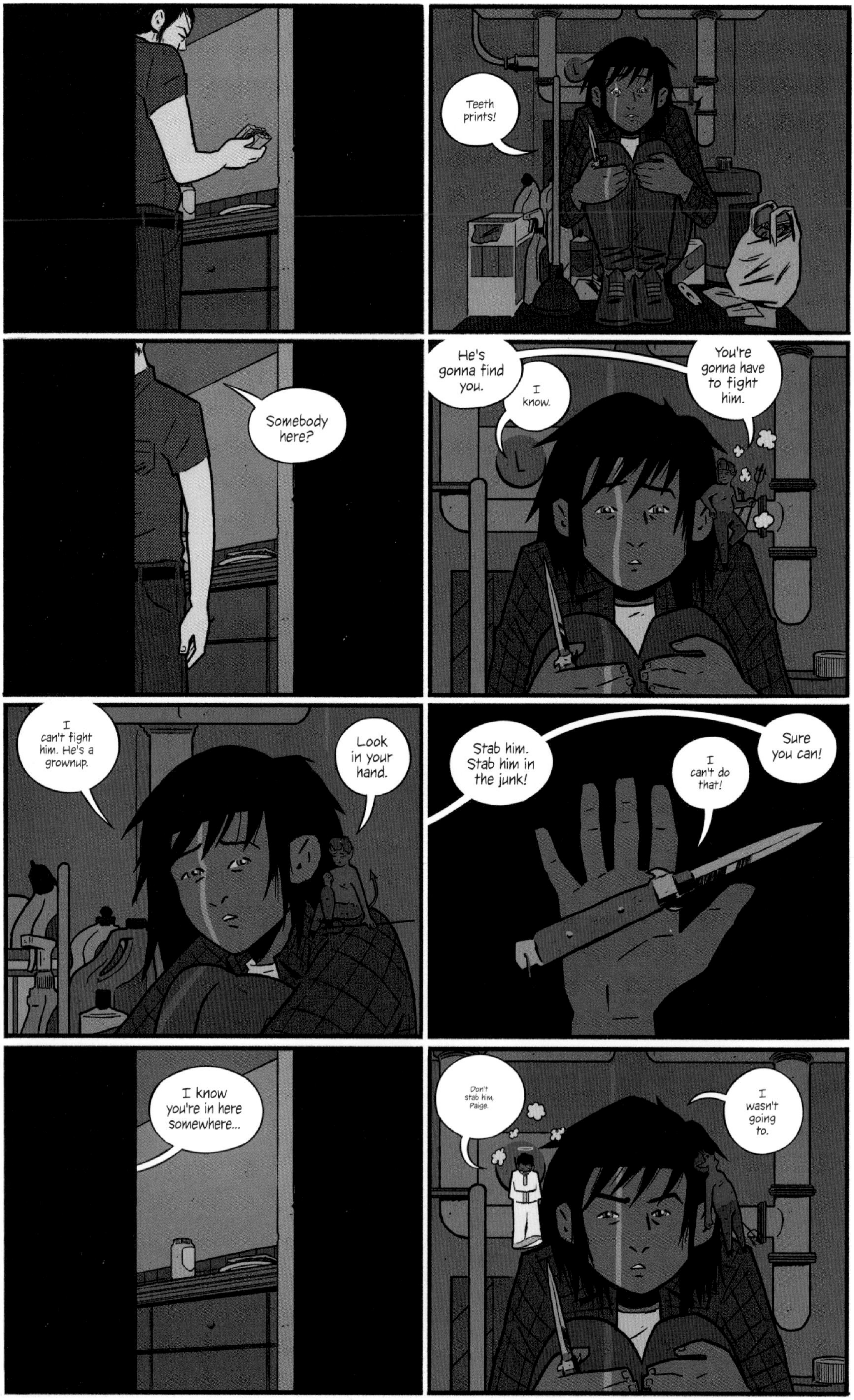
Teeth prints!
Somebody here?
He's gonna find you.
I know.
You're gonna have to fight him.
I can't fight him. He's a grownup.
Look in your hand.
Stab him. Stab him in the junk!
I can't do that!
Sure you can!
I know you're in here somewhere...
Don't stab him, Paige.
I wasn't going to.

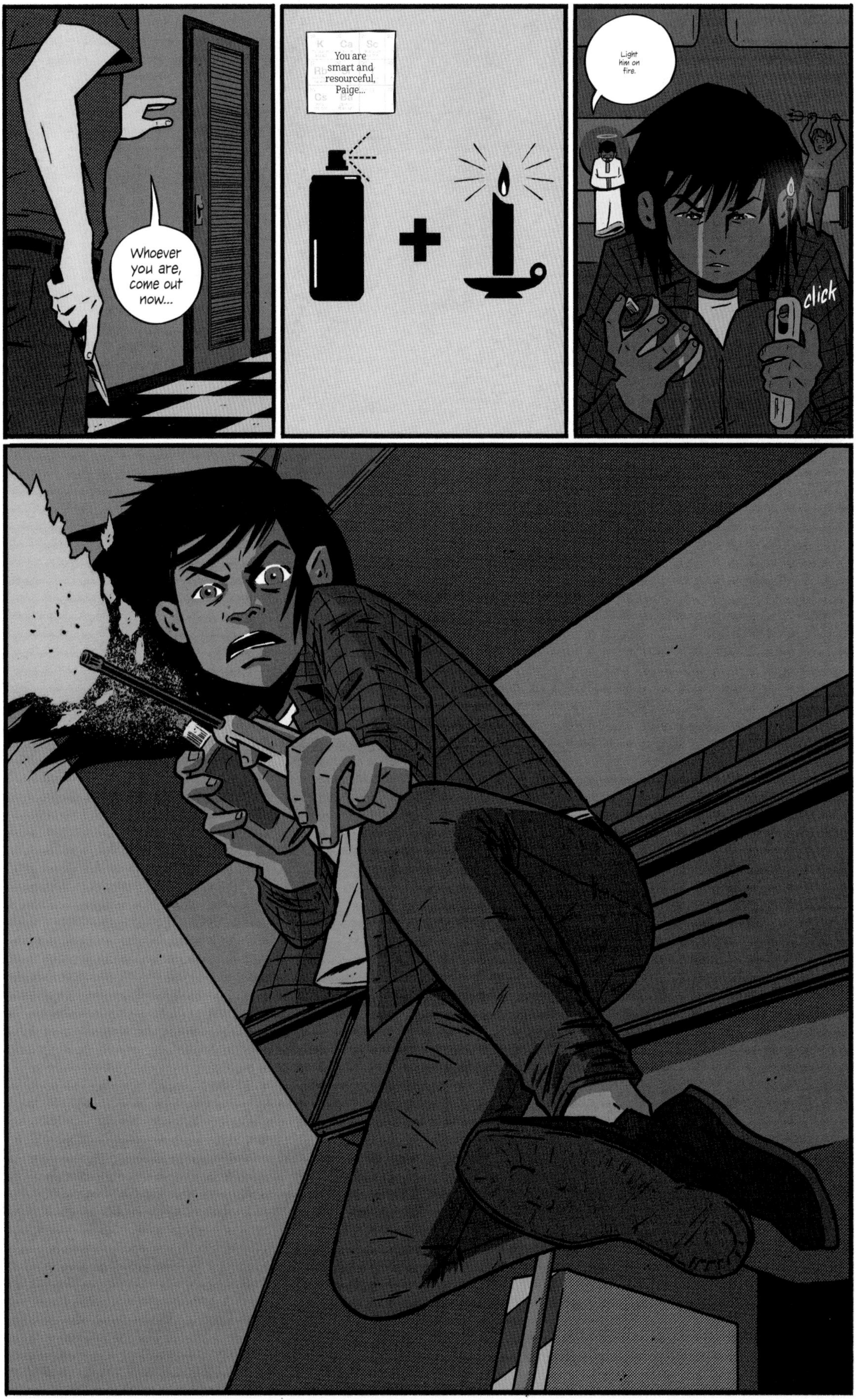

Whoever you are, come out now...
You are smart and resourceful, Paige...
Light him on fire.
click

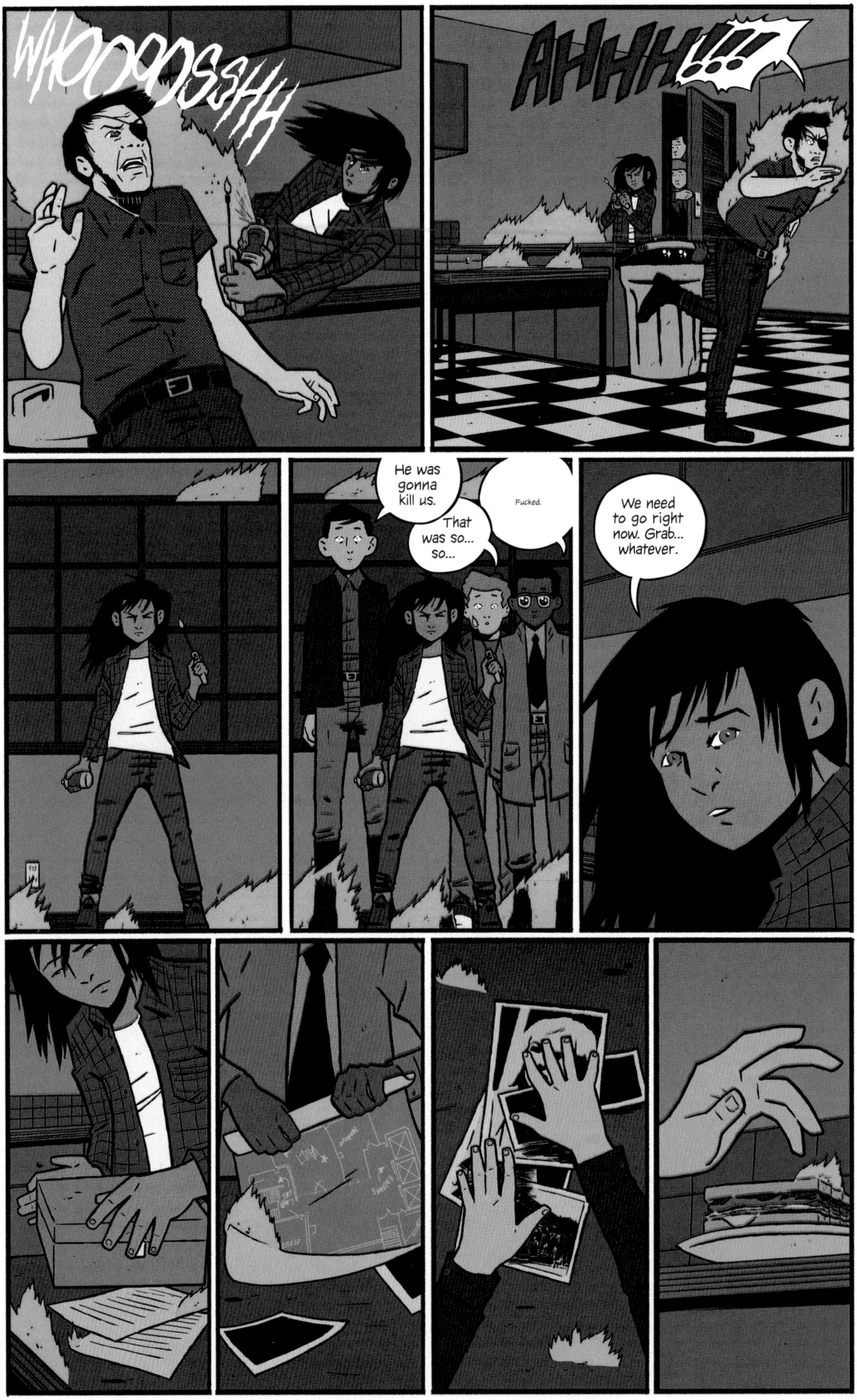
WHOOOOSSHH
AHHH!!!
He was gonna kill us.
That was so... so...
Fucked.
We need to go right now. Grab... whatever.

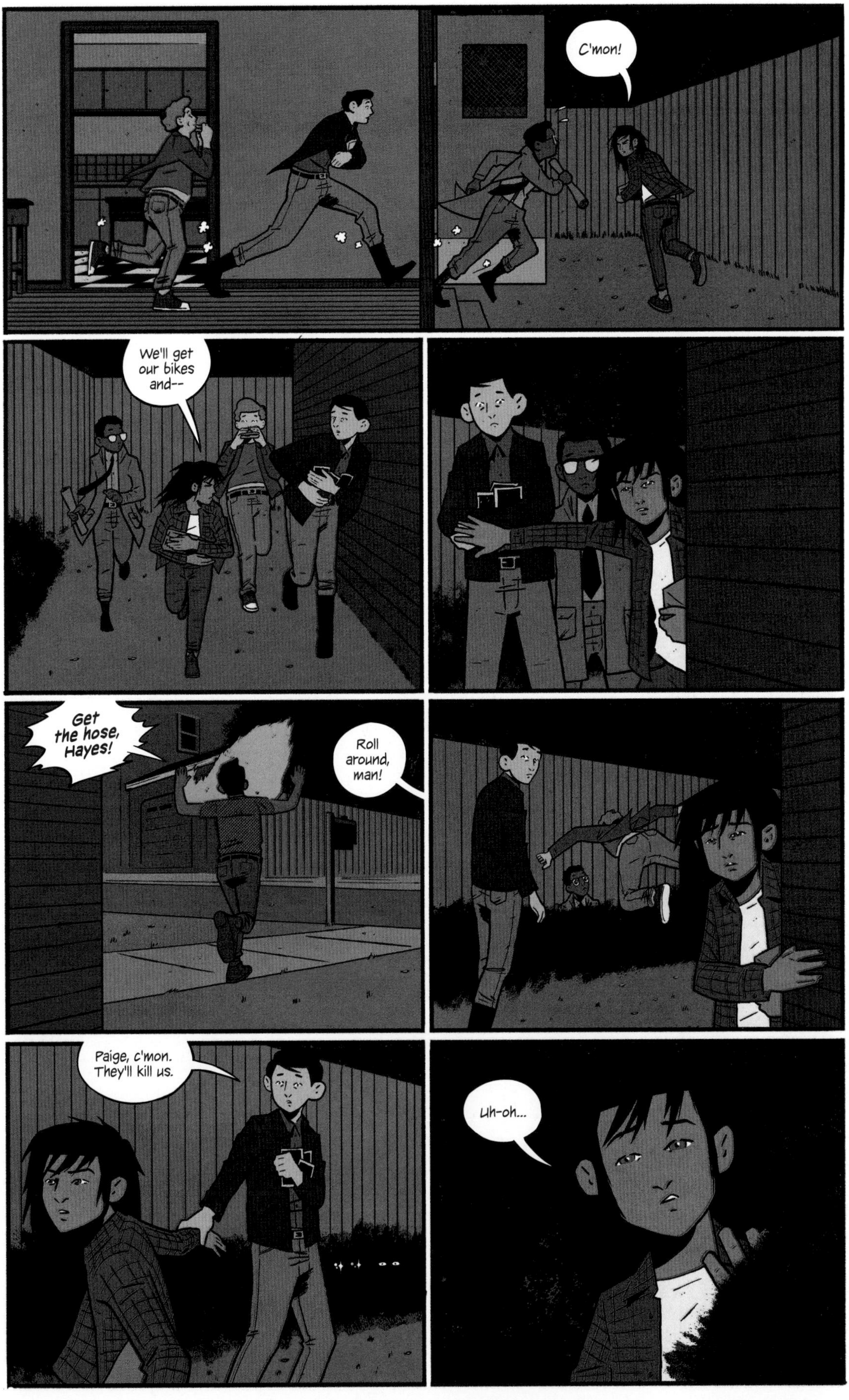
C'mon!
We'll get our bikes and--
Get the hose, Hayes!
Roll around, man!
Paige, c'mon. They'll kill us.
Uh-oh...

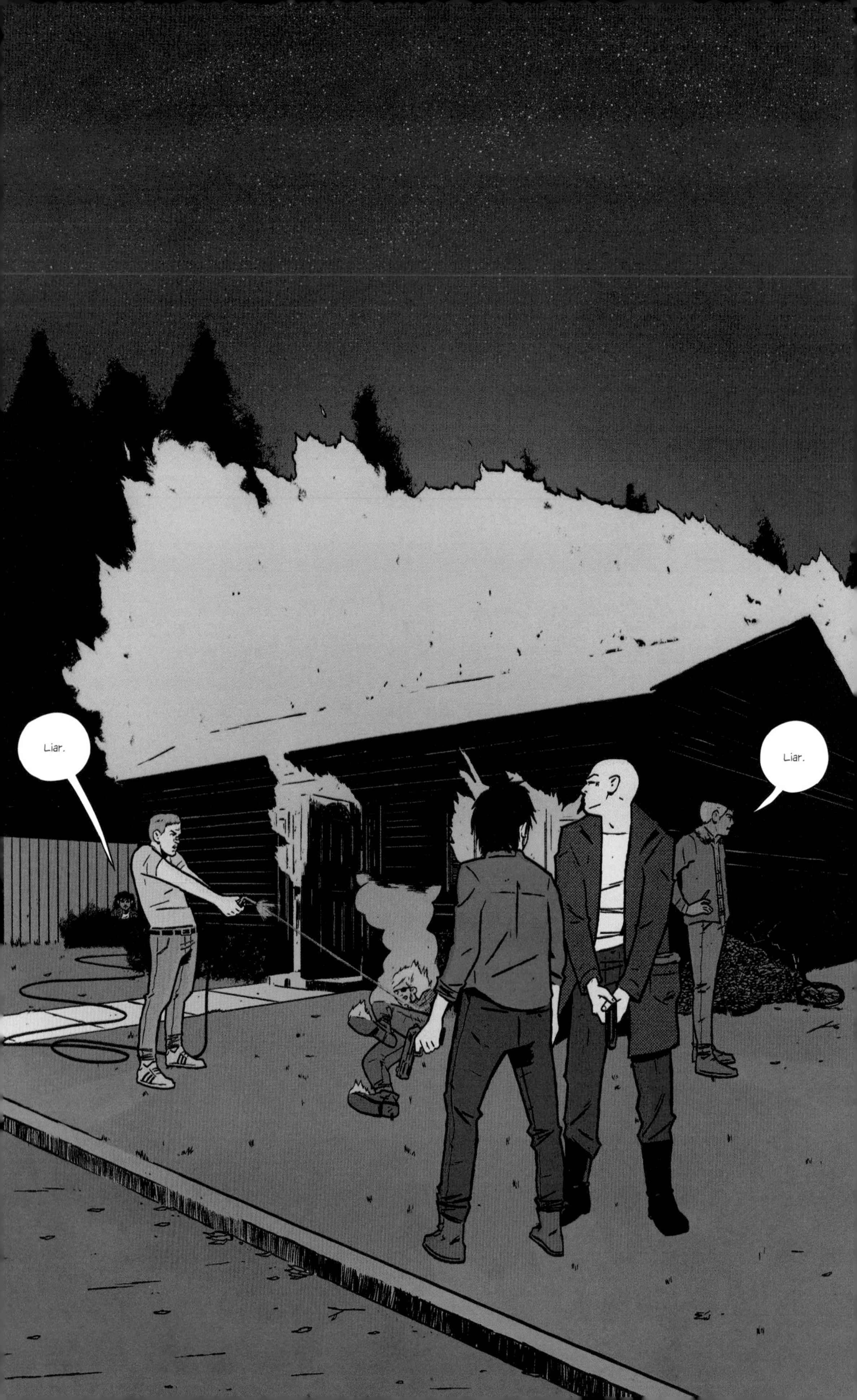
Liar.
Liar.

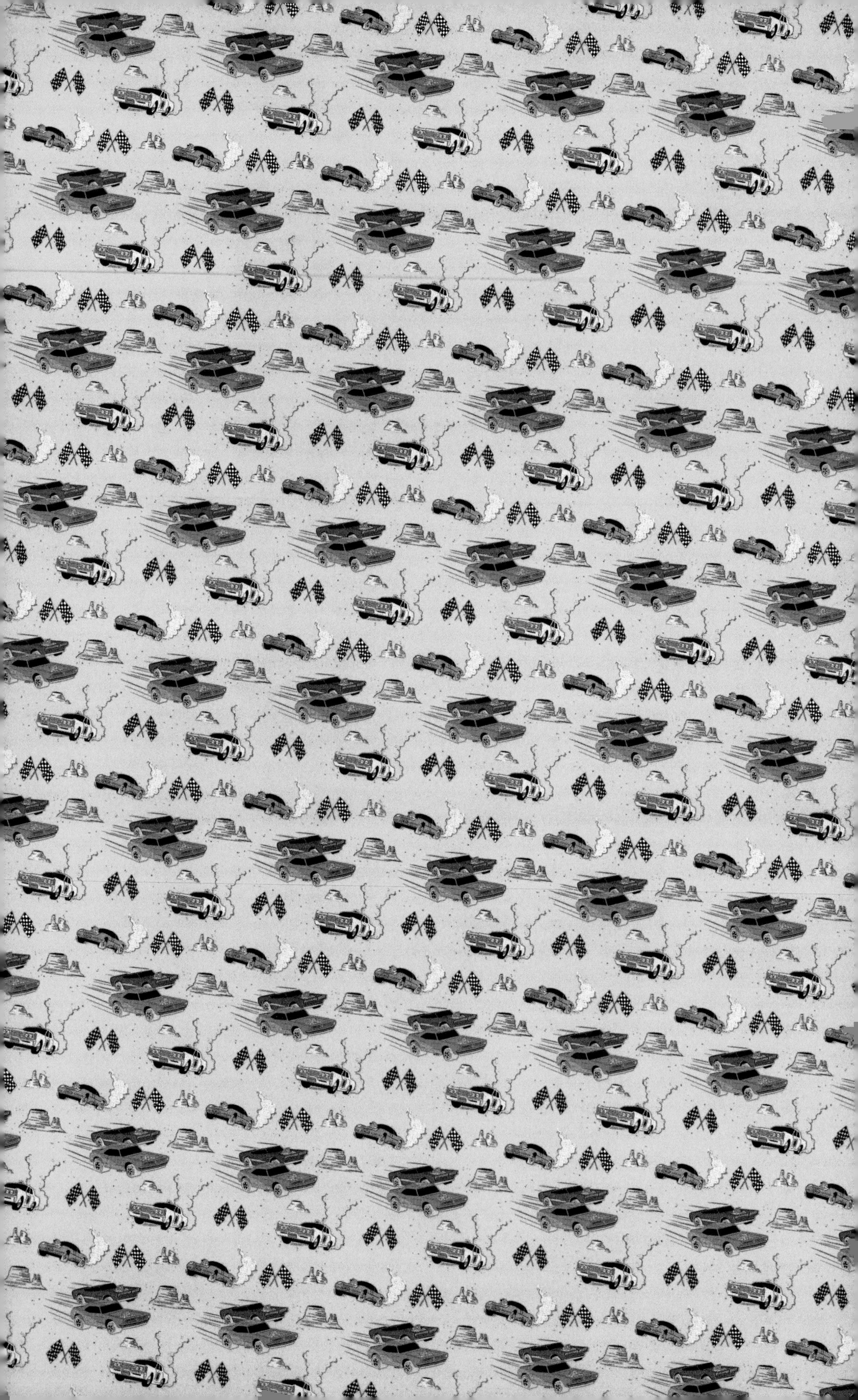

CHAPTER THREE

Leave the gum.
Take the cannoli.

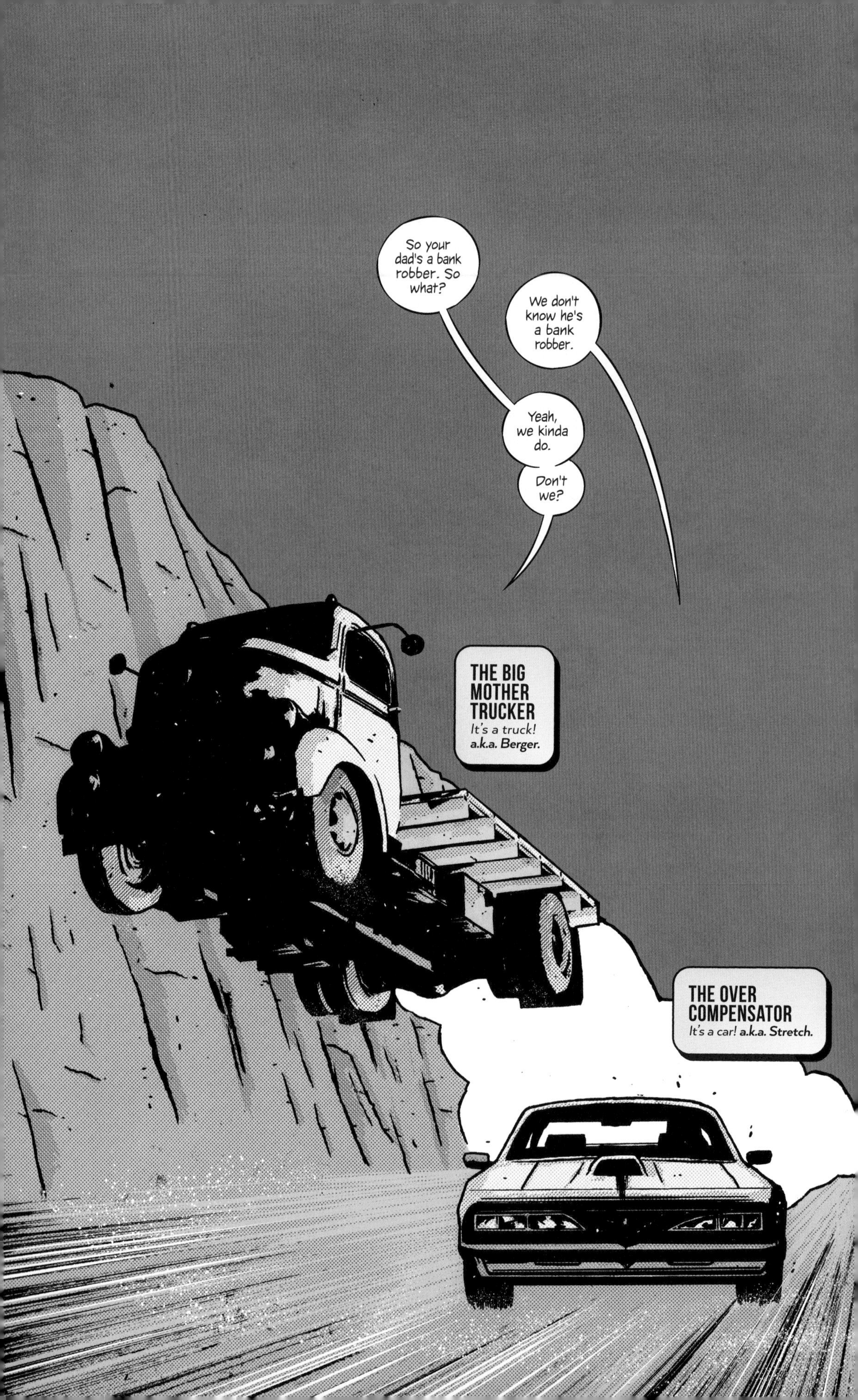
So your dad's a bank robber. So what?
We don't know he's a bank robber.
Yeah, we kinda do.
Don't we?
THE BIG MOTHER TRUCKER
It's a truck! a.k.a. Berger.
THE OVER COMPENSATOR
It's a car! a.k.a. Stretch.

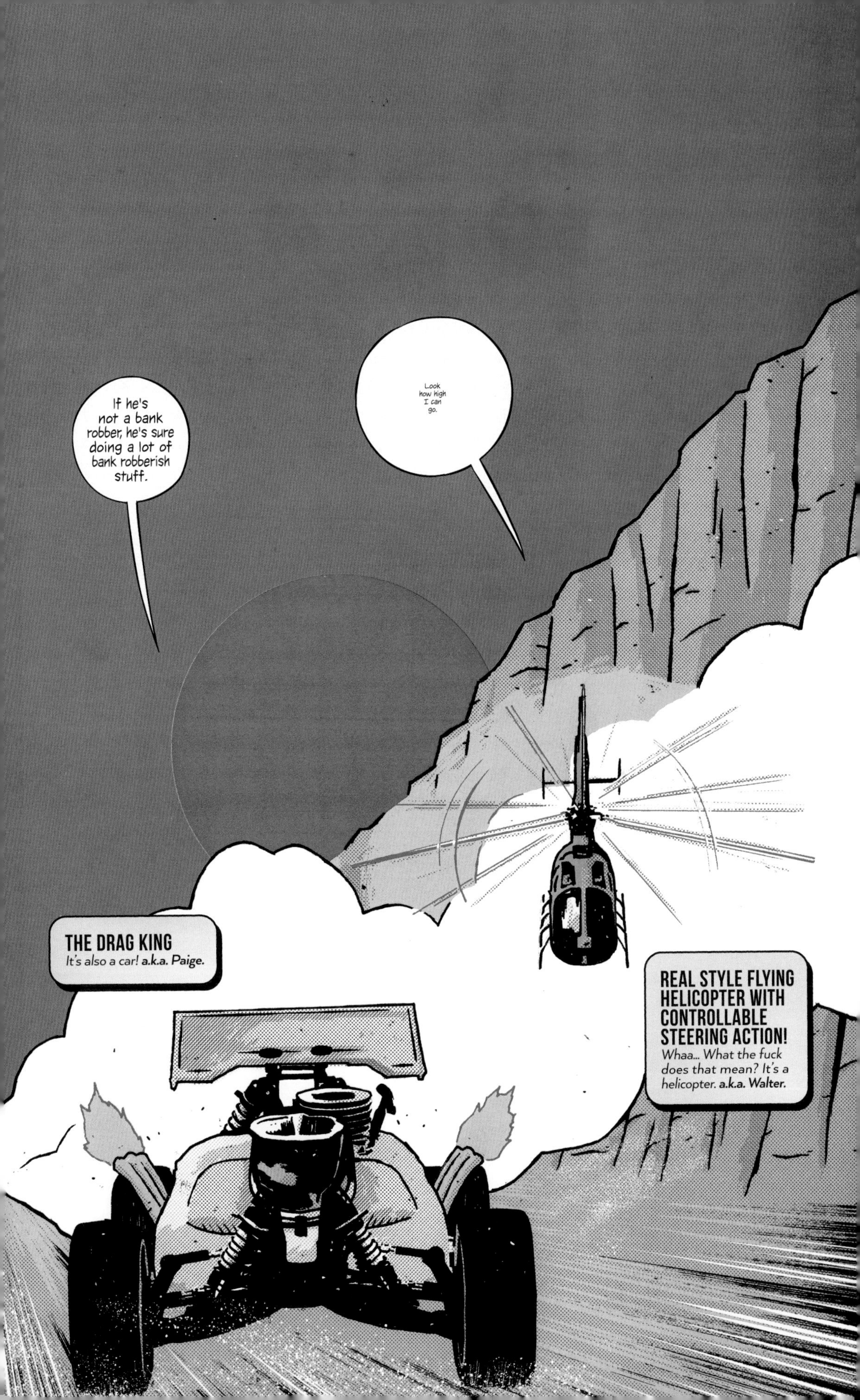
If he's not a bank robber, he's sure doing a lot of bank robberish stuff.
Look how high I can go.
THE DRAG KING
It's also a car! a.k.a. Paige.
REAL STYLE FLYING HELICOPTER WITH CONTROLLABLE STEERING ACTION!
Whaa... What the fuck does that mean? It's a helicopter. a.k.a. Walter.

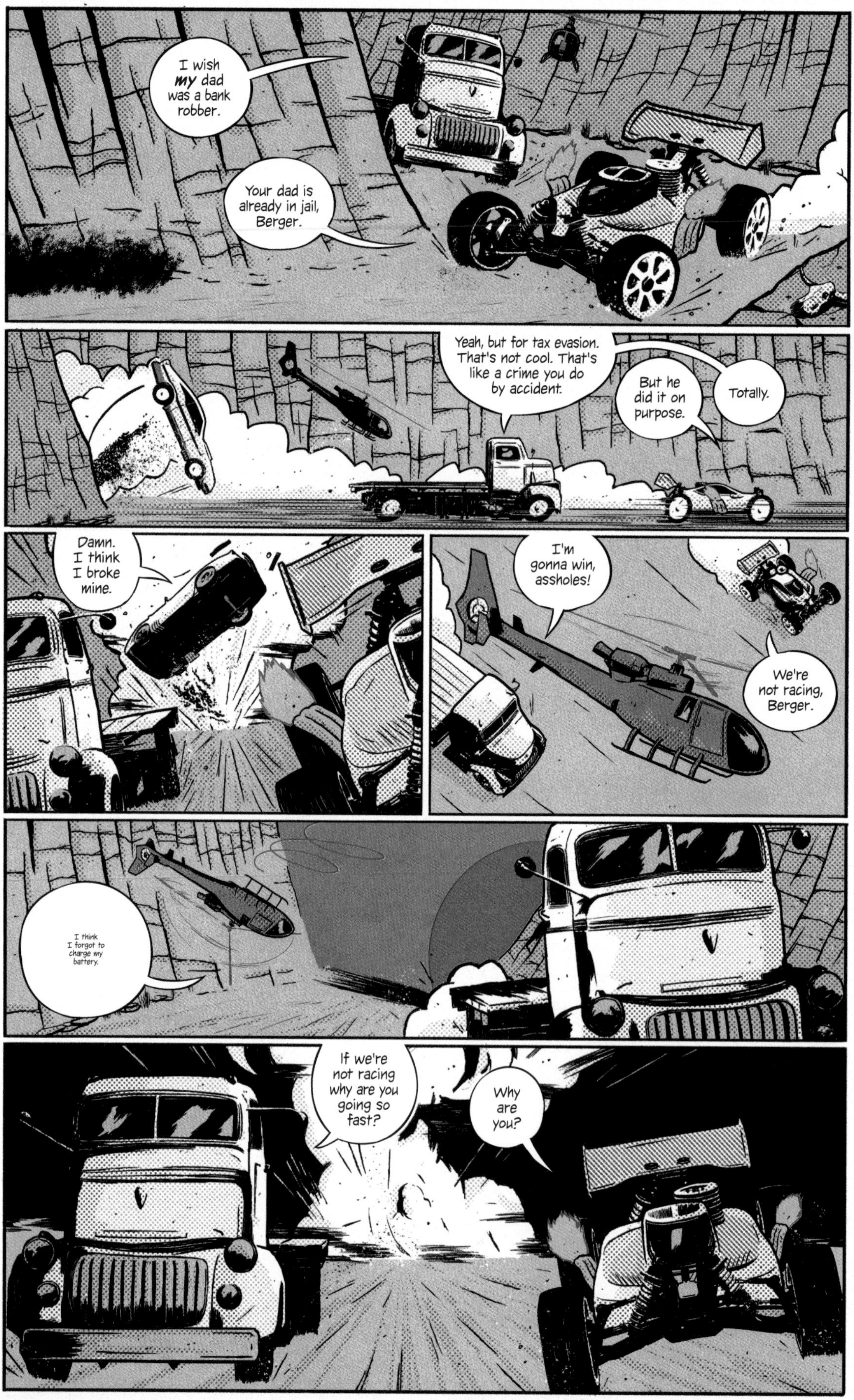
I wish *my* dad was a bank robber.
Your dad is already in jail, Berger.
Yeah, but for tax evasion. That's not cool. That's like a crime you do by accident.
But he did it on purpose.
Totally.
Damn. I think I broke mine.
I'm gonna win, assholes!
We're not racing, Berger.
I think I forgot to charge my battery.
If we're not racing why are you going so fast?
Why are you?

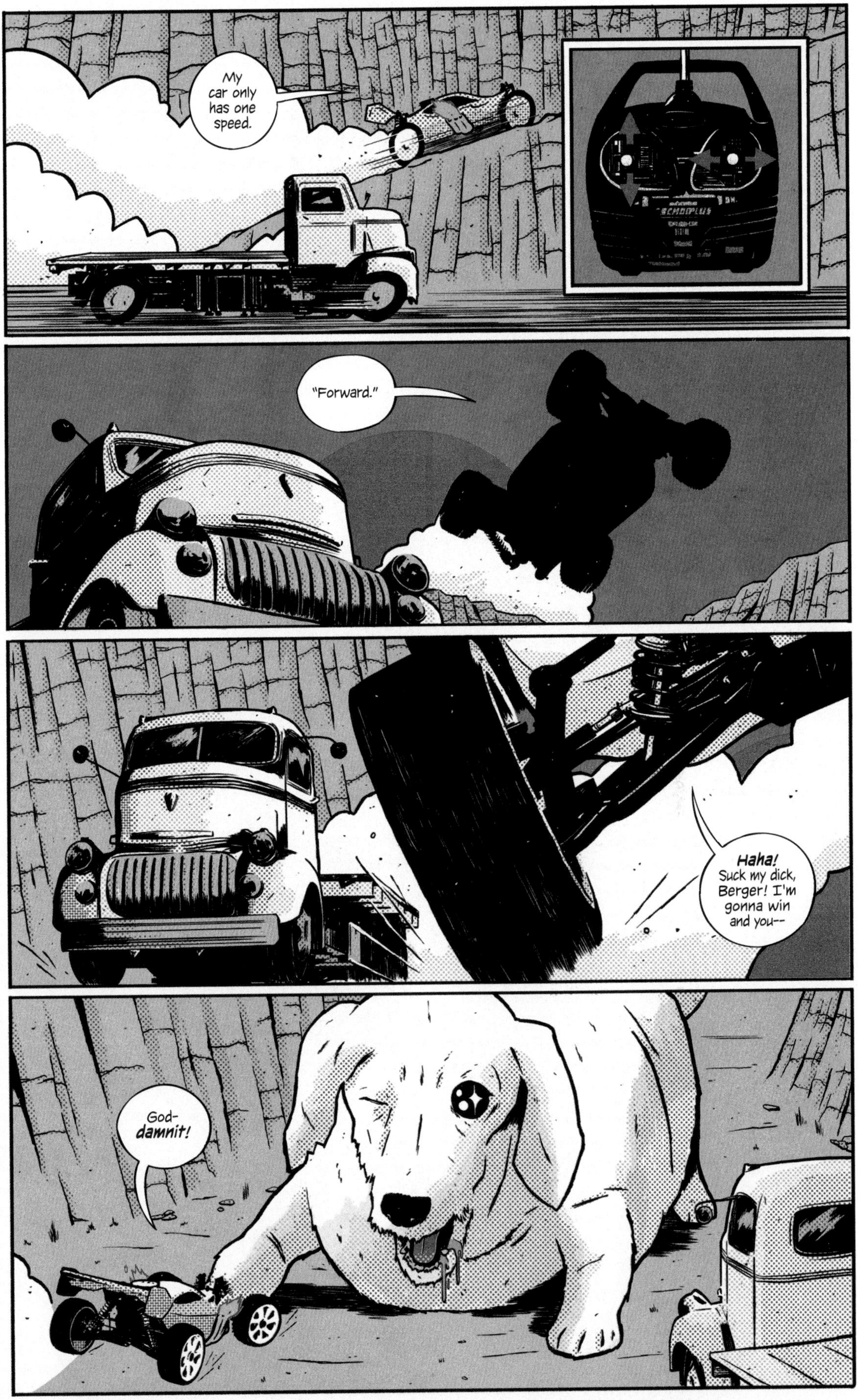

My car only has one speed.
"Forward."
Haha! Suck my dick, Berger! I'm gonna win and you--
God-damnit!

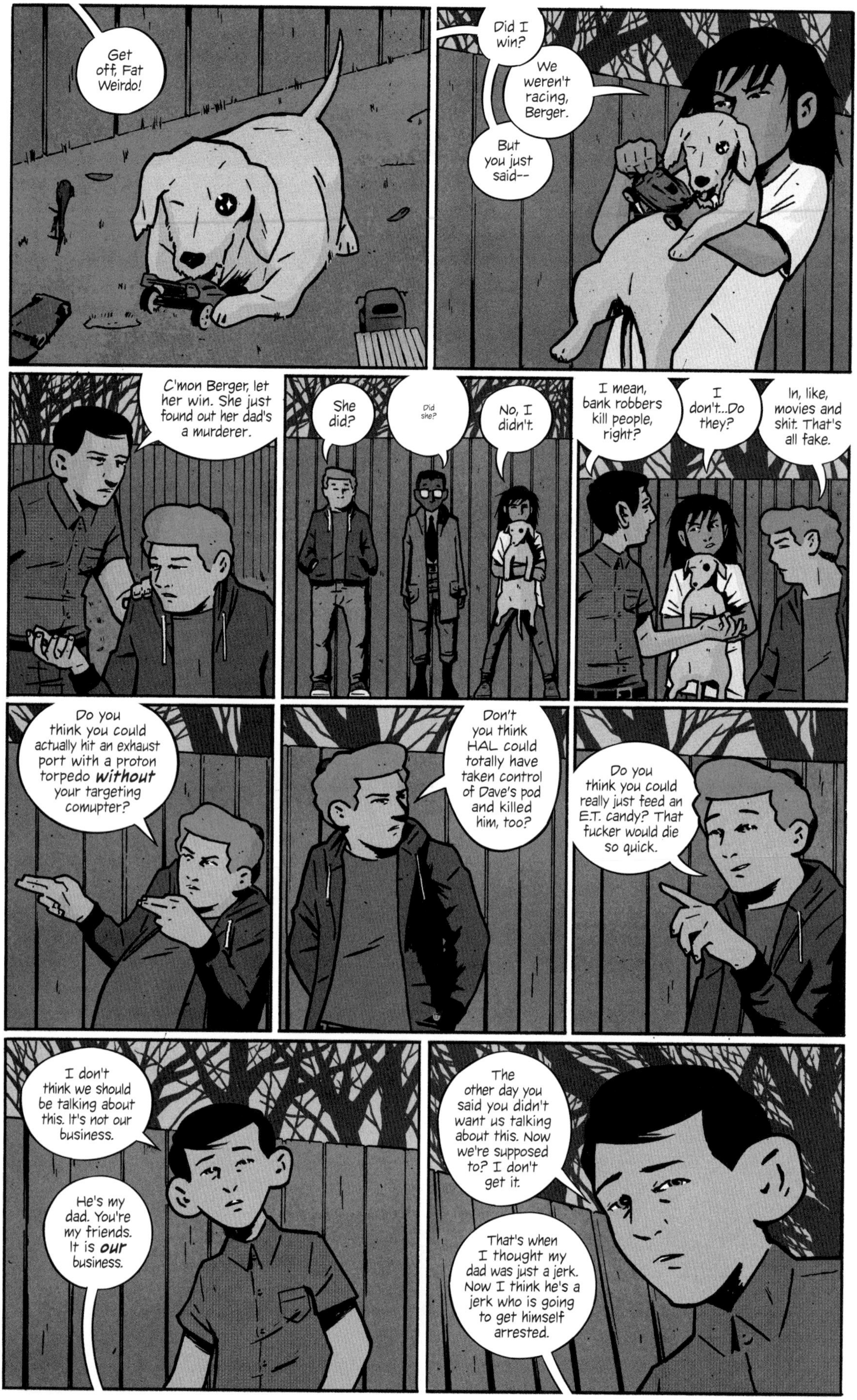
Get off, Fat Weirdo!
Did I win?
We weren't racing, Berger.
But you just said--
C'mon Berger, let her win. She just found out her dad's a murderer.
She did?
Did she?
No, I didn't.
I mean, bank robbers kill people, right?
I don't...Do they?
In, like, movies and shit. That's all fake.
Do you think you could actually hit an exhaust port with a proton torpedo *without* your targeting comupter?
Don't you think HAL could totally have taken control of Dave's pod and killed him, too?
Do you think you could really just feed an E.T. candy? That fucker would die so quick.
I don't think we should be talking about this. It's not our business.
He's my dad. You're my friends. It is *our* business.
The other day you said you didn't want us talking about this. Now we're supposed to? I don't get it.
That's when I thought my dad was just a jerk. Now I think he's a jerk who is going to get himself arrested.

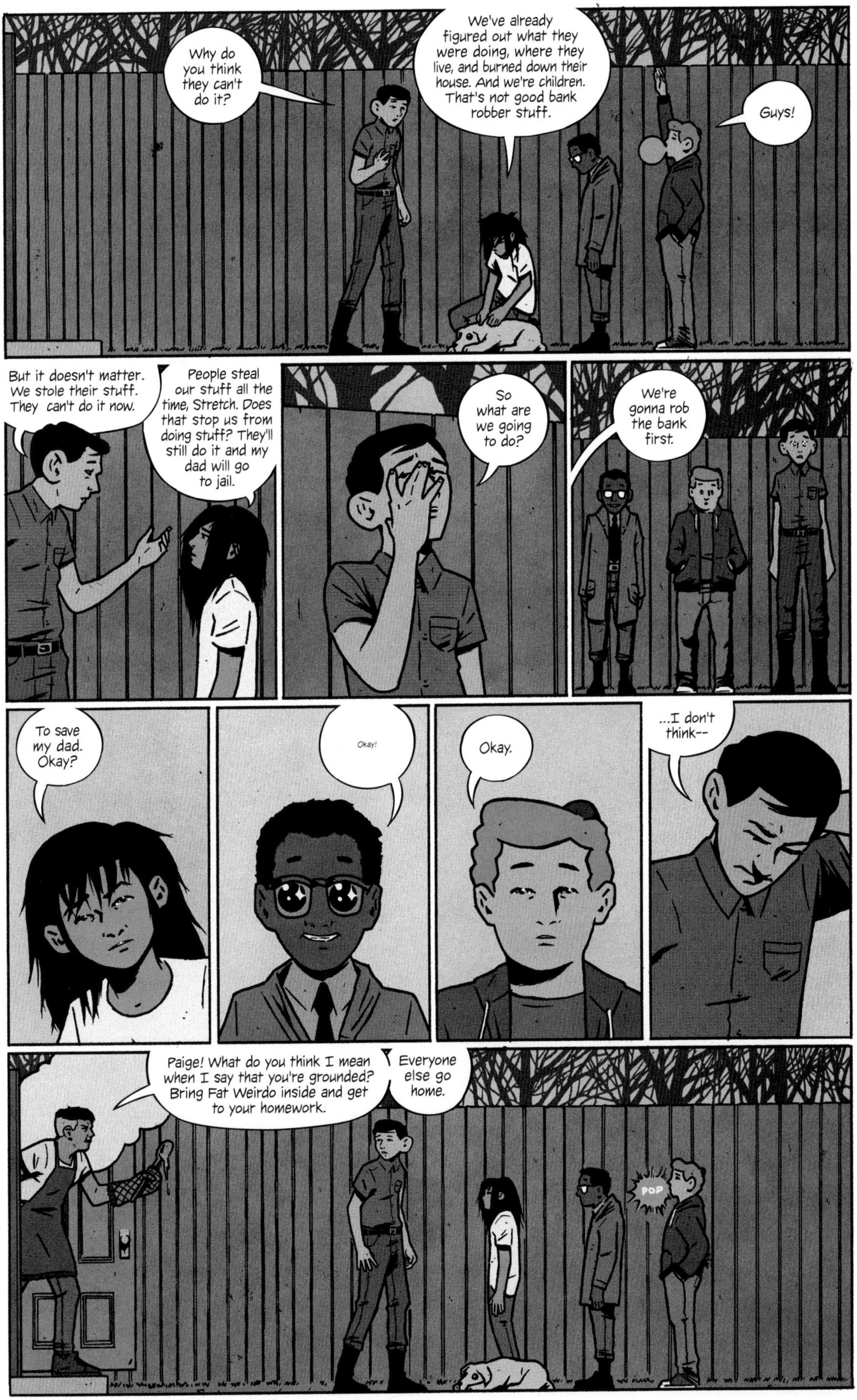
Why do you think they can't do it?
We've already figured out what they were doing, where they live, and burned down their house. And we're children. That's not good bank robber stuff.
Guys!
But it doesn't matter. We stole their stuff. They can't do it now.
People steal our stuff all the time, Stretch. Does that stop us from doing stuff? They'll still do it and my dad will go to jail.
So what are we going to do?
We're gonna rob the bank first.
To save my dad. Okay?
Okay!
Okay.
...I don't think--
Paige! What do you think I mean when I say that you're grounded? Bring Fat Weirdo inside and get to your homework.
Everyone else go home.
POP

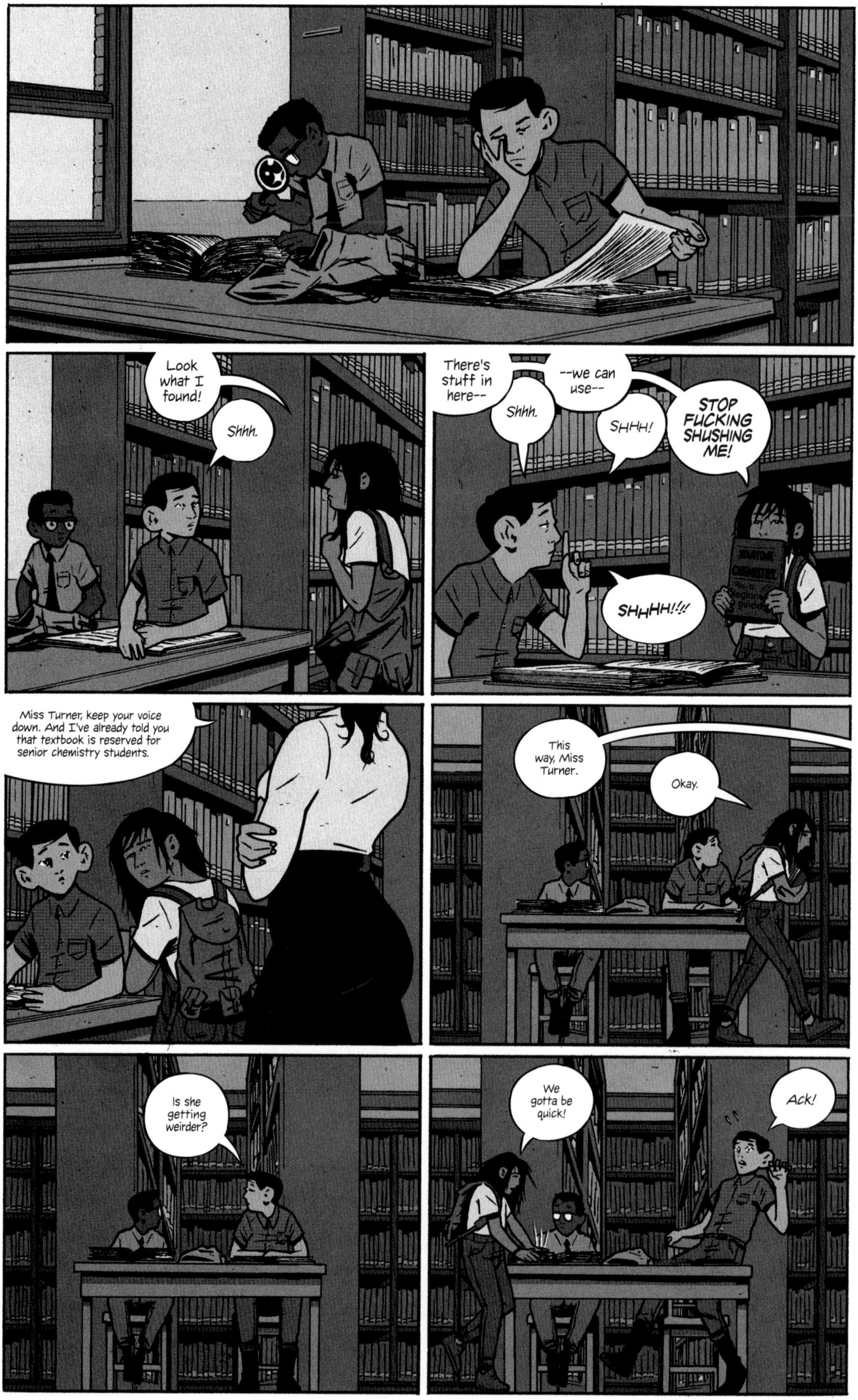
Look what I found!
Shhh.
There's stuff in here--
Shhh.
--we can use--
SHHH!
STOP FUCKING SHUSHING ME!
SHHHH!!!!
Miss Turner, keep your voice down. And I've already told you that textbook is reserved for senior chemistry students.
This way, Miss Turner.
Okay.
Is she getting weirder?
We gotta be quick!
Ack!

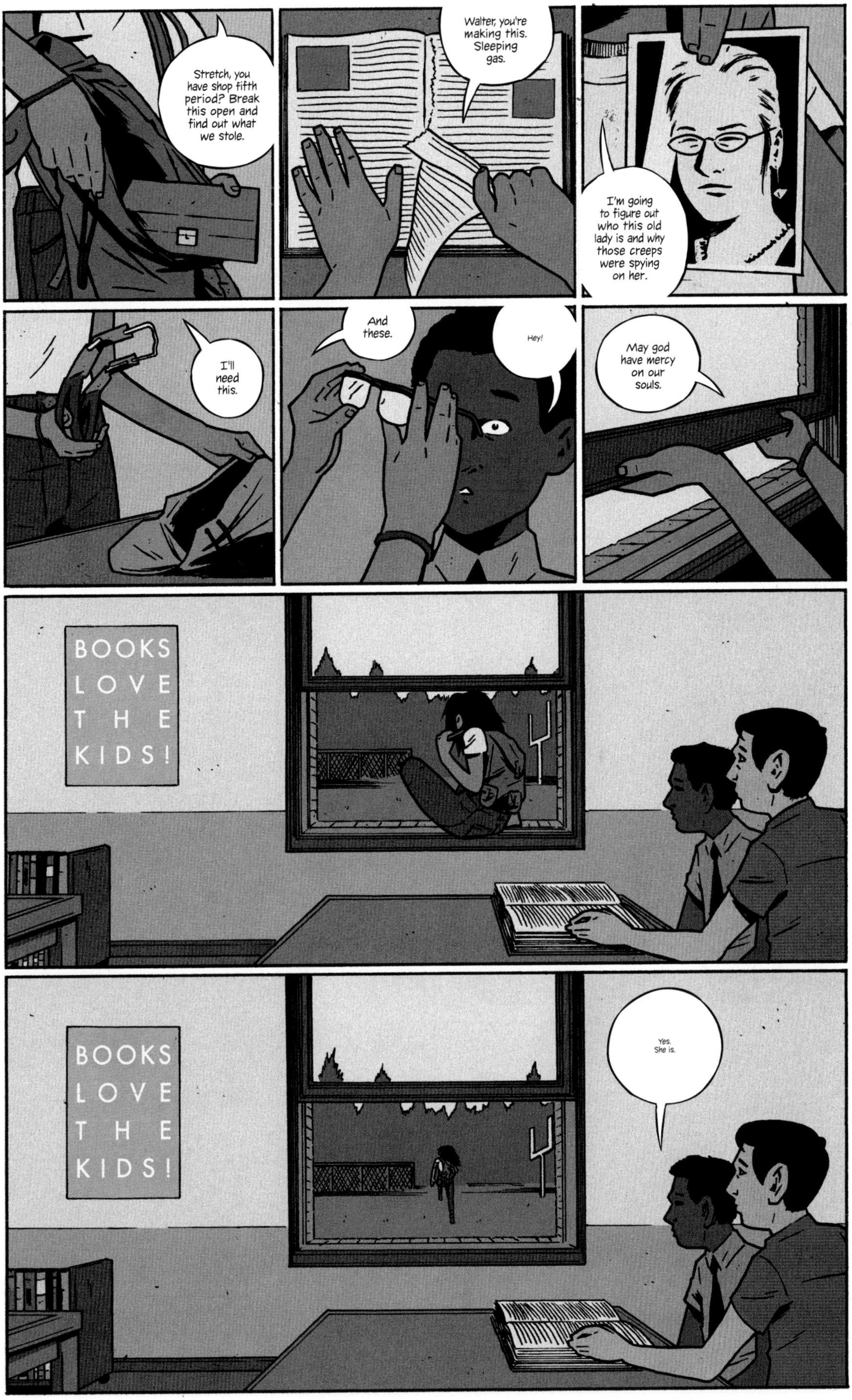
Stretch, you have shop fifth period? Break this open and find out what we stole.
Walter, you're making this. Sleeping gas.
I'm going to figure out who this old lady is and why those creeps were spying on her.
I'll need this.
And these.
Hey!
May god have mercy on our souls.
BOOKS LOVE THE KIDS!
BOOKS LOVE THE KIDS!
Yes. She is.

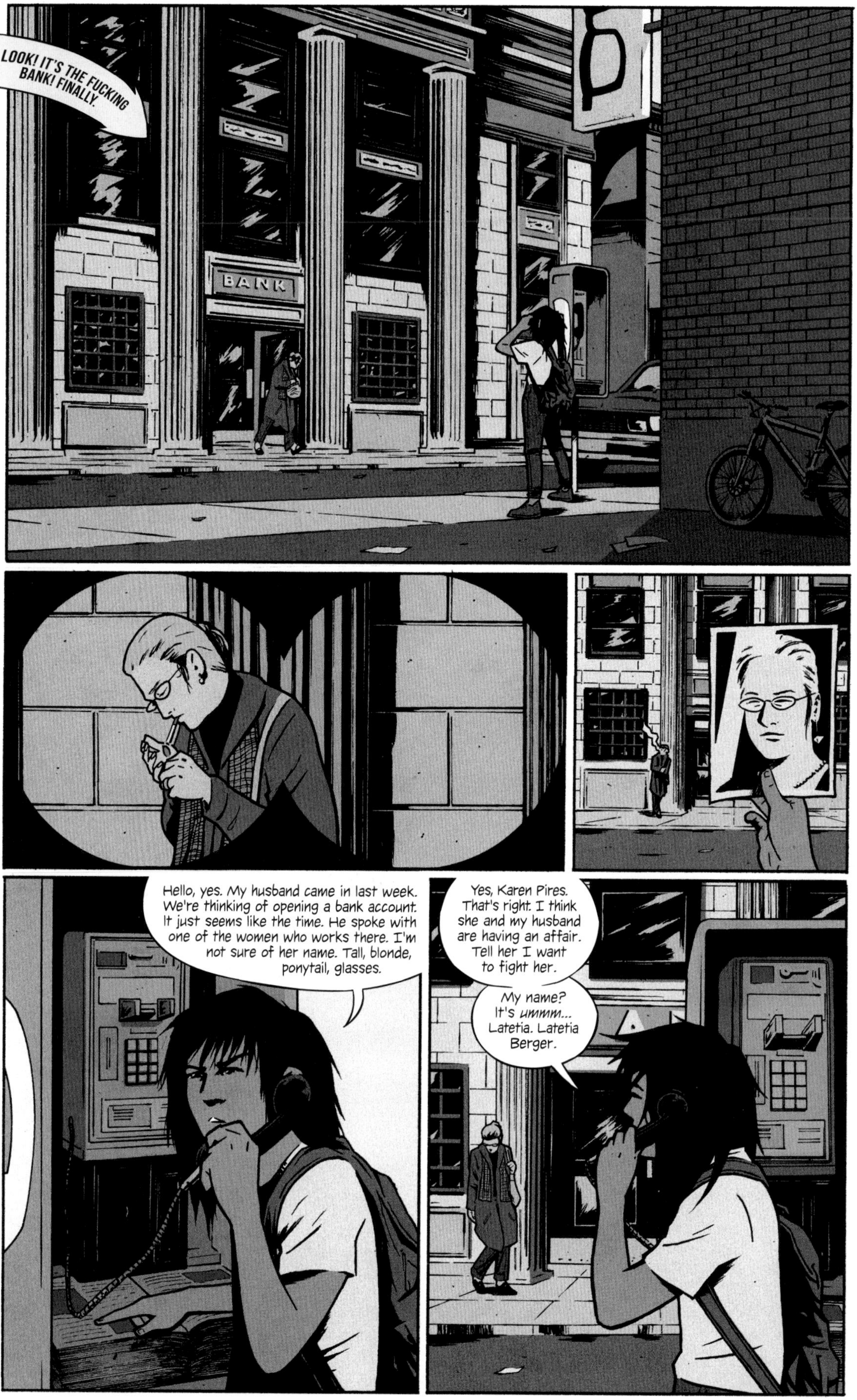
LOOK! IT'S THE FUCKING BANK! FINALLY.
BANK
Hello, yes. My husband came in last week. We're thinking of opening a bank account. It just seems like the time. He spoke with one of the women who works there. I'm not sure of her name. Tall, blonde, ponytail, glasses.
Yes, Karen Pires. That's right. I think she and my husband are having an affair. Tell her I want to fight her.
My name? It's *ummm*... Latetia. Latetia Berger.

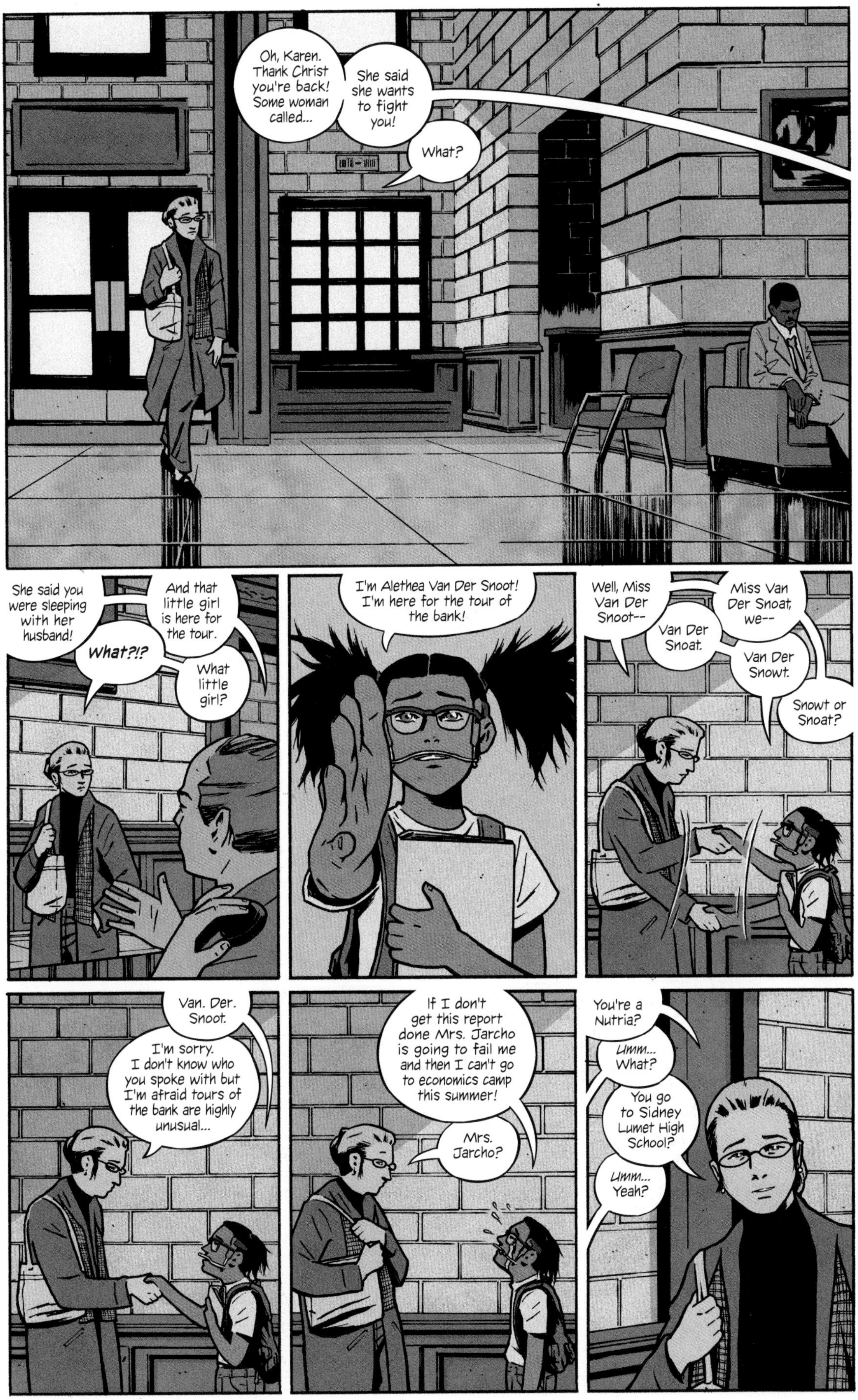
Oh, Karen. Thank Christ you're back! Some woman called...
She said she wants to fight you!
What?
She said you were sleeping with her husband!
What?!?
And that little girl is here for the tour.
What little girl?
I'm Alethea Van Der Snoot! I'm here for the tour of the bank!
Well, Miss Van Der Snoot--
Van Der Snoat.
Miss Van Der Snoat, we--
Van Der Snowt.
Snowt or Snoat?
Van. Der. Snoot.
I'm sorry. I don't know who you spoke with but I'm afraid tours of the bank are highly unusual...
If I don't get this report done Mrs. Jarcho is going to fail me and then I can't go to economics camp this summer!
Mrs. Jarcho?
You're a Nutria?
Umm... What?
You go to Sidney Lumet High School?
Umm... Yeah?

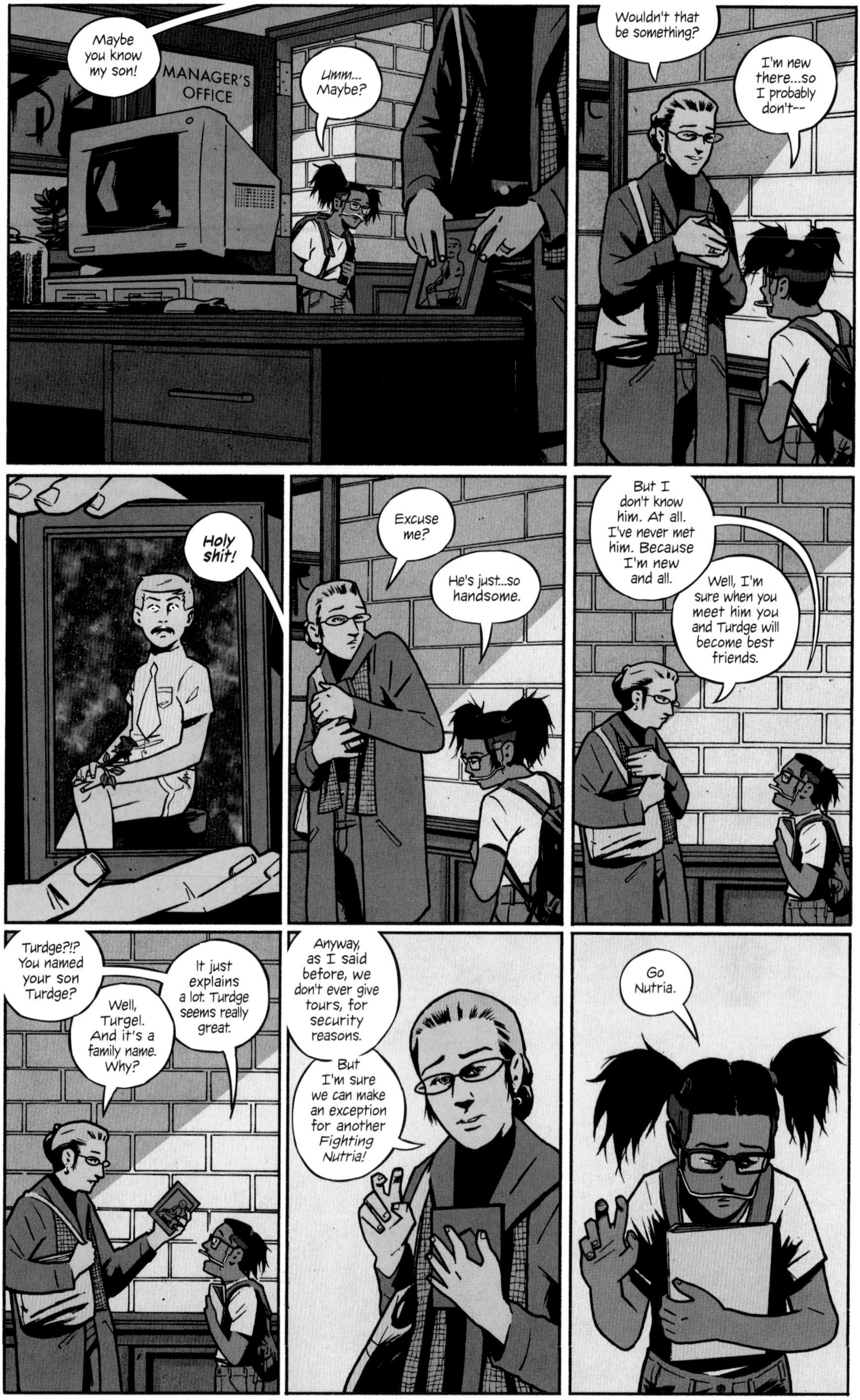
Maybe you know my son!
MANAGER'S OFFICE
Umm... Maybe?
Wouldn't that be something?
I'm new there...so I probably don't--
Holy shit!
Excuse me?
He's just...so handsome.
But I don't know him. At all. I've never met him. Because I'm new and all.
Well, I'm sure when you meet him you and Turdge will become best friends.
Turdge?!? You named your son Turdge?
Well, Turgel. And it's a family name. Why?
It just explains a lot. Turdge seems really great.
Anyway, as I said before, we don't ever give tours, for security reasons.
But I'm sure we can make an exception for another Fighting Nutria!
Go Nutria.

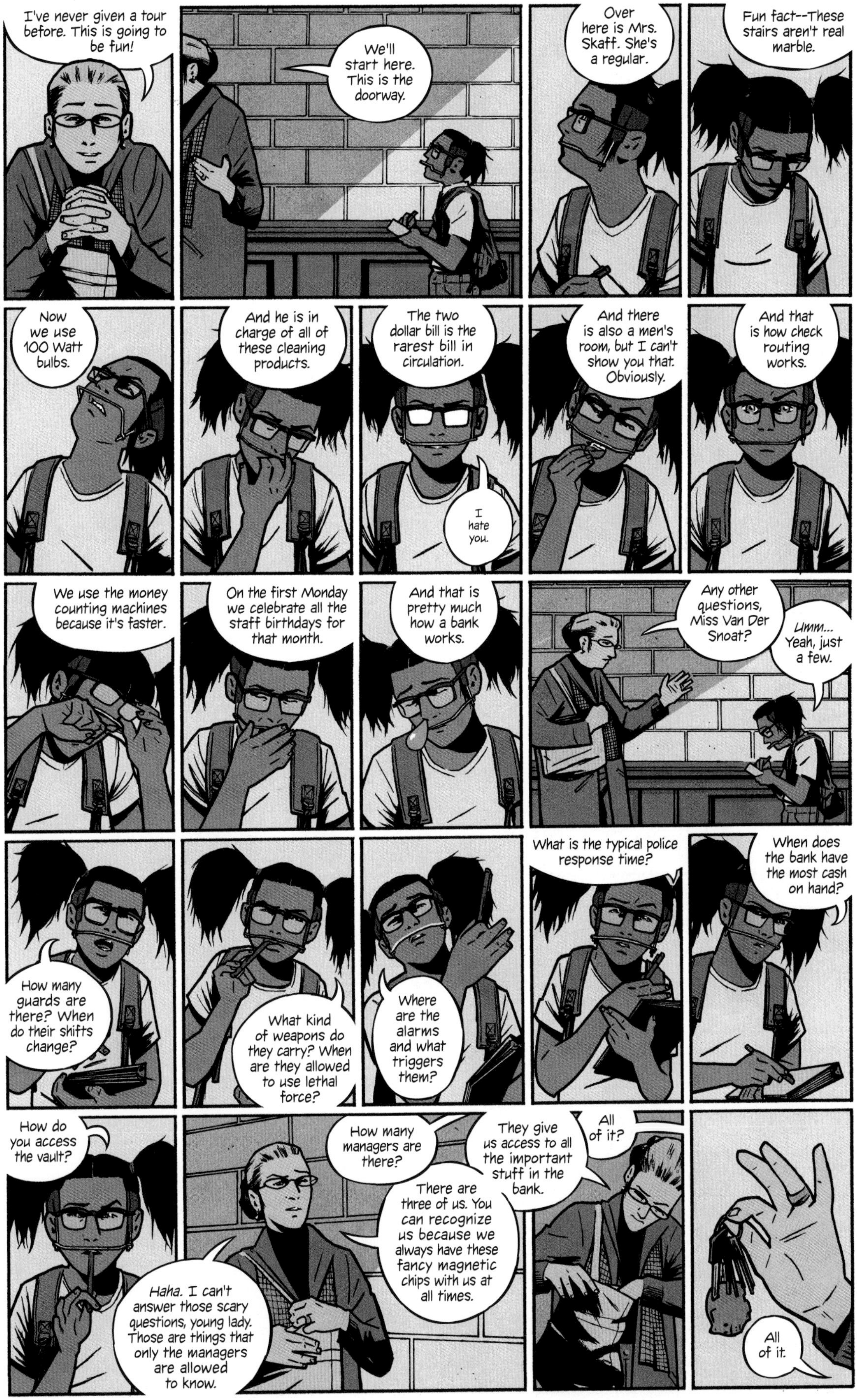
I've never given a tour before. This is going to be fun!
We'll start here. This is the doorway.
Over here is Mrs. Skaff. She's a regular.
Fun fact--These stairs aren't real marble.
Now we use 100 Watt bulbs.
And he is in charge of all of these cleaning products.
The two dollar bill is the rarest bill in circulation.
I hate you.
And there is also a men's room, but I can't show you that. Obviously.
And that is how check routing works.
We use the money counting machines because it's faster.
On the first Monday we celebrate all the staff birthdays for that month.
And that is pretty much how a bank works.
Any other questions, Miss Van Der Snoat?
Umm... Yeah, just a few.
How many guards are there? When do their shifts change?
What kind of weapons do they carry? When are they allowed to use lethal force?
Where are the alarms and what triggers them?
What is the typical police response time?
When does the bank have the most cash on hand?
How do you access the vault?
Haha. I can't answer those scary questions, young lady. Those are things that only the managers are allowed to know.
How many managers are there?
There are three of us. You can recognize us because we always have these fancy magnetic chips with us at all times.
They give us access to all the important stuff in the bank.
All of it?
All of it.

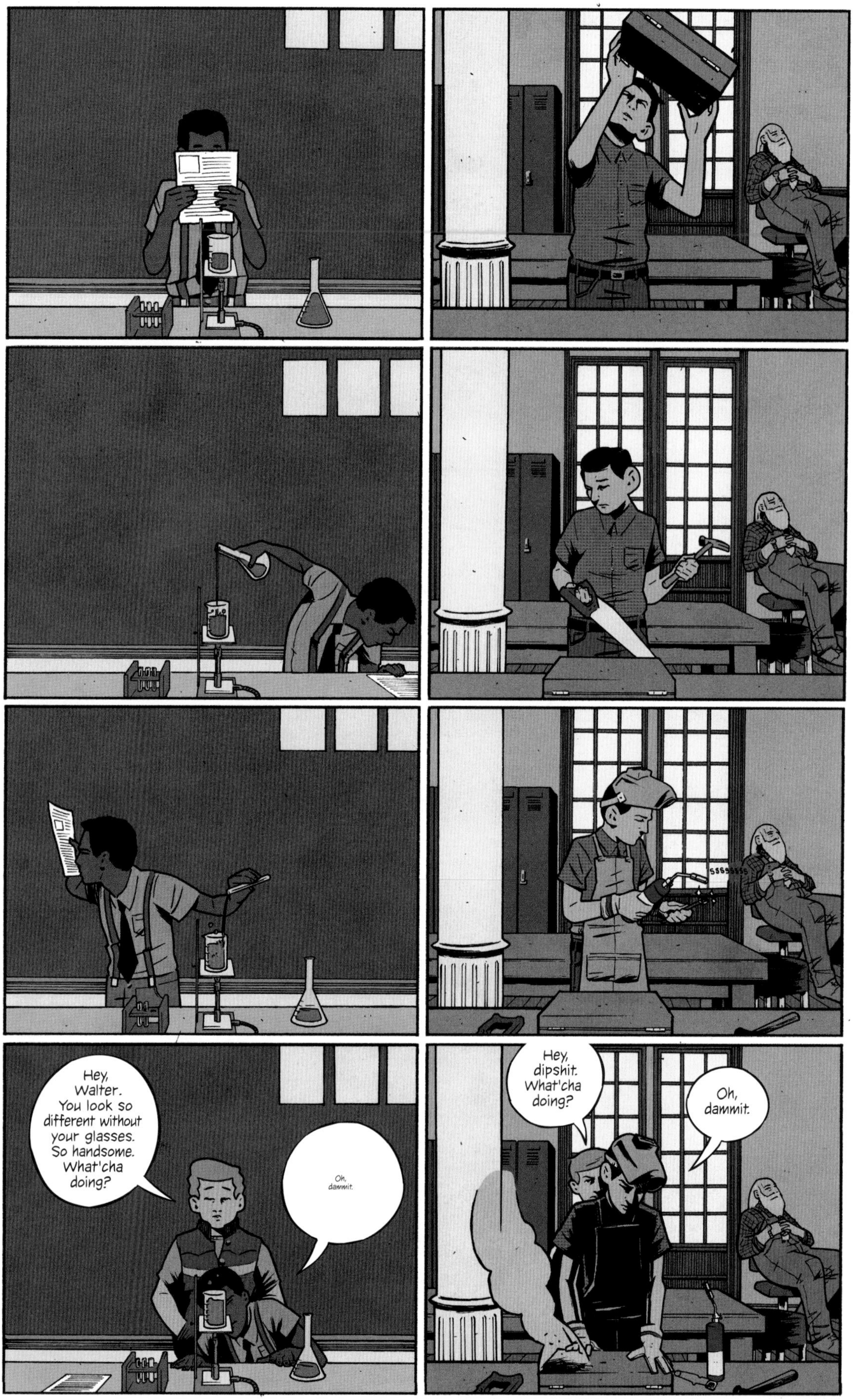

SSSSSSSS
Hey, Walter. You look so different without your glasses. So handsome. What'cha doing?
Oh, dammit.
Hey, dipshit. What'cha doing?
Oh, dammit.

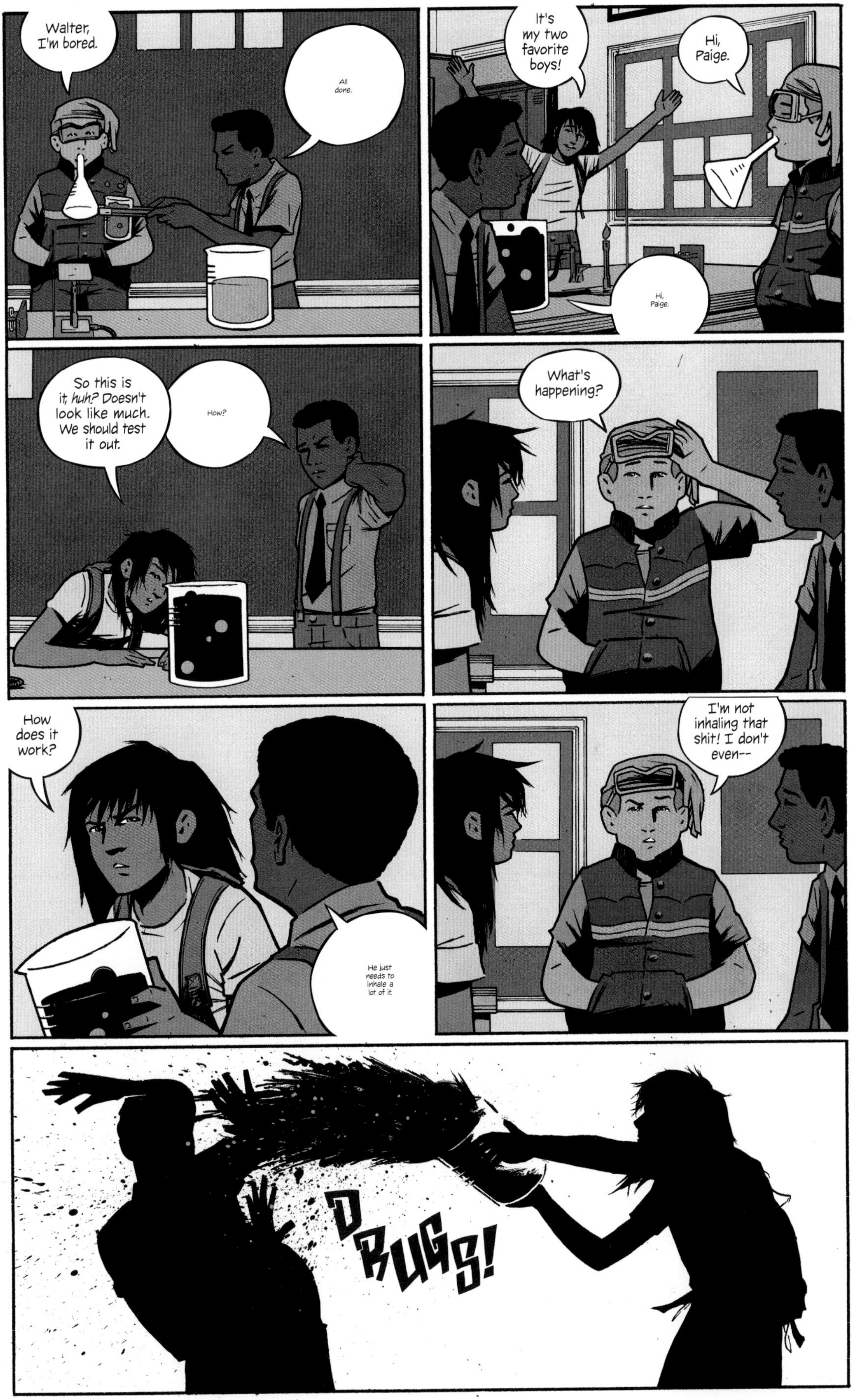
Walter, I'm bored.
All done.
It's my two favorite boys!
Hi, Paige.
Hi, Paige.
So this is it, *huh?* Doesn't look like much. We should test it out.
How?
What's happening?
How does it work?
He just needs to inhale a lot of it.
I'm not inhaling that shit! I don't even--
DRUGS!

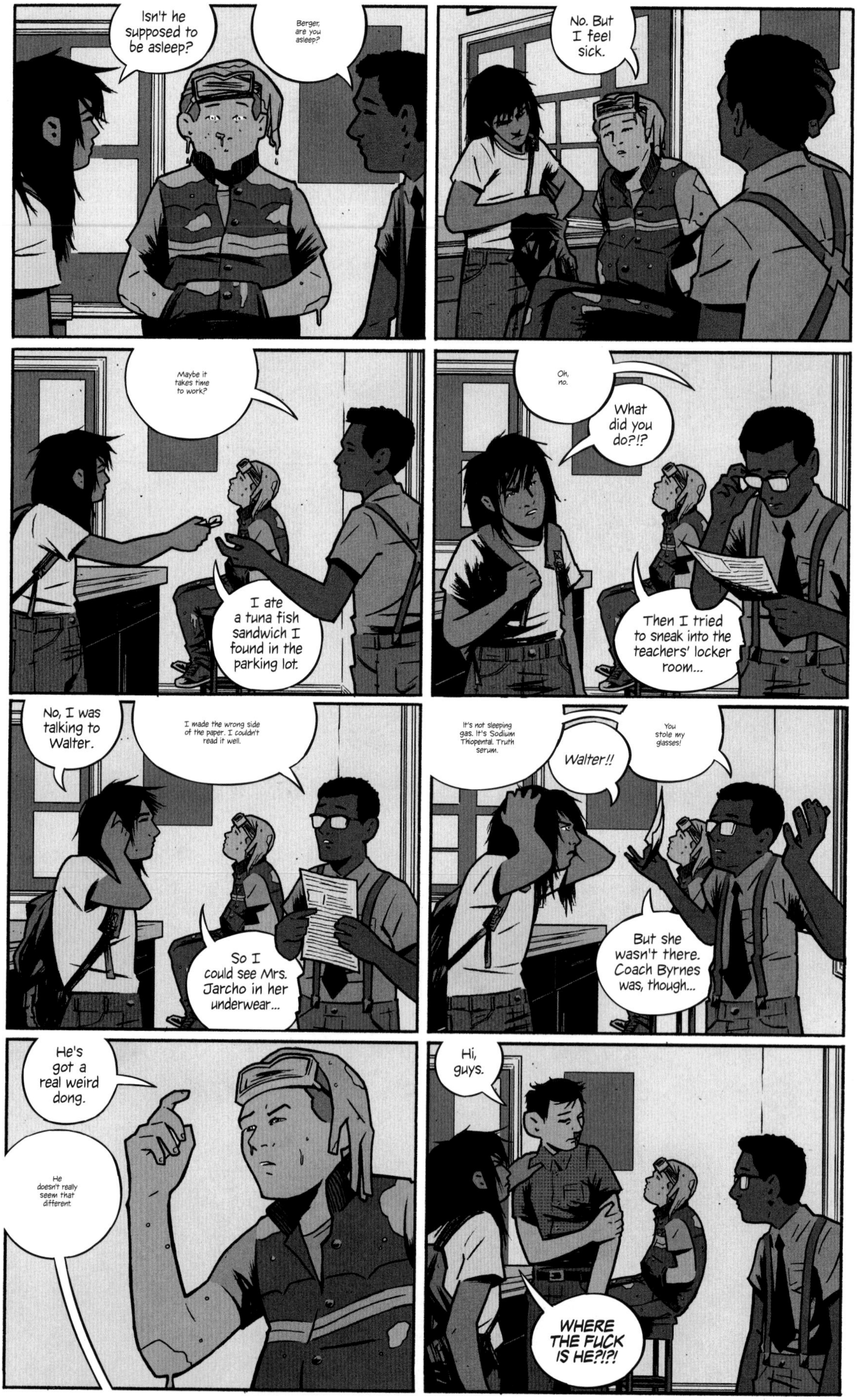
Isn't he supposed to be asleep?
Berger, are you asleep?
No. But I feel sick.
Maybe it takes time to work?
I ate a tuna fish sandwich I found in the parking lot.
Oh, no.
What did you do?!?
Then I tried to sneak into the teachers' locker room...
No, I was talking to Walter.
I made the wrong side of the paper. I couldn't read it well.
So I could see Mrs. Jarcho in her underwear...
It's not sleeping gas. It's Sodium Thiopental. Truth serum.
Walter!!
You stole my glasses!
But she wasn't there. Coach Byrnes was, though...
He's got a real weird dong.
He doesn't really seem that different.
Hi, guys.
WHERE THE FUCK IS HE?!?!

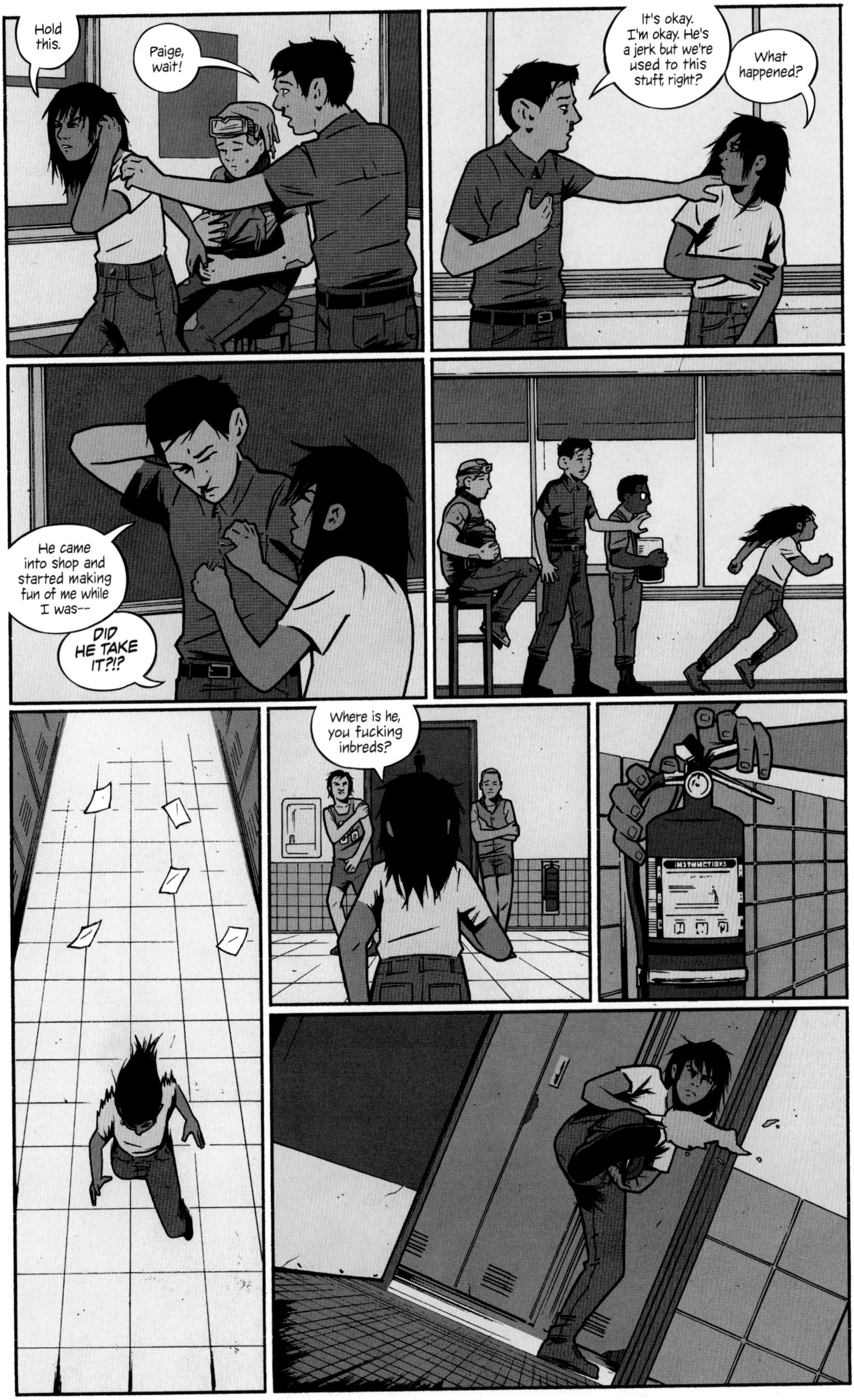
Hold this.
Paige, wait!
It's okay. I'm okay. He's a jerk but we're used to this stuff, right?
What happened?
He came into shop and started making fun of me while I was--
DID HE TAKE IT?!?
Where is he, you fucking inbreds?
INSTRUCTIONS

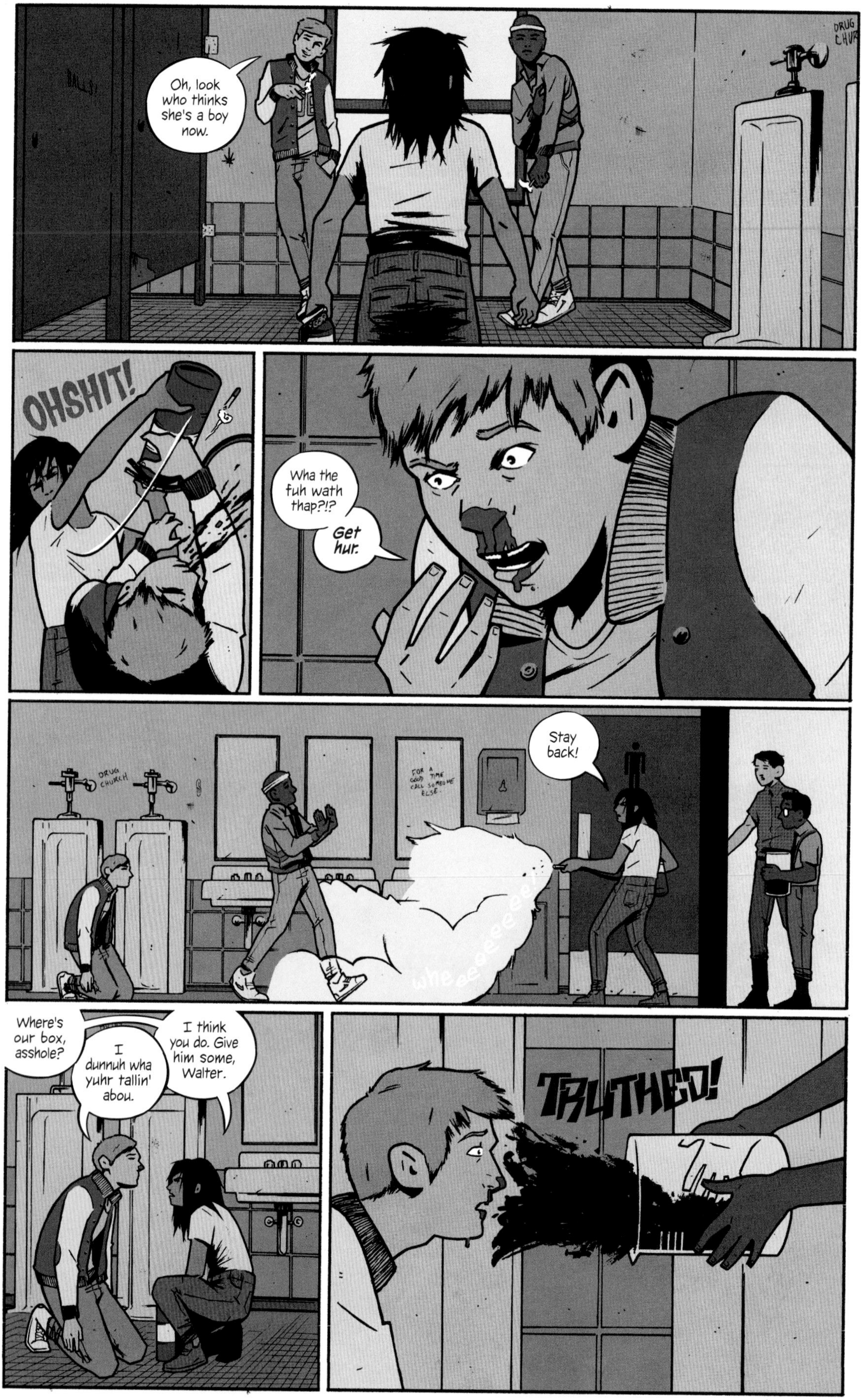

DRUG CHUR
Oh, look who thinks she's a boy now.
OHSHIT!
Wha the fuh wath thap?!?
Get hur.
DRUG CHURCH
FOR A GOOD TIME CALL SOMEONE ELSE.
Stay back!
wheeeeeeee!
Where's our box, asshole?
I dunnuh wha yuhr tallin' abou.
I think you do. Give him some, Walter.
TRUTHED!

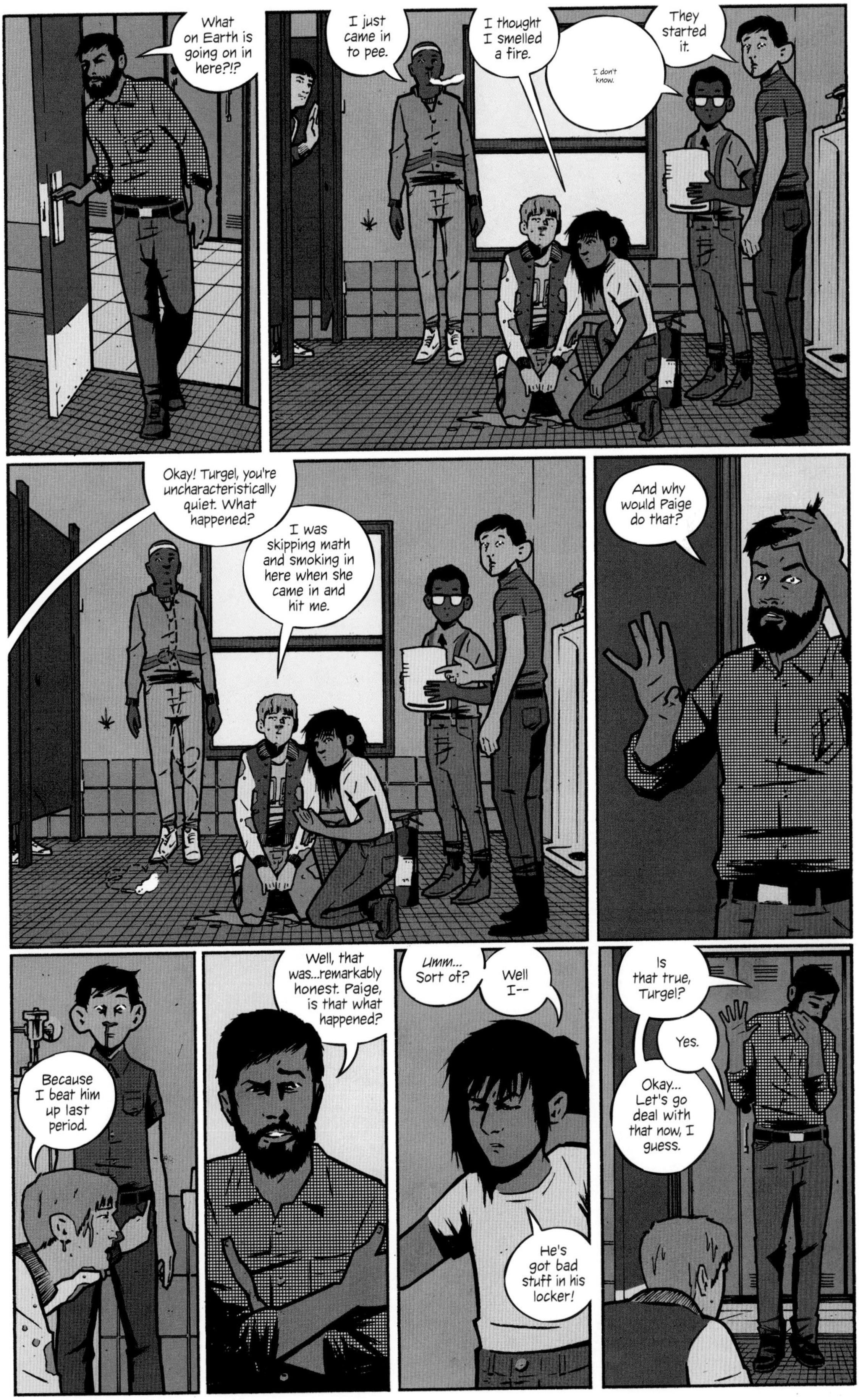
What on Earth is going on in here?!?
I just came in to pee.
I thought I smelled a fire.
I don't know.
They started it.
Okay! Turgel, you're uncharacteristically quiet. What happened?
I was skipping math and smoking in here when she came in and hit me.
And why would Paige do that?
Because I beat him up last period.
Well, that was...remarkably honest. Paige, is that what happened?
Umm... Sort of?
Well I--
He's got bad stuff in his locker!
Is that true, Turgel?
Yes.
Okay... Let's go deal with that now, I guess.

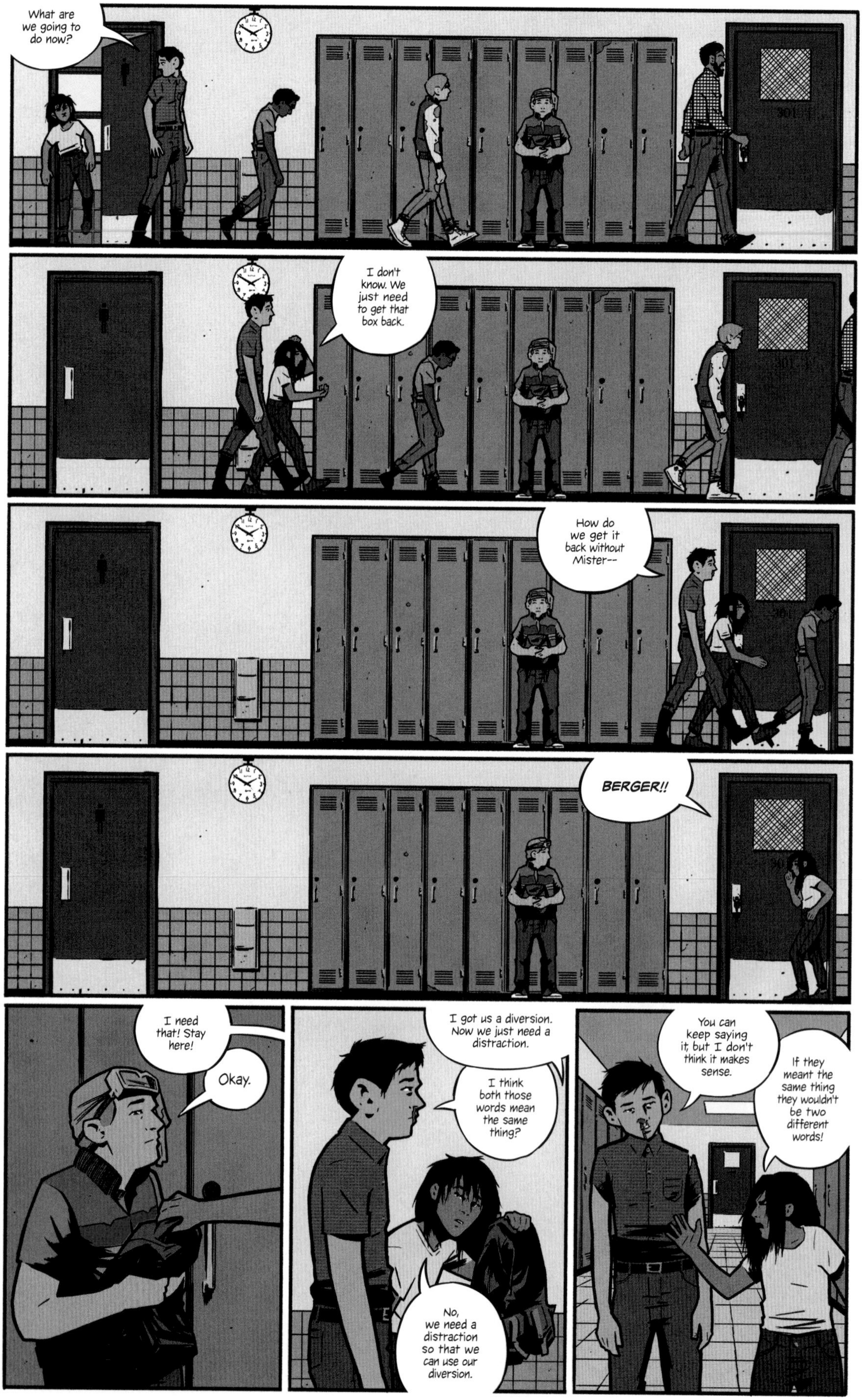

What are we going to do now?
I don't know. We just need to get that box back.
How do we get it back without Mister--
BERGER!!
I need that! Stay here!
Okay.
I got us a diversion. Now we just need a distraction.
I think both those words mean the same thing?
No, we need a distraction so that we can use our diversion.
You can keep saying it, but I don't think it makes sense.
If they meant the same thing they wouldn't be two different words!

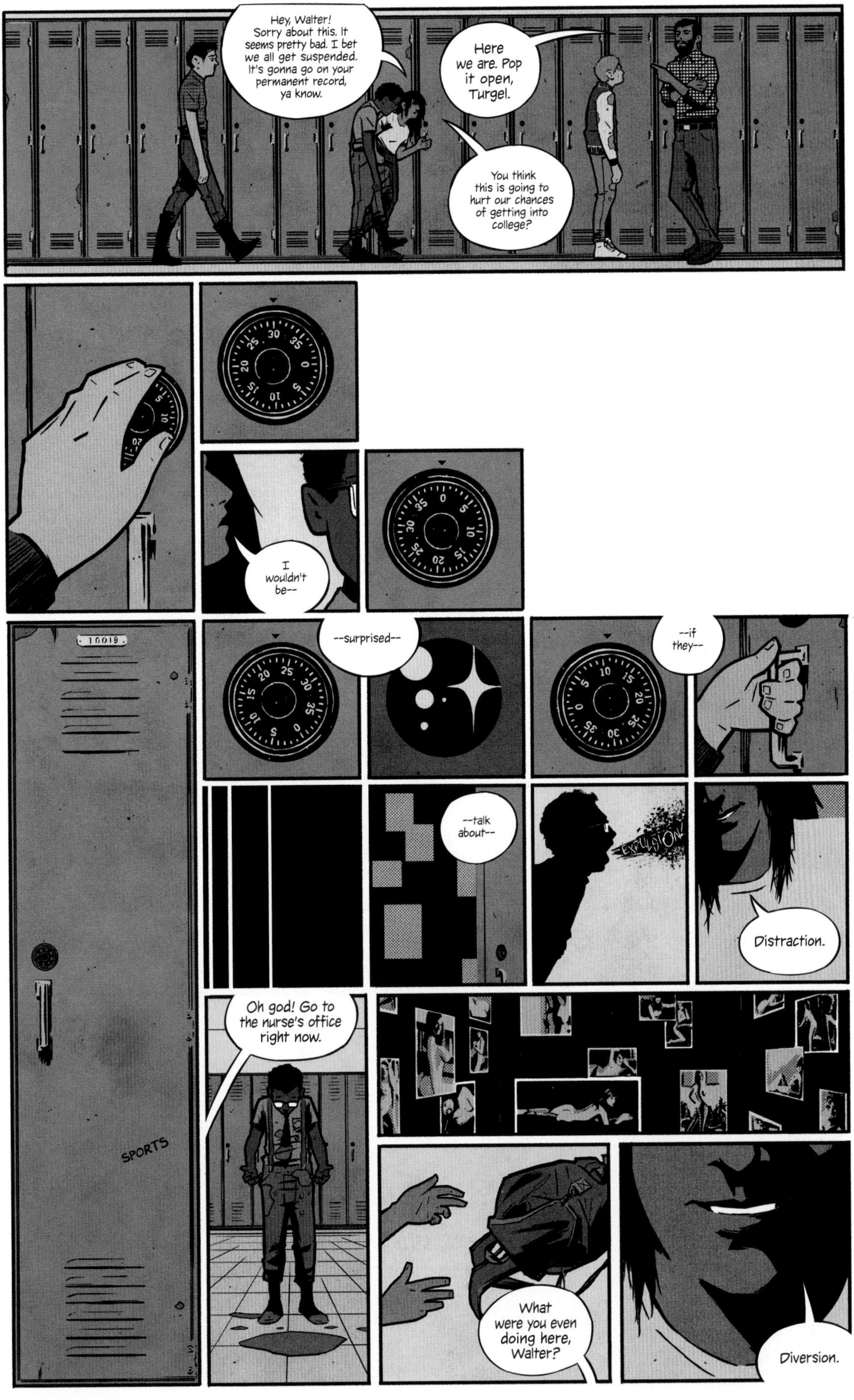
Hey, Walter! Sorry about this. It seems pretty bad. I bet we all get suspended. It's gonna go on your permanent record, ya know.
Here we are. Pop it open, Turgel.
You think this is going to hurt our chances of getting into college?
I wouldn't be--
10019
--surprised--
--if they--
--talk about--
EXPULSION!
Distraction.
SPORTS
Oh god! Go to the nurse's office right now.
What were you even doing here, Walter?
Diversion.

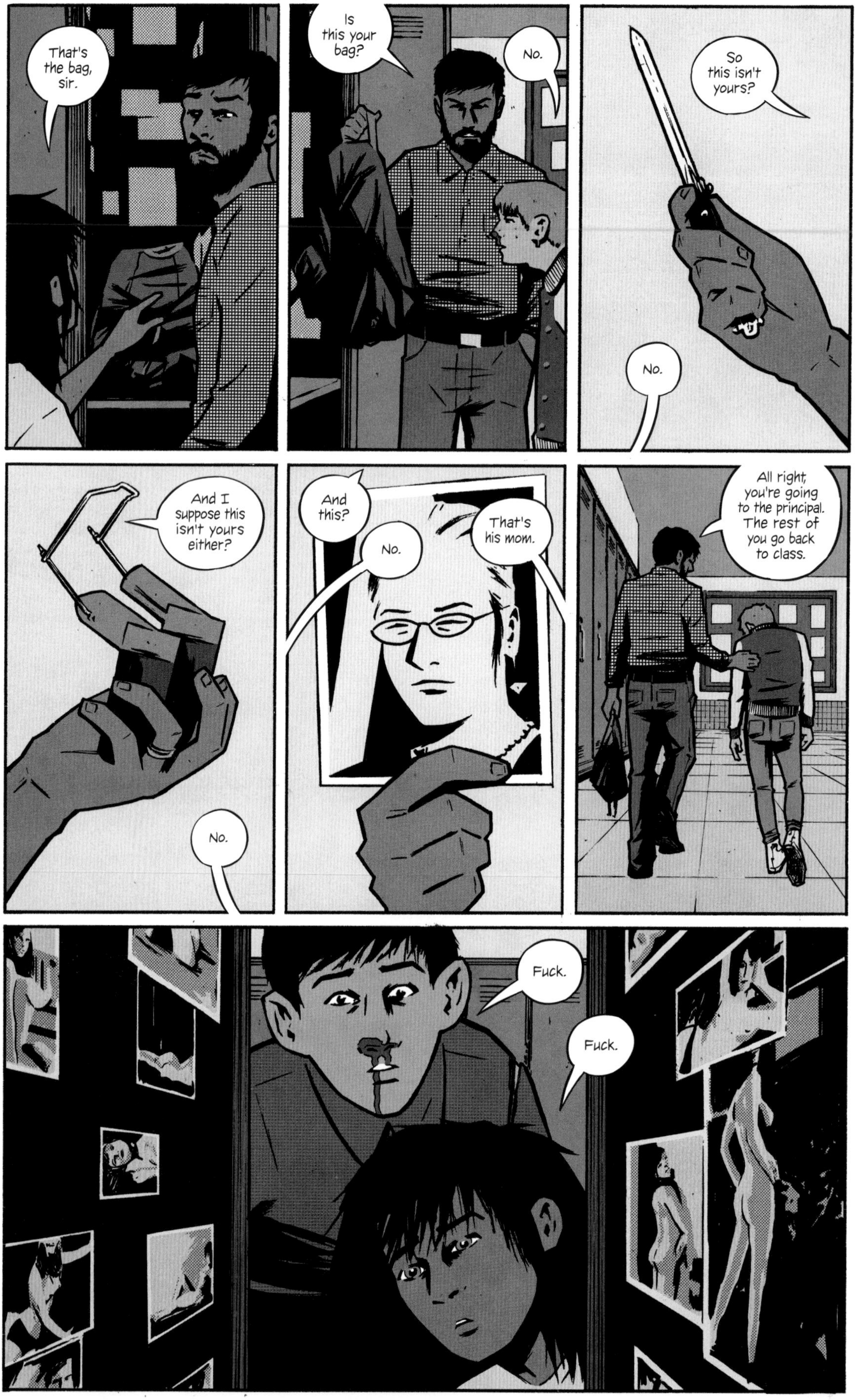
That's the bag, sir.
Is this your bag?
No.
So this isn't yours?
No.
And I suppose this isn't yours either?
No.
And this?
No.
That's his mom.
All right, you're going to the principal. The rest of you go back to class.
Fuck.
Fuck.

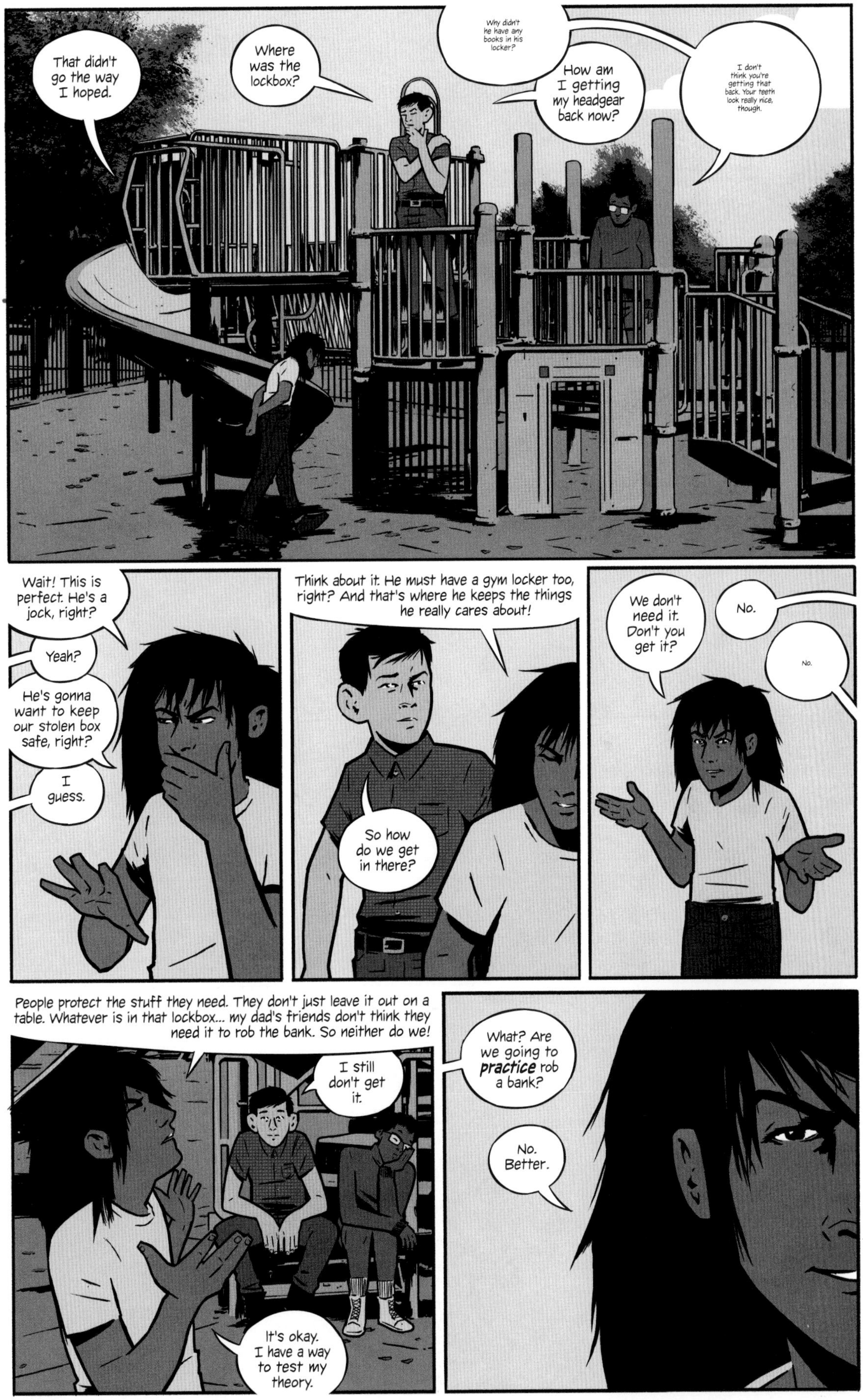
That didn't go the way I hoped.
Where was the lockbox?
Why didn't he have any books in his locker?
How am I getting my headgear back now?
I don't think you're getting that back. Your teeth look really nice, though.
Wait! This is perfect. He's a jock, right?
Yeah?
He's gonna want to keep our stolen box safe, right?
I guess.
Think about it. He must have a gym locker too, right? And that's where he keeps the things he really cares about!
So how do we get in there?
We don't need it. Don't you get it?
No.
No.
People protect the stuff they need. They don't just leave it out on a table. Whatever is in that lockbox... my dad's friends don't think they need it to rob the bank. So neither do we!
I still don't get it.
It's okay. I have a way to test my theory.
What? Are we going to *practice* rob a bank?
No. Better.

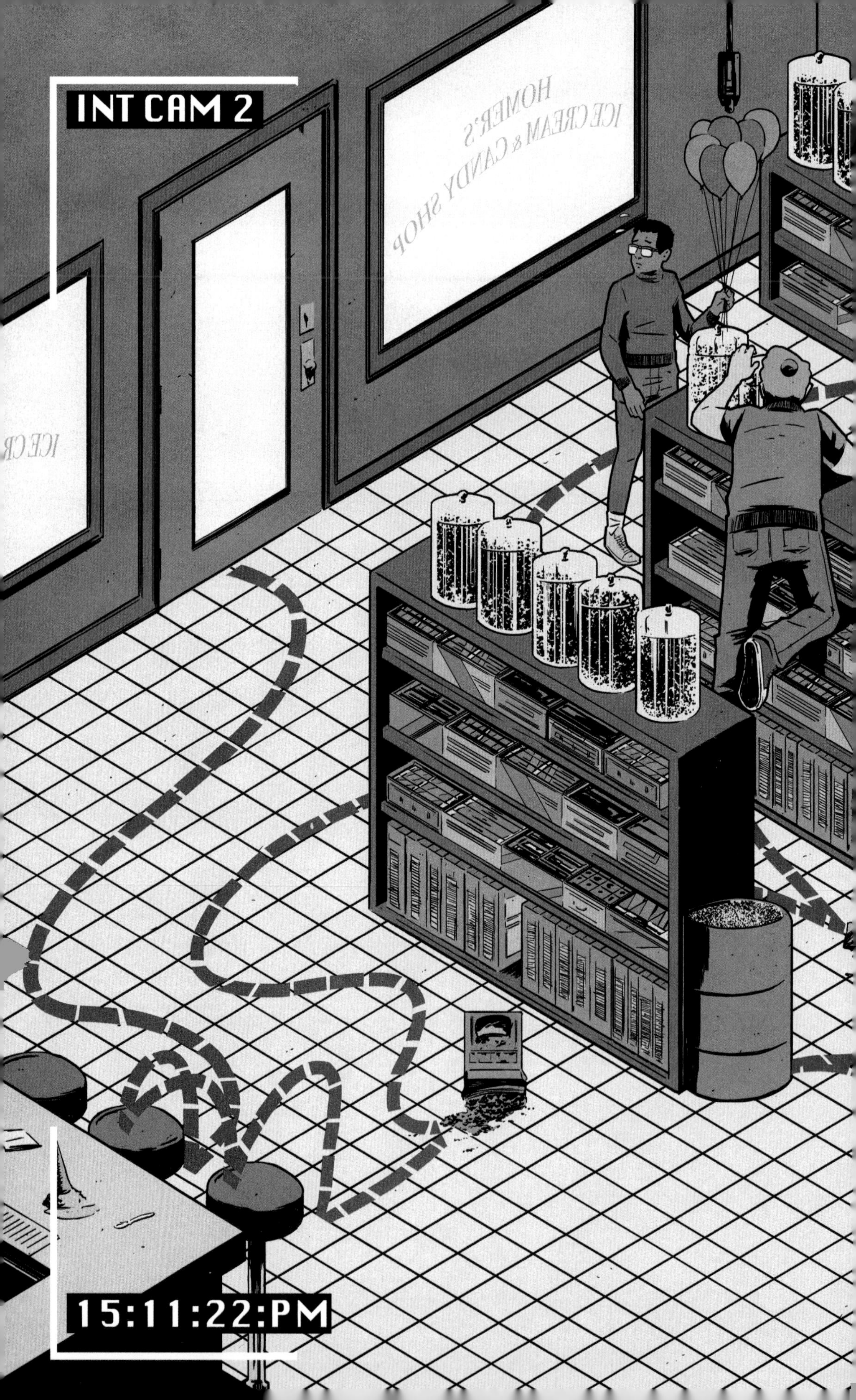
INT CAM 2
HOMER'S
ICE CREAM & CANDY SHOP
15:11:22:PM

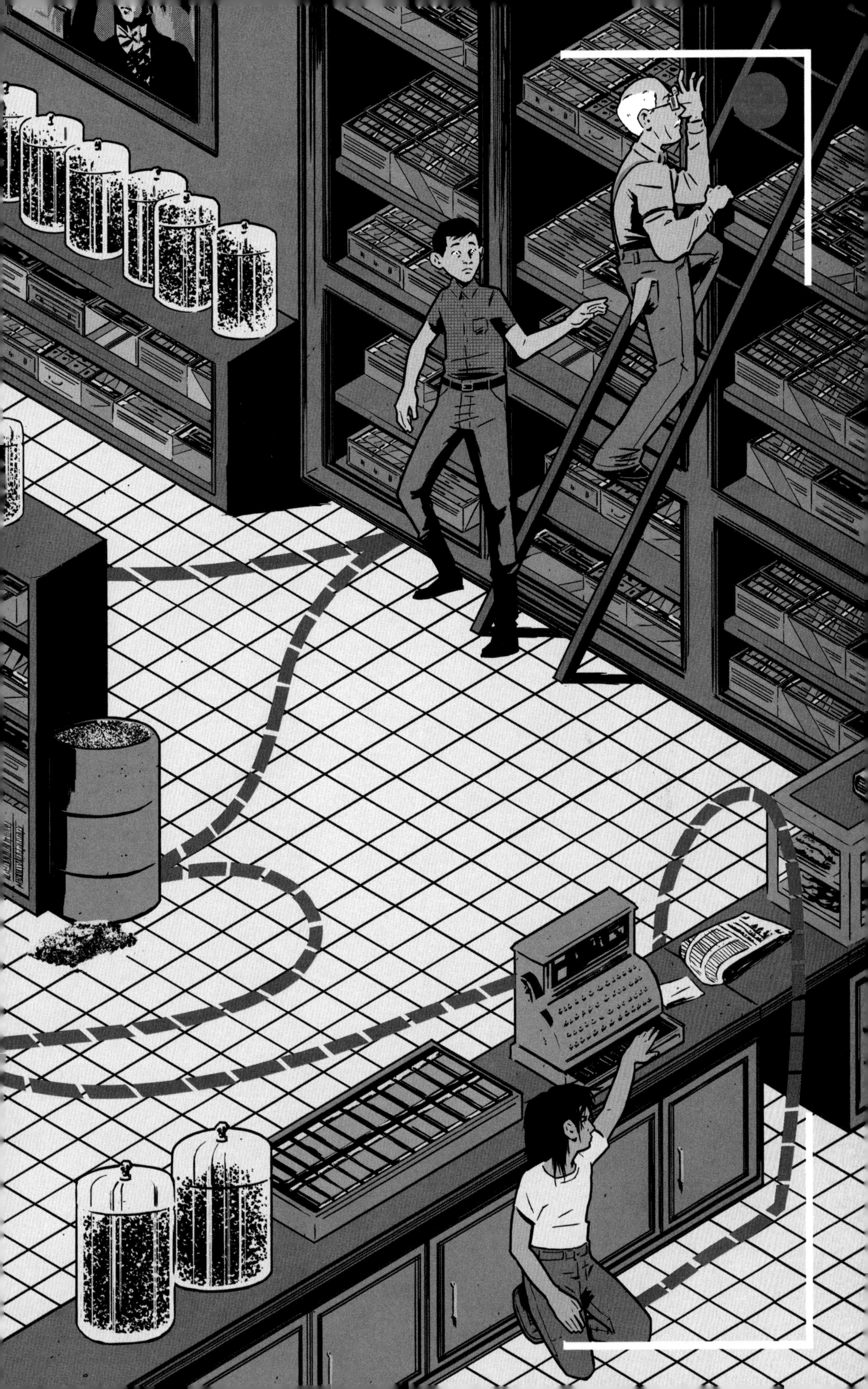

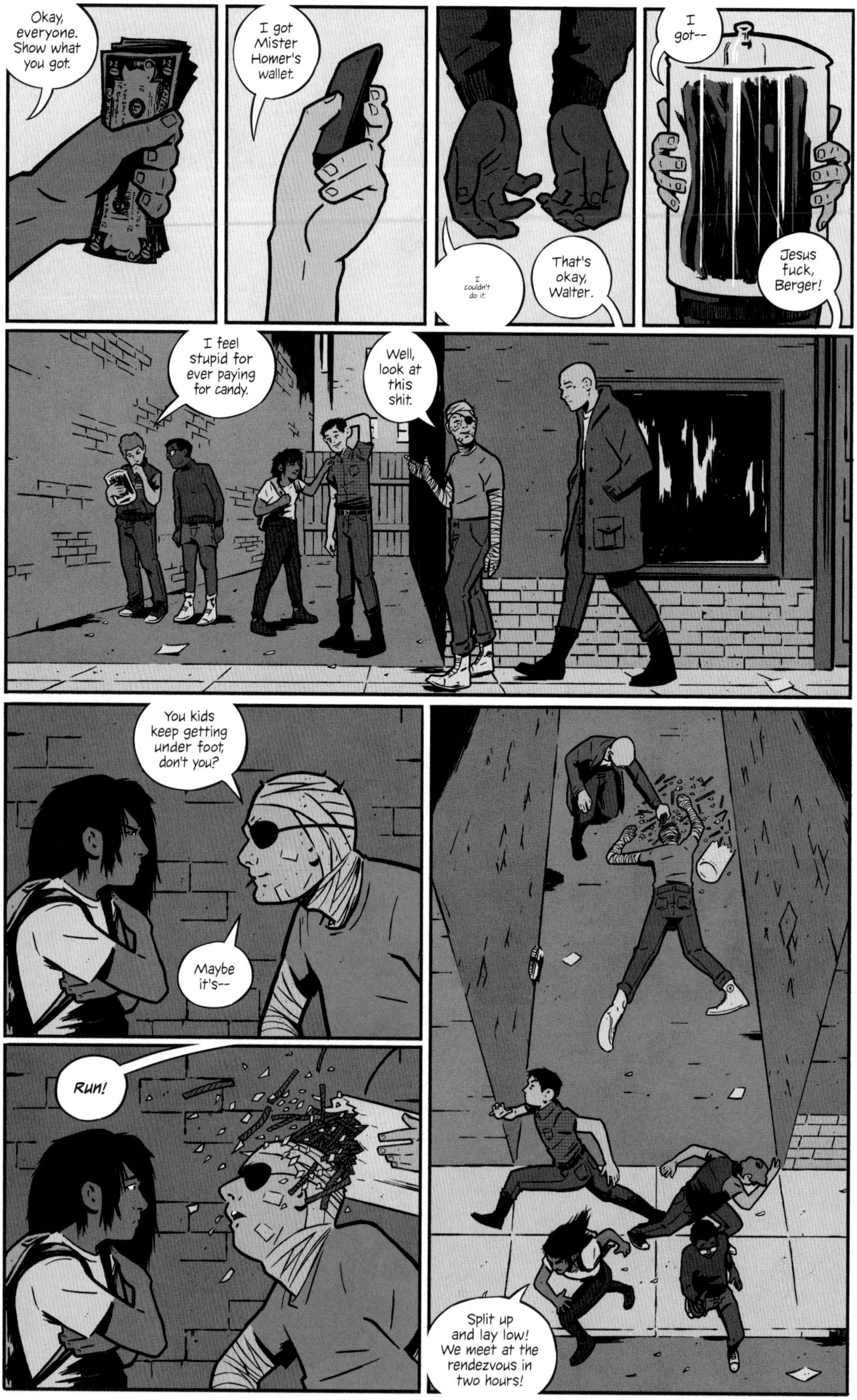
Okay, everyone. Show what you got.
I got Mister Homer's wallet.
I couldn't do it.
That's okay, Walter.
I got--
Jesus fuck, Berger!
I feel stupid for ever paying for candy.
Well, look at this shit.
You kids keep getting under foot, don't you?
Maybe it's--
Run!
Split up and lay low! We meet at the rendezvous in two hours!

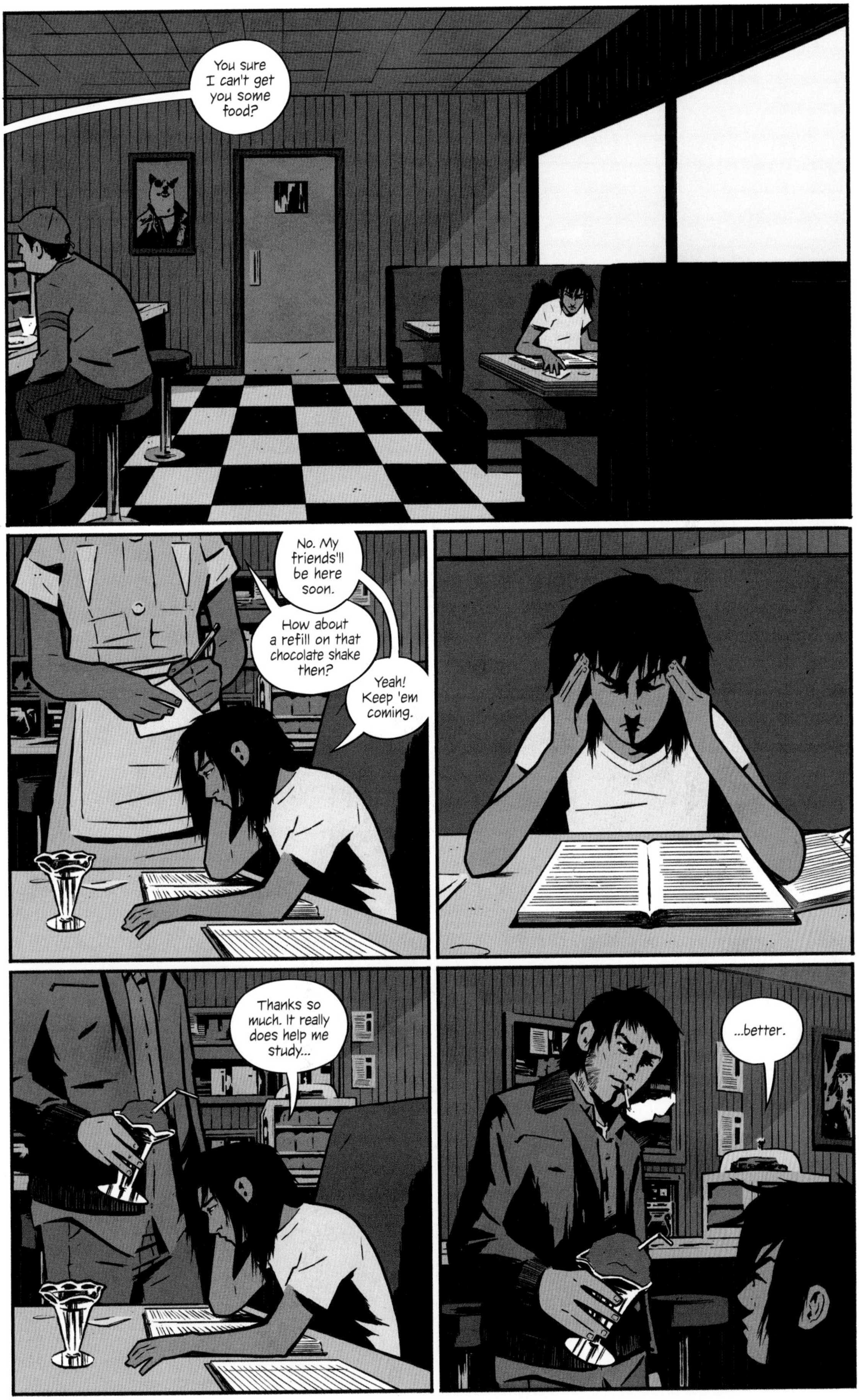

You sure I can't get you some food?
No. My friends'll be here soon.
How about a refill on that chocolate shake then?
Yeah! Keep 'em coming.
Thanks so much. It really does help me study...
...better.

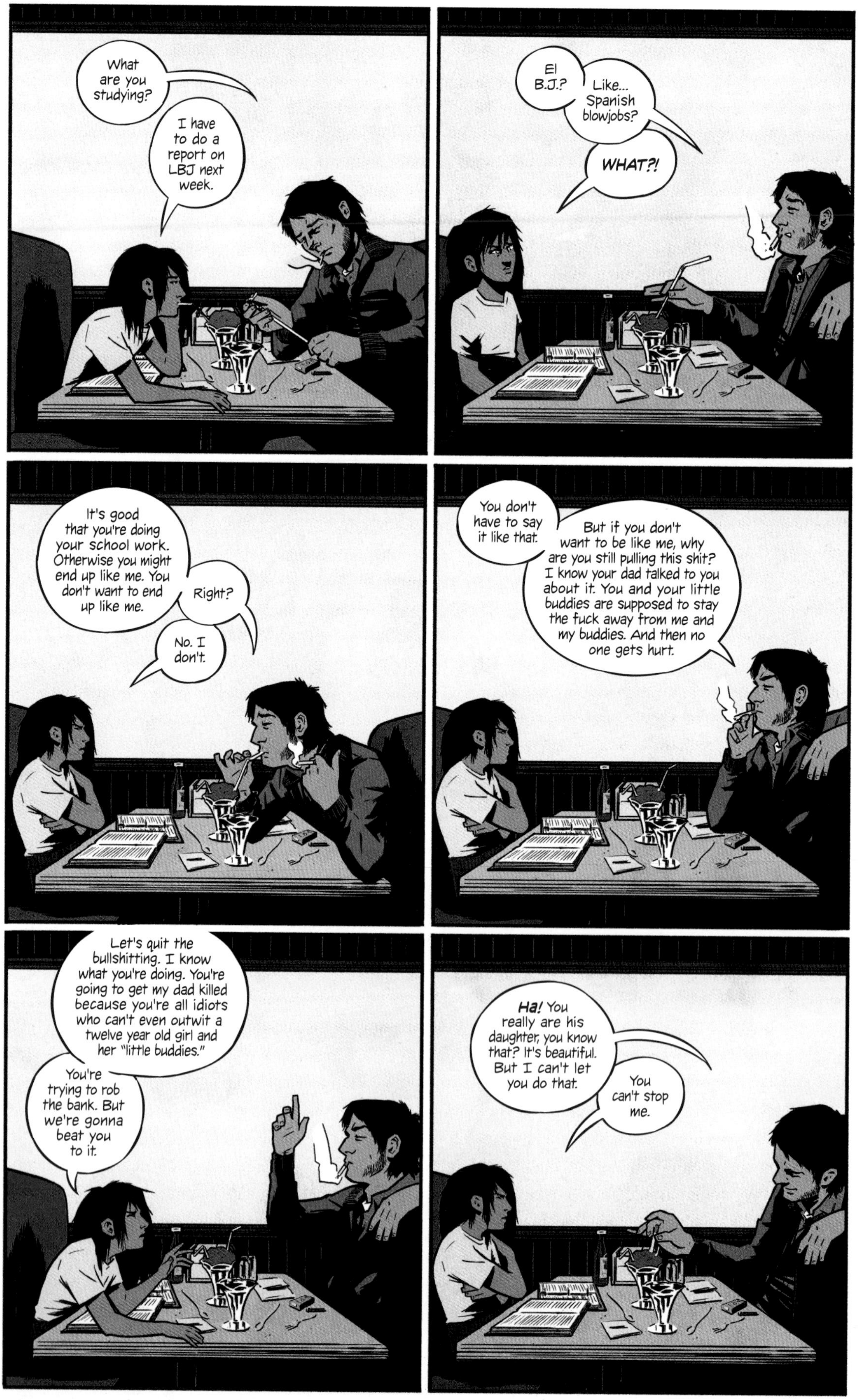

What are you studying?
I have to do a report on LBJ next week.
El B.J.?
Like... Spanish blowjobs?
WHAT?!
It's good that you're doing your school work. Otherwise you might end up like me. You don't want to end up like me.
Right?
No. I don't.
You don't have to say it like that.
But if you don't want to be like me, why are you still pulling this shit? I know your dad talked to you about it. You and your little buddies are supposed to stay the fuck away from me and my buddies. And then no one gets hurt.
Let's quit the bullshitting. I know what you're doing. You're going to get my dad killed because you're all idiots who can't even outwit a twelve year old girl and her "little buddies."
You're trying to rob the bank. But we're gonna beat you to it.
Ha! You really are his daughter, you know that? It's beautiful. But I can't let you do that.
You can't stop me.

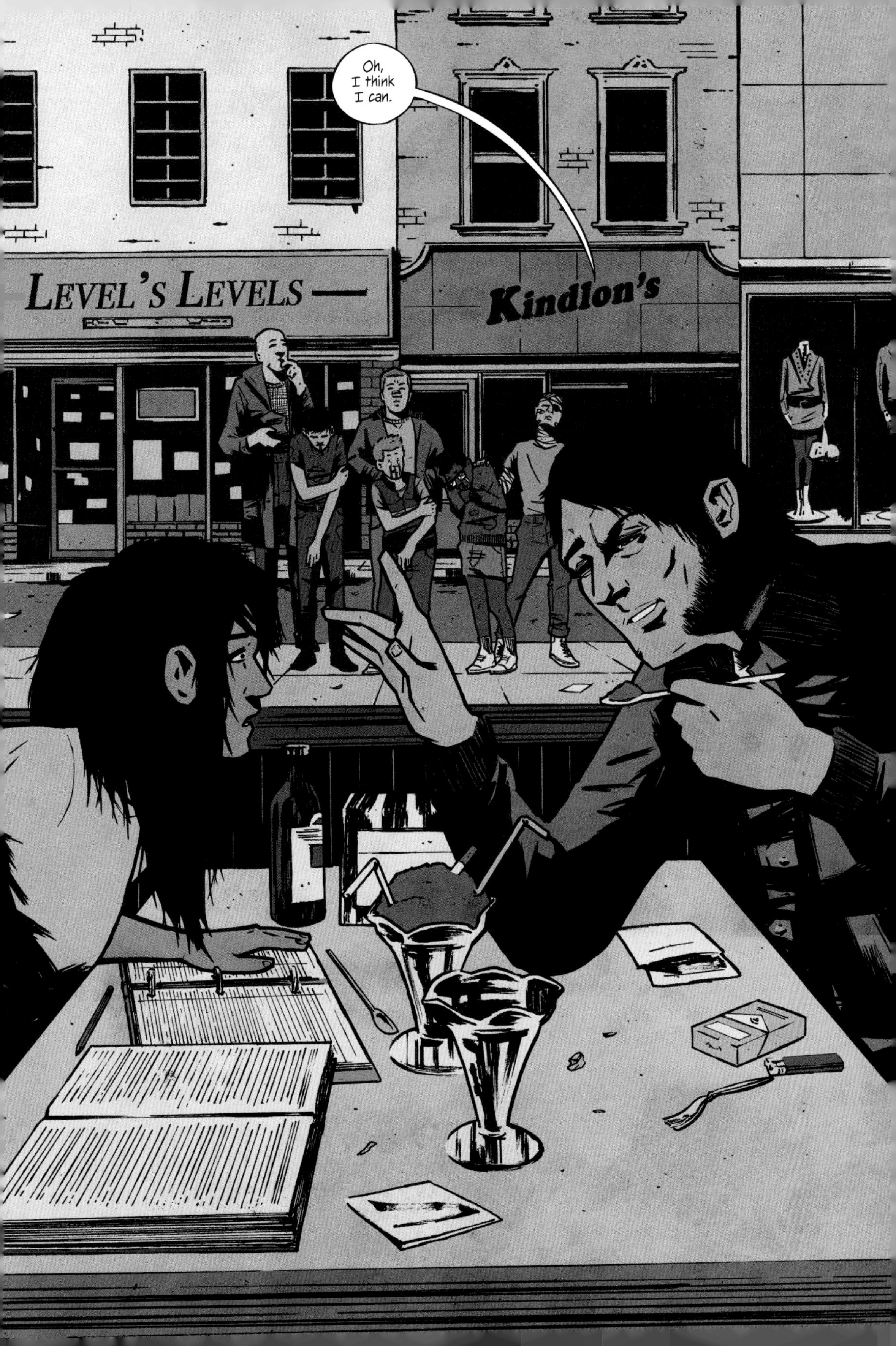
Oh, I think I can.
LEVEL'S LEVELS
Kindlon's

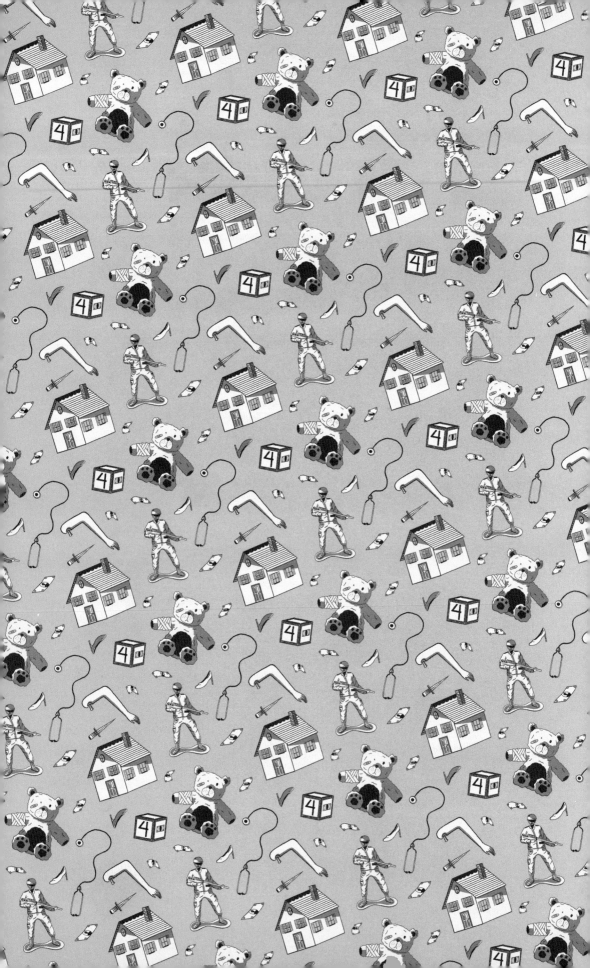

CHAPTER FOUR

Say hello
to my little friends.

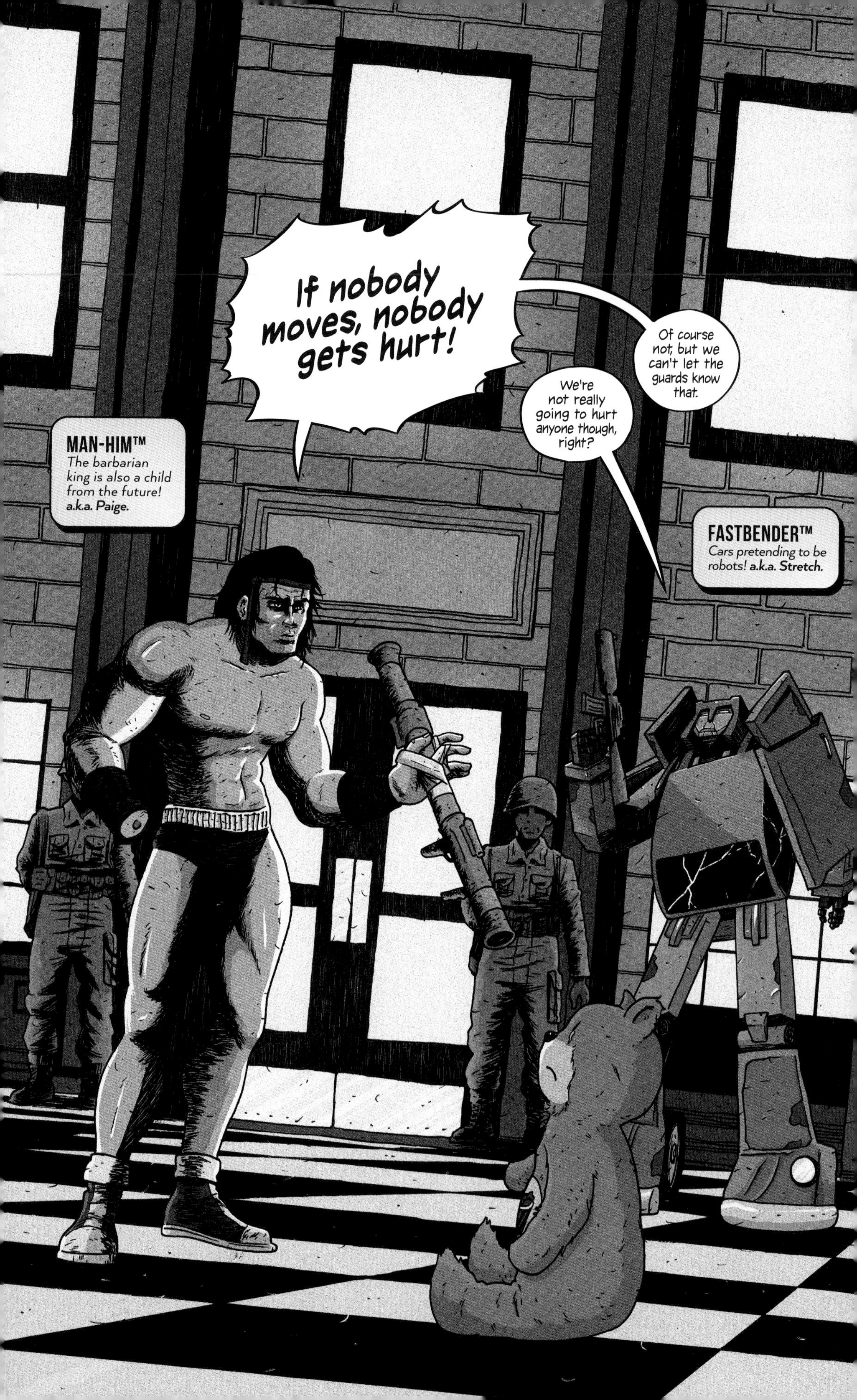
If nobody moves, nobody gets hurt!
We're not really going to hurt anyone though, right?
Of course not, but we can't let the guards know that.
MAN-HIM™
The barbarian king is also a child from the future! a.k.a. Paige.
FASTBENDER™
Cars pretending to be robots! a.k.a. Stretch.

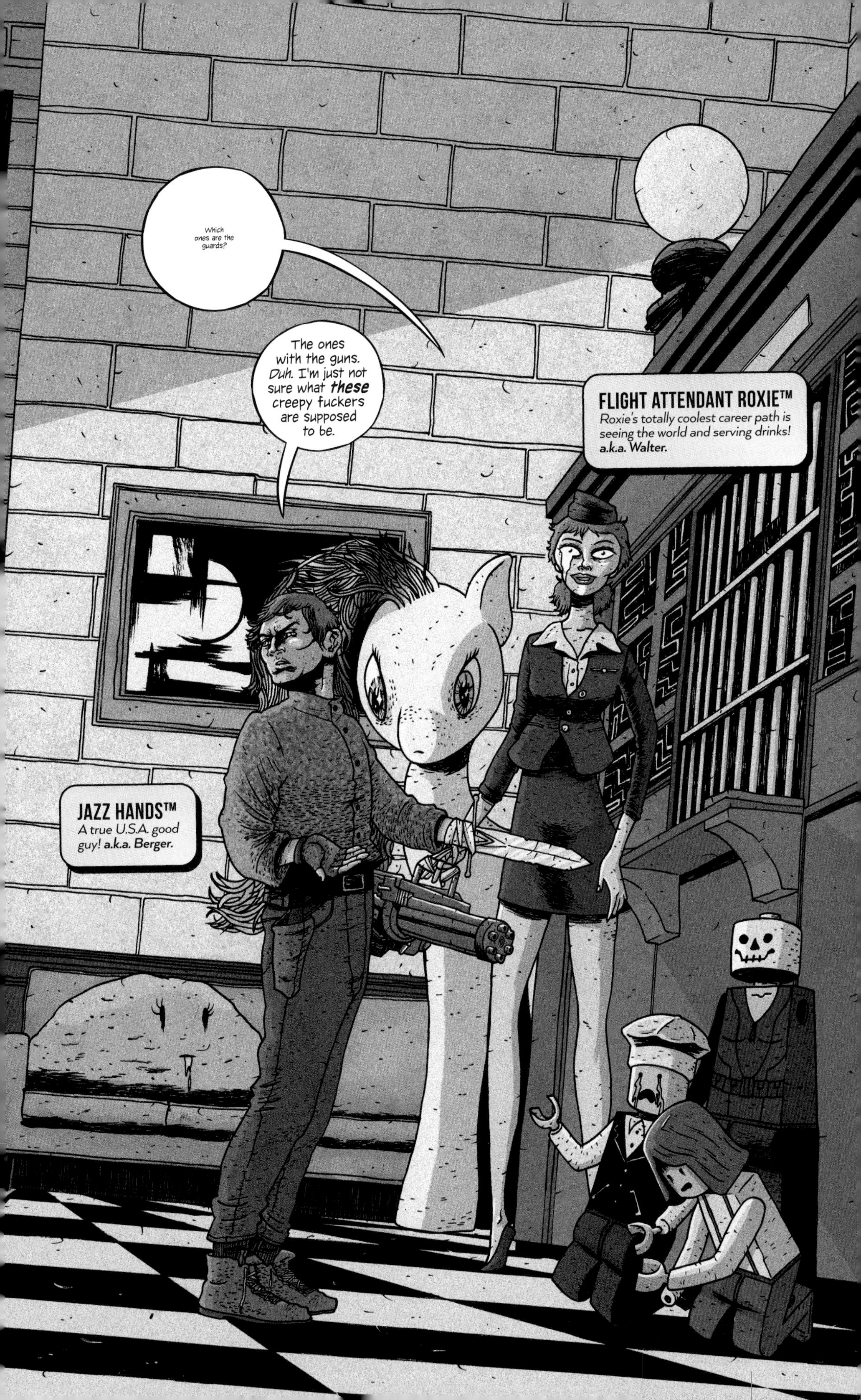

Which ones are the guards?
The ones with the guns. *Duh.* I'm just not sure what ***these*** creepy fuckers are supposed to be.
FLIGHT ATTENDANT ROXIE™
Roxie's totally coolest career path is seeing the world and serving drinks! **a.k.a. Walter.**
JAZZ HANDS™
A true U.S.A. good guy! **a.k.a. Berger.**

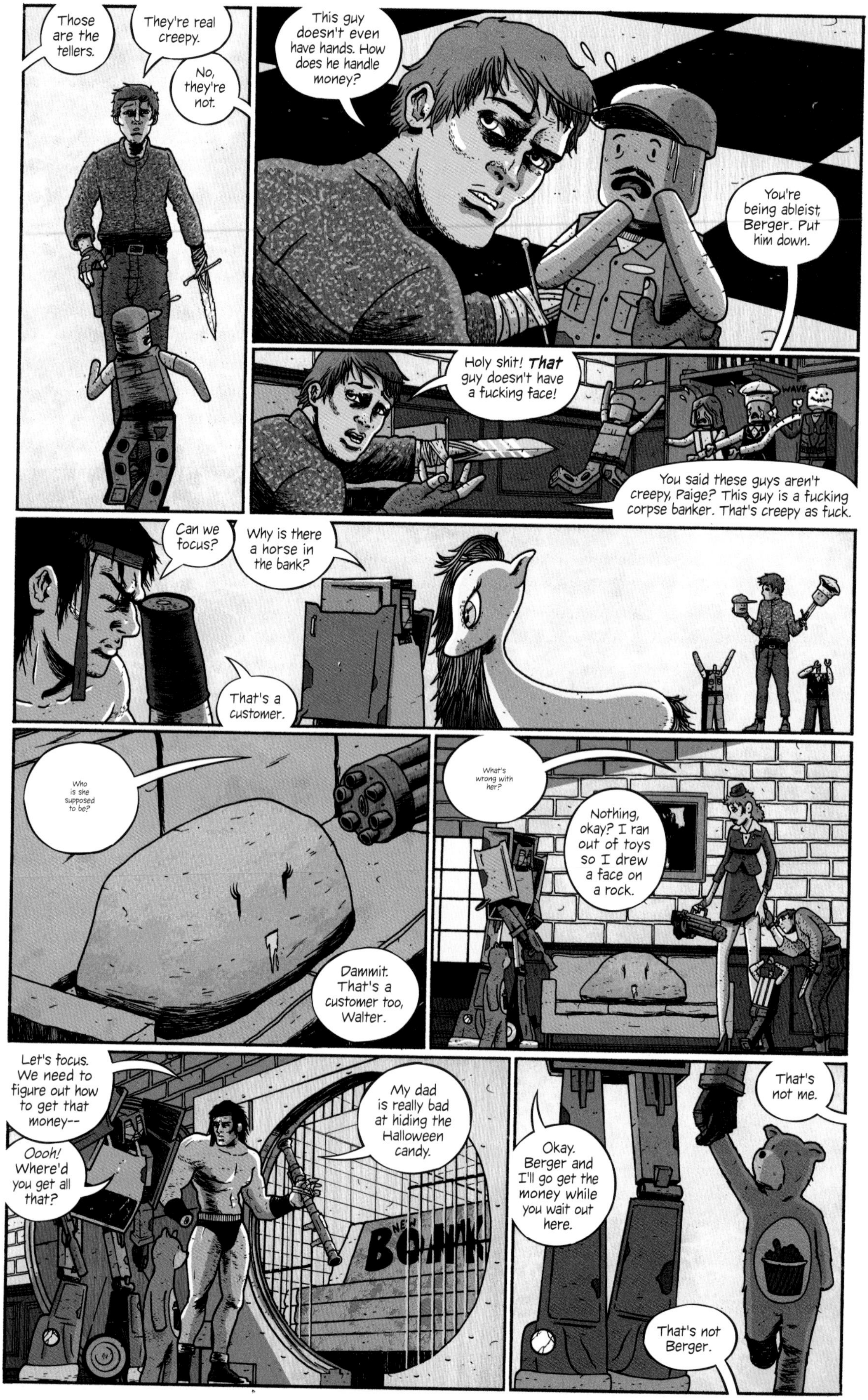

Those are the tellers.
They're real creepy.
No, they're not.
This guy doesn't even have hands. How does he handle money?
You're being ableist, Berger. Put him down.
Holy shit! *That* guy doesn't have a fucking face!
You said these guys aren't creepy, Paige? This guy is a fucking corpse banker. That's creepy as fuck.
Can we focus?
Why is there a horse in the bank?
That's a customer.
Who is she supposed to be?
Dammit. That's a customer too, Walter.
What's wrong with her?
Nothing, okay? I ran out of toys so I drew a face on a rock.
Let's focus. We need to figure out how to get that money--
Oooh! Where'd you get all that?
My dad is really bad at hiding the Halloween candy.
That's not me.
Okay. Berger and I'll go get the money while you wait out here.
That's not Berger.

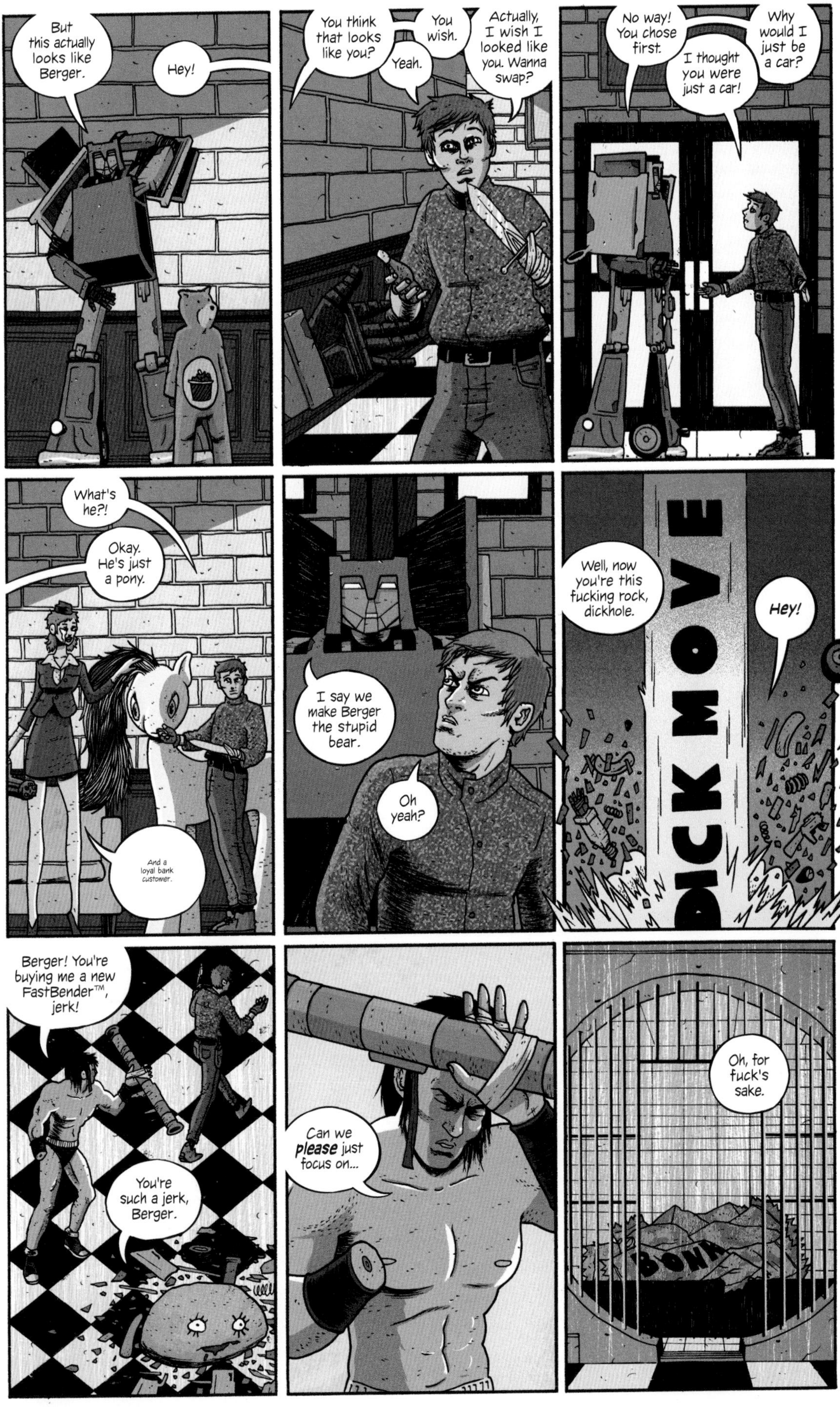

But this actually looks like Berger.
Hey!
You think that looks like you?
You wish.
Yeah.
Actually, I wish I looked like you. Wanna swap?
No way! You chose first.
Why would I just be a car?
I thought you were just a car!
What's he?!
Okay. He's just a pony.
And a loyal bank customer.
I say we make Berger the stupid bear.
Oh yeah?
Well, now you're this fucking rock, dickhole.
DICK MOVE
Hey!
Berger! You're buying me a new FastBender™, jerk!
You're such a jerk, Berger.
Can we ***please*** just focus on...
Oh, for fuck's sake.

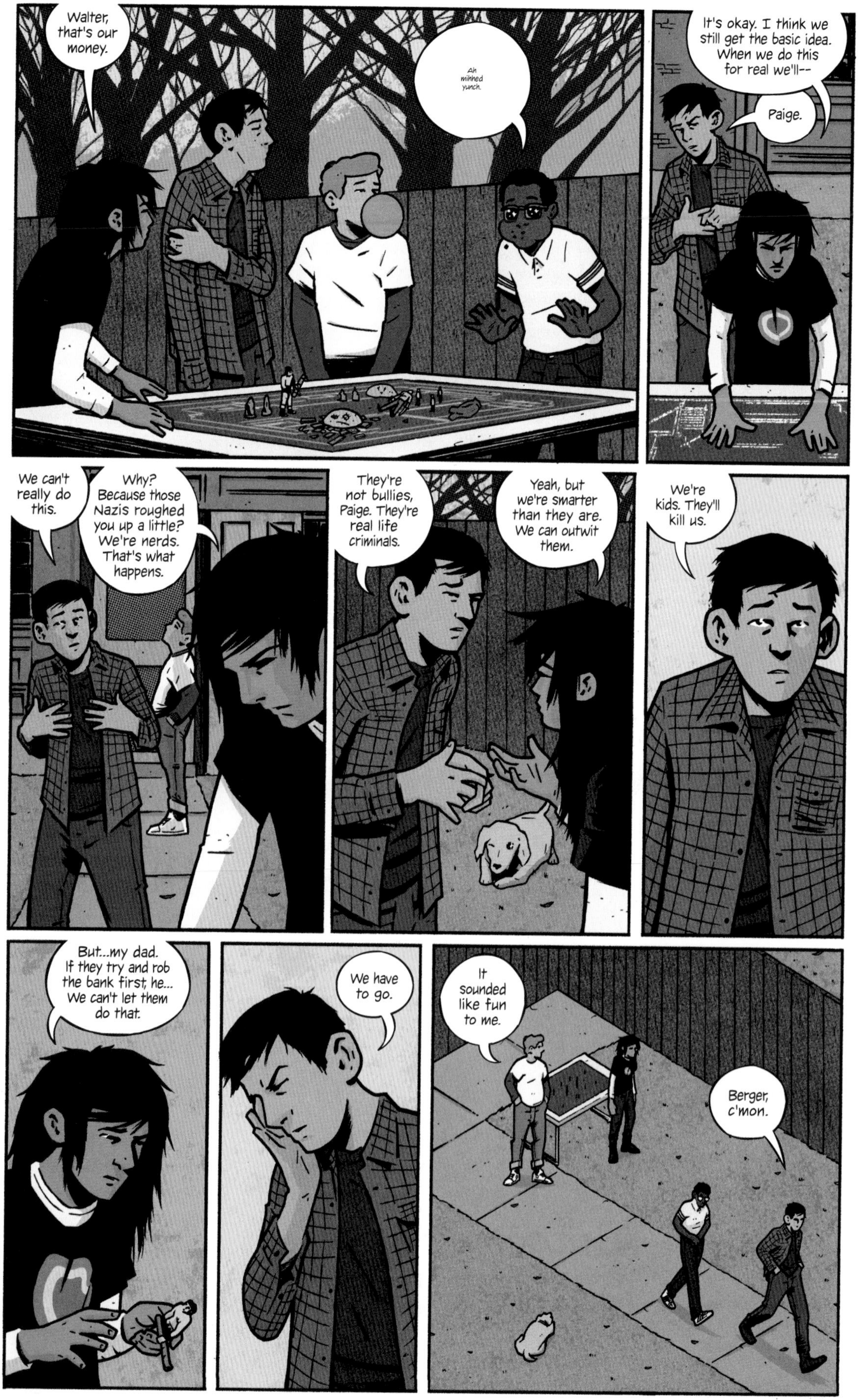

Walter, that's our money.
Ah mihhed yunch.
It's okay. I think we still get the basic idea. When we do this for real we'll--
Paige.
We can't really do this.
Why? Because those Nazis roughed you up a little? We're nerds. That's what happens.
They're not bullies, Paige. They're real life criminals.
Yeah, but we're smarter than they are. We can outwit them.
We're kids. They'll kill us.
But...my dad. If they try and rob the bank first, he... We can't let them do that.
We have to go.
It sounded like fun to me.
Berger, c'mon.

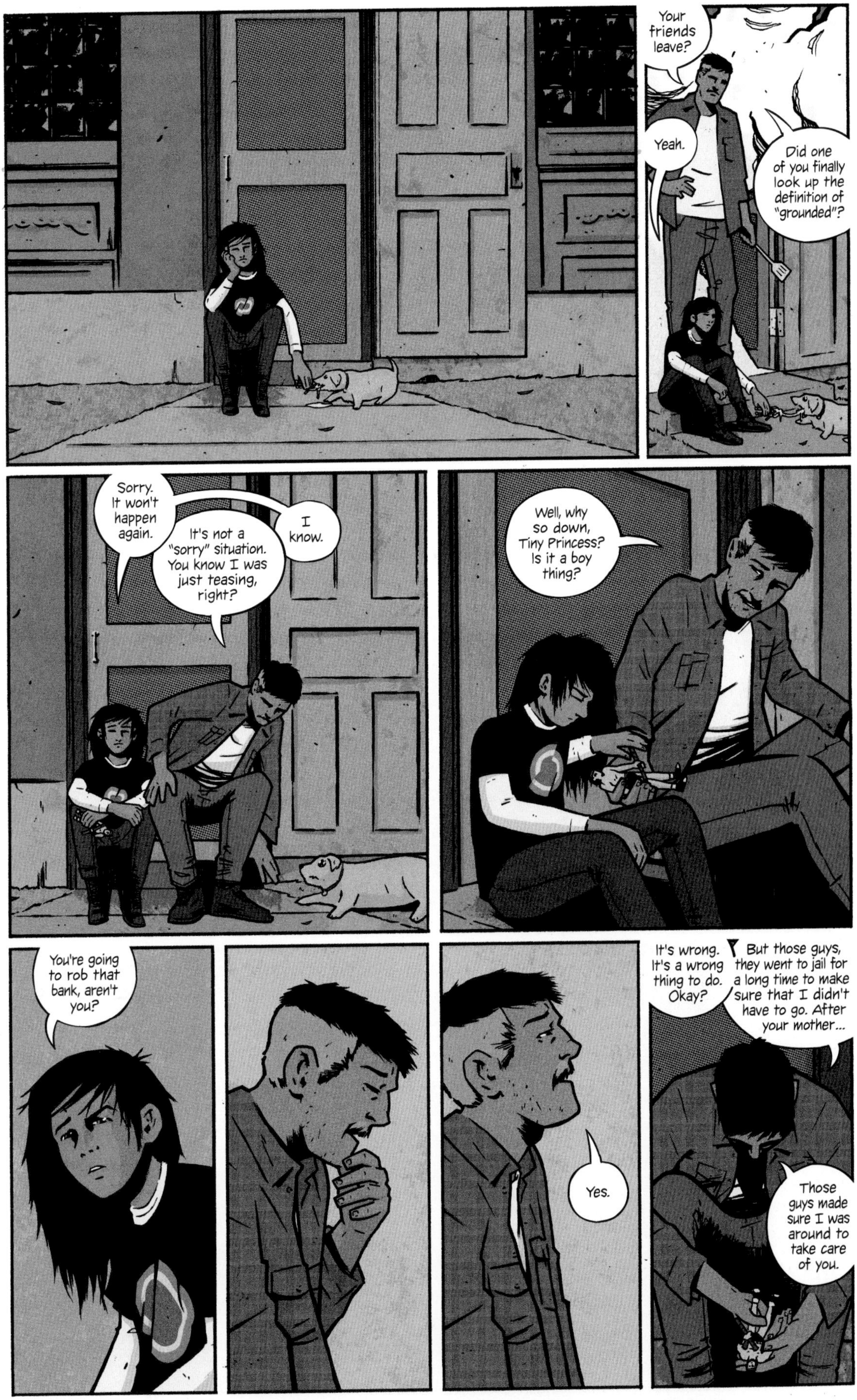
Your friends leave?
Yeah.
Did one of you finally look up the definition of "grounded"?
Sorry. It won't happen again.
It's not a "sorry" situation. You know I was just teasing, right?
I know.
Well, why so down, Tiny Princess? Is it a boy thing?
You're going to rob that bank, aren't you?
Yes.
It's wrong. It's a wrong thing to do. Okay?
But those guys, they went to jail for a long time to make sure that I didn't have to go. After your mother...
Those guys made sure I was around to take care of you.

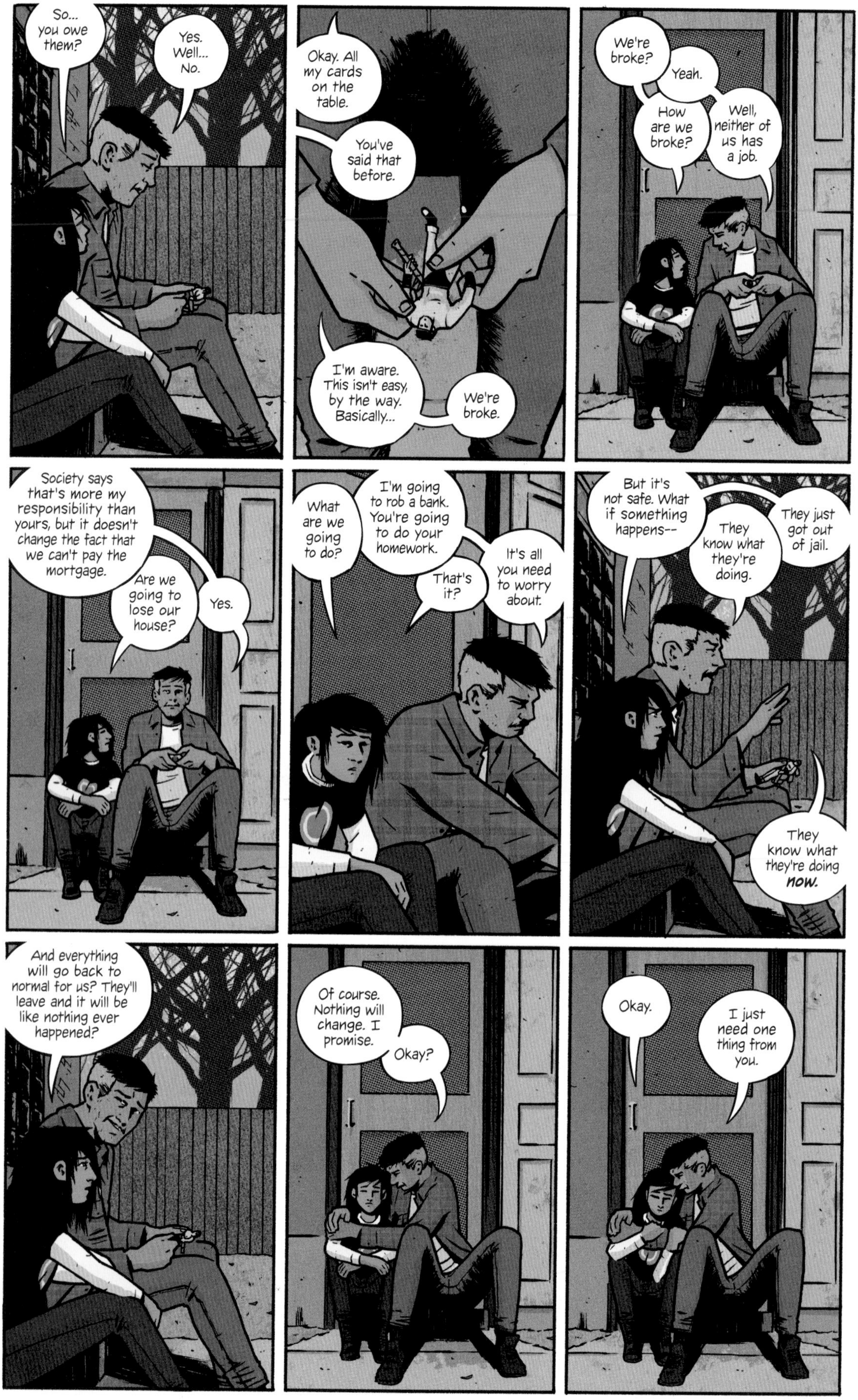
So... you owe them?
Yes. Well... No.
Okay. All my cards on the table.
You've said that before.
I'm aware. This isn't easy, by the way. Basically...
We're broke.
We're broke?
Yeah.
How are we broke?
Well, neither of us has a job.
Society says that's more my responsibility than yours, but it doesn't change the fact that we can't pay the mortgage.
Are we going to lose our house?
Yes.
What are we going to do?
I'm going to rob a bank. You're going to do your homework.
That's it?
It's all you need to worry about.
But it's not safe. What if something happens--
They know what they're doing.
They just got out of jail.
They know what they're doing **now.**
And everything will go back to normal for us? They'll leave and it will be like nothing ever happened?
Of course. Nothing will change. I promise.
Okay?
Okay.
I just need one thing from you.

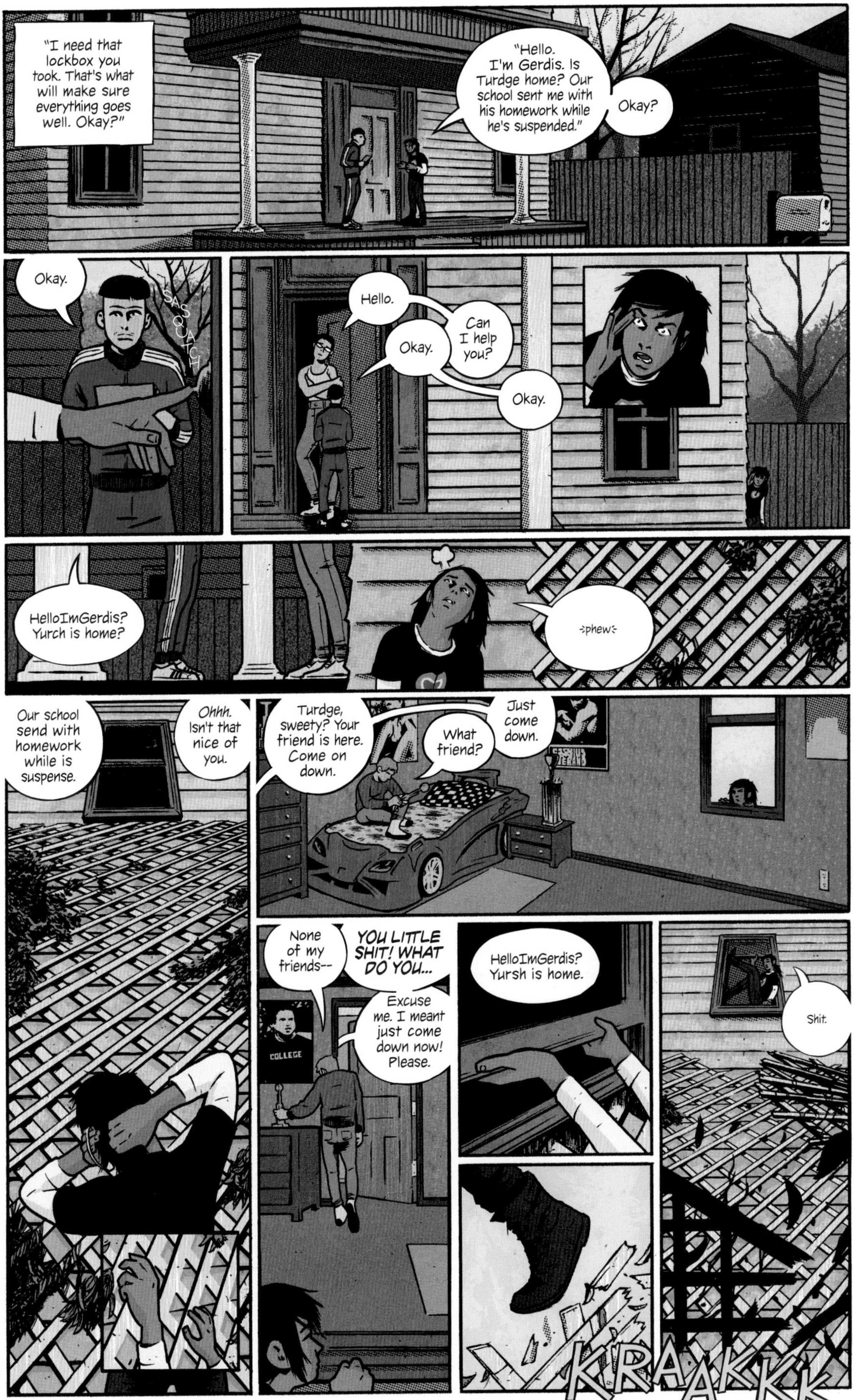
"I need that lockbox you took. That's what will make sure everything goes well. Okay?"
"Hello. I'm Gerdis. Is Turdge home? Our school sent me with his homework while he's suspended."
Okay?
Okay.
SASQUATCH
Hello.
Can I help you?
Okay.
Okay.
HelloImGerdis? Yurch is home?
phew
Our school send with homework while is suspense.
Ohhh. Isn't that nice of you.
Turdge, sweety? Your friend is here. Come on down.
What friend?
Just come down.
None of my friends--
YOU LITTLE SHIT! WHAT DO YOU...
Excuse me. I meant just come down now! Please.
COLLEGE
HelloImGerdis? Yursh is home.
Shit.
KRAAKKK

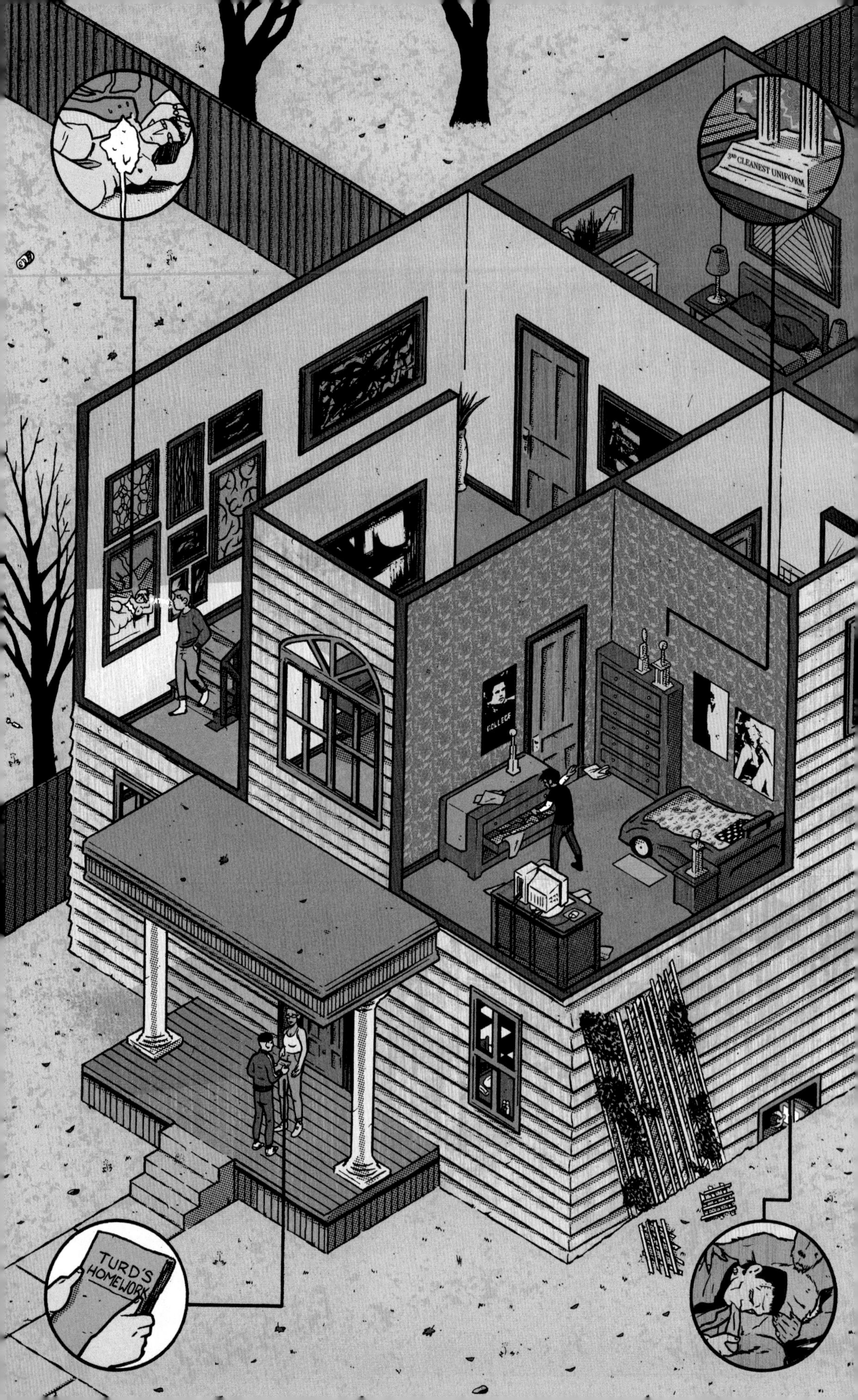
3RD CLEANEST UNIFORM
COLLEGE
TURD'S HOMEWORK

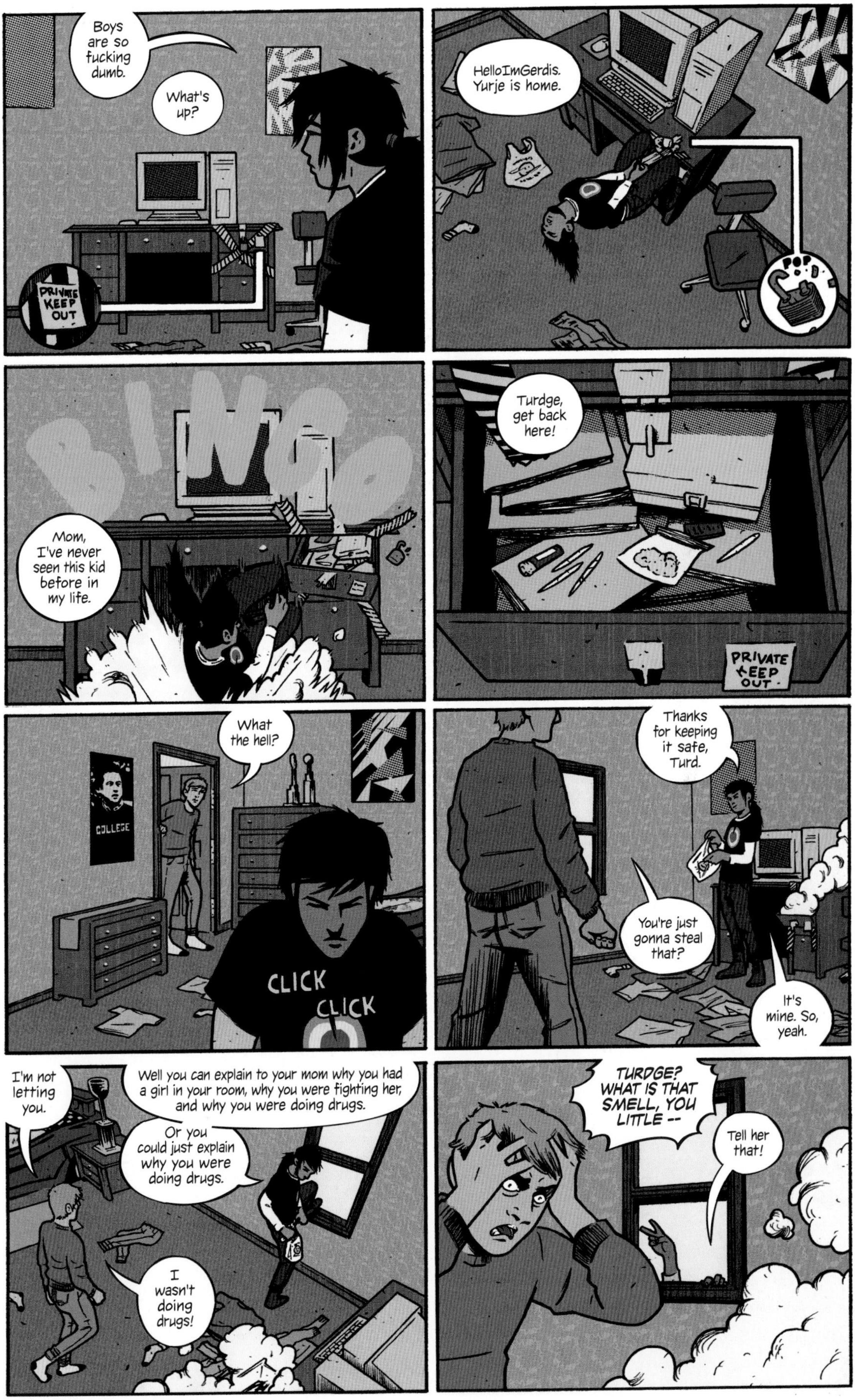

Boys are so fucking dumb.
What's up?
PRIVATE KEEP OUT
HelloImGerdis. Yurje is home.
BINGO
Mom, I've never seen this kid before in my life.
Turdge, get back here!
PRIVATE KEEP OUT
What the hell?
COLLEGE
CLICK CLICK
Thanks for keeping it safe, Turd.
You're just gonna steal that?
It's mine. So, yeah.
I'm not letting you.
Well you can explain to your mom why you had a girl in your room, why you were fighting her, and why you were doing drugs.
Or you could just explain why you were doing drugs.
I wasn't doing drugs!
TURDGE? WHAT IS THAT SMELL, YOU LITTLE --
Tell her that!

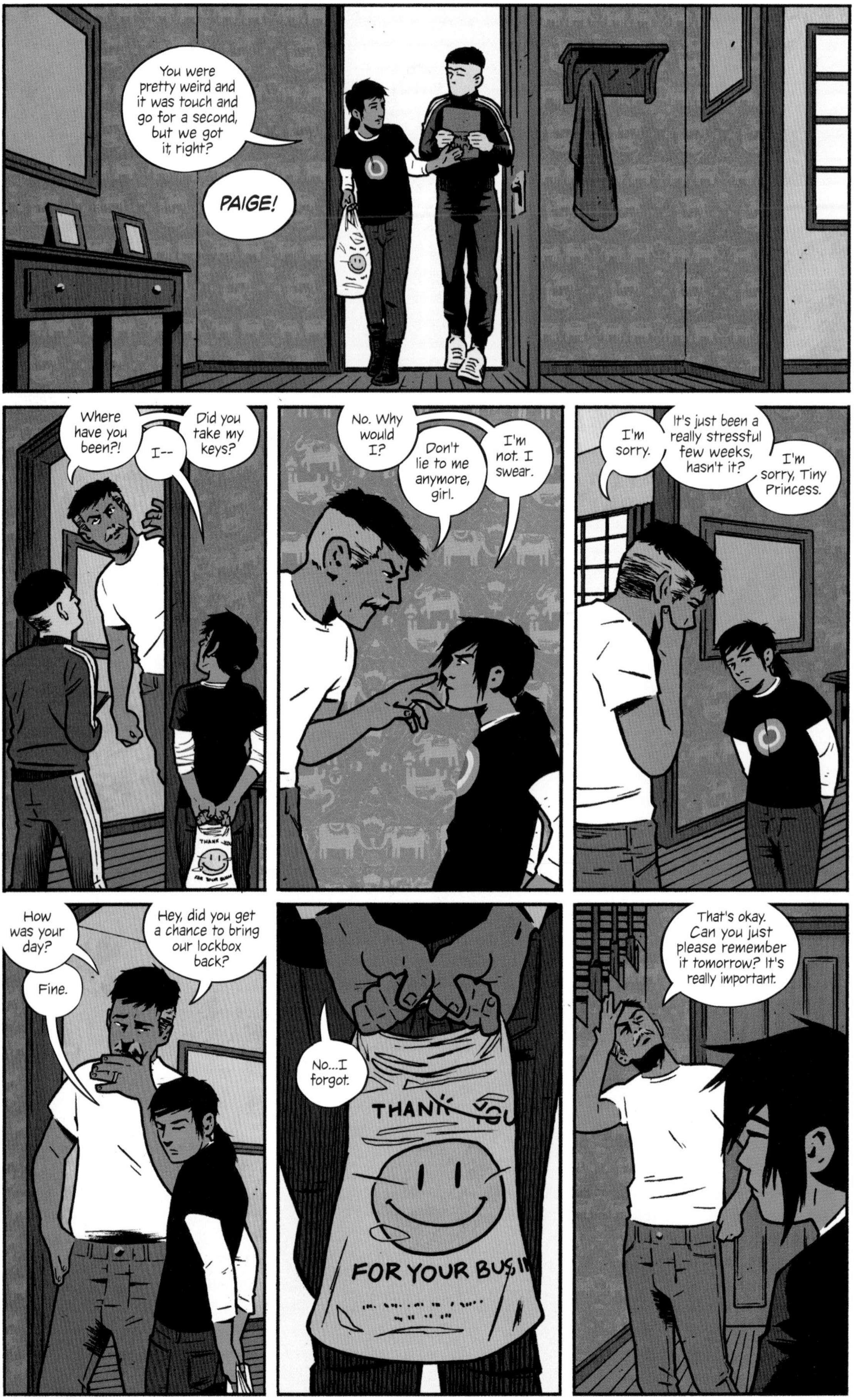
You were pretty weird and it was touch and go for a second, but we got it right?
PAIGE!
Where have you been?!
I--
Did you take my keys?
No. Why would I?
Don't lie to me anymore, girl.
I'm not. I swear.
I'm sorry.
It's just been a really stressful few weeks, hasn't it?
I'm sorry, Tiny Princess.
How was your day?
Fine.
Hey, did you get a chance to bring our lockbox back?
No...I forgot.
THANK YOU
FOR YOUR BUSI
That's okay. Can you just please remember it tomorrow? It's really important.

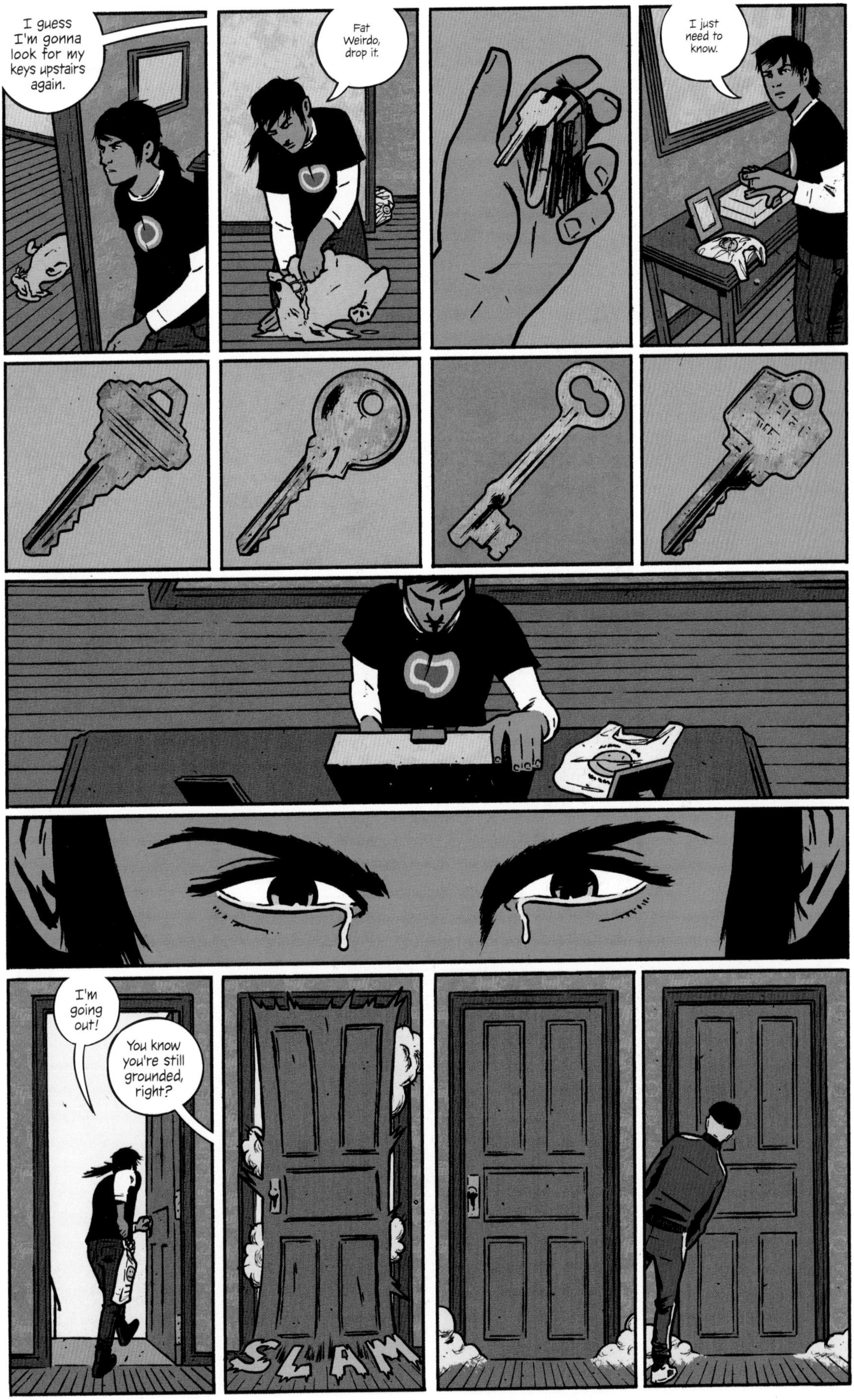
I guess I'm gonna look for my keys upstairs again.
Fat Weirdo, drop it.
I just need to know.
I'm going out!
You know you're still grounded, right?
SLAM

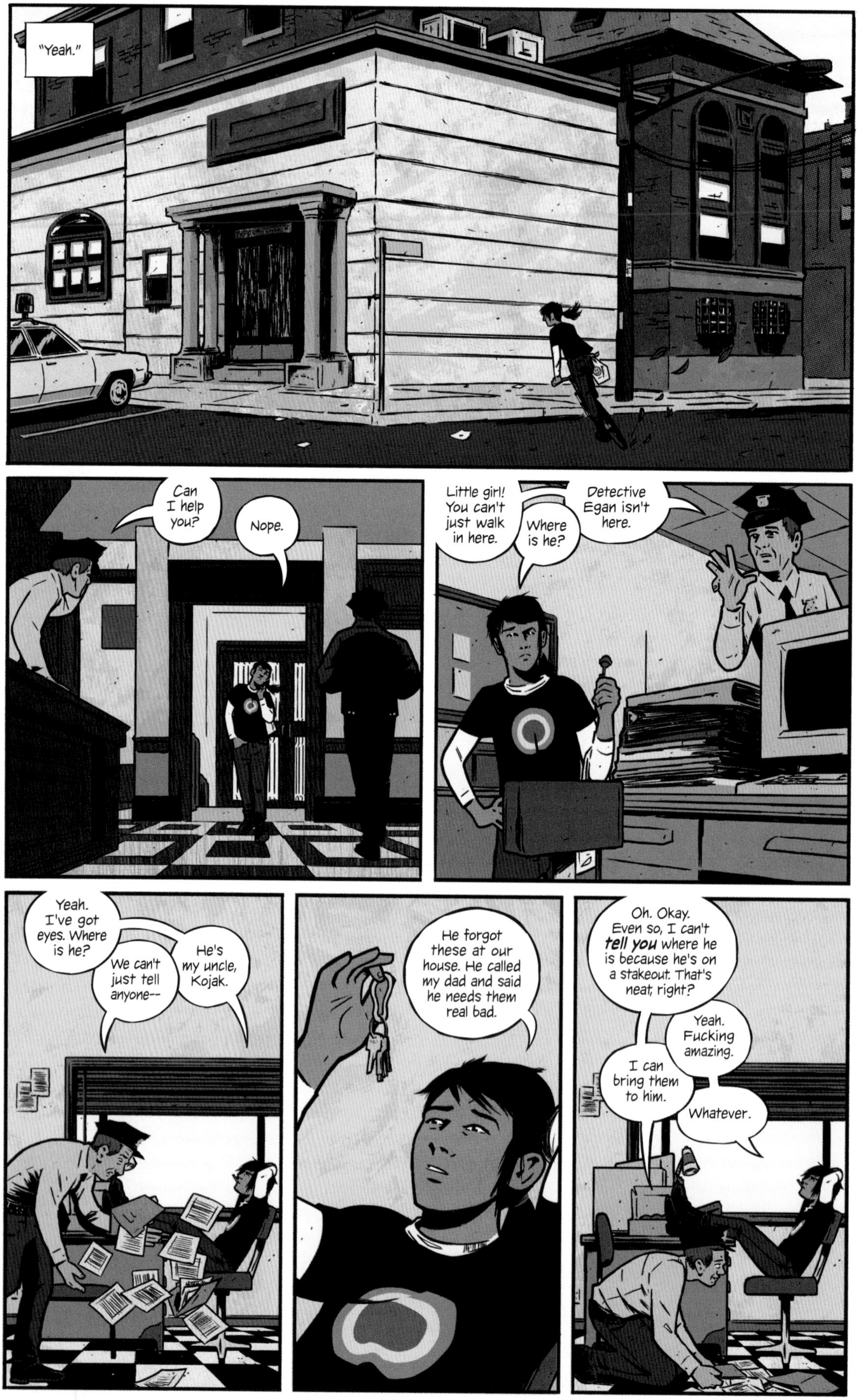
"Yeah."
Can I help you?
Nope.
Little girl! You can't just walk in here.
Where is he?
Detective Egan isn't here.
Yeah. I've got eyes. Where is he?
We can't just tell anyone--
He's my uncle, Kojak.
He forgot these at our house. He called my dad and said he needs them real bad.
Oh. Okay. Even so, I can't **tell you** where he is because he's on a stakeout. That's neat, right?
Yeah. Fucking amazing.
I can bring them to him.
Whatever.

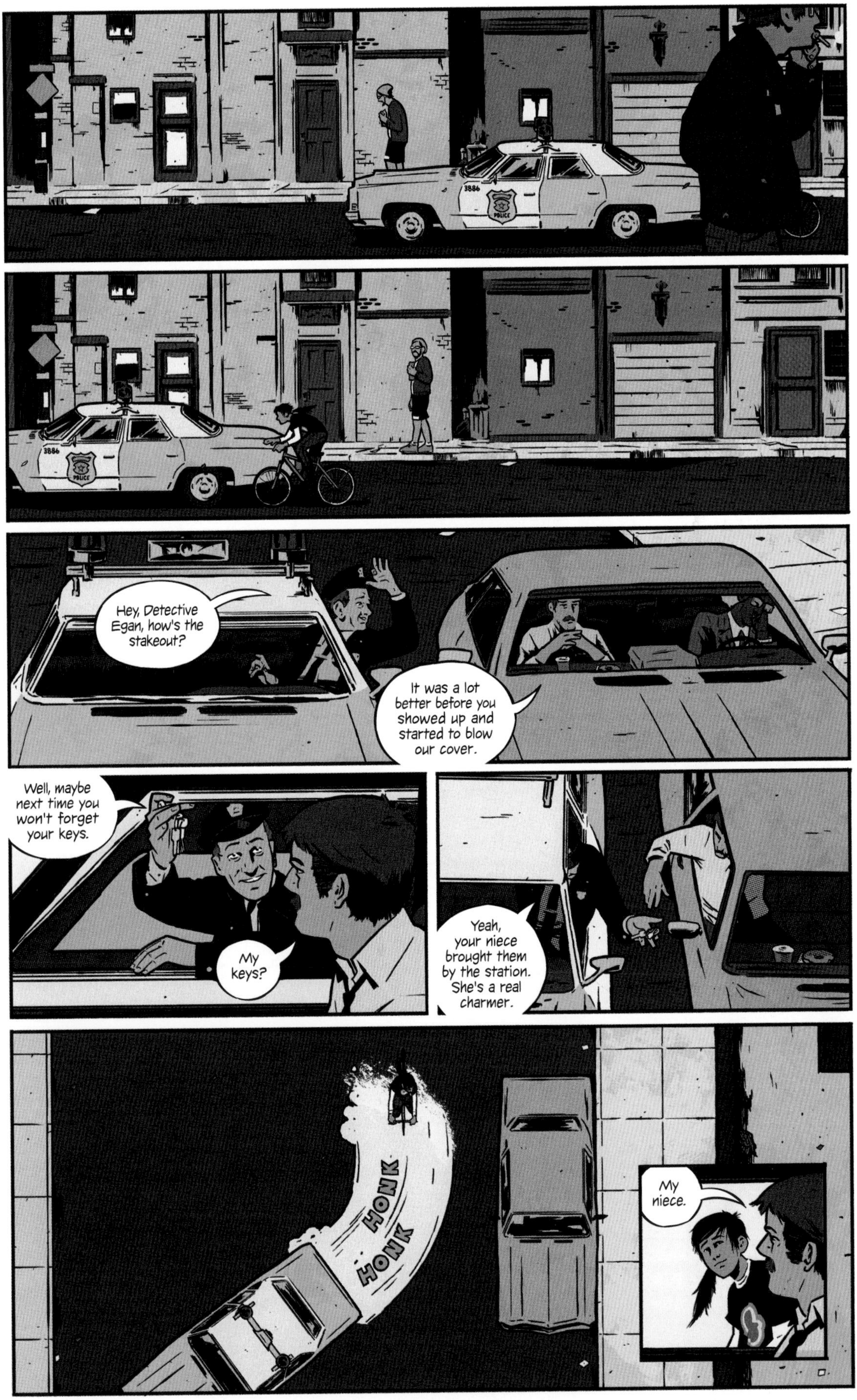
3886
POLICE
3886
POLICE
Hey, Detective Egan, how's the stakeout?
It was a lot better before you showed up and started to blow our cover.
Well, maybe next time you won't forget your keys.
My keys?
Yeah, your niece brought them by the station. She's a real charmer.
HONK HONK
My niece.

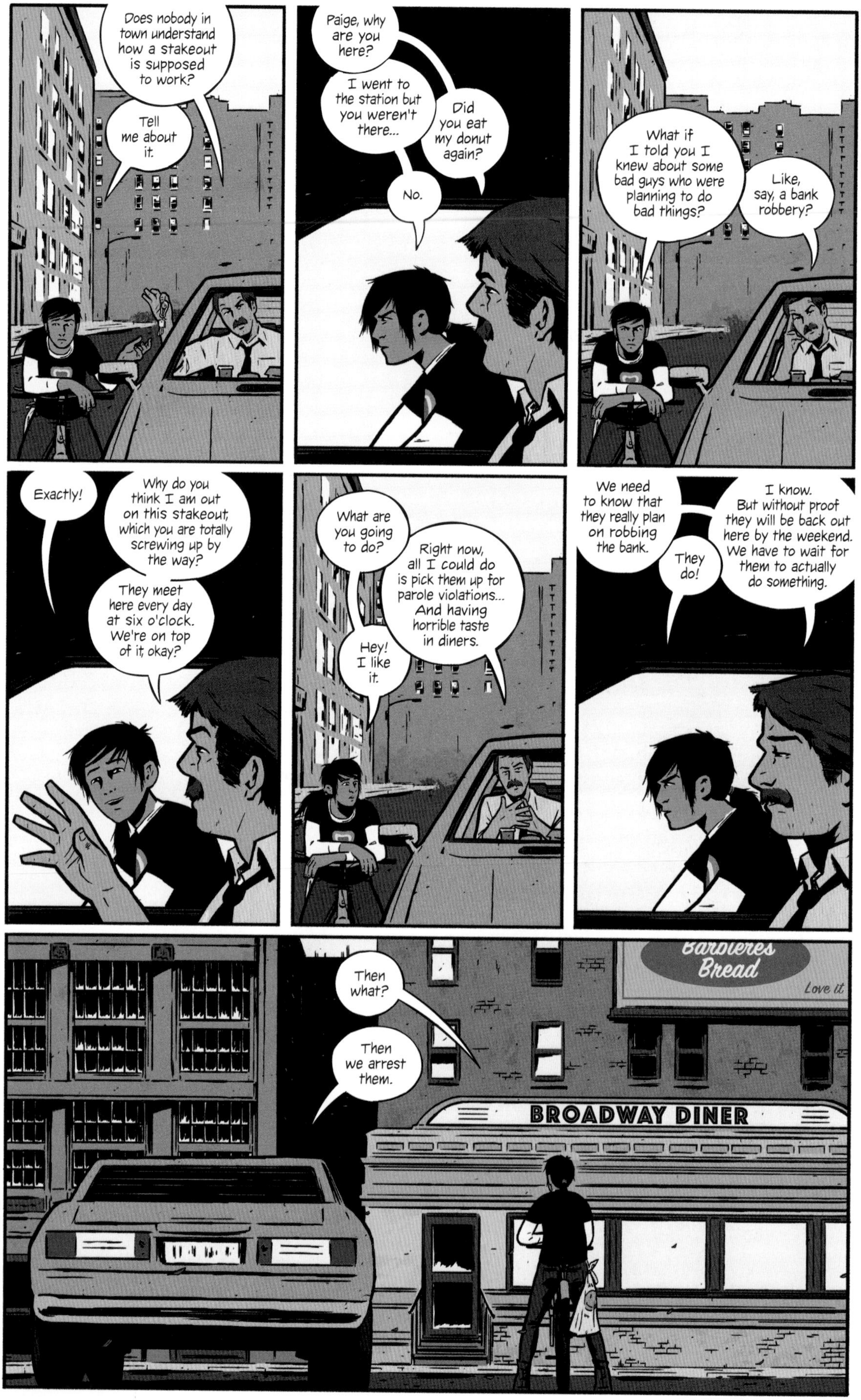
Does nobody in town understand how a stakeout is supposed to work?
Tell me about it.
Paige, why are you here?
I went to the station but you weren't there...
Did you eat my donut again?
No.
What if I told you I knew about some bad guys who were planning to do bad things?
Like, say, a bank robbery?
Exactly!
Why do you think I am out on this stakeout, which you are totally screwing up by the way?
They meet here every day at six o'clock. We're on top of it, okay?
What are you going to do?
Right now, all I could do is pick them up for parole violations... And having horrible taste in diners.
Hey! I like it.
We need to know that they really plan on robbing the bank.
They do!
I know. But without proof they will be back out here by the weekend. We have to wait for them to actually do something.
Barbieres Bread
Love it
Then what?
Then we arrest them.
BROADWAY DINER

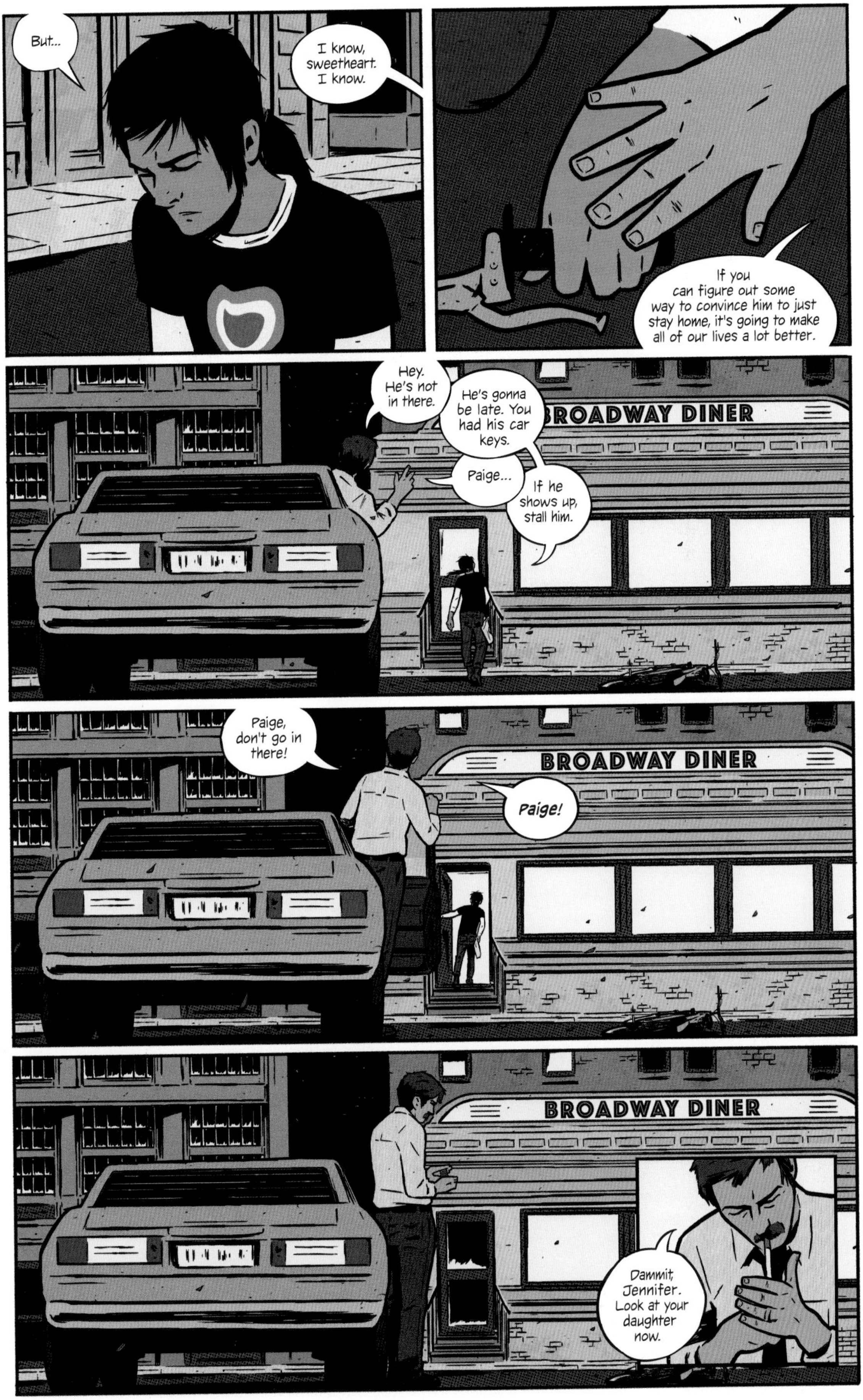
But...
I know, sweetheart. I know.
If you can figure out some way to convince him to just stay home, it's going to make all of our lives a lot better.
Hey. He's not in there.
He's gonna be late. You had his car keys.
BROADWAY DINER
Paige...
If he shows up, stall him.
Paige, don't go in there!
BROADWAY DINER
Paige!
BROADWAY DINER
Dammit, Jennifer. Look at your daughter now.

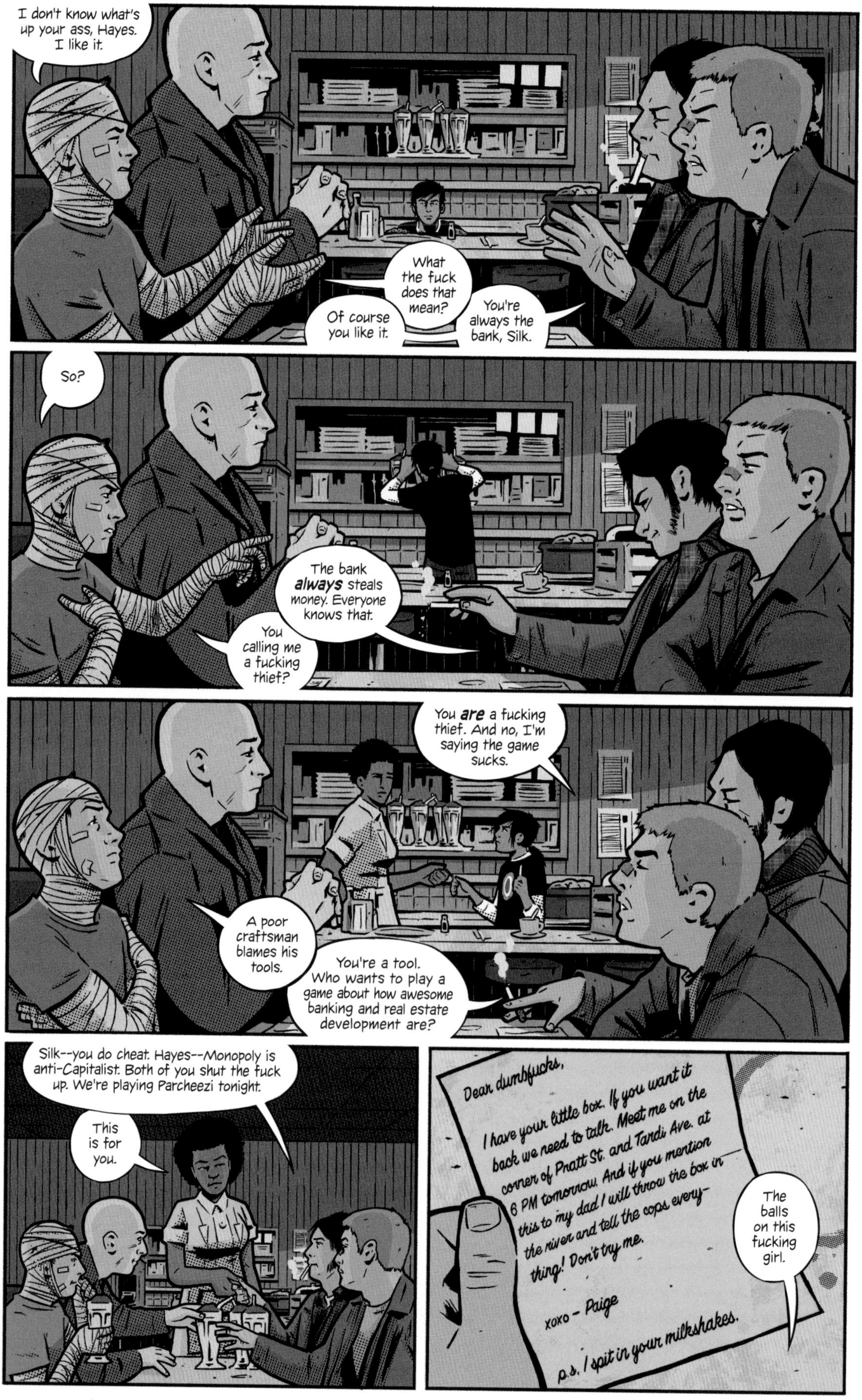

I don't know what's up your ass, Hayes. I like it.
What the fuck does that mean?
Of course you like it.
You're always the bank, Silk.
So?
The bank **always** steals money. Everyone knows that.
You calling me a fucking thief?
You **are** a fucking thief. And no, I'm saying the game sucks.
A poor craftsman blames his tools.
You're a tool. Who wants to play a game about how awesome banking and real estate development are?
Silk--you do cheat. Hayes--Monopoly is anti-Capitalist. Both of you shut the fuck up. We're playing Parcheezi tonight.
This is for you.
Dear dumbfucks,
I have your little box. If you want it back we need to talk. Meet me on the corner of Pratt St. and Tardi Ave. at 6 PM tomorrow. And if you mention this to my dad I will throw the box in the river and tell the cops everything! Don't try me.
xoxo – Paige
p.s. I spit in your milkshakes.
The balls on this fucking girl.

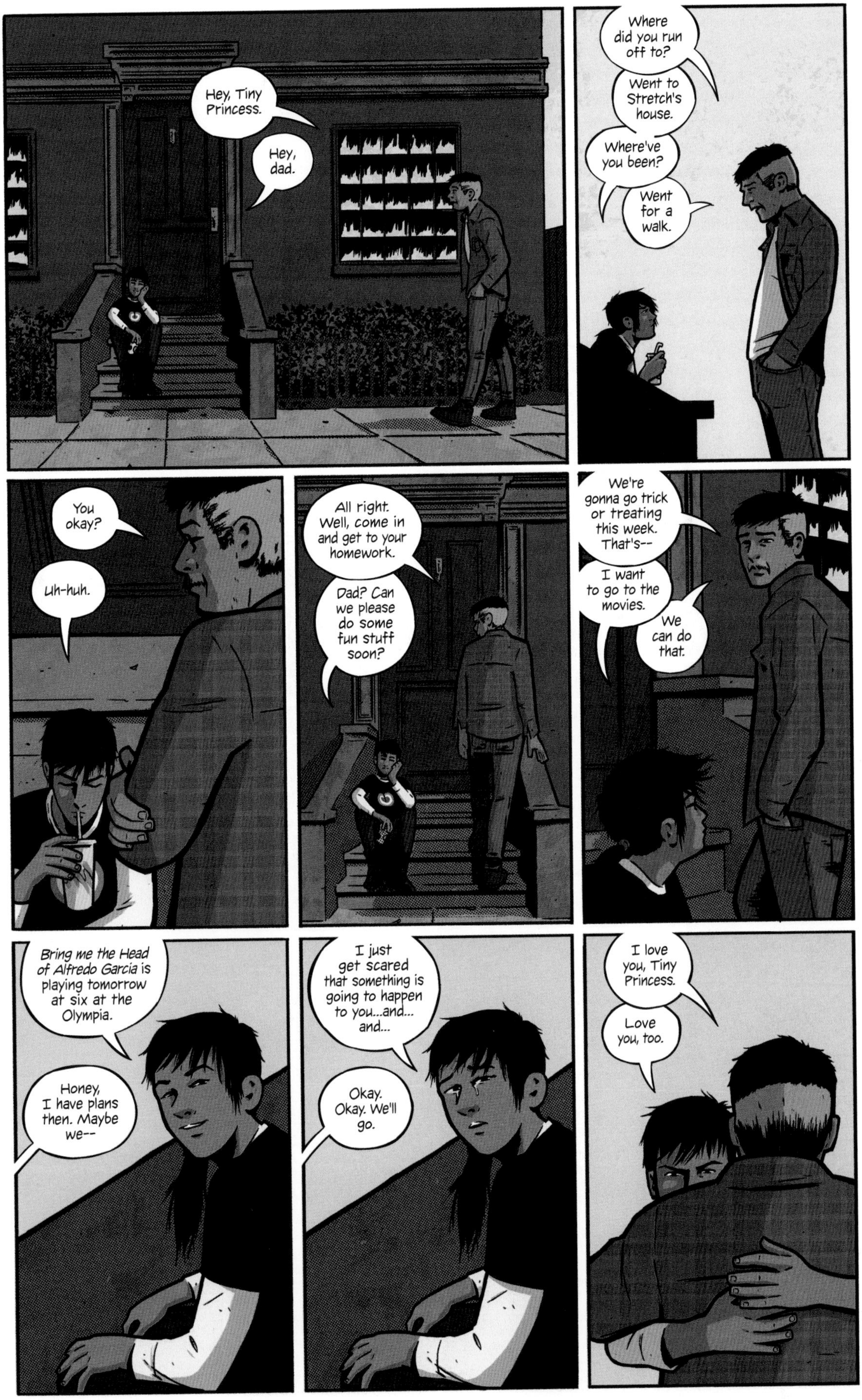
Hey, Tiny Princess.
Hey, dad.
Where did you run off to?
Went to Stretch's house.
Where've you been?
Went for a walk.
You okay?
Uh-huh.
All right. Well, come in and get to your homework.
Dad? Can we please do some fun stuff soon?
We're gonna go trick or treating this week. That's--
I want to go to the movies.
We can do that.
Bring me the Head of Alfredo Garcia is playing tomorrow at six at the Olympia.
Honey, I have plans then. Maybe we--
I just get scared that something is going to happen to you...and... and...
Okay. Okay. We'll go.
I love you, Tiny Princess.
Love you, too.

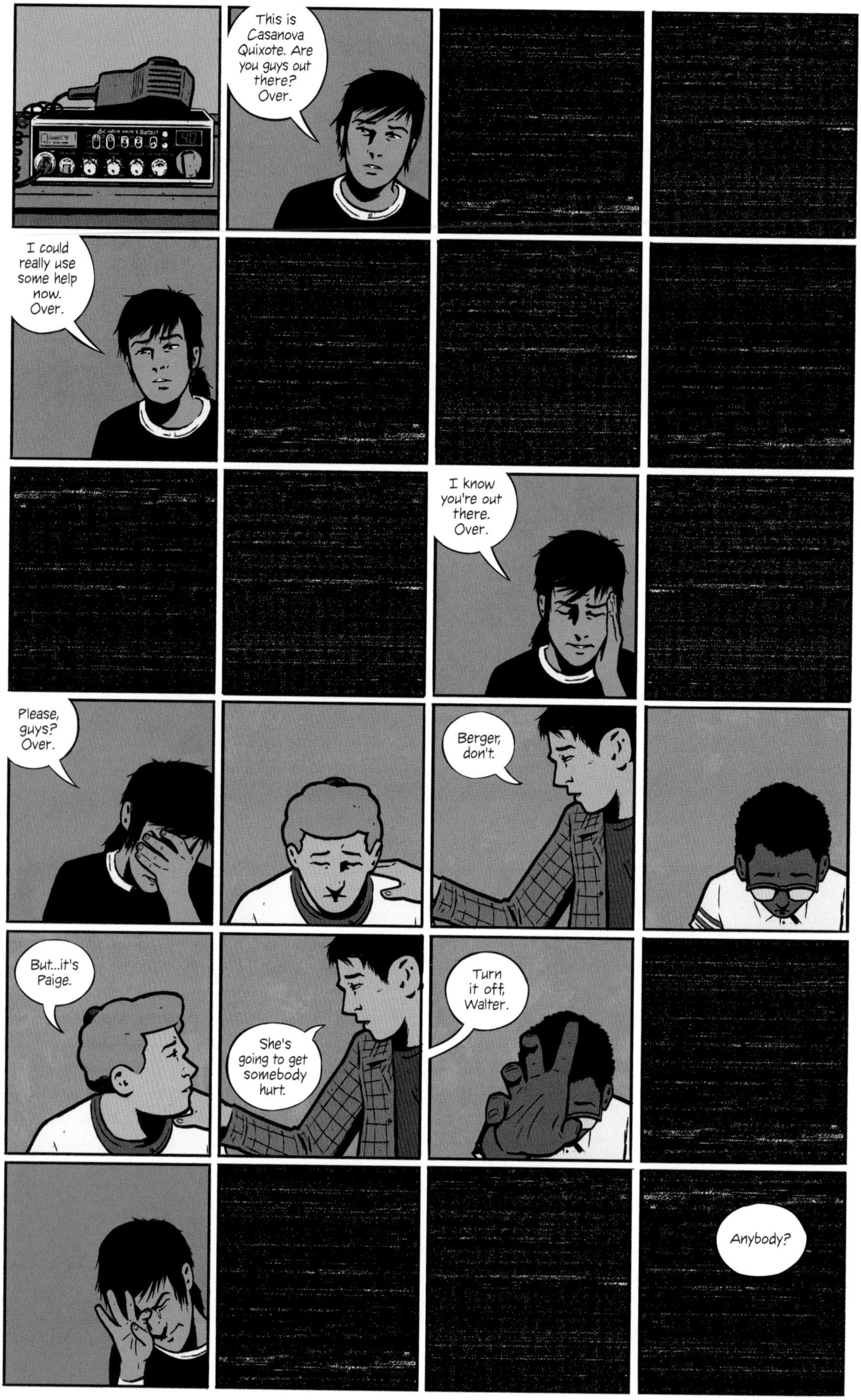
This is Casanova Quixote. Are you guys out there? Over.
I could really use some help now. Over.
I know you're out there. Over.
Please, guys? Over.
Berger, don't.
But...it's Paige.
She's going to get somebody hurt.
Turn it off, Walter.
Anybody?

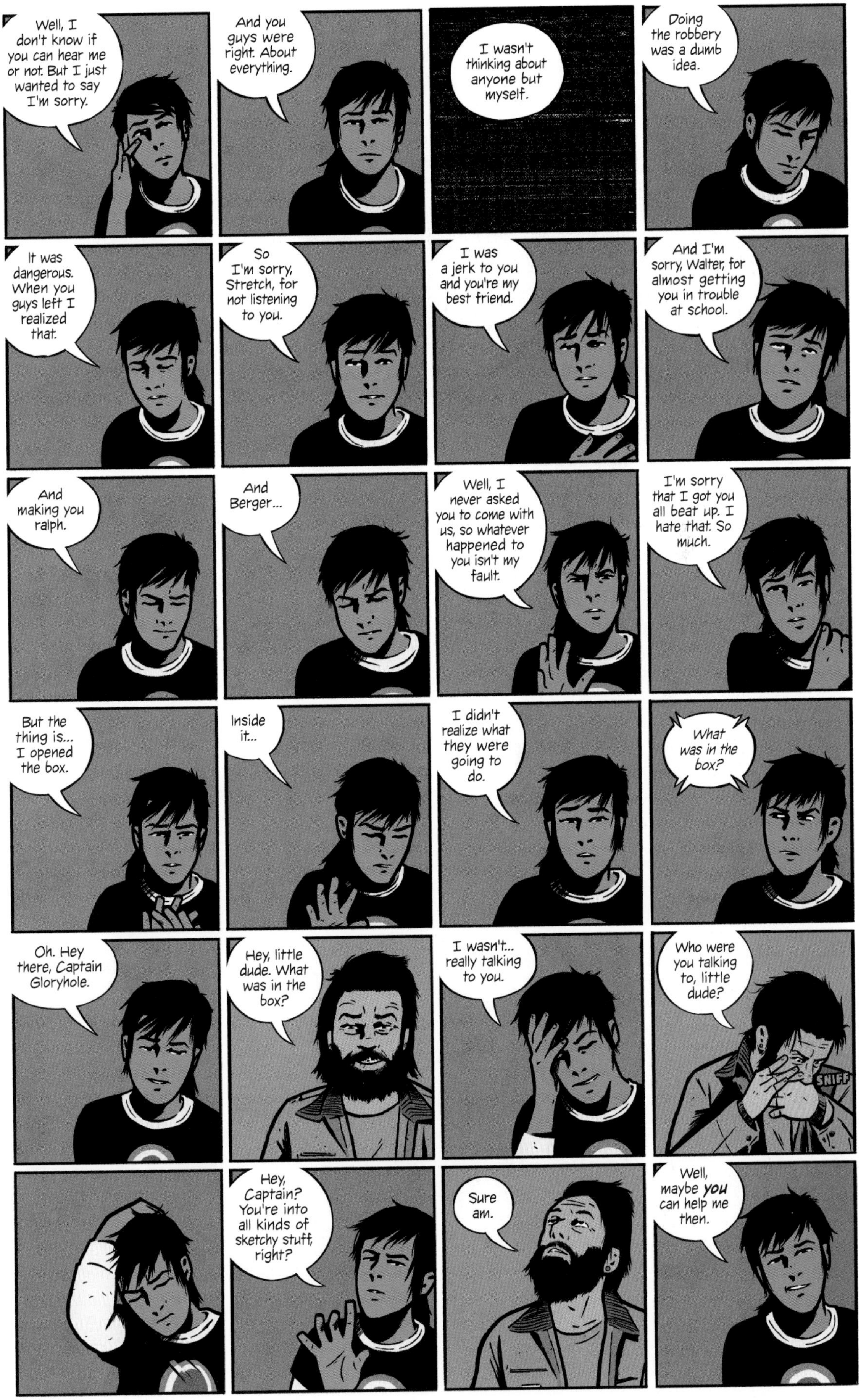
Well, I don't know if you can hear me or not. But I just wanted to say I'm sorry.
And you guys were right. About everything.
I wasn't thinking about anyone but myself.
Doing the robbery was a dumb idea.
It was dangerous. When you guys left I realized that.
So I'm sorry, Stretch, for not listening to you.
I was a jerk to you and you're my best friend.
And I'm sorry, Walter, for almost getting you in trouble at school.
And making you ralph.
And Berger...
Well, I never asked you to come with us, so whatever happened to you isn't my fault.
I'm sorry that I got you all beat up. I hate that. So much.
But the thing is... I opened the box.
Inside it...
I didn't realize what they were going to do.
What was in the box?
Oh. Hey there, Captain Gloryhole.
Hey, little dude. What was in the box?
I wasn't... really talking to you.
Who were you talking to, little dude?
SNIFF
Hey, Captain? You're into all kinds of sketchy stuff, right?
Sure am.
Well, maybe YOU can help me then.

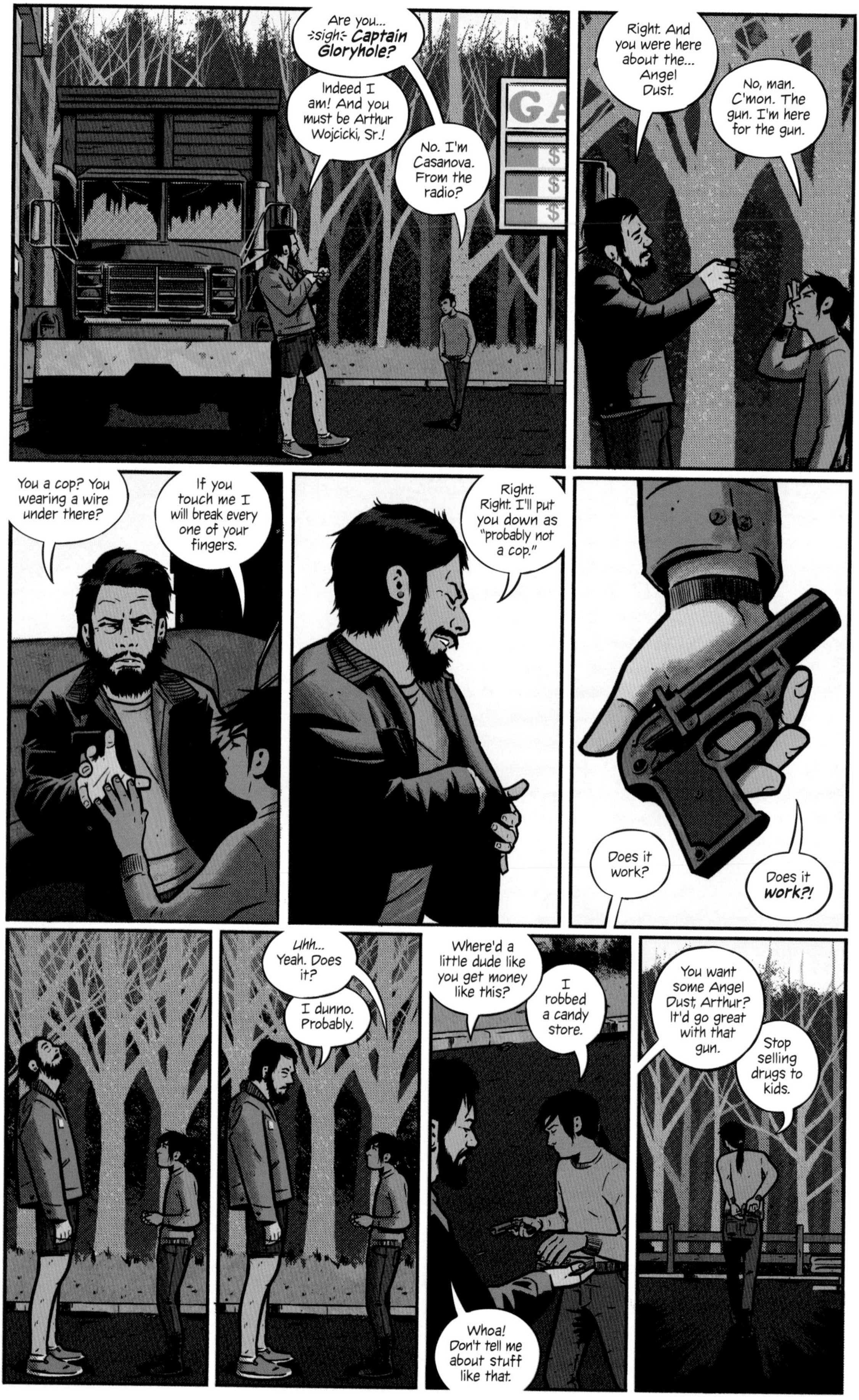
Are you... ⋟sigh⋞ Captain Gloryhole?
Indeed I am! And you must be Arthur Wojcicki, Sr.!
No. I'm Casanova. From the radio?
GA
Right. And you were here about the... Angel Dust.
No, man. C'mon. The gun. I'm here for the gun.
You a cop? You wearing a wire under there?
If you touch me I will break every one of your fingers.
Right. Right. I'll put you down as "probably not a cop."
Does it work?
Does it work?!
Uhh... Yeah. Does it?
I dunno. Probably.
Where'd a little dude like you get money like this?
I robbed a candy store.
Whoa! Don't tell me about stuff like that.
You want some Angel Dust, Arthur? It'd go great with that gun.
Stop selling drugs to kids.

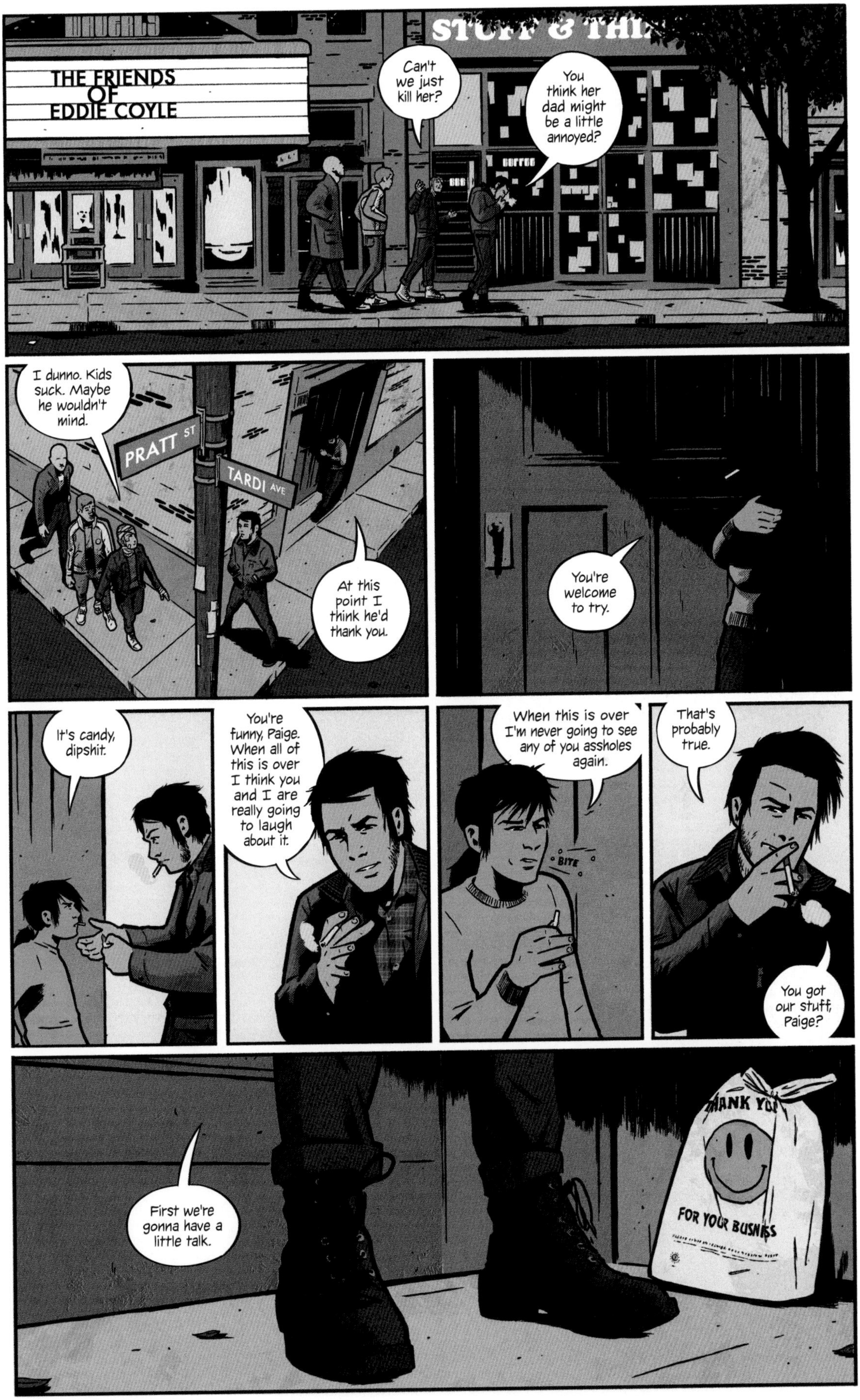
WAVERLY
THE FRIENDS OF EDDIE COYLE
STUFF & THI
Can't we just kill her?
You think her dad might be a little annoyed?
I dunno. Kids suck. Maybe he wouldn't mind.
PRATT ST
TARDI AVE
At this point I think he'd thank you.
You're welcome to try.
It's candy, dipshit.
You're funny, Paige. When all of this is over I think you and I are really going to laugh about it.
When this is over I'm never going to see any of you assholes again.
BITE
That's probably true.
You got our stuff, Paige?
First we're gonna have a little talk.
THANK YO
FOR YOUR BUSNSS

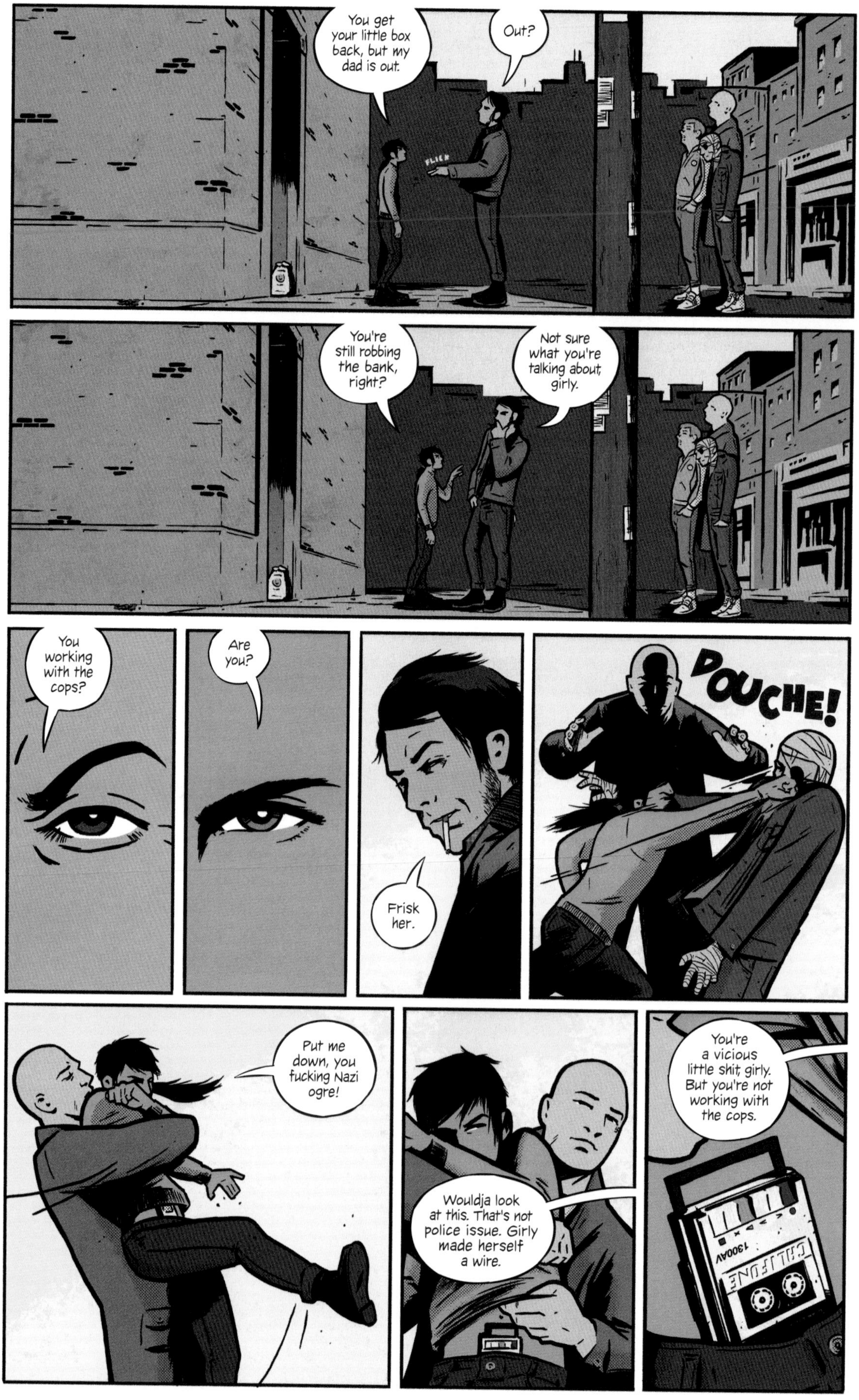
You get your little box back, but my dad is out.
Out?
FLICK
You're still robbing the bank, right?
Not sure what you're talking about, girly.
You working with the cops?
Are you?
Frisk her.
DOUCHE!
Put me down, you fucking Nazi ogre!
Wouldja look at this. That's not police issue. Girly made herself a wire.
You're a vicious little shit, girly. But you're not working with the cops.

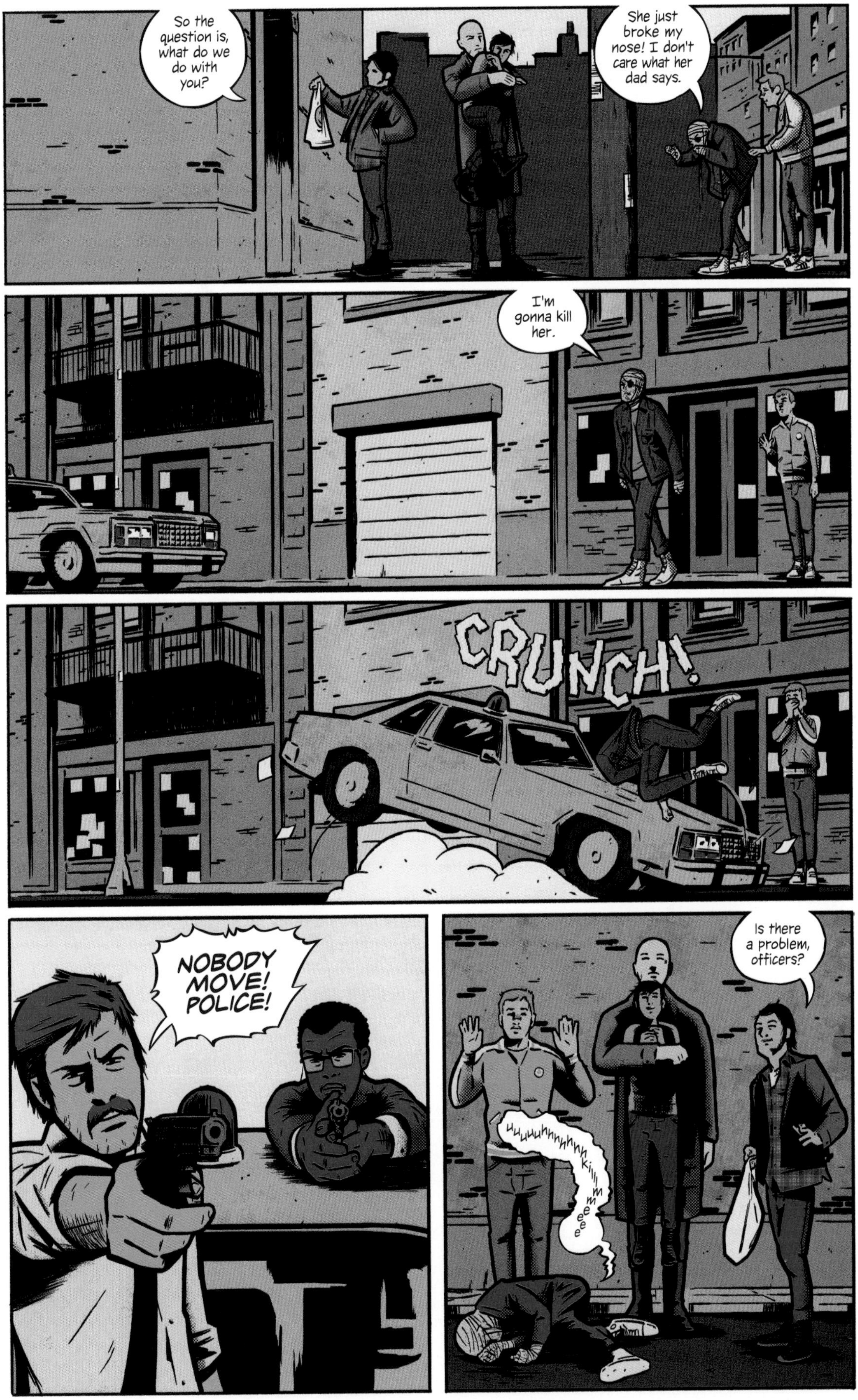
So the question is, what do we do with you?
She just broke my nose! I don't care what her dad says.
I'm gonna kill her.
CRUNCH!
NOBODY MOVE! POLICE!
Is there a problem, officers?
uuuuuhhhhhnnkillllmmeeee

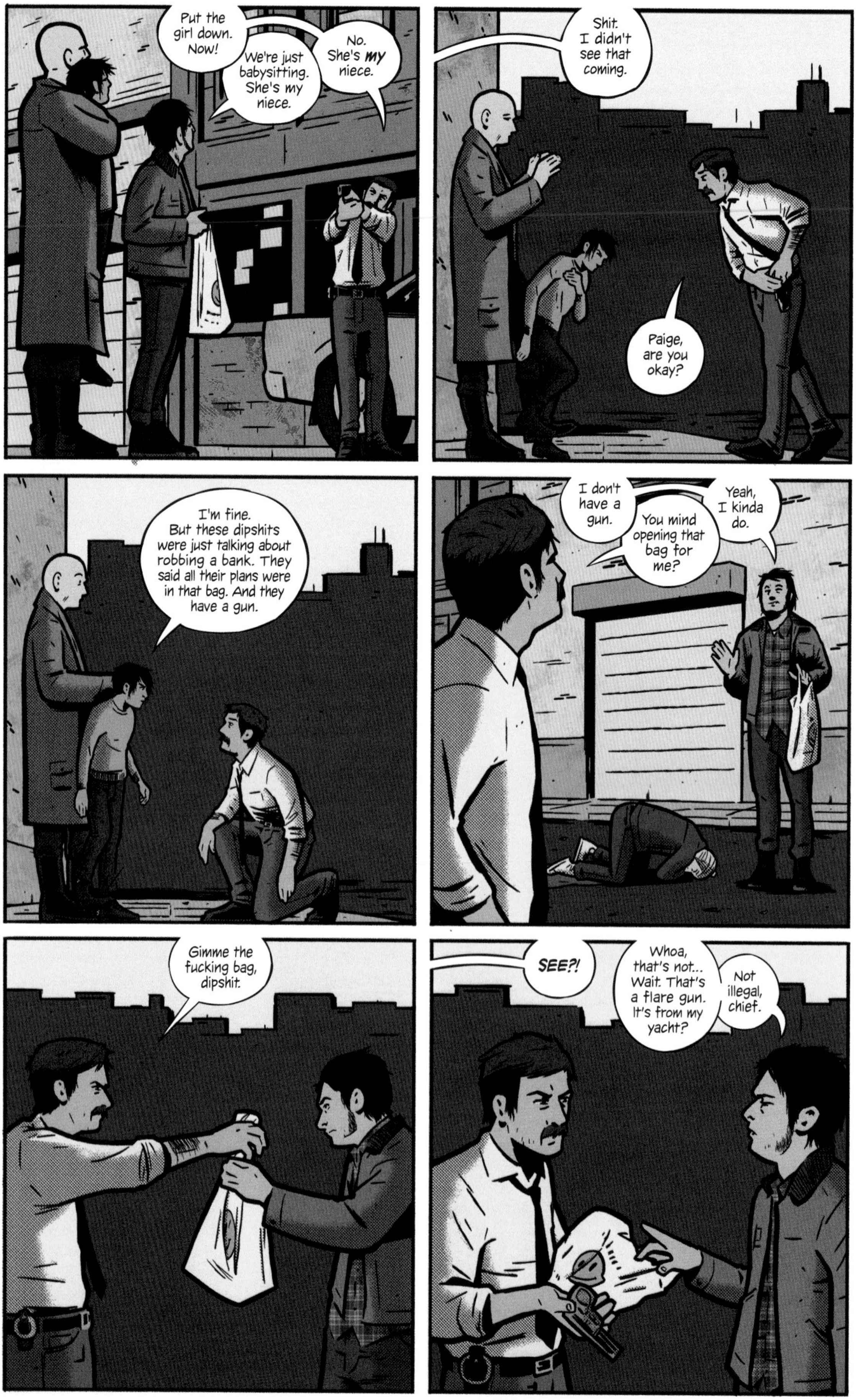
Put the girl down. Now!
We're just babysitting. She's my niece.
No. She's **my** niece.
Shit. I didn't see that coming.
Paige, are you okay?
I'm fine. But these dipshits were just talking about robbing a bank. They said all their plans were in that bag. And they have a gun.
I don't have a gun.
You mind opening that bag for me?
Yeah, I kinda do.
Gimme the fucking bag, dipshit.
SEE?!
Whoa, that's not... Wait. That's a flare gun. It's from my yacht?
Not illegal, chief.

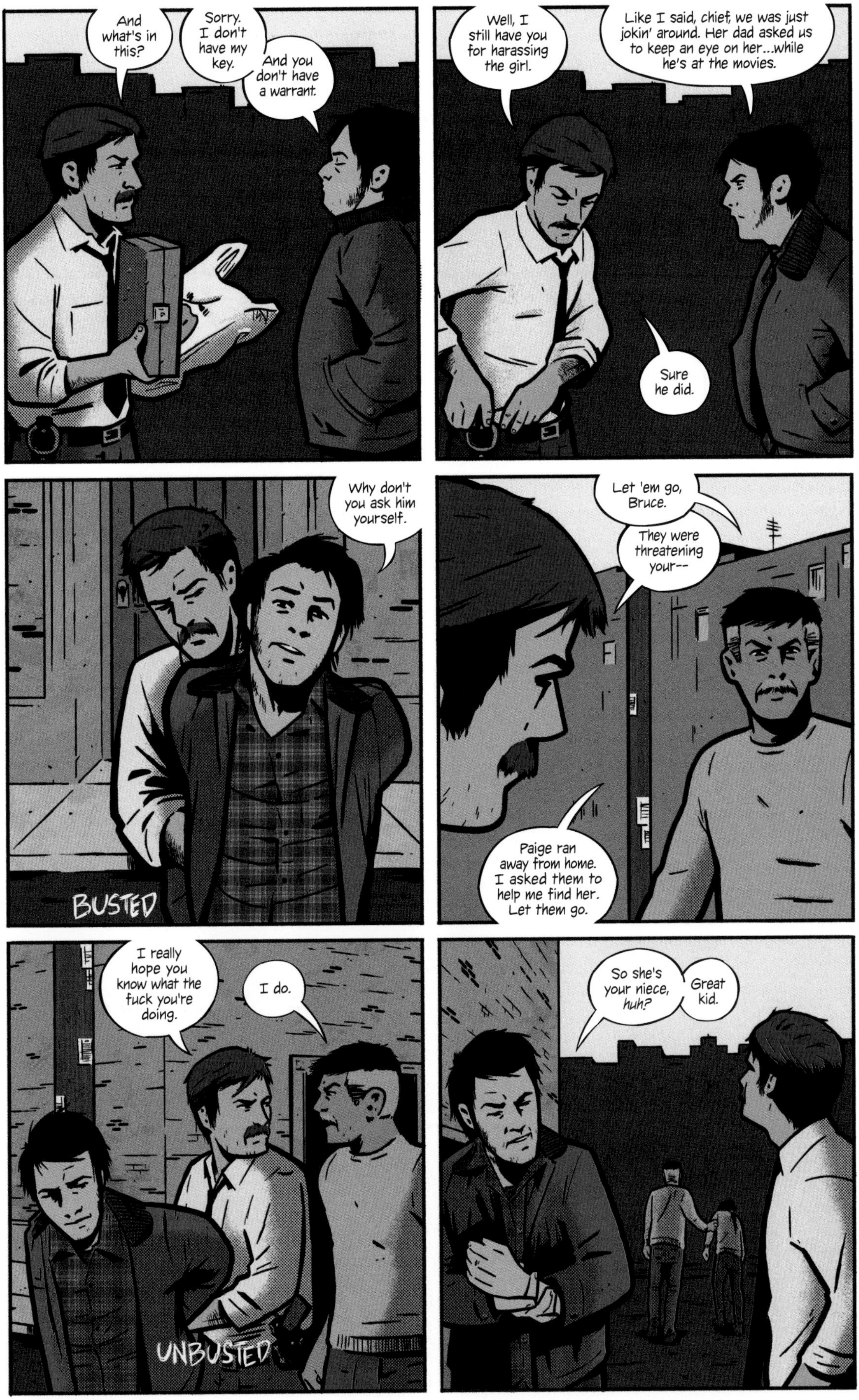

And what's in this?
Sorry. I don't have my key.
And you don't have a warrant.
Well, I still have you for harassing the girl.
Like I said, chief, we was just jokin' around. Her dad asked us to keep an eye on her...while he's at the movies.
Sure he did.
Why don't you ask him yourself.
BUSTED
Let 'em go, Bruce.
They were threatening your--
Paige ran away from home. I asked them to help me find her. Let them go.
I really hope you know what the fuck you're doing.
I do.
UNBUSTED
So she's your niece, *huh?*
Great kid.

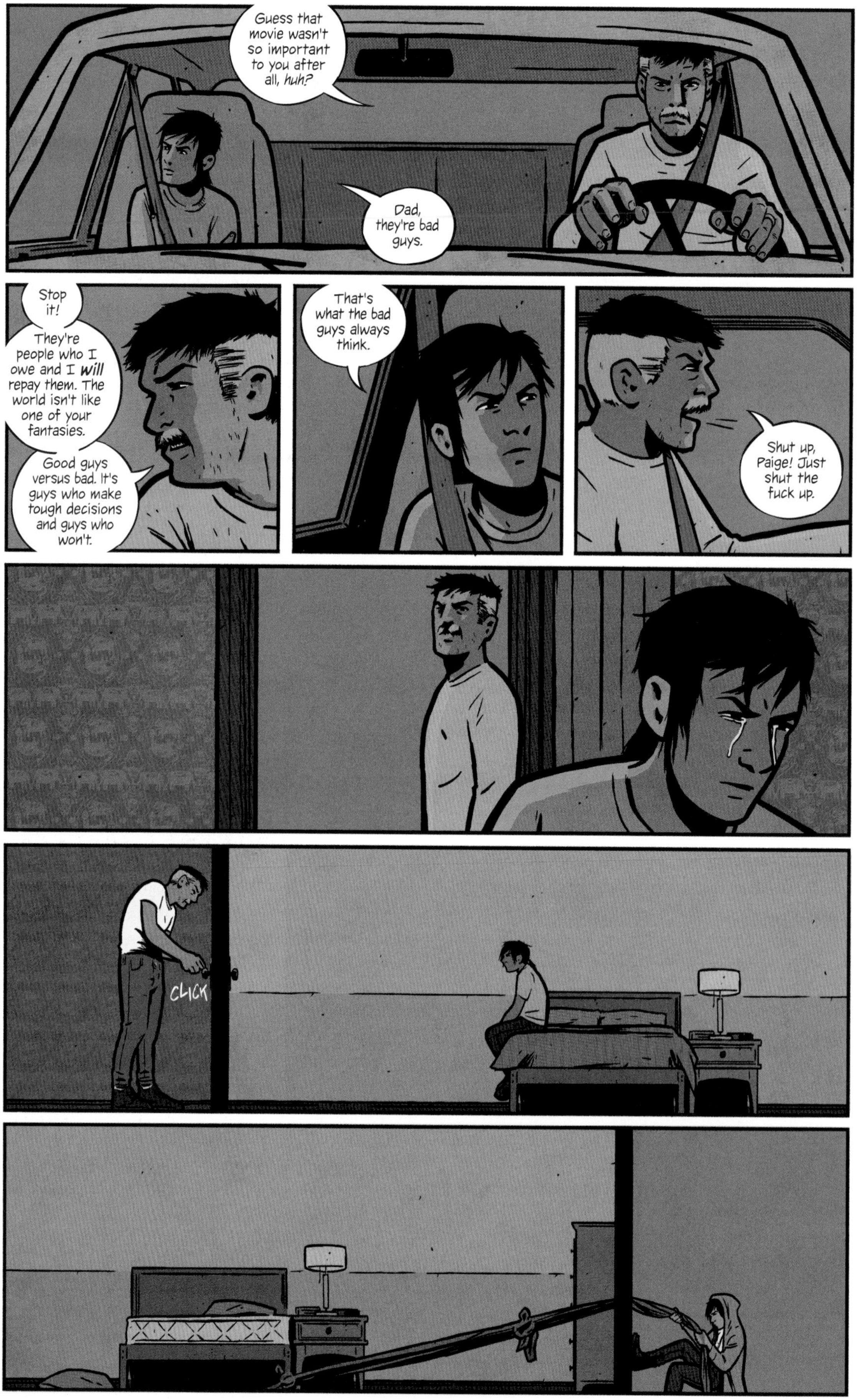
Guess that movie wasn't so important to you after all, *huh?*
Dad, they're bad guys.
Stop it!
They're people who I owe and I ***will*** repay them. The world isn't like one of your fantasies.
Good guys versus bad. It's guys who make tough decisions and guys who won't.
That's what the bad guys always think.
Shut up, Paige! Just shut the fuck up.
CLICK

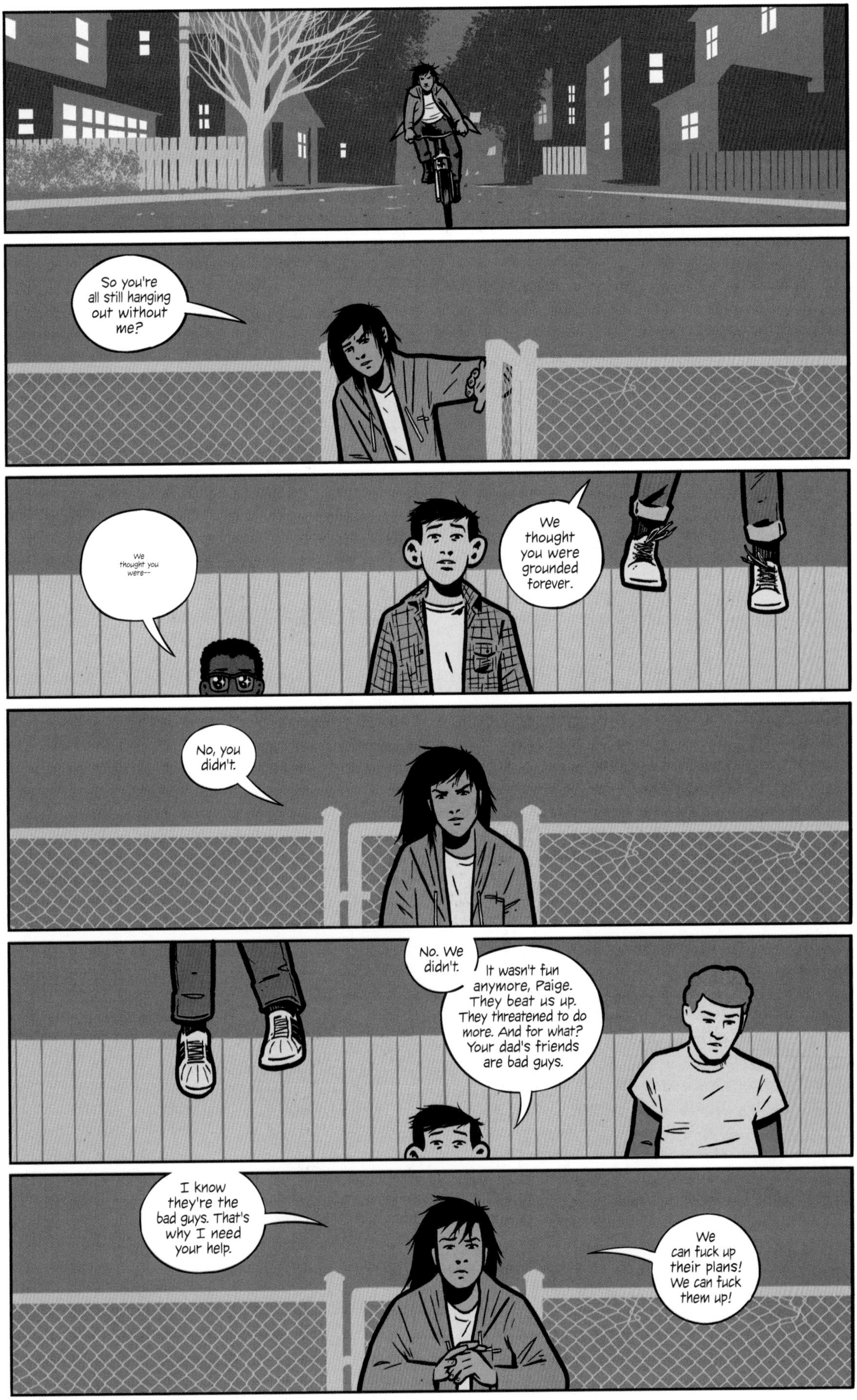
So you're all still hanging out without me?
We thought you were--
We thought you were grounded forever.
No, you didn't.
No. We didn't.
It wasn't fun anymore, Paige. They beat us up. They threatened to do more. And for what? Your dad's friends are bad guys.
I know they're the bad guys. That's why I need your help.
We can fuck up their plans! We can fuck them up!

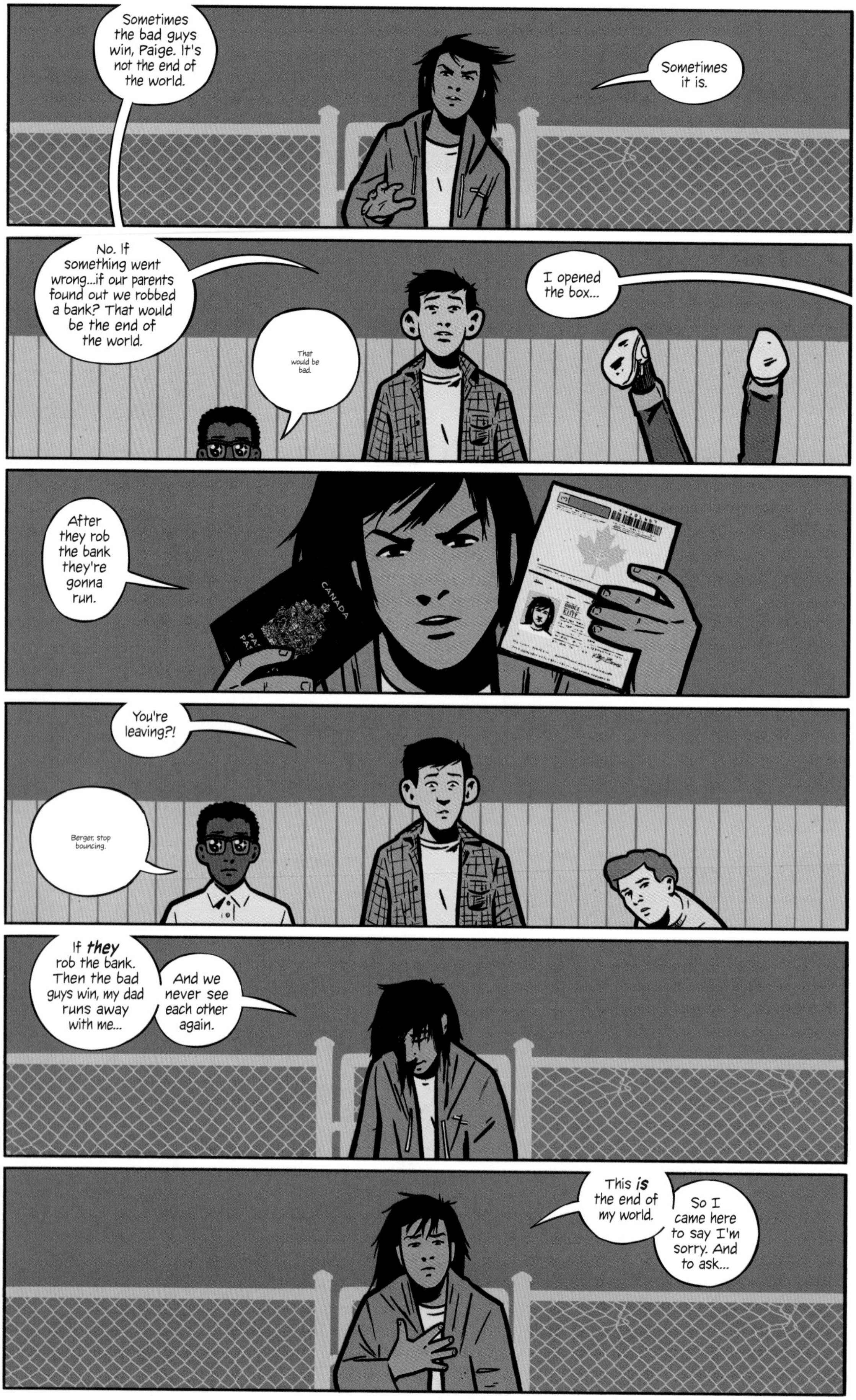
Sometimes the bad guys win, Paige. It's not the end of the world.
Sometimes it is.
No. If something went wrong...if our parents found out we robbed a bank? That would be the end of the world.
That would be bad.
I opened the box...
After they rob the bank they're gonna run.
CANADA
You're leaving?!
Berger, stop bouncing.
If *they* rob the bank. Then the bad guys win, my dad runs away with me...
And we never see each other again.
This *is* the end of my world.
So I came here to say I'm sorry. And to ask...

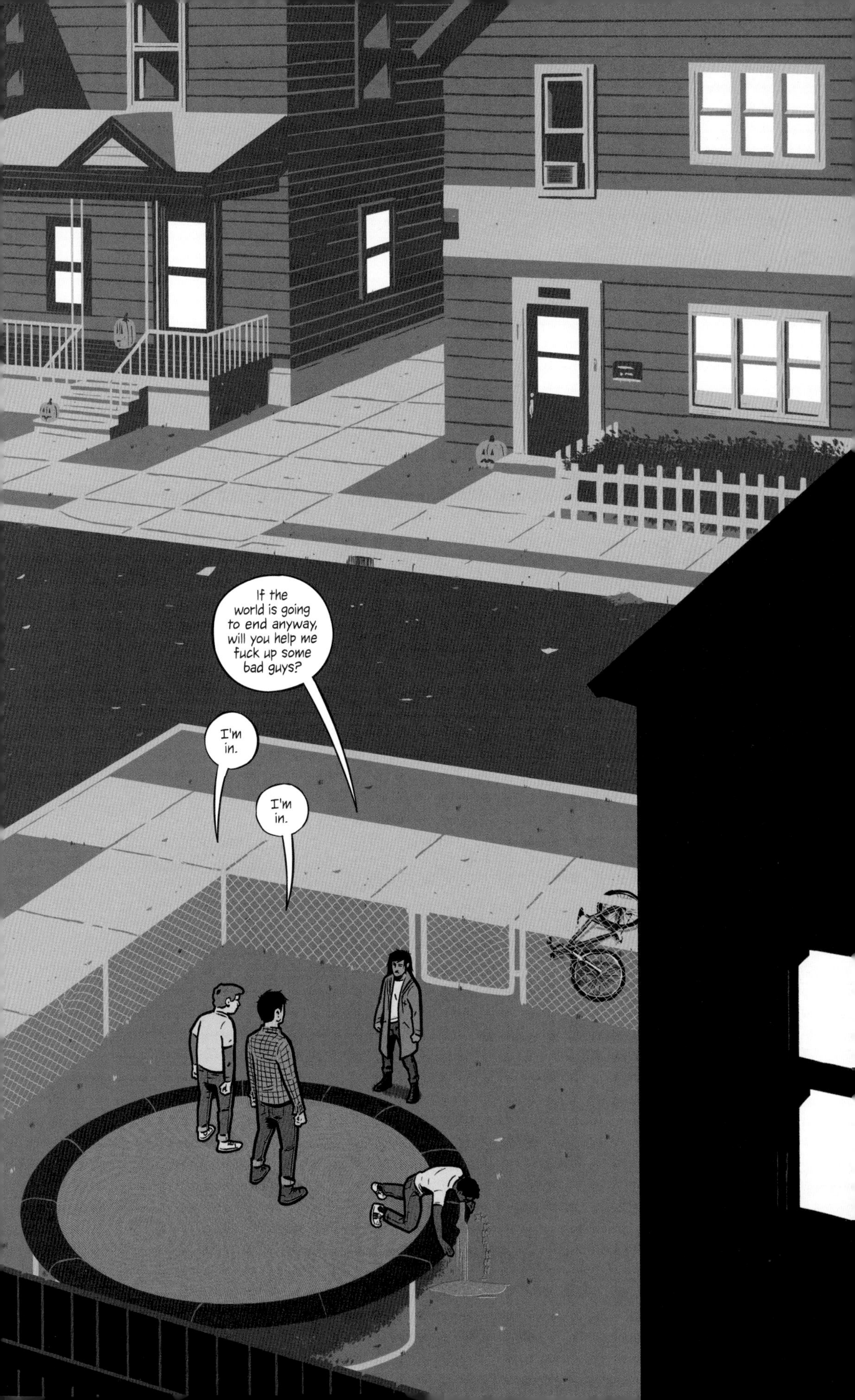
If the world is going to end anyway, will you help me fuck up some bad guys?
I'm in.
I'm in.

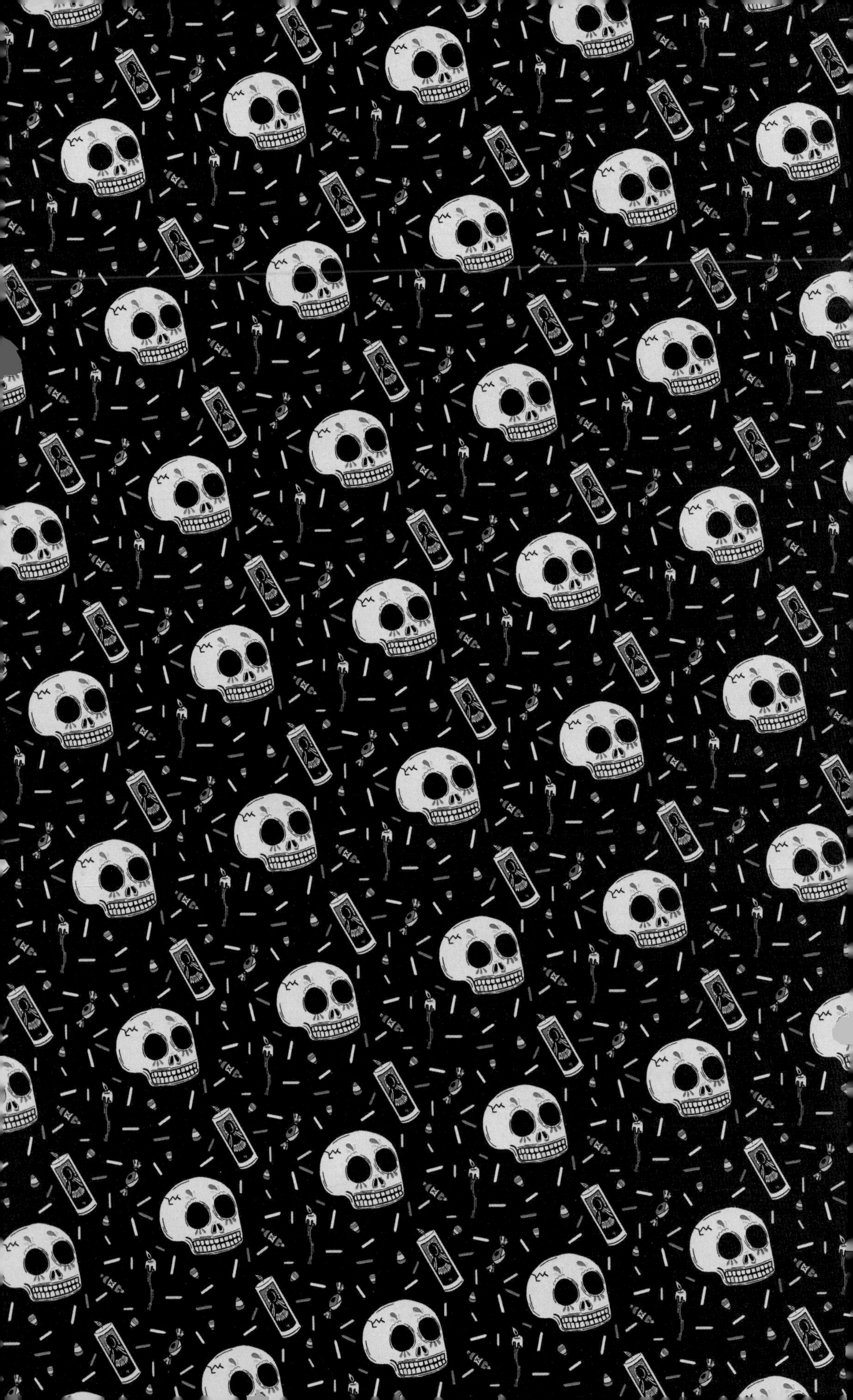

CHAPTER FIVE

WE ROB BANKS?

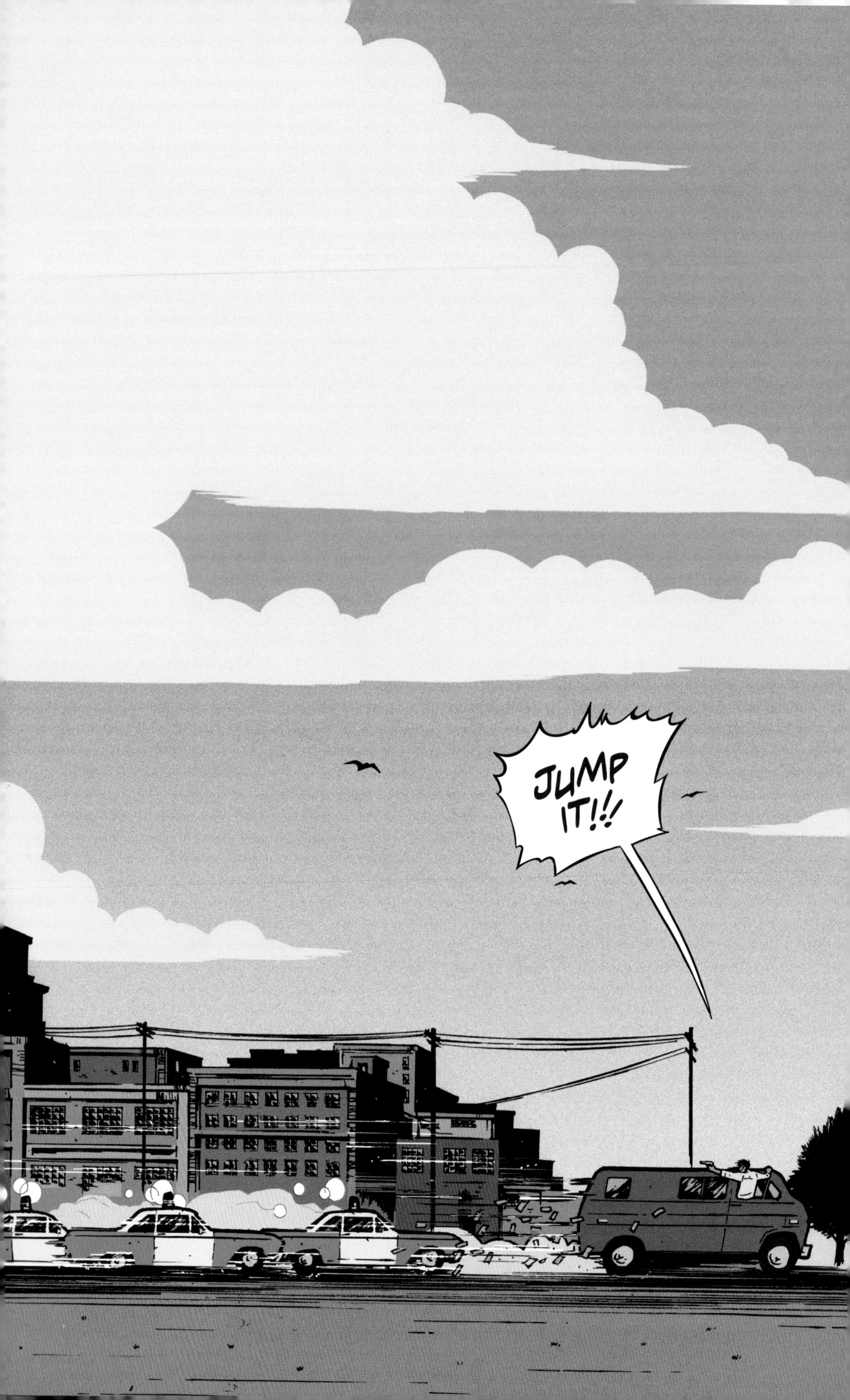
JUMP IT!!!

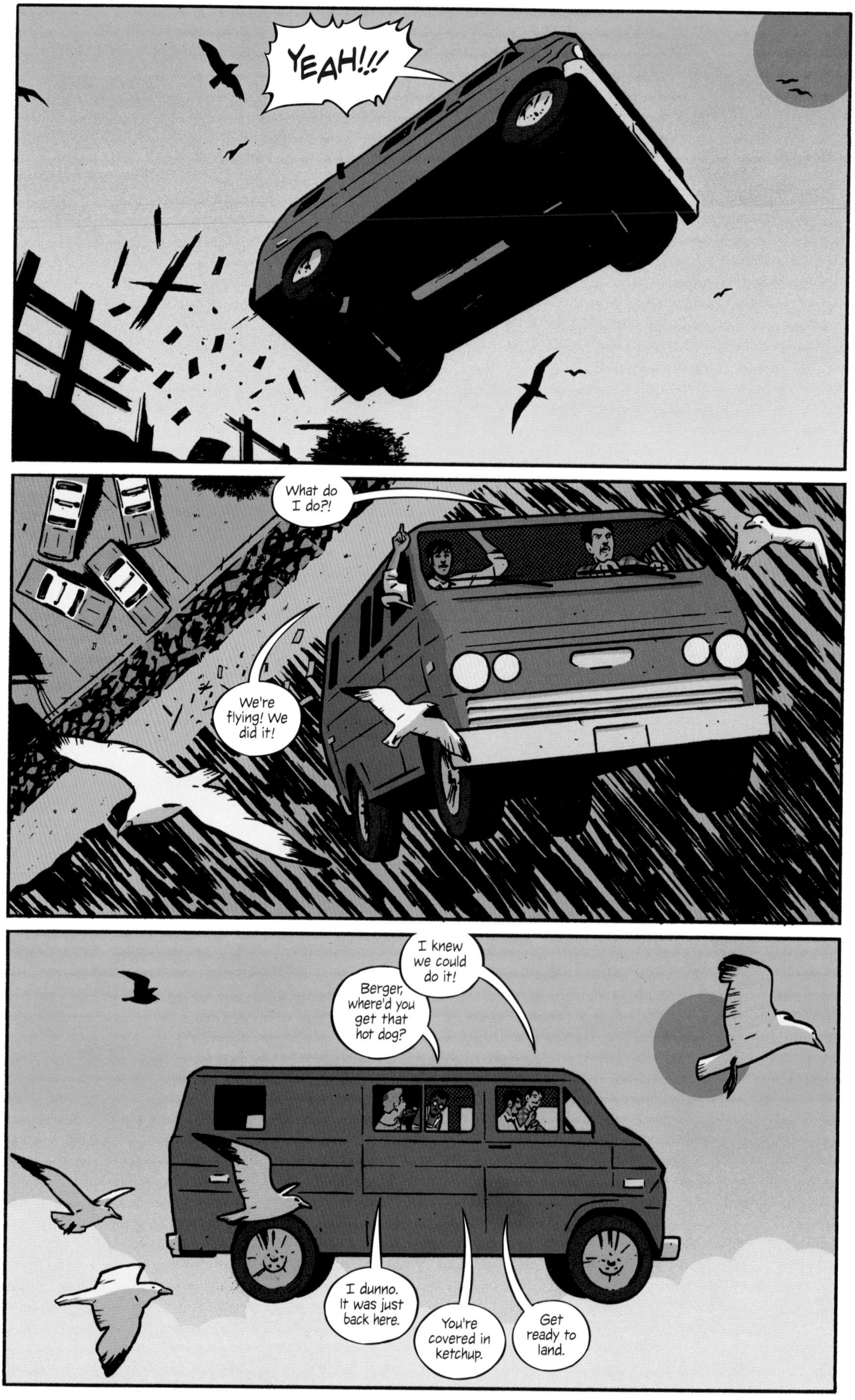
YEAH!!!
What do I do?!
We're flying! We did it!
I knew we could do it!
Berger, where'd you get that hot dog?
I dunno. It was just back here.
You're covered in ketchup.
Get ready to land.

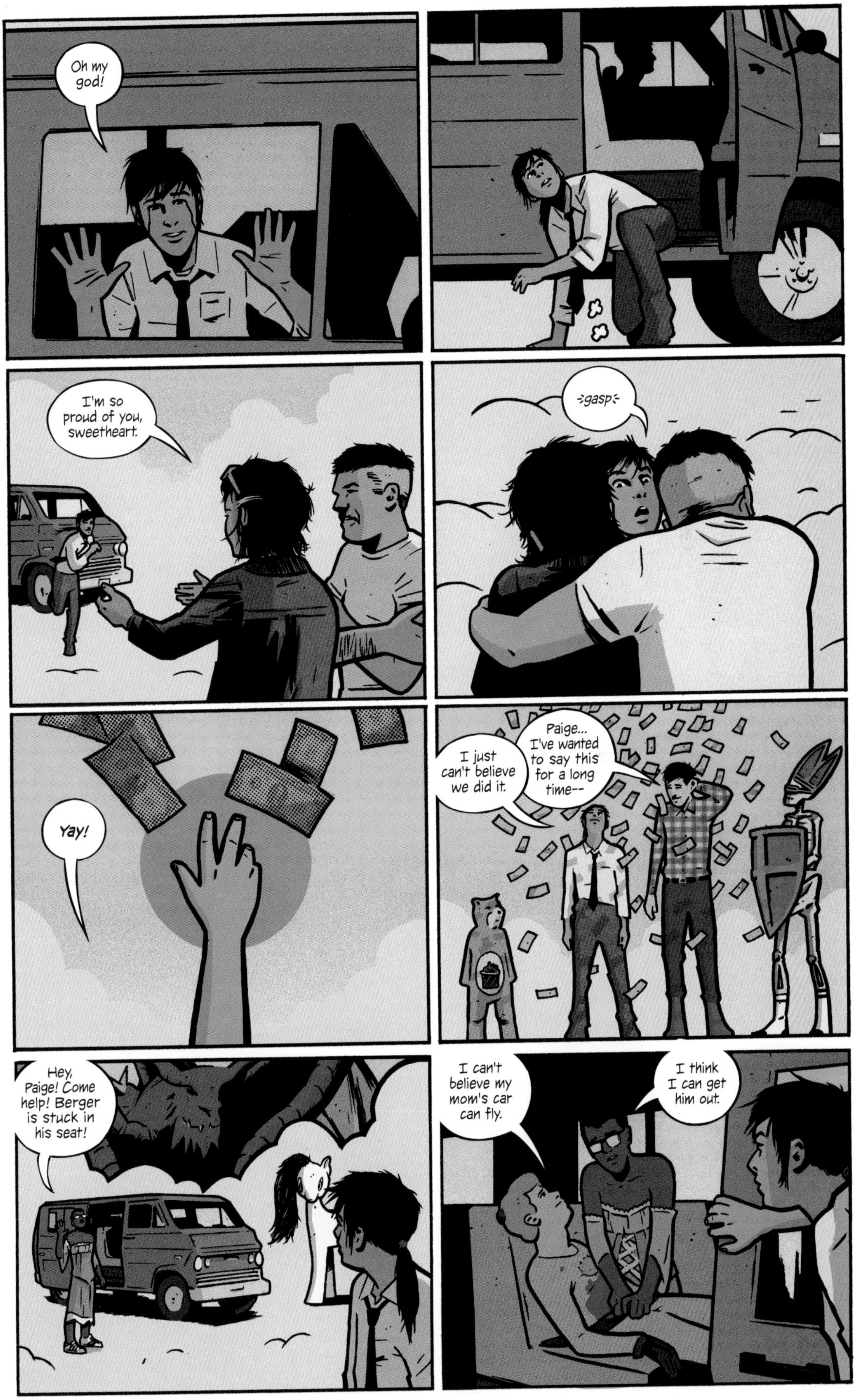
Oh my god!
I'm so proud of you, sweetheart.
gasp
Yay!
I just can't believe we did it.
Paige... I've wanted to say this for a long time--
Hey, Paige! Come help! Berger is stuck in his seat!
I can't believe my mom's car can fly.
I think I can get him out.

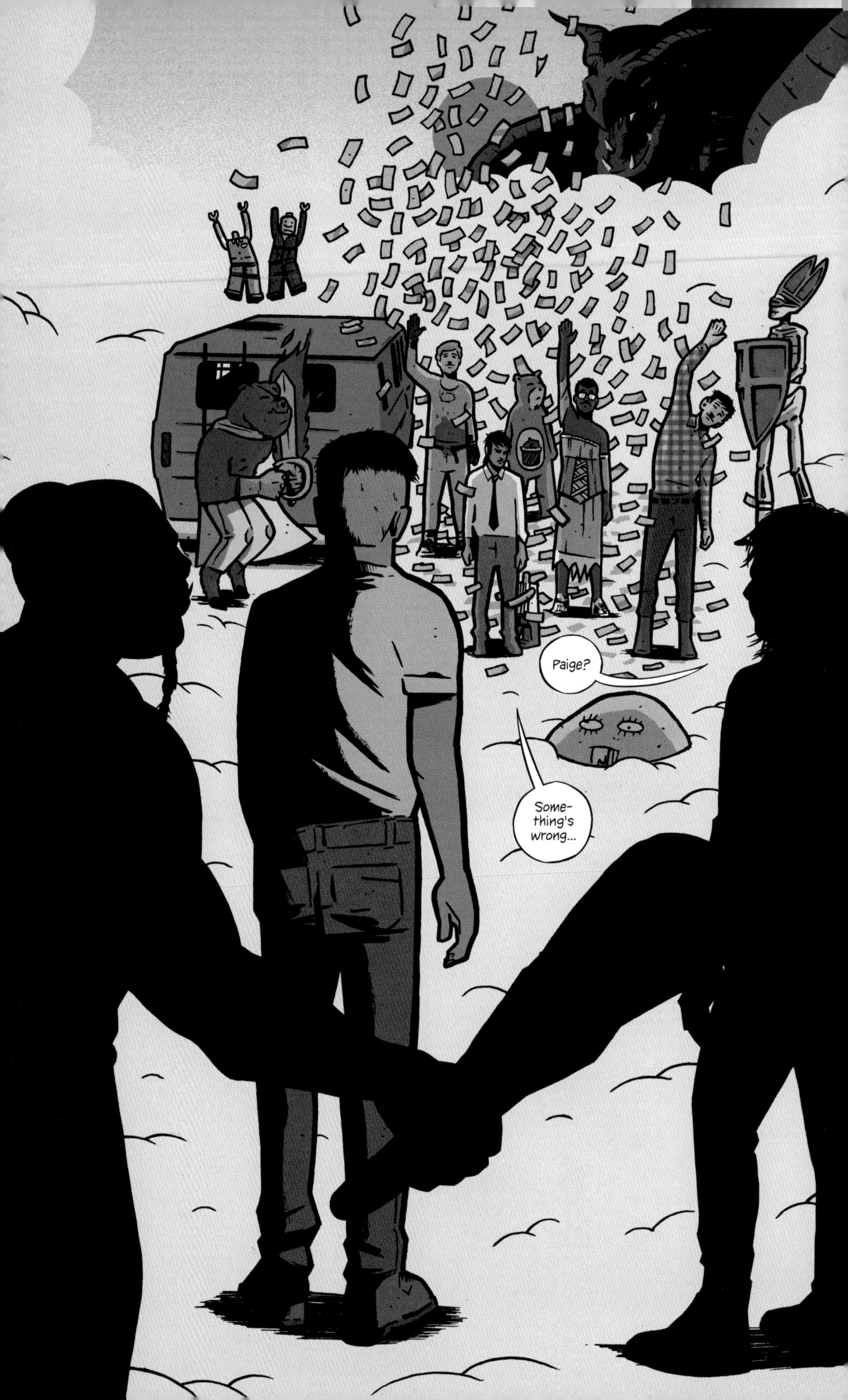
Paige?
Some-thing's wrong...

EARLIER

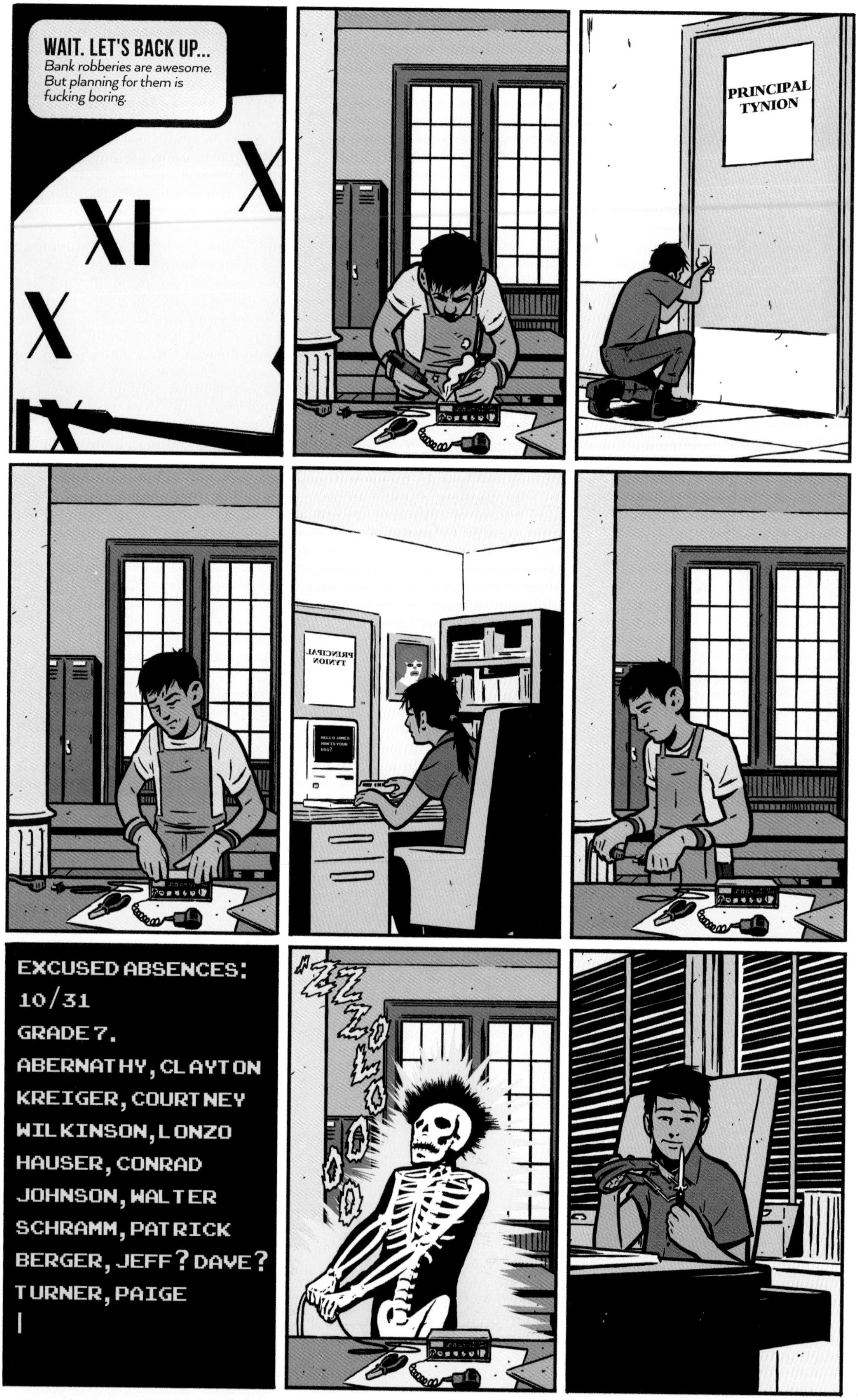
WAIT. LET'S BACK UP...
Bank robberies are awesome. But planning for them is fucking boring.
XI
X
PRINCIPAL TYNION
HELLO JAMES HOW IS YOUR DOG?
EXCUSED ABSENCES:
10/31
GRADE 7.
ABERNATHY, CLAYTON
KREIGER, COURTNEY
WILKINSON, LONZO
HAUSER, CONRAD
JOHNSON, WALTER
SCHRAMM, PATRICK
BERGER, JEFF? DAVE?
TURNER, PAIGE
|

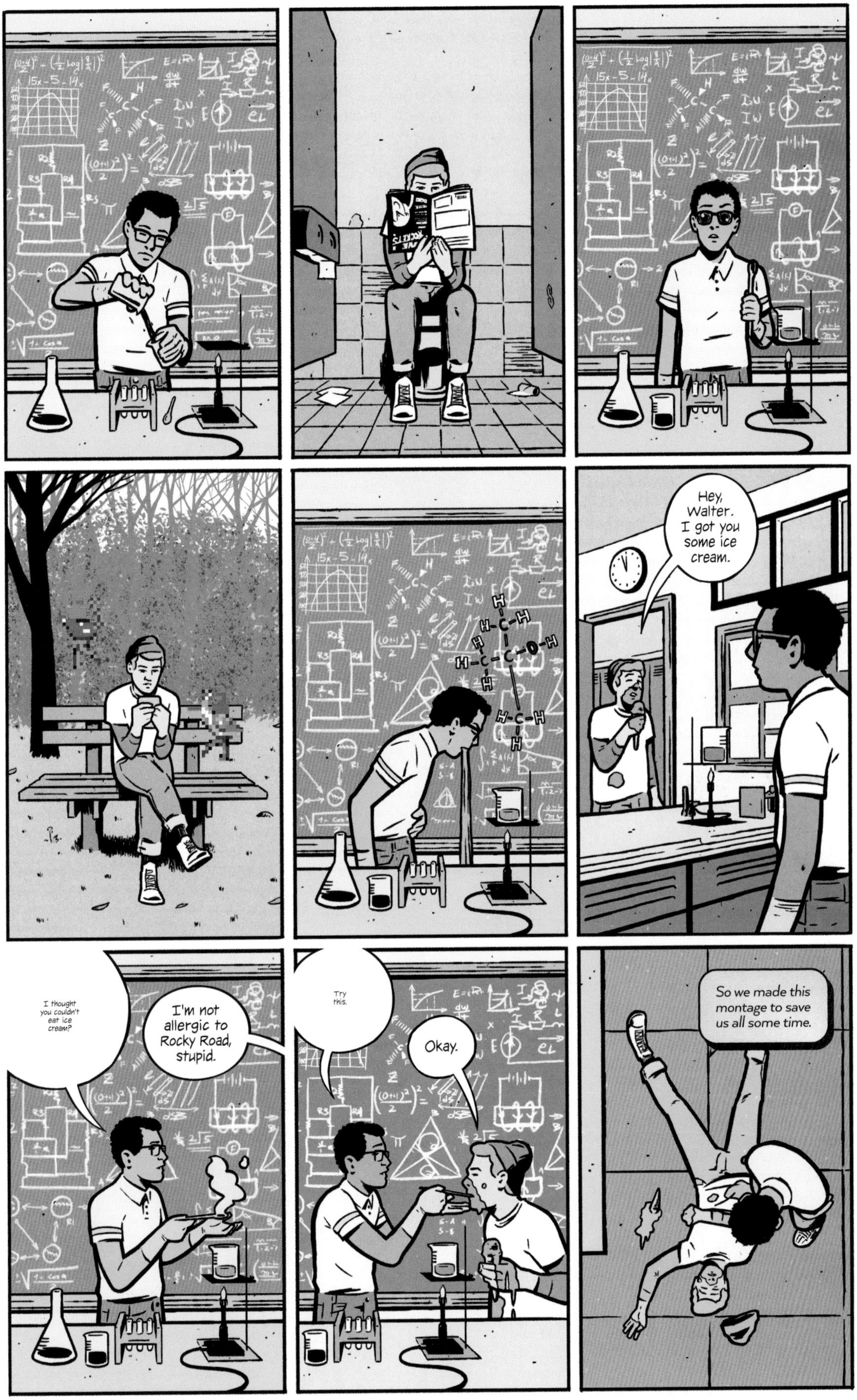
Hey, Walter. I got you some ice cream.
I thought you couldn't eat ice cream?
I'm not allergic to Rocky Road, stupid.
Try this.
Okay.
So we made this montage to save us all some time.

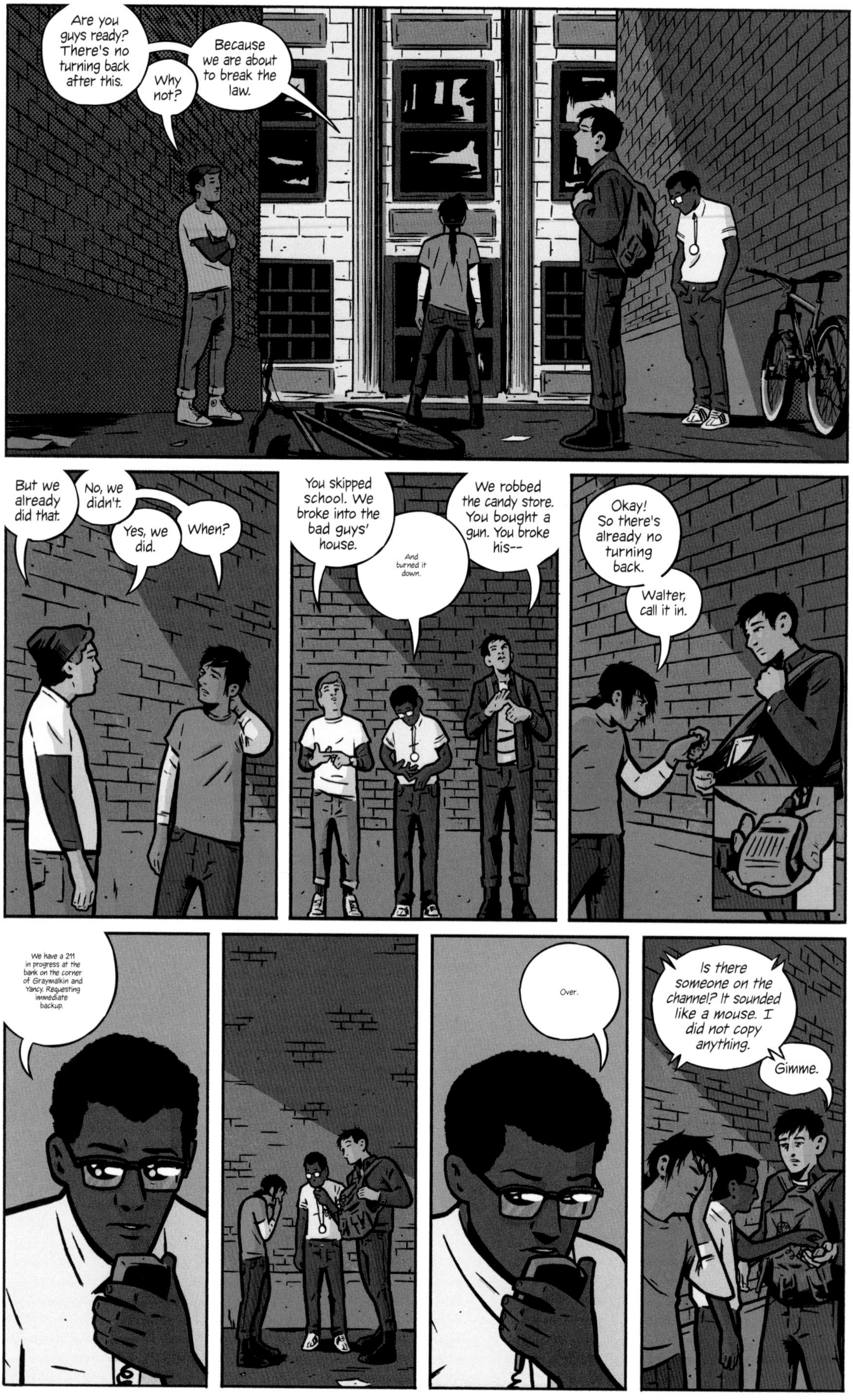

Are you guys ready? There's no turning back after this.
Why not?
Because we are about to break the law.
But we already did that.
No, we didn't.
Yes, we did.
When?
You skipped school. We broke into the bad guys' house.
And burned it down.
We robbed the candy store. You bought a gun. You broke his--
Okay! So there's already no turning back.
Walter, call it in.
We have a 211 in progress at the bank on the corner of Graymalkin and Yancy. Requesting immediate backup.
Over.
Is there someone on the channel? It sounded like a mouse. I did not copy anything.
Gimme.

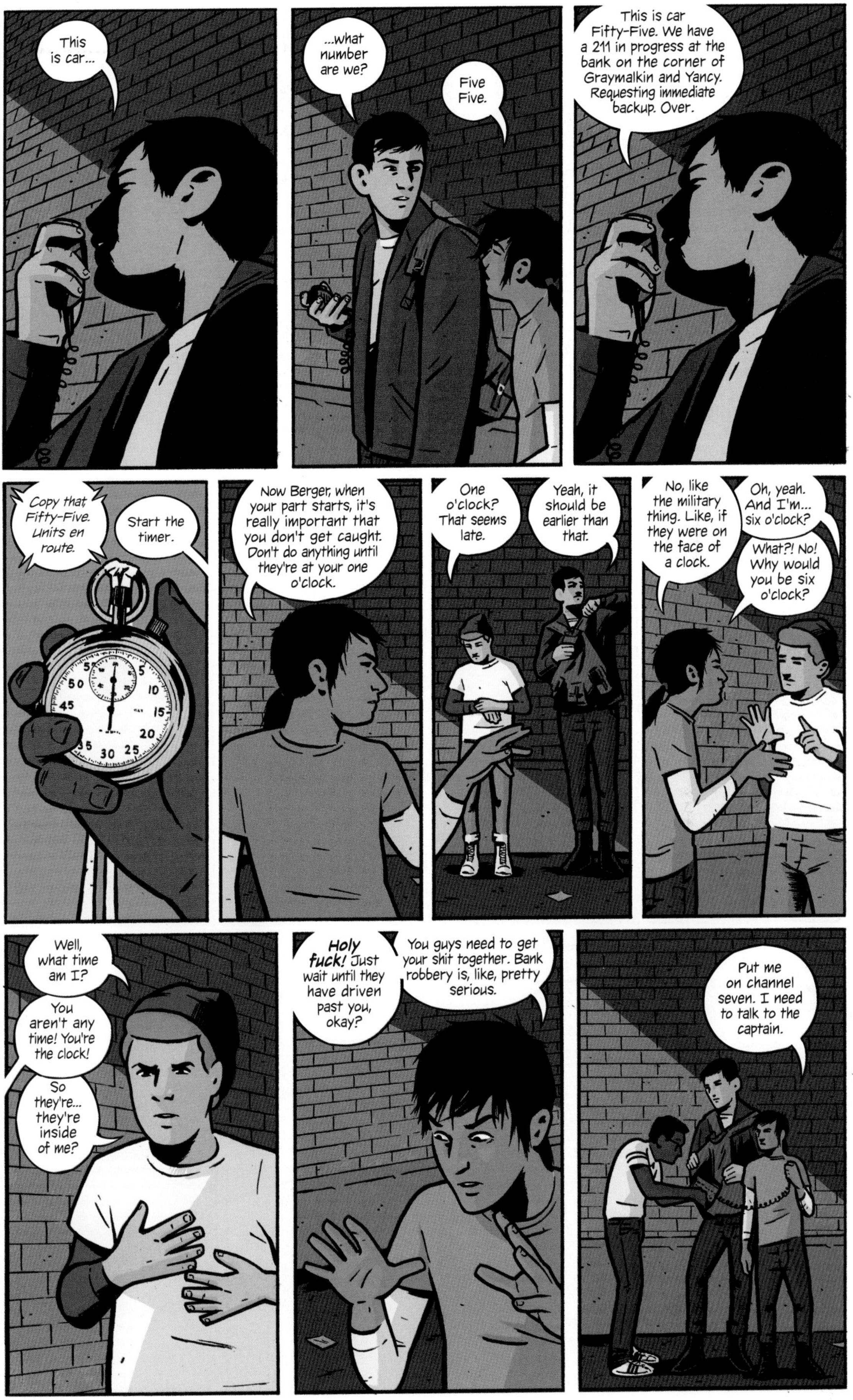
This is car...
...what number are we?
Five Five.
This is car Fifty-Five. We have a 211 in progress at the bank on the corner of Graymalkin and Yancy. Requesting immediate backup. Over.
Copy that, Fifty-Five. Units en route.
Start the timer.
Now Berger, when your part starts, it's really important that you don't get caught. Don't do anything until they're at your one o'clock.
One o'clock? That seems late.
Yeah, it should be earlier than that.
No, like the military thing. Like, if they were on the face of a clock.
Oh, yeah. And I'm... six o'clock?
What?! No! Why would you be six o'clock?
Well, what time am I?
You aren't any time! You're the clock!
So they're... they're inside of me?
Holy fuck! Just wait until they have driven past you, okay?
You guys need to get your shit together. Bank robbery is, like, pretty serious.
Put me on channel seven. I need to talk to the captain.

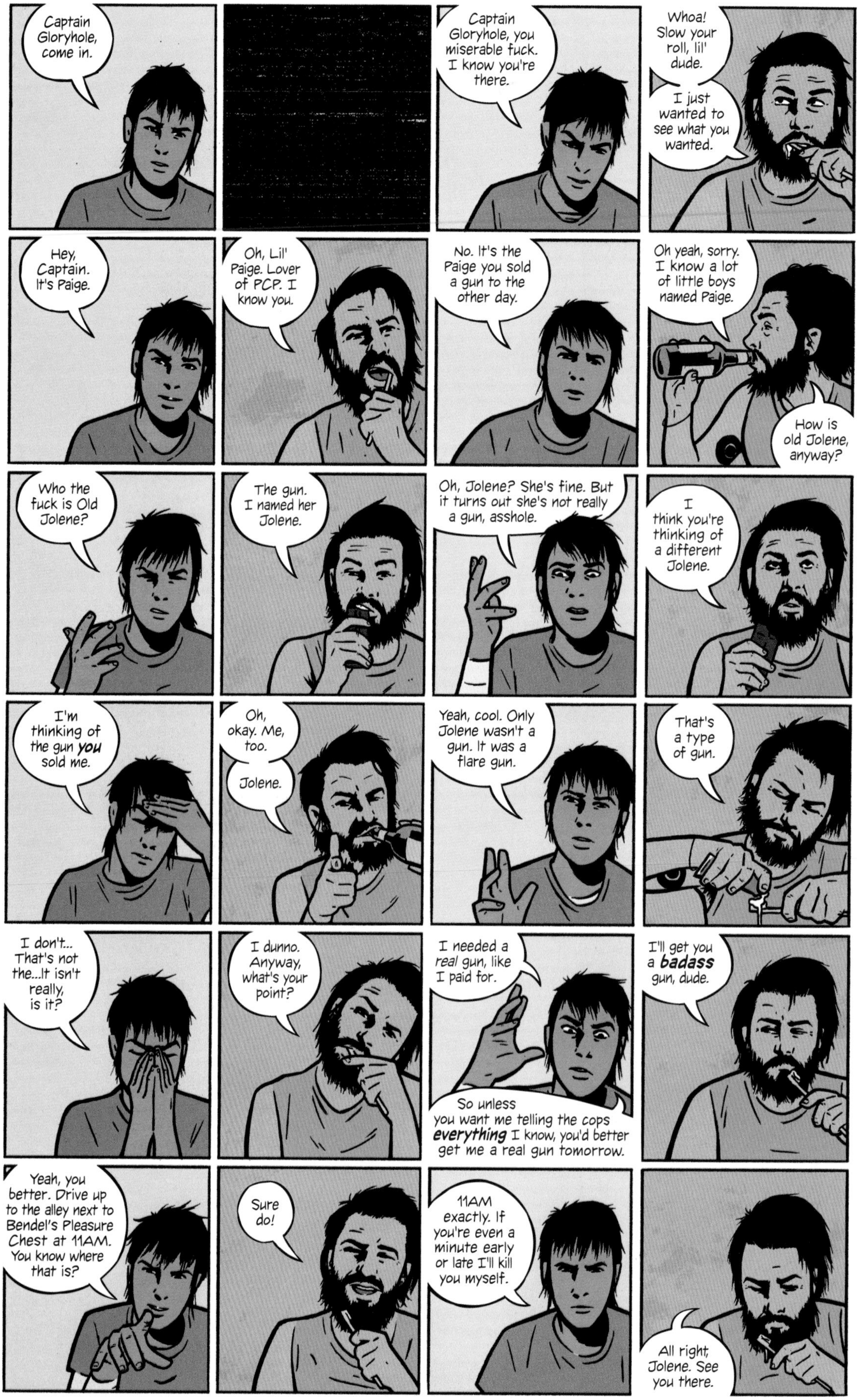

Captain Gloryhole, come in.
Captain Gloryhole, you miserable fuck. I know you're there.
Whoa! Slow your roll, lil' dude.
I just wanted to see what you wanted.
Hey, Captain. It's Paige.
Oh, Lil' Paige. Lover of PCP. I know you.
No. It's the Paige you sold a gun to the other day.
Oh yeah, sorry. I know a lot of little boys named Paige.
How is old Jolene, anyway?
Who the fuck is Old Jolene?
The gun. I named her Jolene.
Oh, Jolene? She's fine. But it turns out she's not really a gun, asshole.
I think you're thinking of a different Jolene.
I'm thinking of the gun *you* sold me.
Oh, okay. Me, too.
Jolene.
Yeah, cool. Only Jolene wasn't a gun. It was a flare gun.
That's a type of gun.
I don't... That's not the...It isn't really, is it?
I dunno. Anyway, what's your point?
I needed a *real* gun, like I paid for.
So unless you want me telling the cops ***everything*** I know, you'd better get me a real gun tomorrow.
I'll get you a ***badass*** gun, dude.
Yeah, you better. Drive up to the alley next to Bendel's Pleasure Chest at 11AM. You know where that is?
Sure do!
11AM exactly. If you're even a minute early or late I'll kill you myself.
All right, Jolene. See you there.

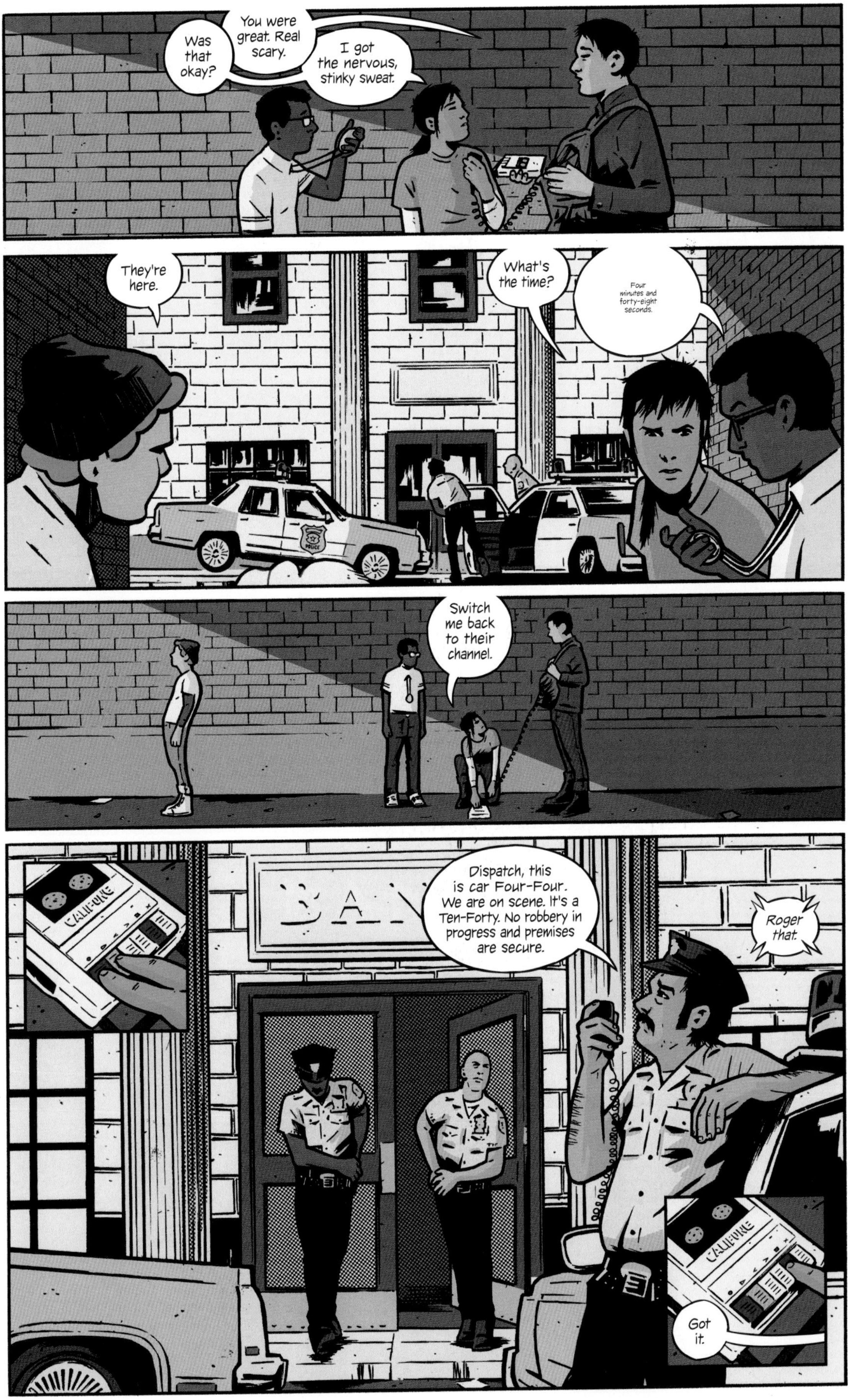
Was that okay?
You were great. Real scary.
I got the nervous, stinky sweat.
They're here.
What's the time?
Four minutes and forty-eight seconds.
Switch me back to their channel.
Dispatch, this is car Four-Four. We are on scene. It's a Ten-Forty. No robbery in progress and premises are secure.
Roger that.
Got it.

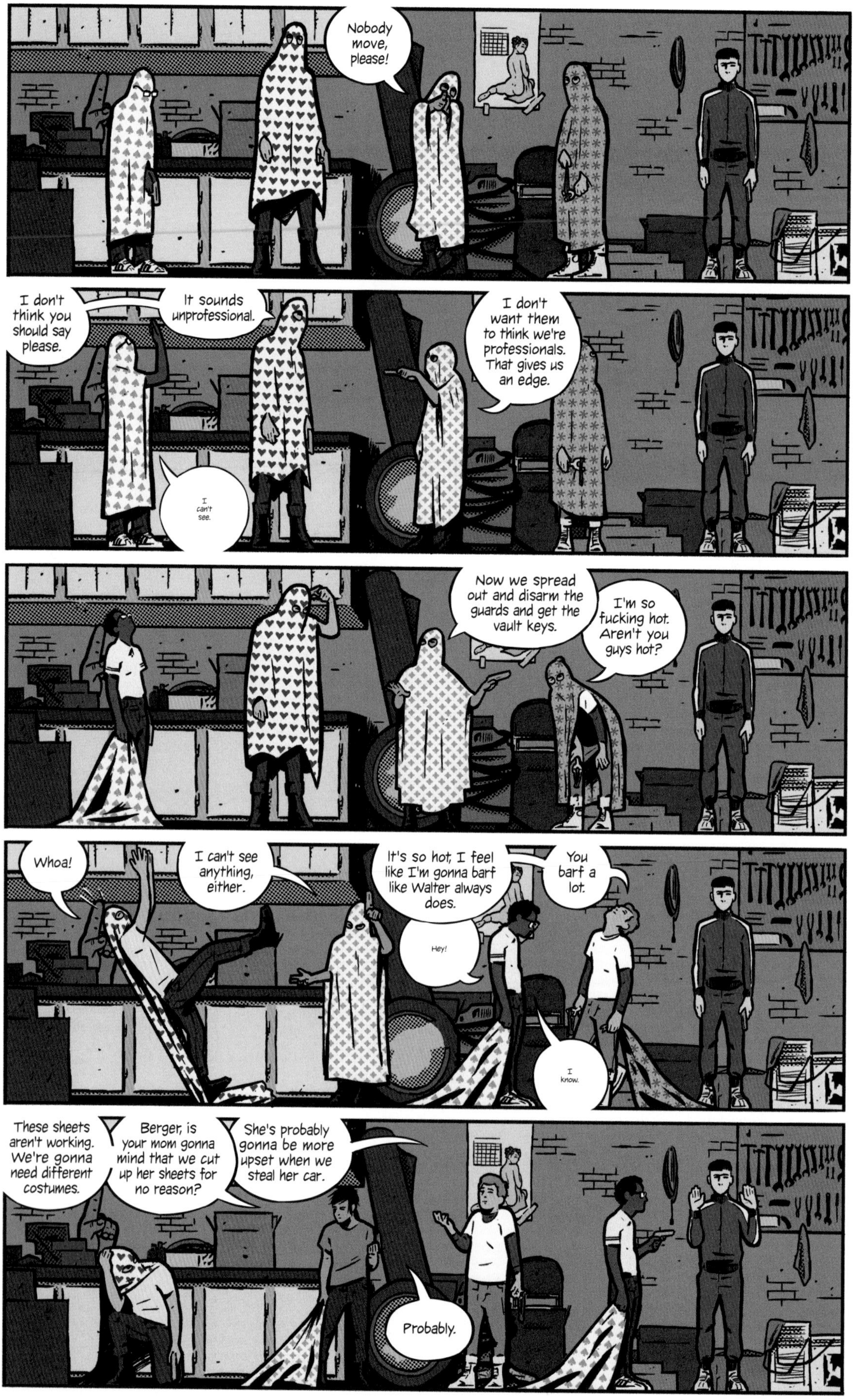
Nobody move, please!
I don't think you should say please.
It sounds unprofessional.
I don't want them to think we're professionals. That gives us an edge.
I can't see.
Now we spread out and disarm the guards and get the vault keys.
I'm so fucking hot. Aren't you guys hot?
Whoa!
I can't see anything, either.
It's so hot, I feel like I'm gonna barf like Walter always does.
You barf a lot.
Hey!
I know.
These sheets aren't working. We're gonna need different costumes.
Berger, is your mom gonna mind that we cut up her sheets for no reason?
She's probably gonna be more upset when we steal her car.
Probably.

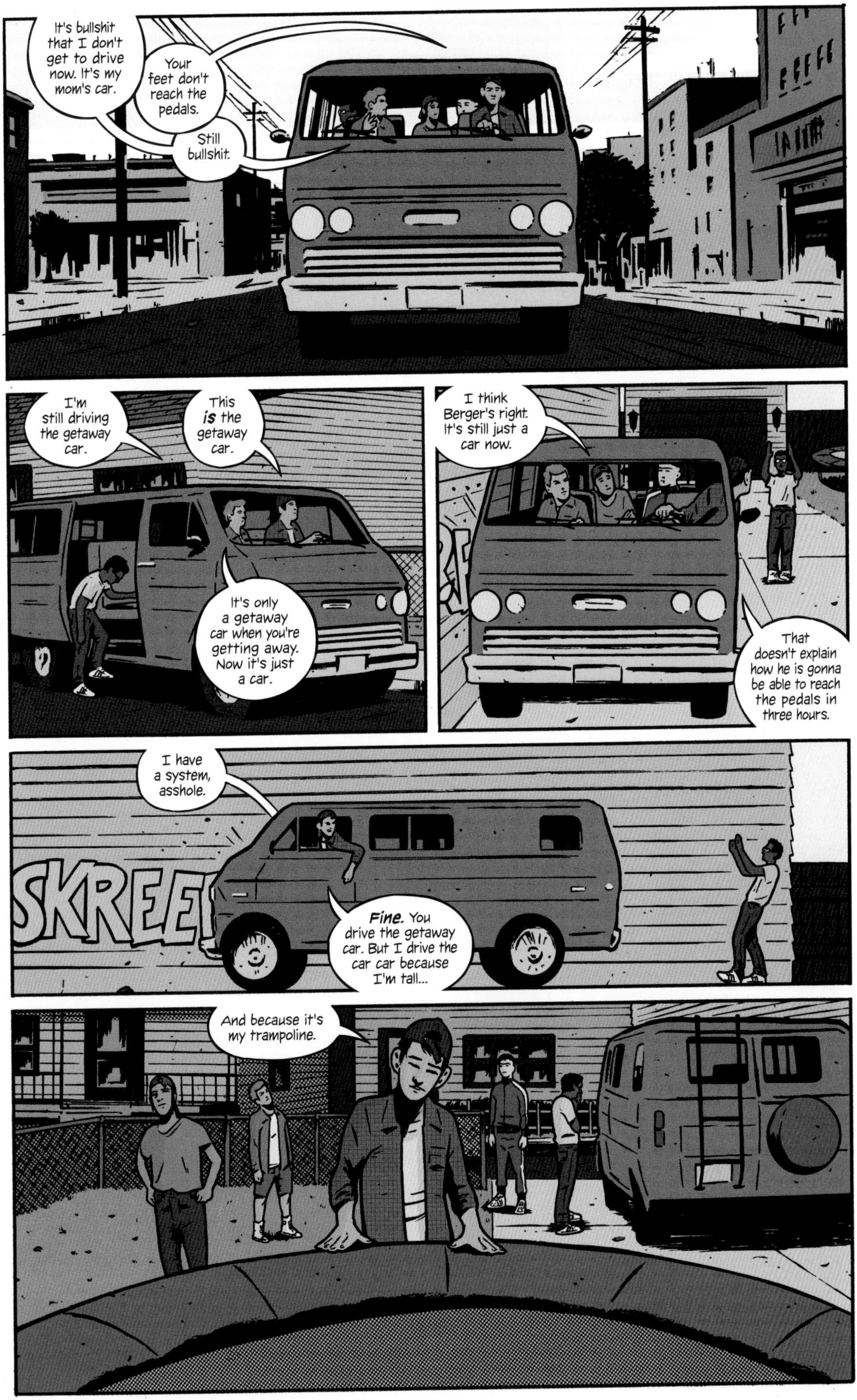
It's bullshit that I don't get to drive now. It's my mom's car.
Your feet don't reach the pedals.
Still bullshit.
I'm still driving the getaway car.
This *is* the getaway car.
It's only a getaway car when you're getting away. Now it's just a car.
I think Berger's right. It's still just a car now.
That doesn't explain how he is gonna be able to reach the pedals in three hours.
I have a system, asshole.
SKREE
Fine. You drive the getaway car. But I drive the car car because I'm tall...
And because it's my trampoline.

All right, boys. You know I don't really like to give speeches....

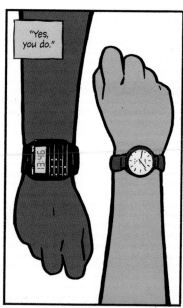

"Yes, you do."

"No, I don't."

"You kinda do though."

"Whatever... that's not the point..."

"...Shit. I forgot what I was gonna say..."

"It's something about giving speeches. Right, Paige?"

"Yeah, I know that... umm...was..."

Fuck it. Doesn't matter.

Let's go rob a bank or whatever.

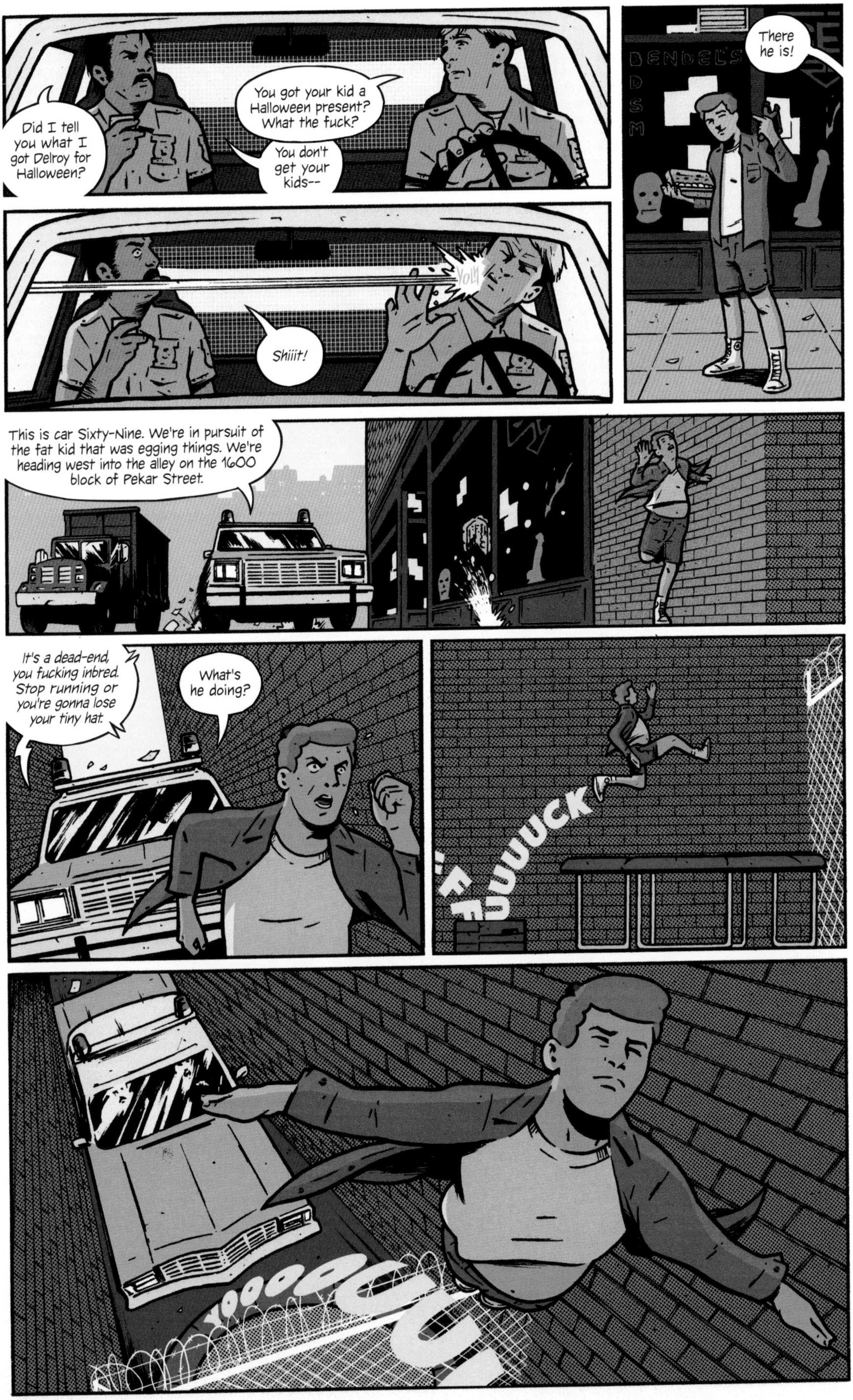

Did I tell you what I got Delroy for Halloween?
You got your kid a Halloween present? What the fuck?
You don't get your kids--
There he is!
BENDEL'S
DSM
YOLK
Shiiit!
This is car Sixty-Nine. We're in pursuit of the fat kid that was egging things. We're heading west into the alley on the 1600 block of Pekar Street.
It's a dead-end, you fucking inbred. Stop running or you're gonna lose your tiny hat.
What's he doing?
FFUUUUCK
YOOOOOU

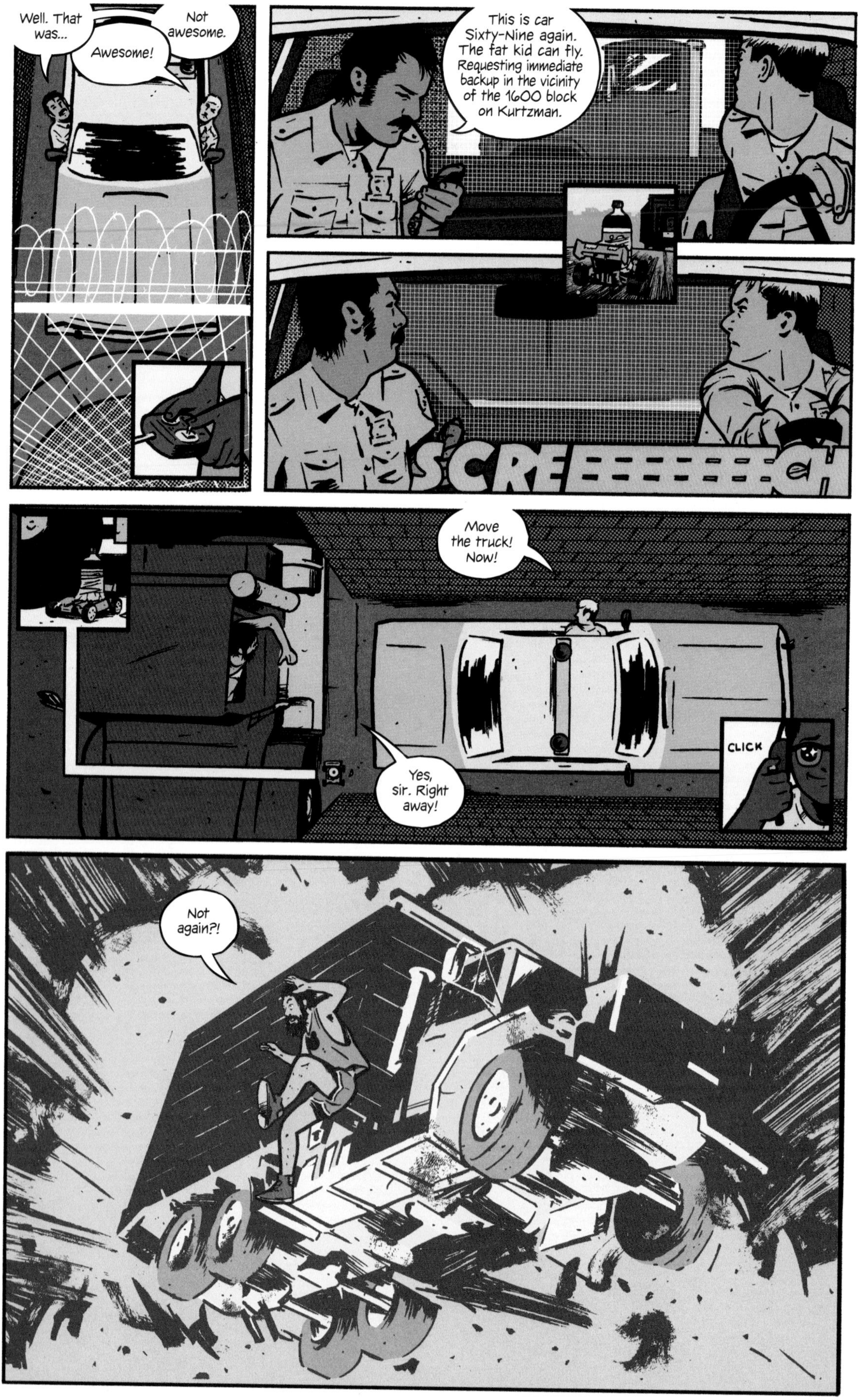
Well. That was...
Awesome!
Not awesome.
This is car Sixty-Nine again. The fat kid can fly. Requesting immediate backup in the vicinity of the 1600 block on Kurtzman.
SCREEEEEEEECH
Move the truck! Now!
Yes, sir. Right away!
CLICK
Not again?!

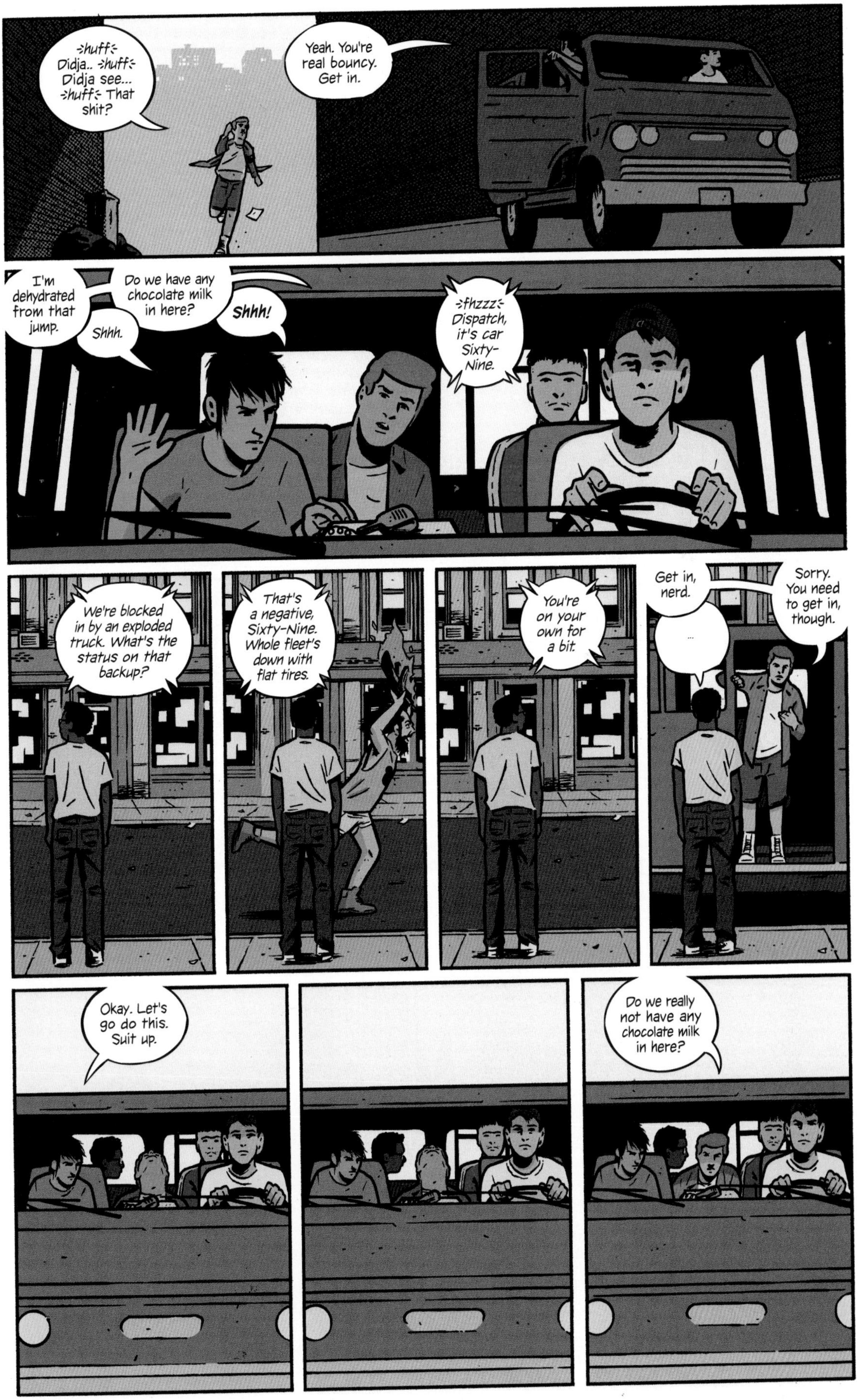

=huff= Didja.. =huff= Didja see... =huff= That shit?
Yeah. You're real bouncy. Get in.
I'm dehydrated from that jump.
Do we have any chocolate milk in here?
Shhh.
Shhh!
=fhzzz= Dispatch, it's car Sixty-Nine.
We're blocked in by an exploded truck. What's the status on that backup?
That's a negative, Sixty-Nine. Whole fleet's down with flat tires.
You're on your own for a bit.
Get in, nerd.
...
Sorry. You need to get in, though.
Okay. Let's go do this. Suit up.
Do we really not have any chocolate milk in here?

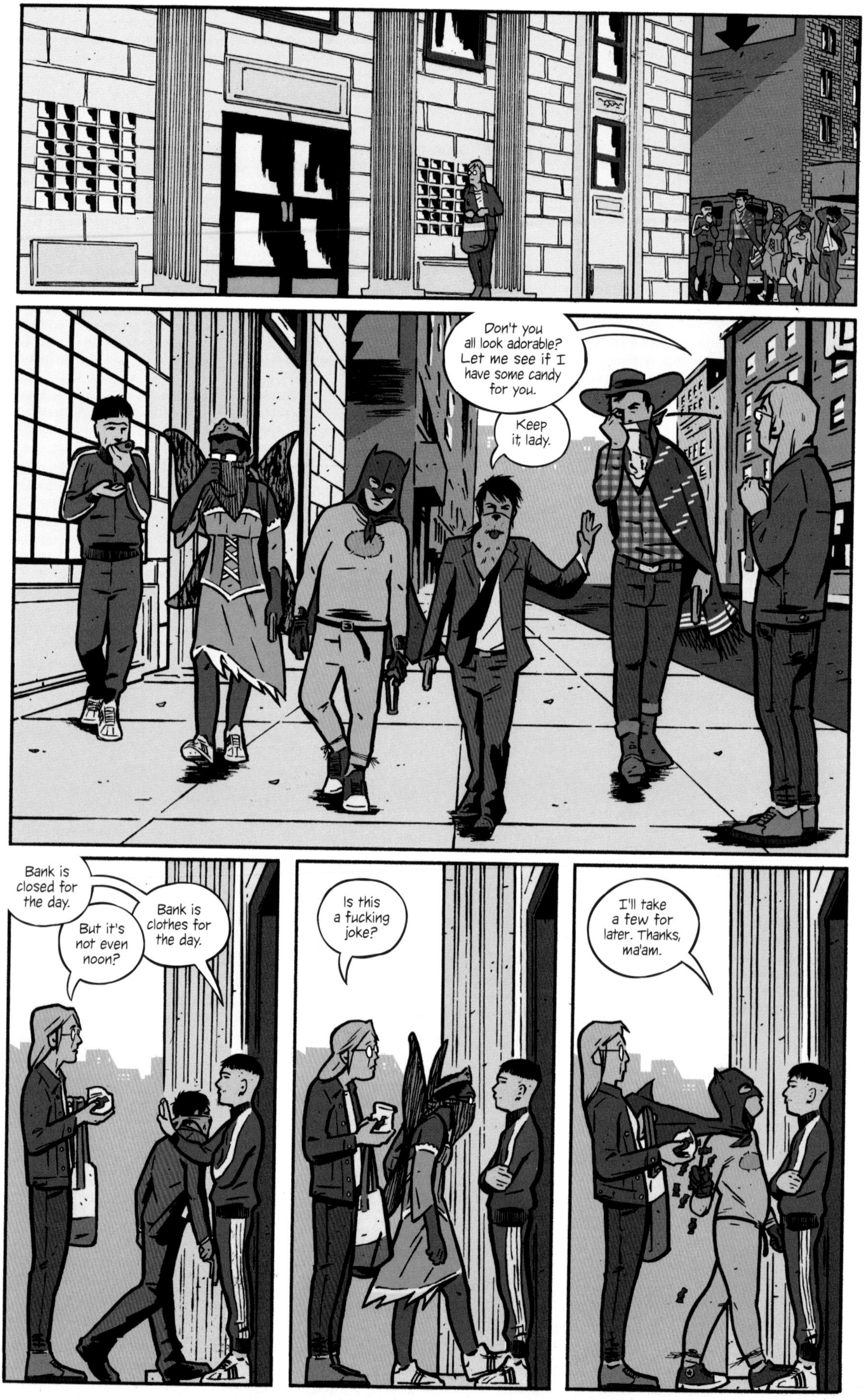
Don't you all look adorable? Let me see if I have some candy for you.
Keep it, lady.
Bank is closed for the day.
But it's not even noon?
Bank is clothes for the day.
Is this a fucking joke?
I'll take a few for later. Thanks, ma'am.

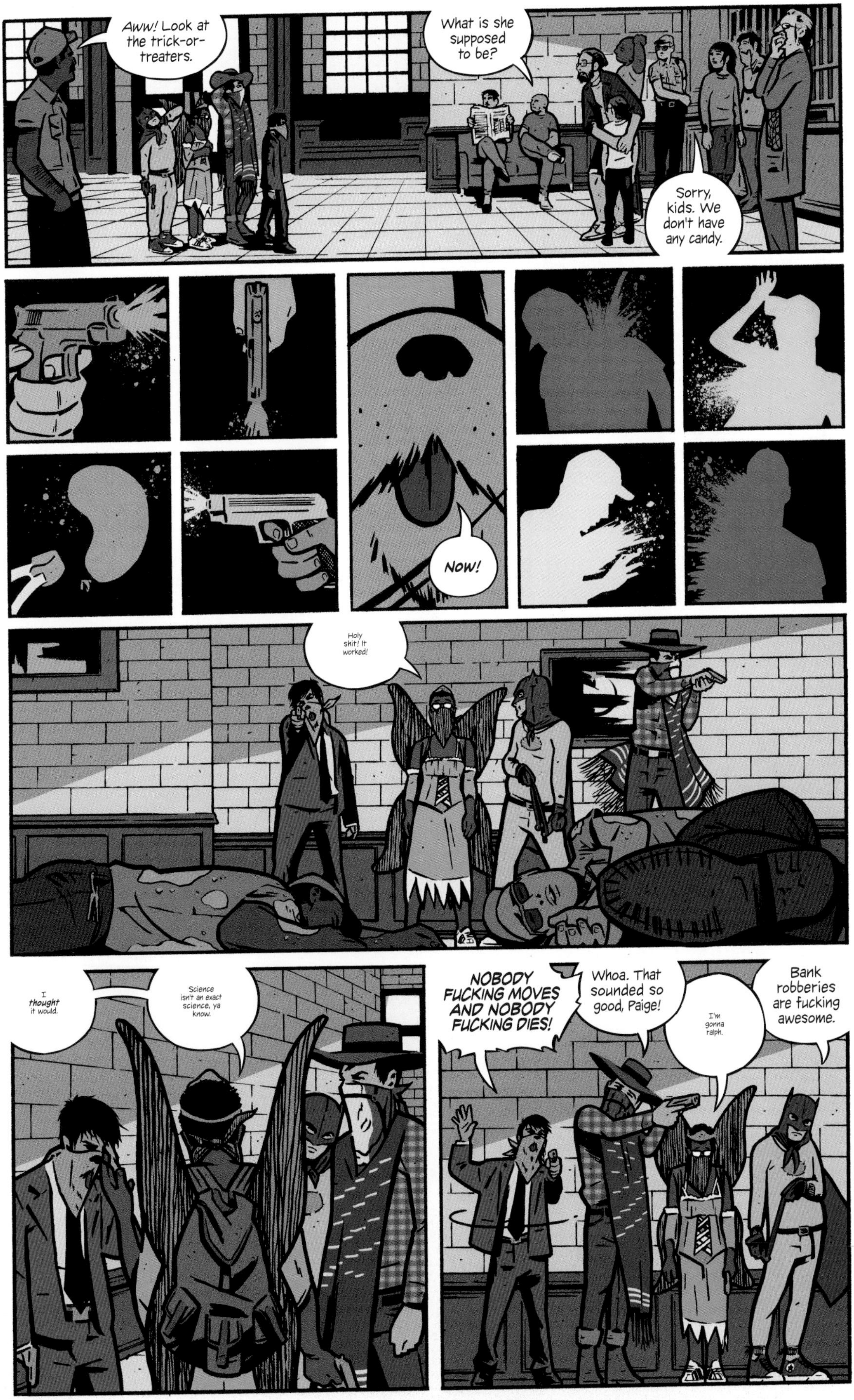
Aww! Look at the trick-or-treaters.
What is she supposed to be?
Sorry, kids. We don't have any candy.
NOW!
Holy shit! It worked!
I *thought* it would.
Science isn't an exact science, ya know.
NOBODY FUCKING MOVES AND NOBODY FUCKING DIES!
Whoa. That sounded so good, Paige!
I'm gonna ralph.
Bank robberies are fucking awesome.

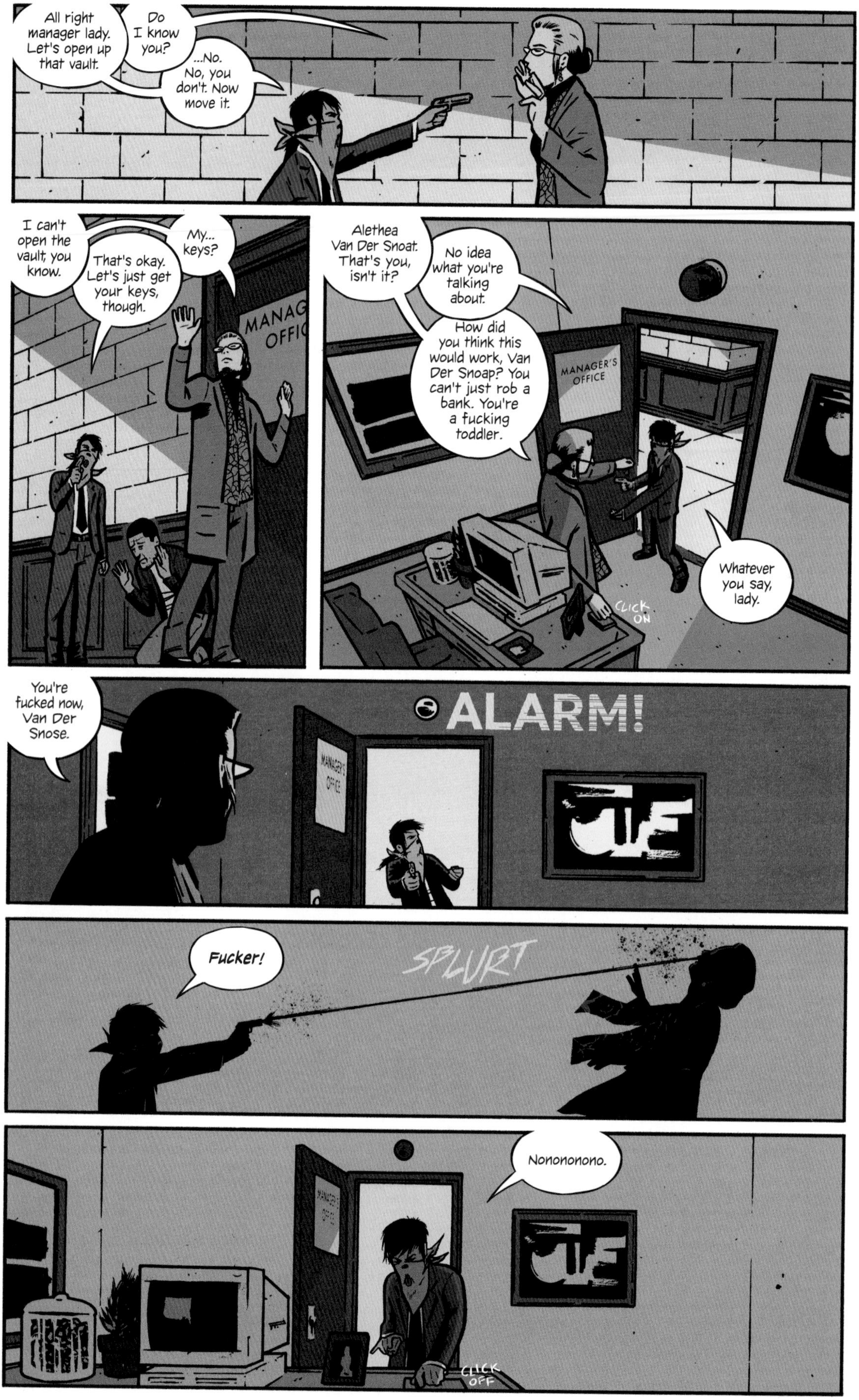
All right manager lady. Let's open up that vault.
Do I know you?
...No. No, you don't. Now move it.
I can't open the vault, you know.
That's okay. Let's just get your keys, though.
My... keys?
MANAGER'S OFFICE
Alethea Van Der Snoat. That's you, isn't it?
No idea what you're talking about.
How did you think this would work, Van Der Snoap? You can't just rob a bank. You're a fucking toddler.
MANAGER'S OFFICE
Whatever you say, lady.
CLICK ON
You're fucked now, Van Der Snose.
ALARM!
MANAGER'S OFFICE
Fucker!
SPLURT
Nononononono.
CLICK OFF

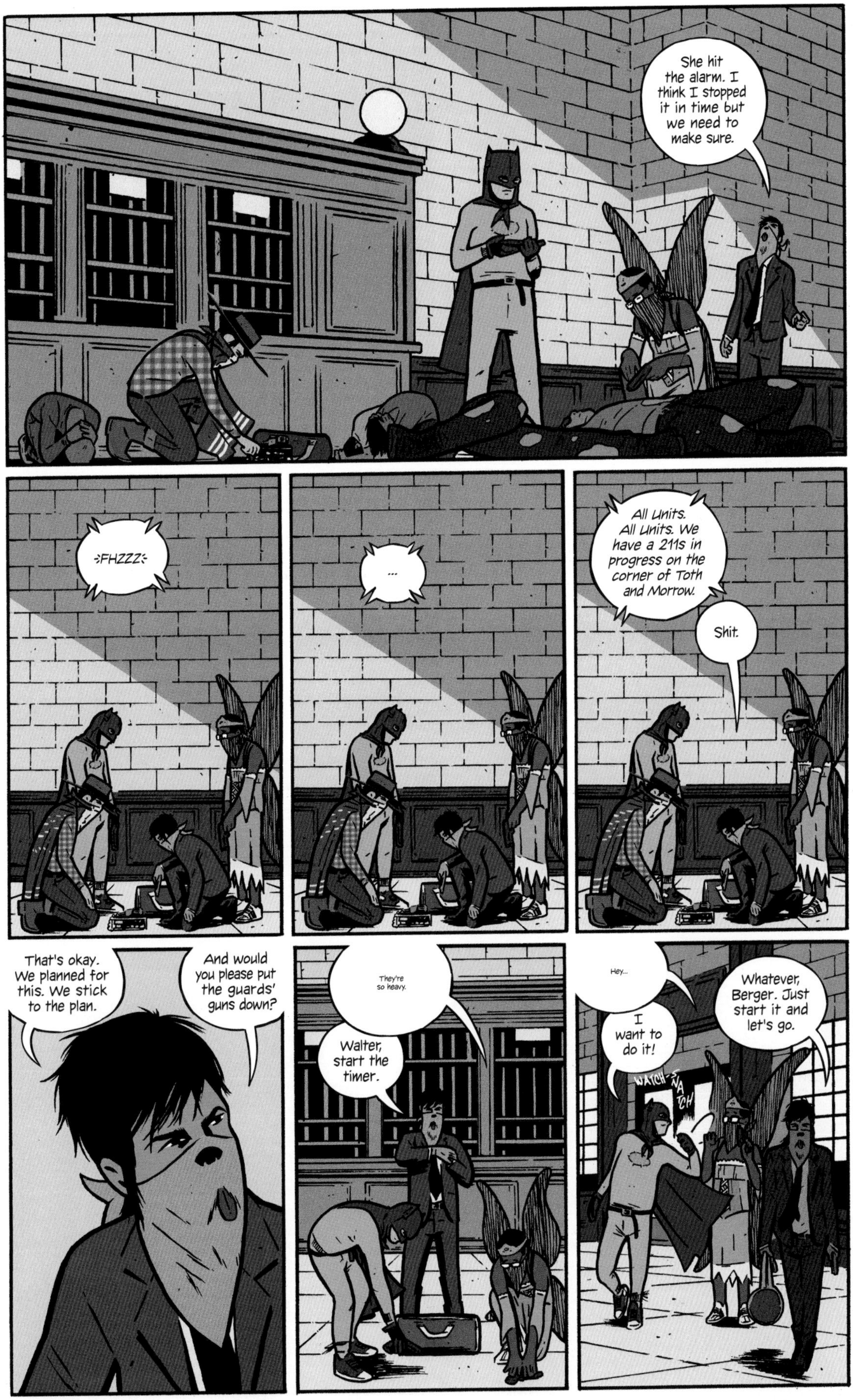

She hit the alarm. I think I stopped it in time but we need to make sure.
-FHZZZ-
...
All Units. All Units. We have a 211s in progress on the corner of Toth and Morrow.
Shit.
That's okay. We planned for this. We stick to the plan.
And would you please put the guards' guns down?
They're so heavy.
Walter, start the timer.
Hey...
I want to do it!
Whatever, Berger. Just start it and let's go.
WATCH-SNATCH

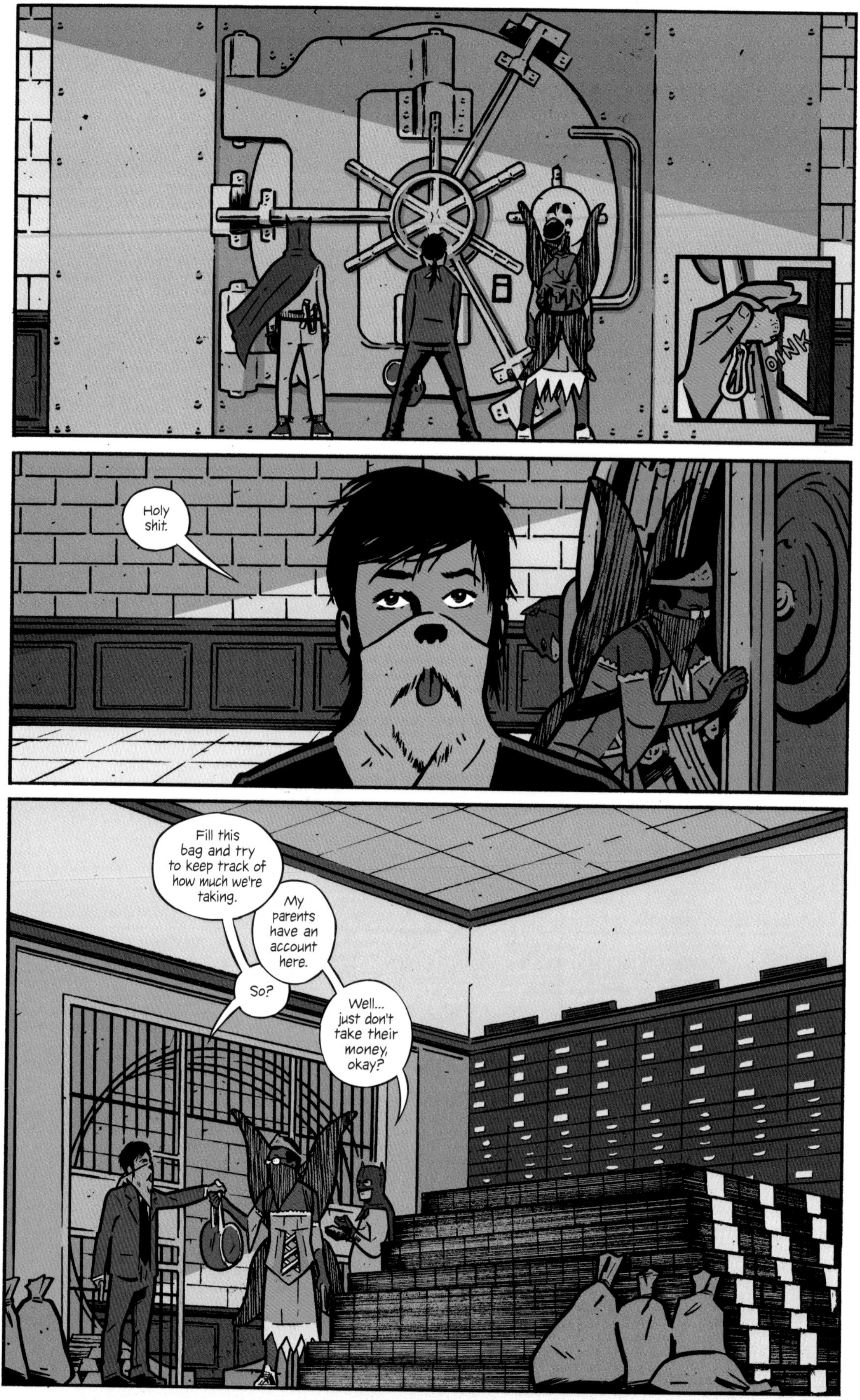
OINK
Holy shit.
Fill this bag and try to keep track of how much we're taking.
My parents have an account here.
So?
Well... just don't take their money, okay?

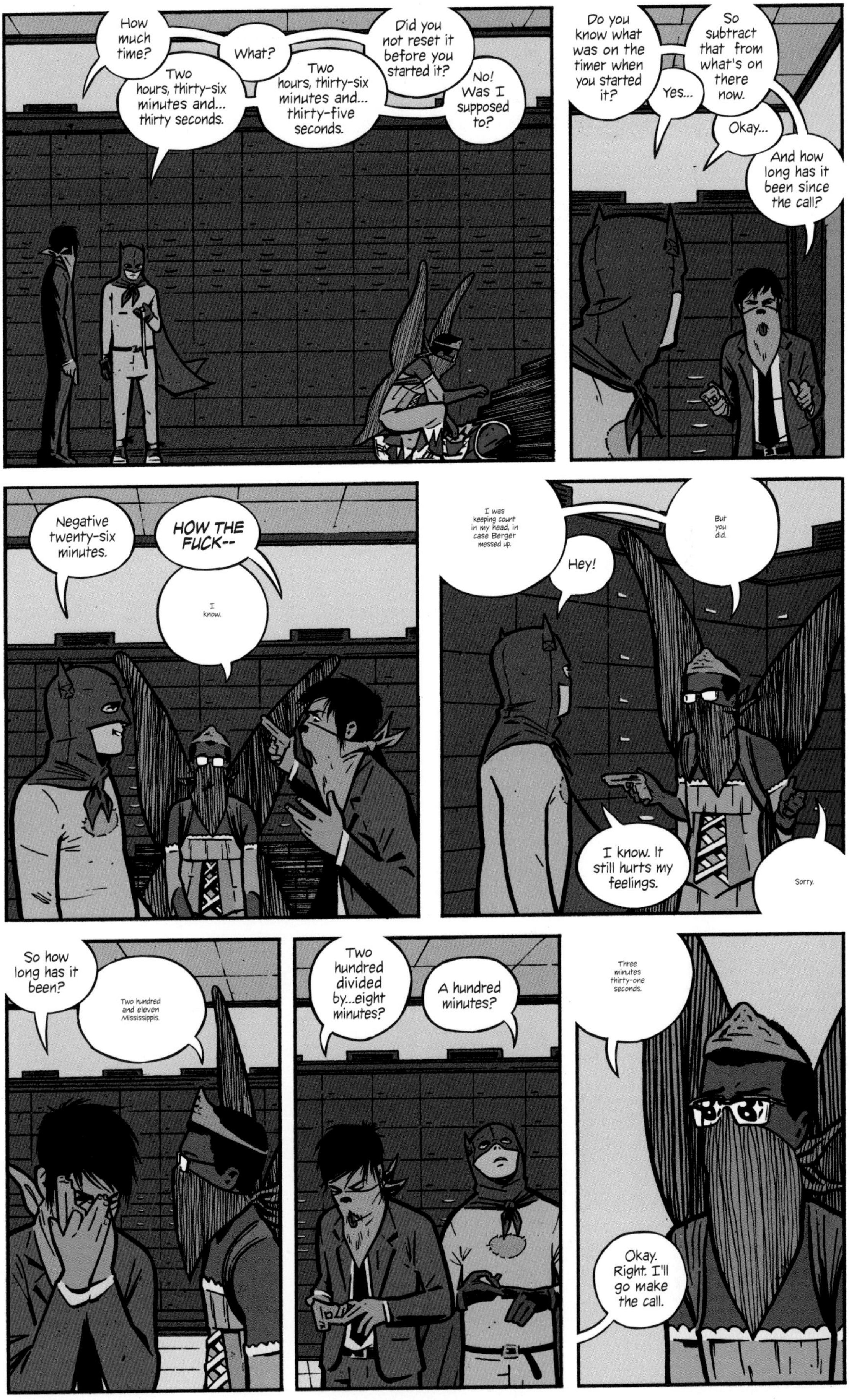
How much time?
Two hours, thirty-six minutes and... thirty seconds.
What?
Two hours, thirty-six minutes and... thirty-five seconds.
Did you not reset it before you started it?
No! Was I supposed to?
Do you know what was on the timer when you started it?
Yes...
So subtract that from what's on there now.
Okay...
And how long has it been since the call?
Negative twenty-six minutes.
HOW THE FUCK--
I know.
I was keeping count in my head, in case Berger messed up.
Hey!
But you did.
I know. It still hurts my feelings.
Sorry.
So how long has it been?
Two hundred and eleven Mississippis.
Two hundred divided by...eight minutes?
A hundred minutes?
Three minutes thirty-one seconds.
Okay. Right. I'll go make the call.

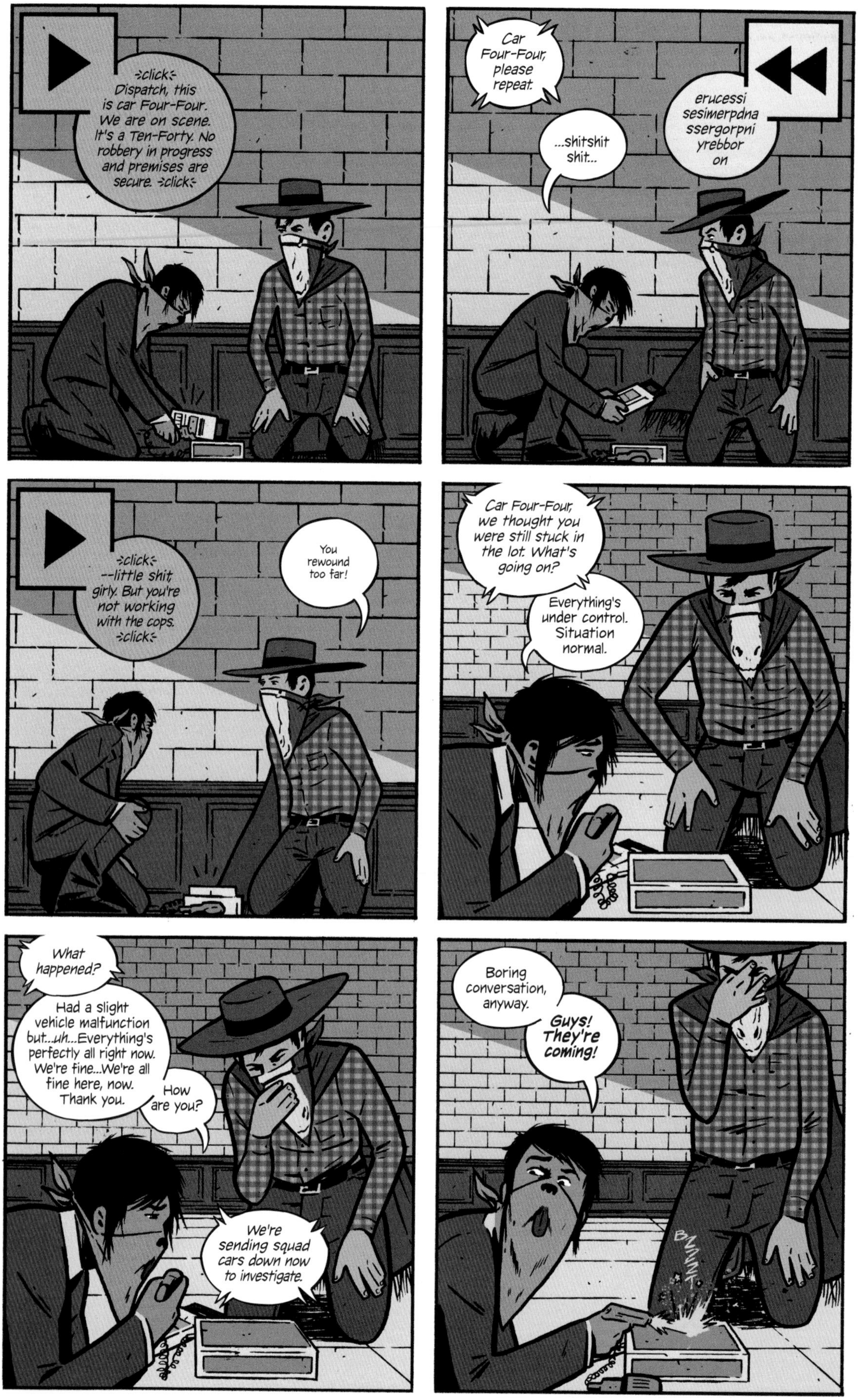
>click< Dispatch, this is car Four-Four. We are on scene. It's a Ten-Forty. No robbery in progress and premises are secure. >click<
Car Four-Four, please repeat.
...shitshit shit...
erucessi sesimerpdna ssergorpni yrebbor on
>click< --little shit, girly. But you're not working with the cops. >click<
You rewound too far!
Car Four-Four, we thought you were still stuck in the lot. What's going on?
Everything's under control. Situation normal.
What happened?
Had a slight vehicle malfunction but...uh...Everything's perfectly all right now. We're fine...We're all fine here, now. Thank you.
How are you?
We're sending squad cars down now to investigate.
Boring conversation, anyway.
Guys! They're coming!
BZZZT

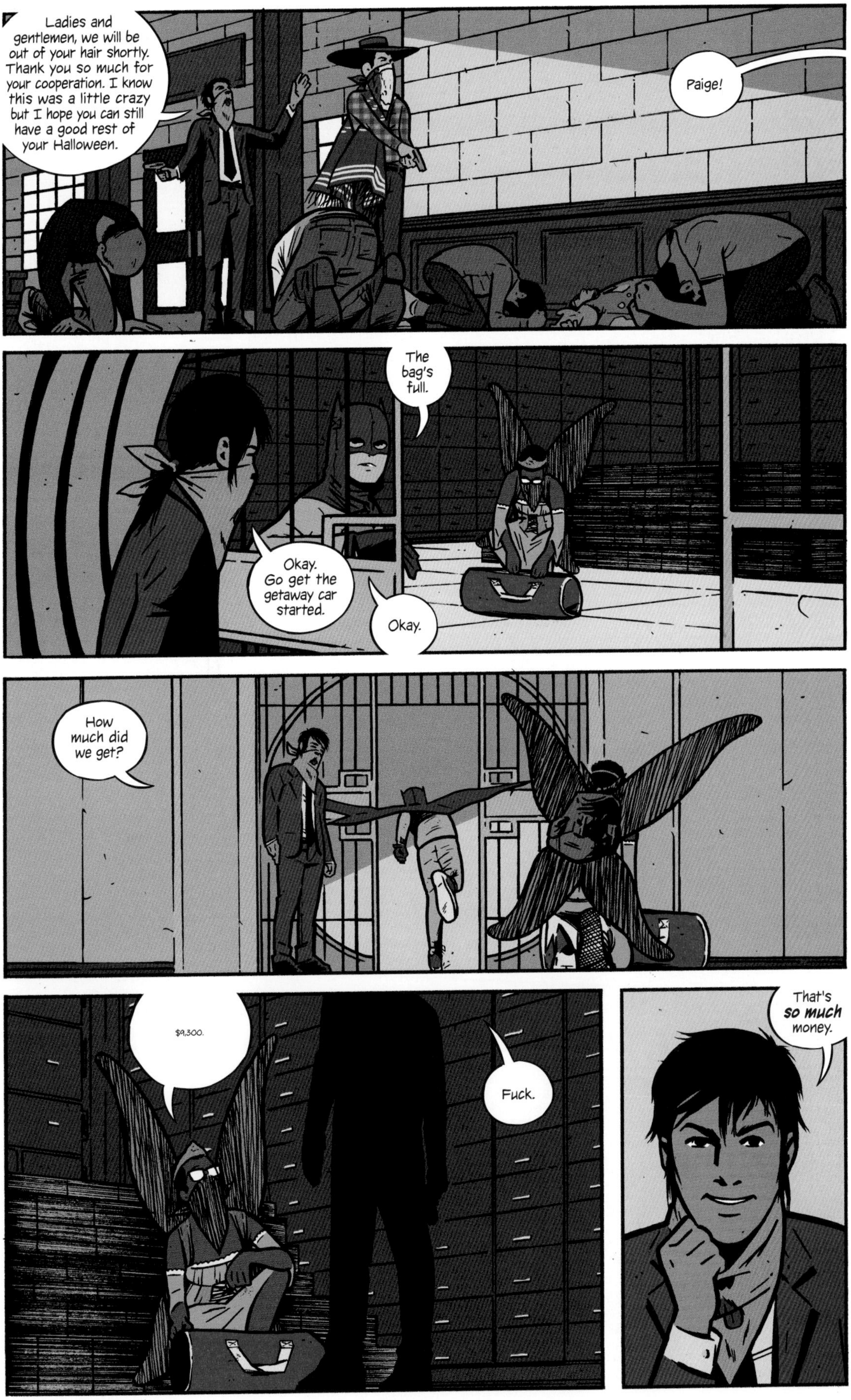
Ladies and gentlemen, we will be out of your hair shortly. Thank you so much for your cooperation. I know this was a little crazy but I hope you can still have a good rest of your Halloween.
Paige!
The bag's full.
Okay. Go get the getaway car started.
Okay.
How much did we get?
$9,300.
Fuck.
That's **so much** money.

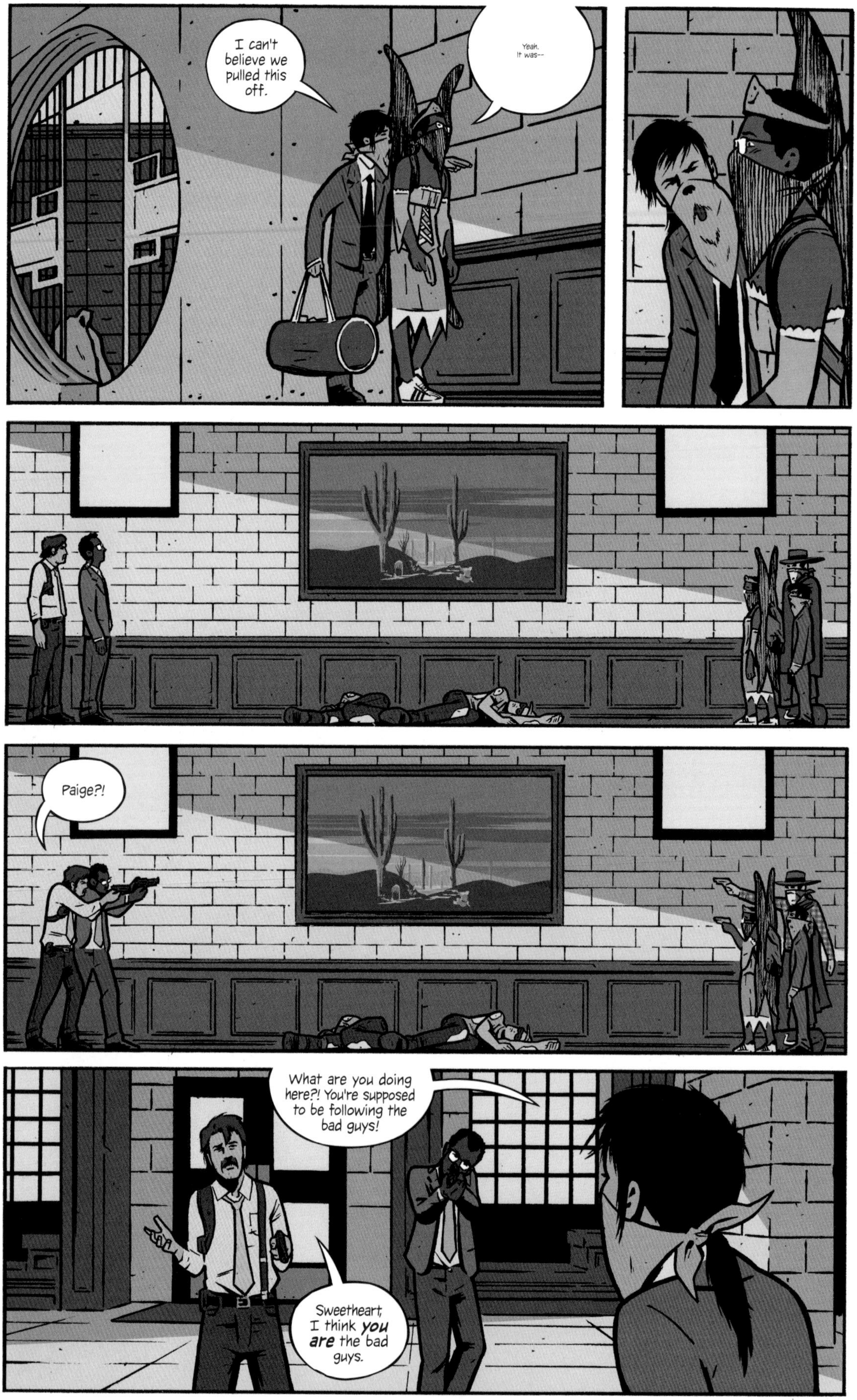
I can't believe we pulled this off.
Yeah. It was--
Paige?!
What are you doing here?! You're supposed to be following the bad guys!
Sweetheart, I think ***you are*** the bad guys.

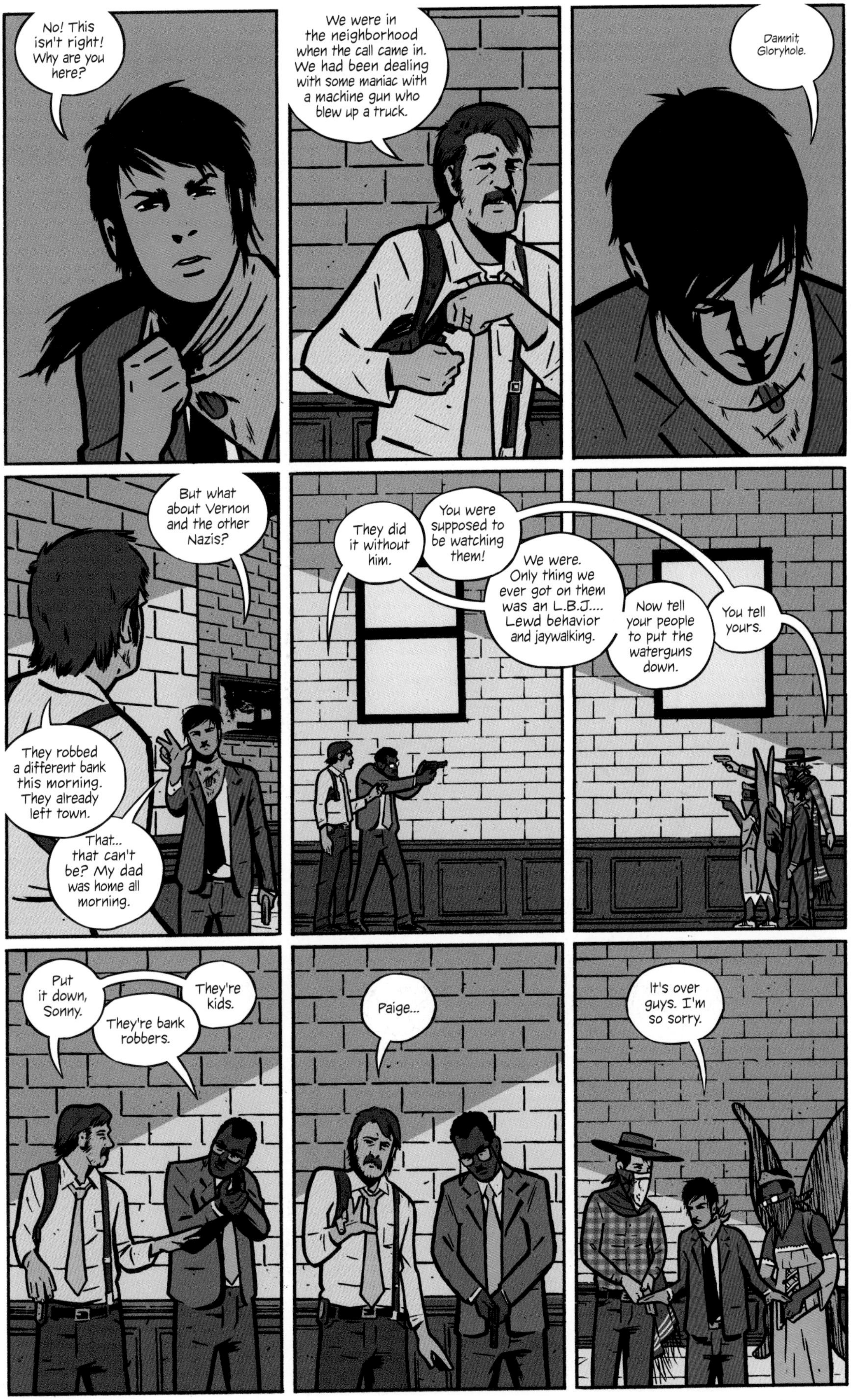
No! This isn't right! Why are you here?
We were in the neighborhood when the call came in. We had been dealing with some maniac with a machine gun who blew up a truck.
Damnit, Gloryhole.
But what about Vernon and the other Nazis?
They robbed a different bank this morning. They already left town.
That... that can't be? My dad was home all morning.
They did it without him.
You were supposed to be watching them!
We were. Only thing we ever got on them was an L.B.J.... Lewd behavior and jaywalking.
Now tell your people to put the waterguns down.
You tell yours.
Put it down, Sonny.
They're kids.
They're bank robbers.
Paige...
It's over guys. I'm so sorry.

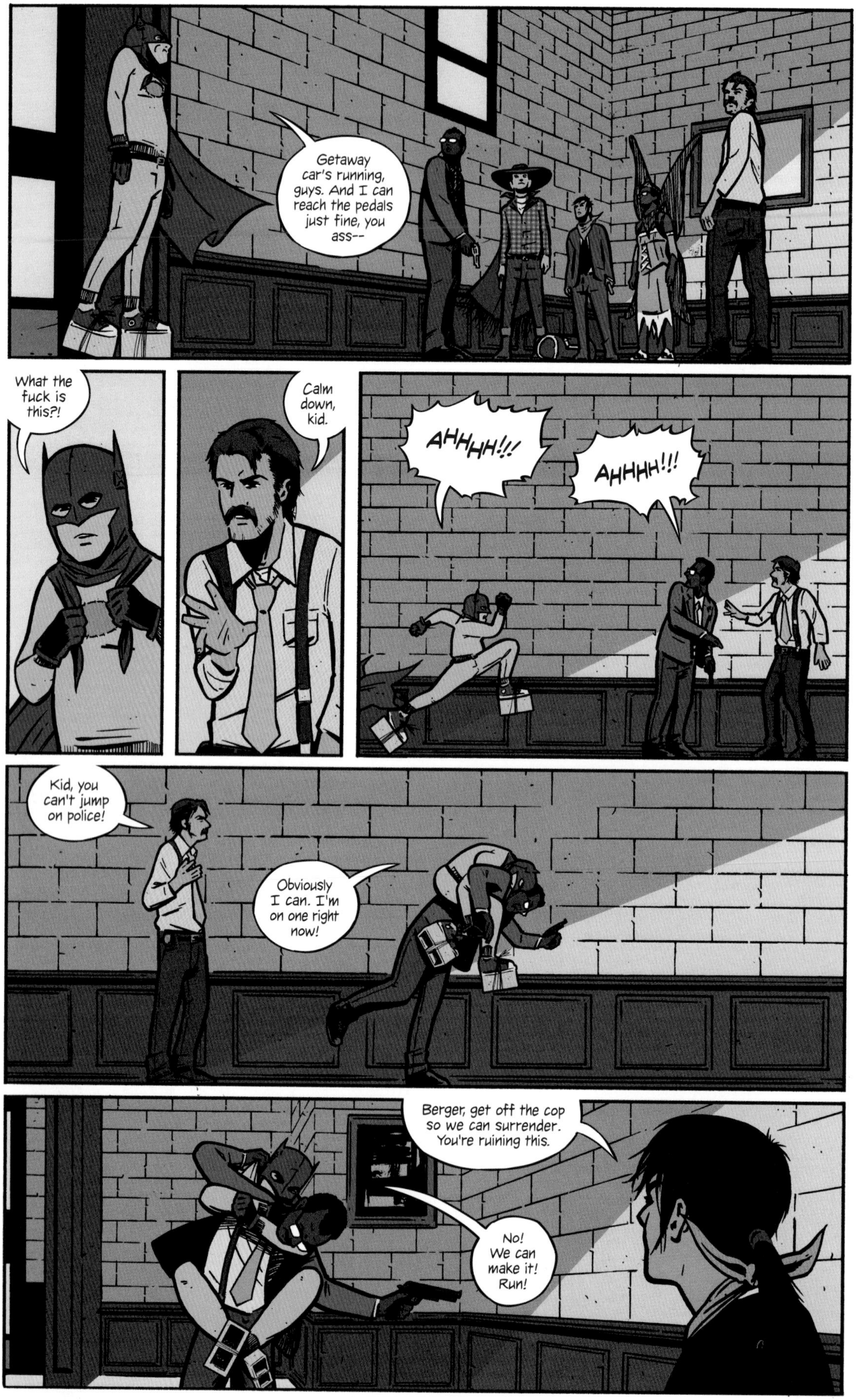
Getaway car's running, guys. And I can reach the pedals just fine, you ass--
What the fuck is this?!
Calm down, kid.
AHHHH!!!
AHHHH!!!
Kid, you can't jump on police!
Obviously I can. I'm on one right now!
Berger, get off the cop so we can surrender. You're ruining this.
No! We can make it! Run!

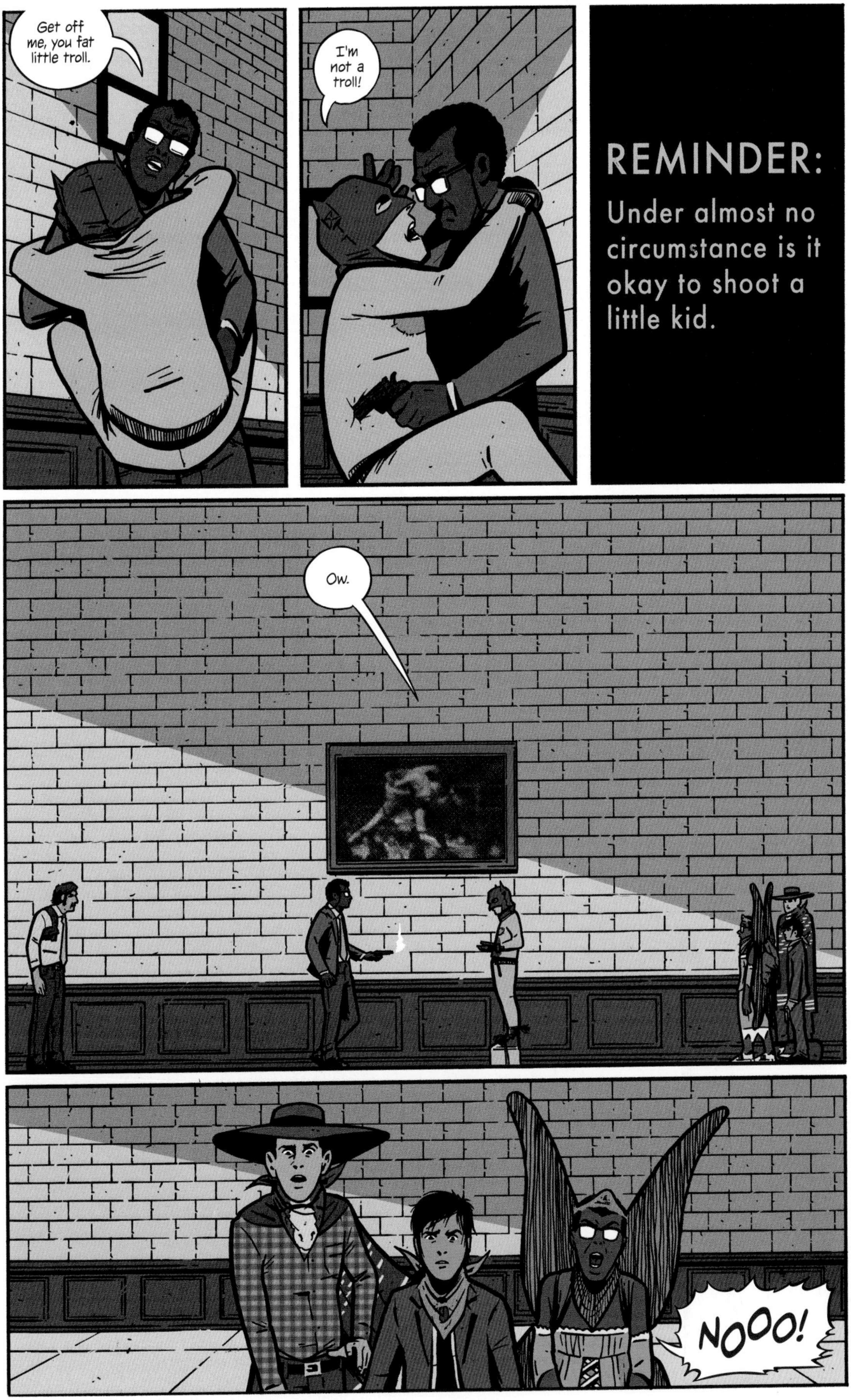
Get off me, you fat little troll.
I'm not a troll!
REMINDER:
Under almost no circumstance is it okay to shoot a little kid.
Ow.
NOOO!

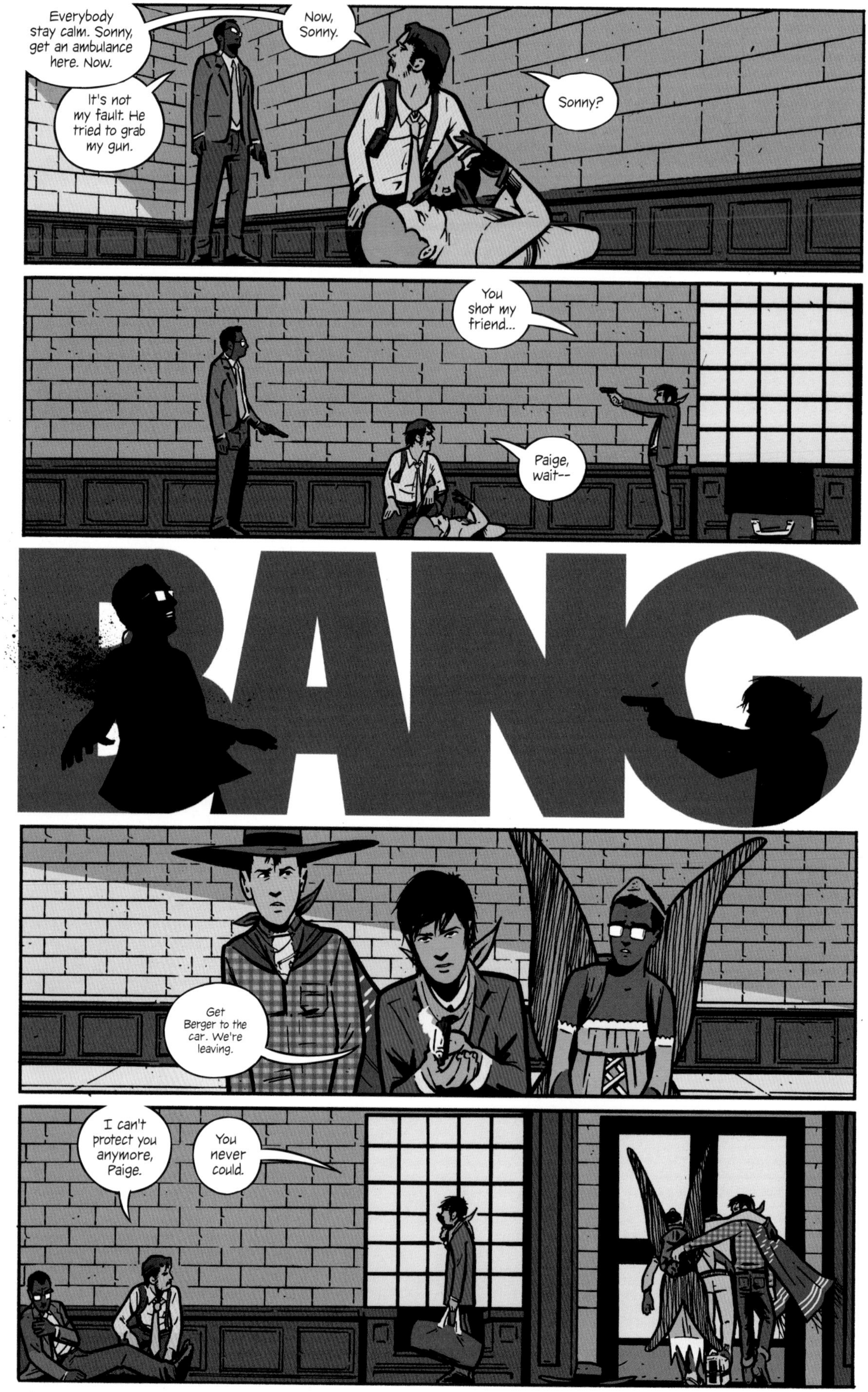
Everybody stay calm. Sonny, get an ambulance here. Now.
Now, Sonny.
It's not my fault. He tried to grab my gun.
Sonny?
You shot my friend...
Paige, wait--
BANG
Get Berger to the car. We're leaving.
I can't protect you anymore, Paige.
You never could.

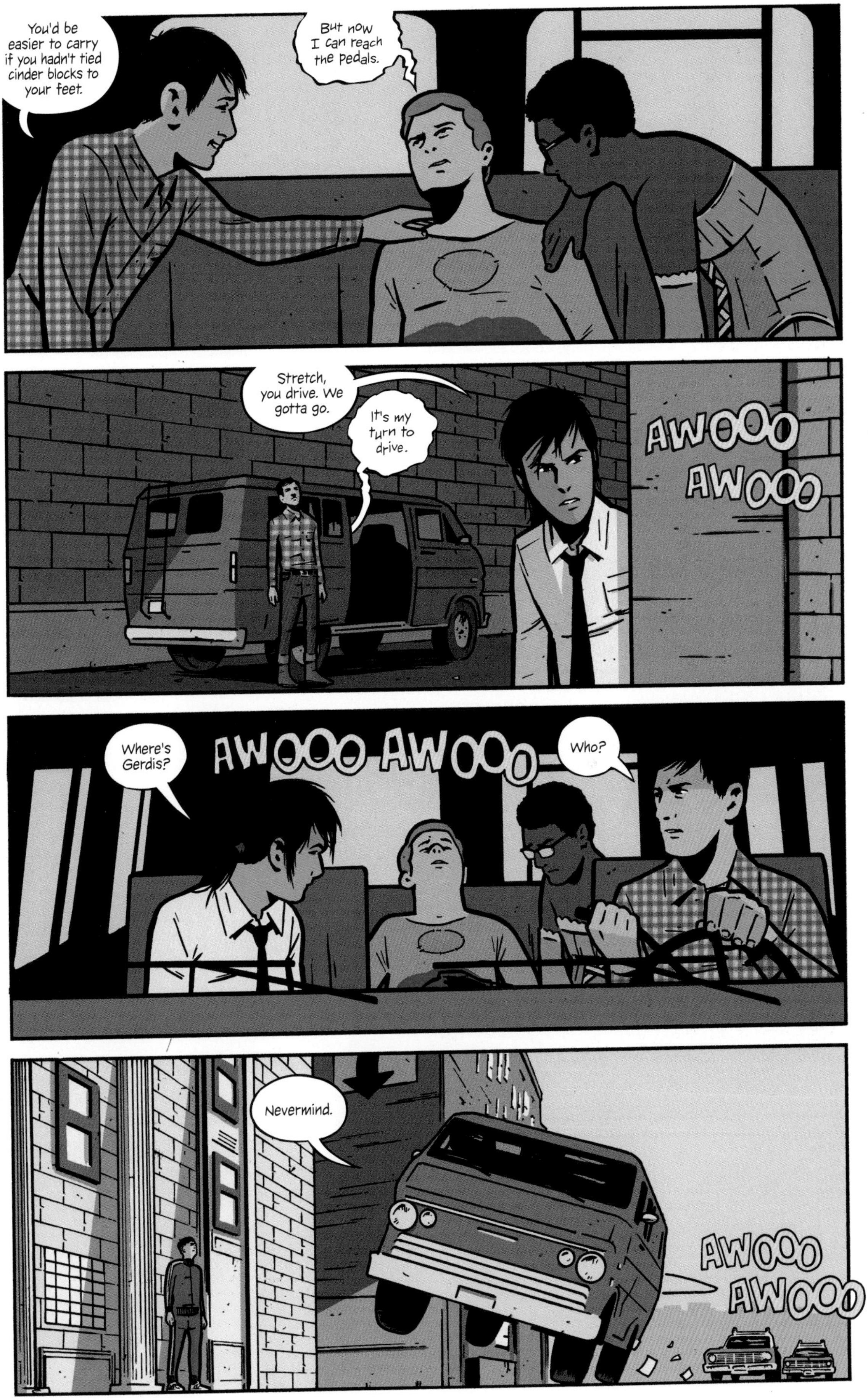
You'd be easier to carry if you hadn't tied cinder blocks to your feet.
But now I can reach the pedals.
Stretch, you drive. We gotta go.
It's my turn to drive.
AWOOO AWOOO
Where's Gerdis?
AWOOO AWOOO
Who?
Nevermind.
AWOOO AWOOO

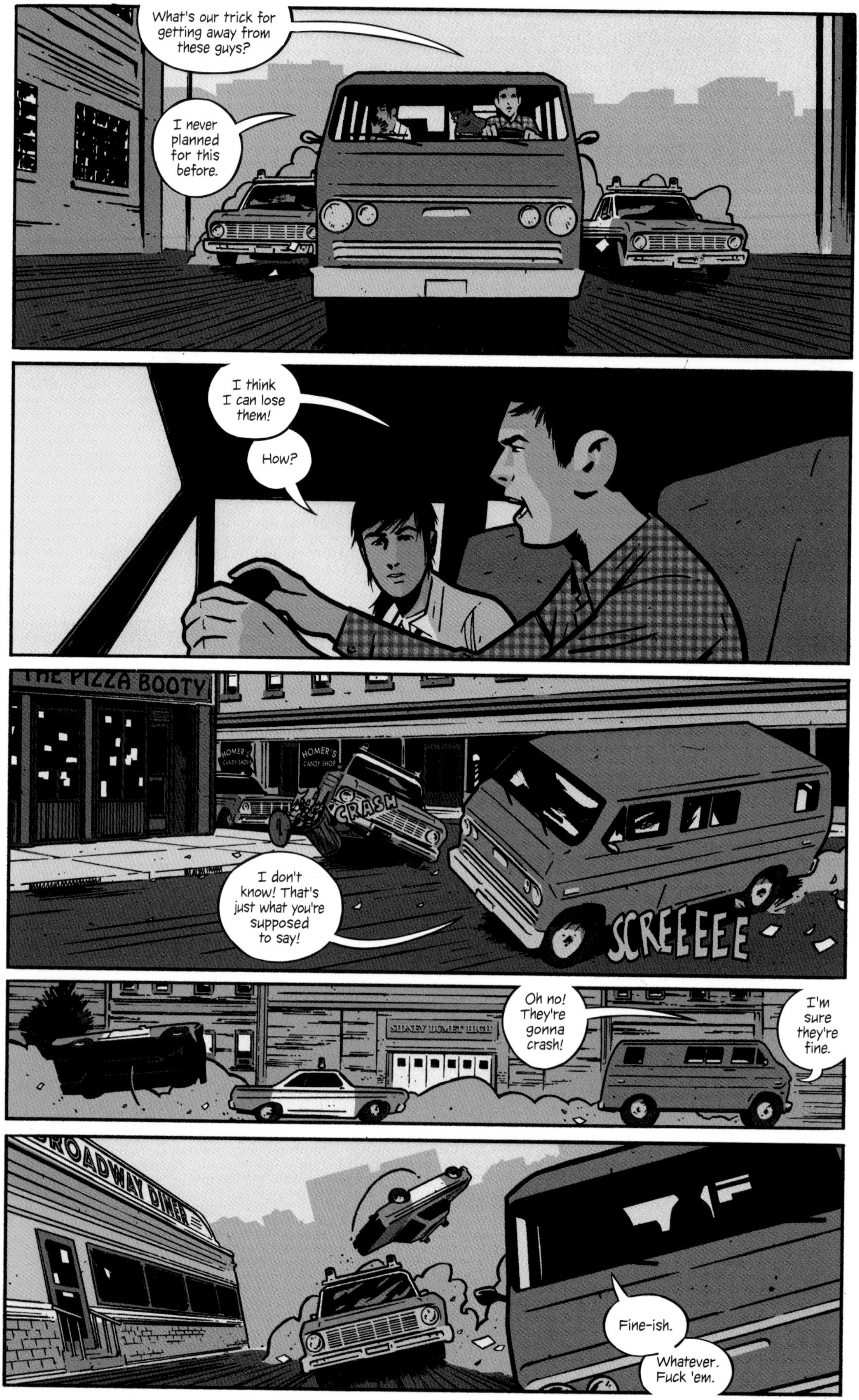
What's our trick for getting away from these guys?
I never planned for this before.
I think I can lose them!
How?
THE PIZZA BOOTY
HOMER'S CANDY SHOP
HOMER'S CANDY SHOP
CRASH
I don't know! That's just what you're supposed to say!
SCREEEEE
SIDNEY LUMET HIGH
Oh no! They're gonna crash!
I'm sure they're fine.
ROADWAY DINER
Fine-ish.
Whatever. Fuck 'em.

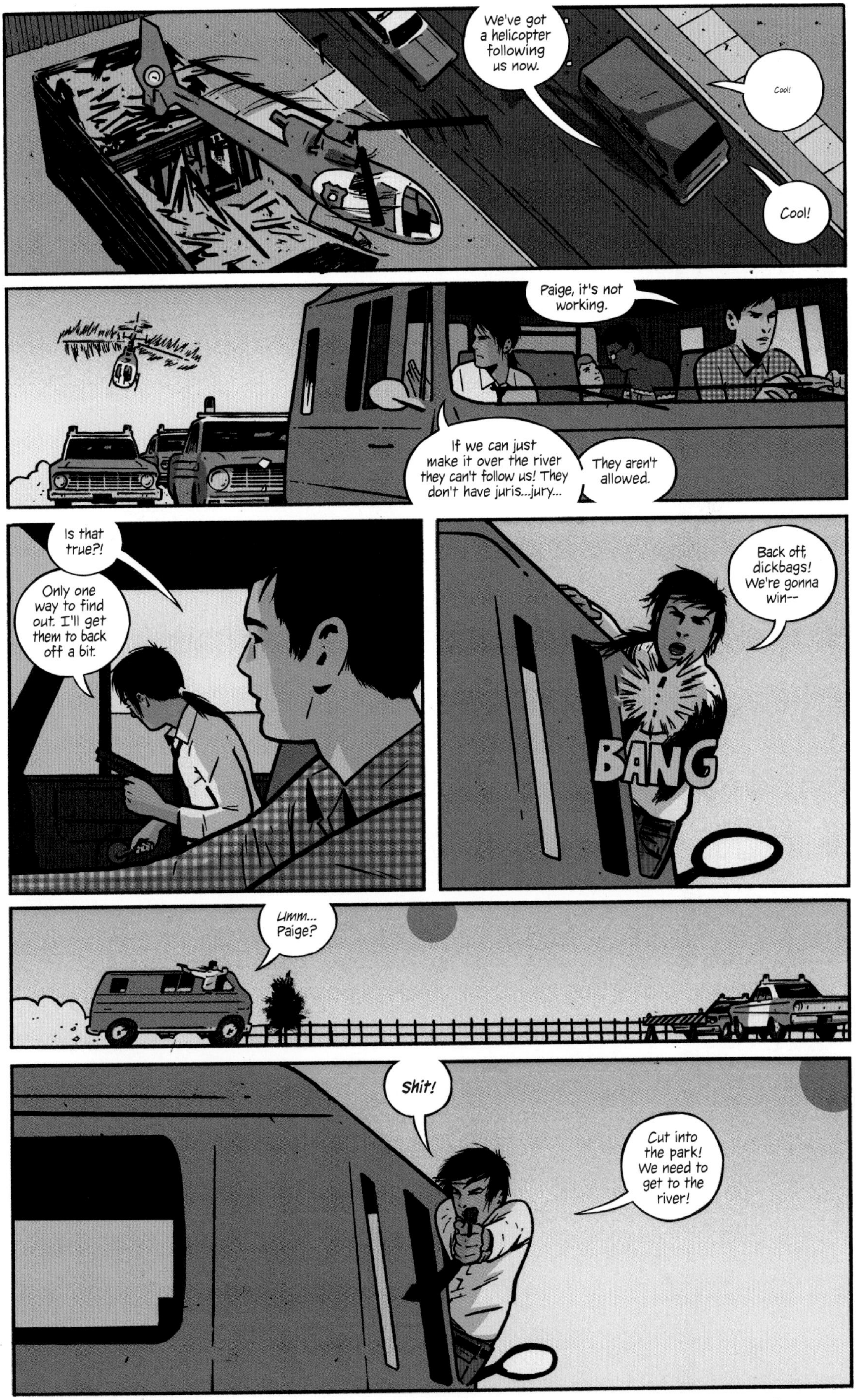
We've got a helicopter following us now.
Cool!
Cool!
Paige, it's not working.
If we can just make it over the river they can't follow us! They don't have juris...jury...
They aren't allowed.
Is that true?!
Only one way to find out. I'll get them to back off a bit.
Back off, dickbags! We're gonna win--
BANG
Umm... Paige?
Shit!
Cut into the park! We need to get to the river!

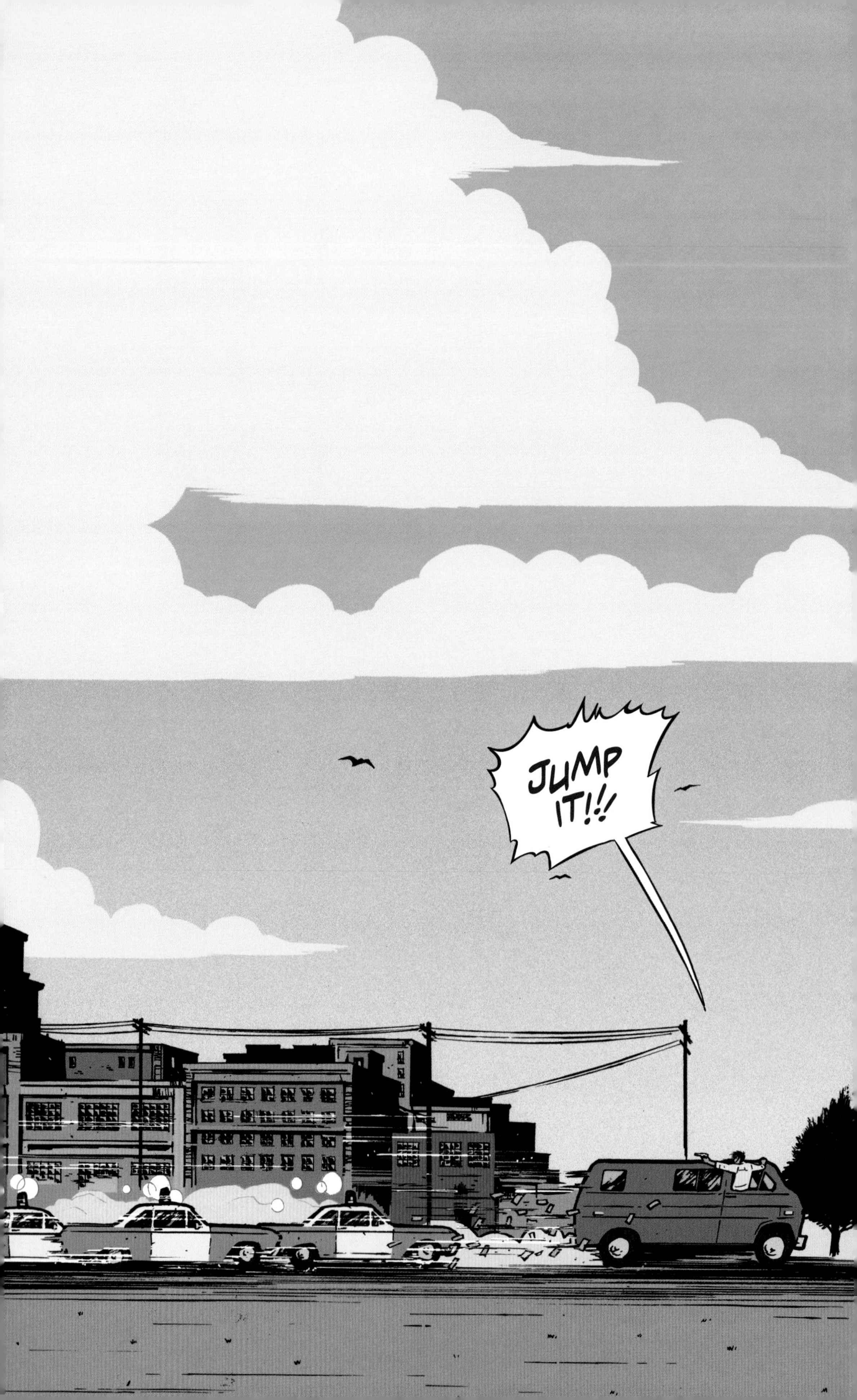
JUMP IT!!!

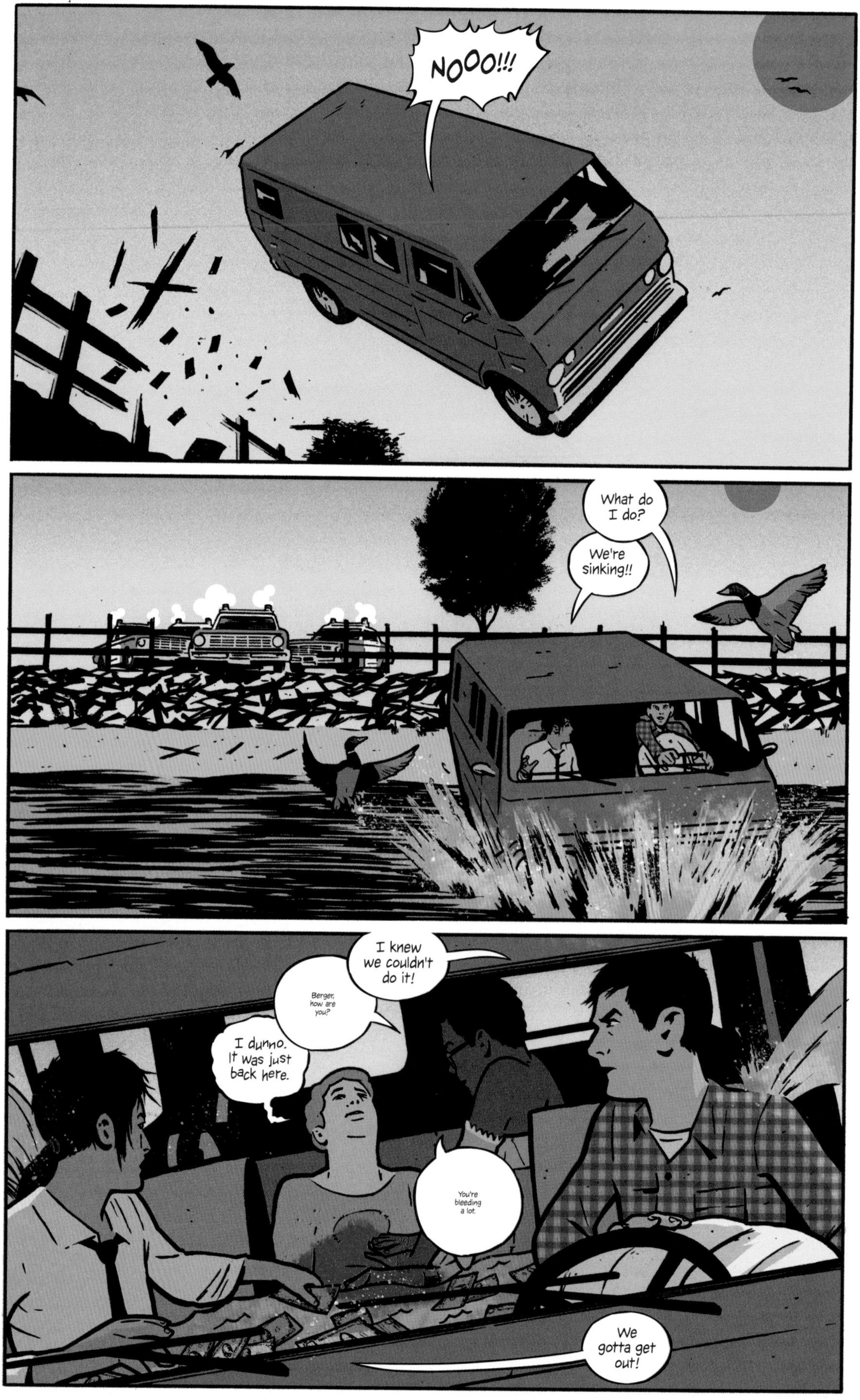
NOOO!!!
What do I do?
We're sinking!!
I knew we couldn't do it!
Berger, how are you?
I dunno. It was just back here.
You're bleeding a lot.
We gotta get out!

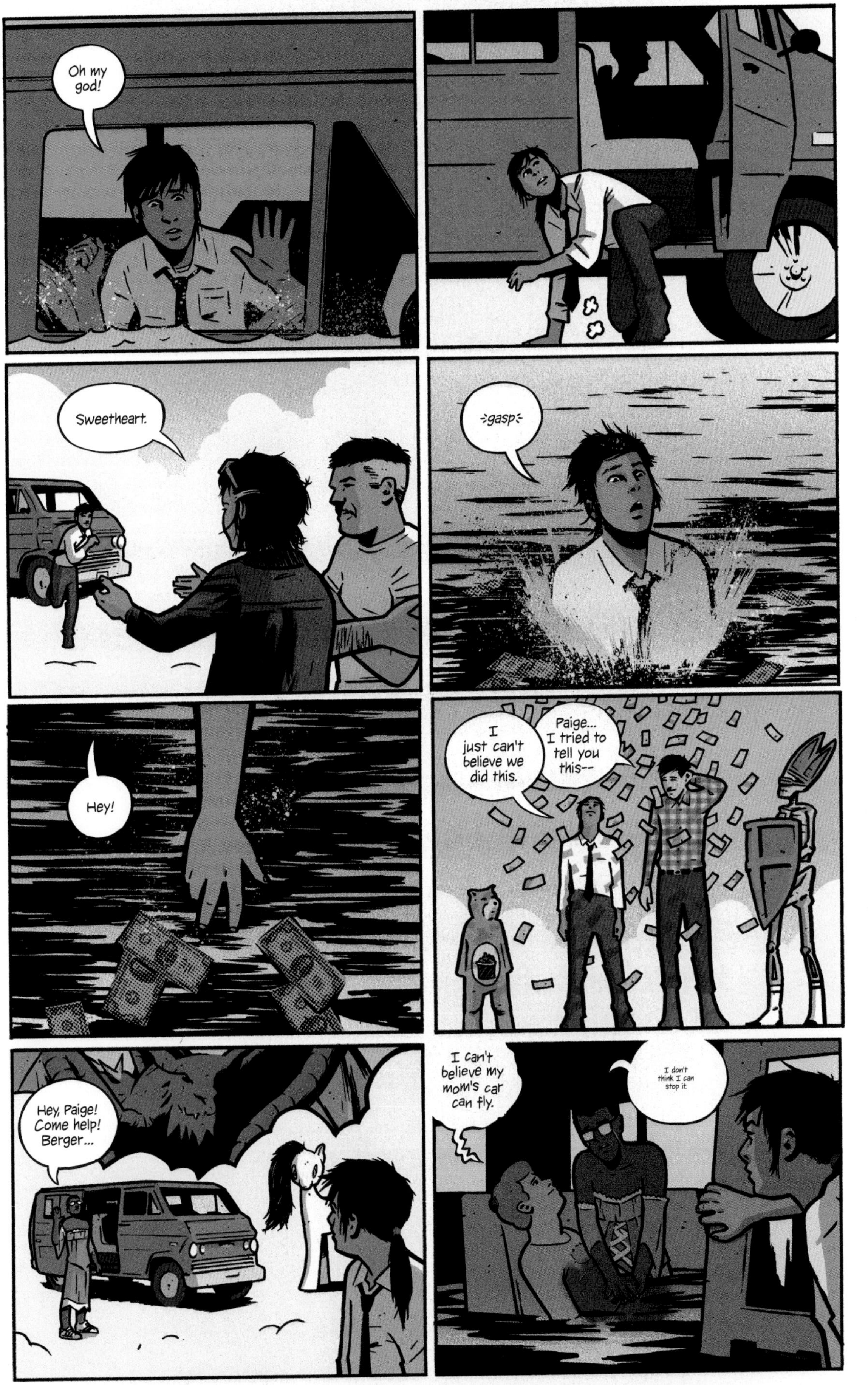
Oh my god!
Sweetheart.
gasp
Hey!
I just can't believe we did this.
Paige... I tried to tell you this--
Hey, Paige! Come help! Berger...
I can't believe my mom's car can fly.
I don't think I can stop it.

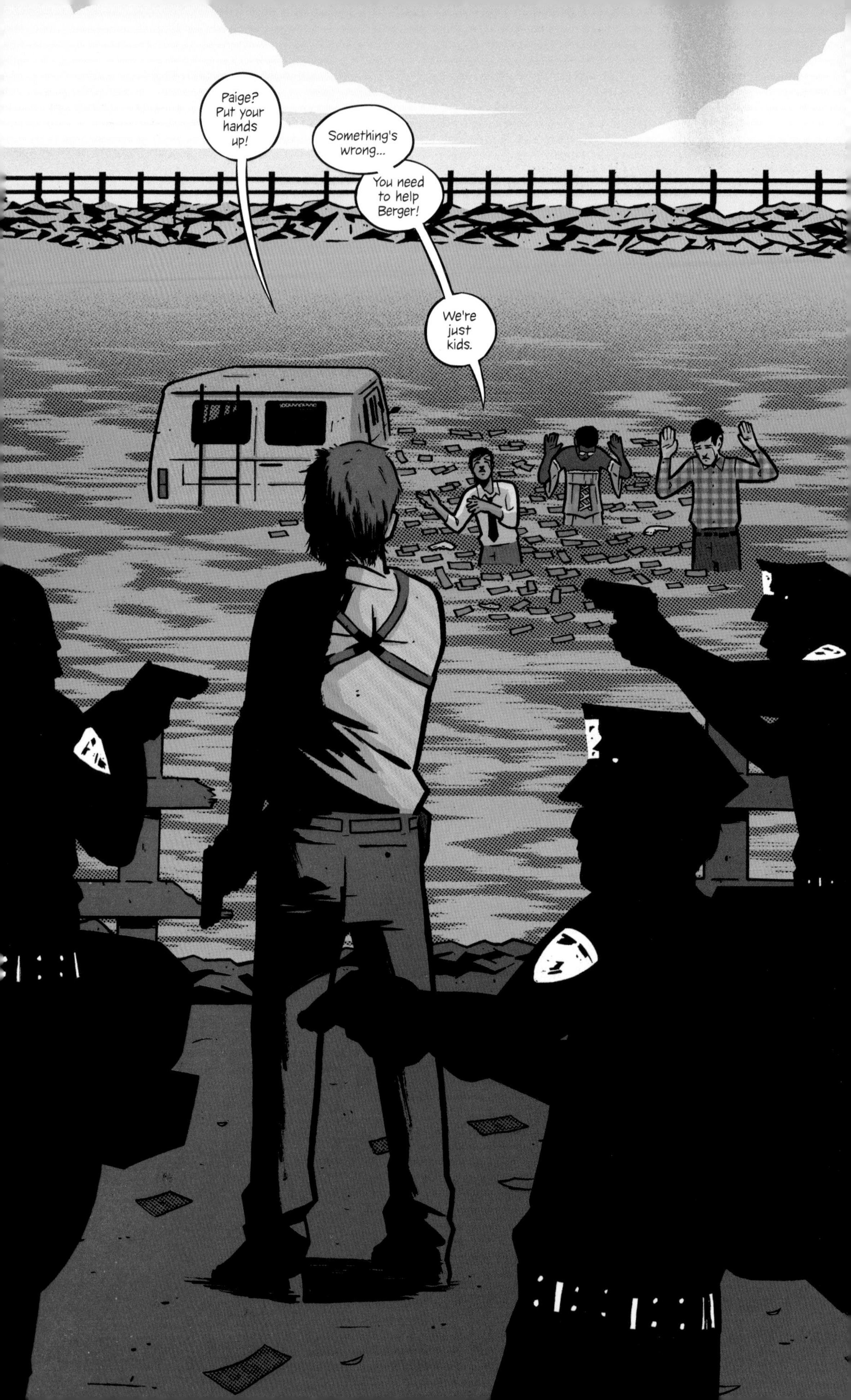
Paige? Put your hands up!
Something's wrong...
You need to help Berger!
We're just kids.

LATER

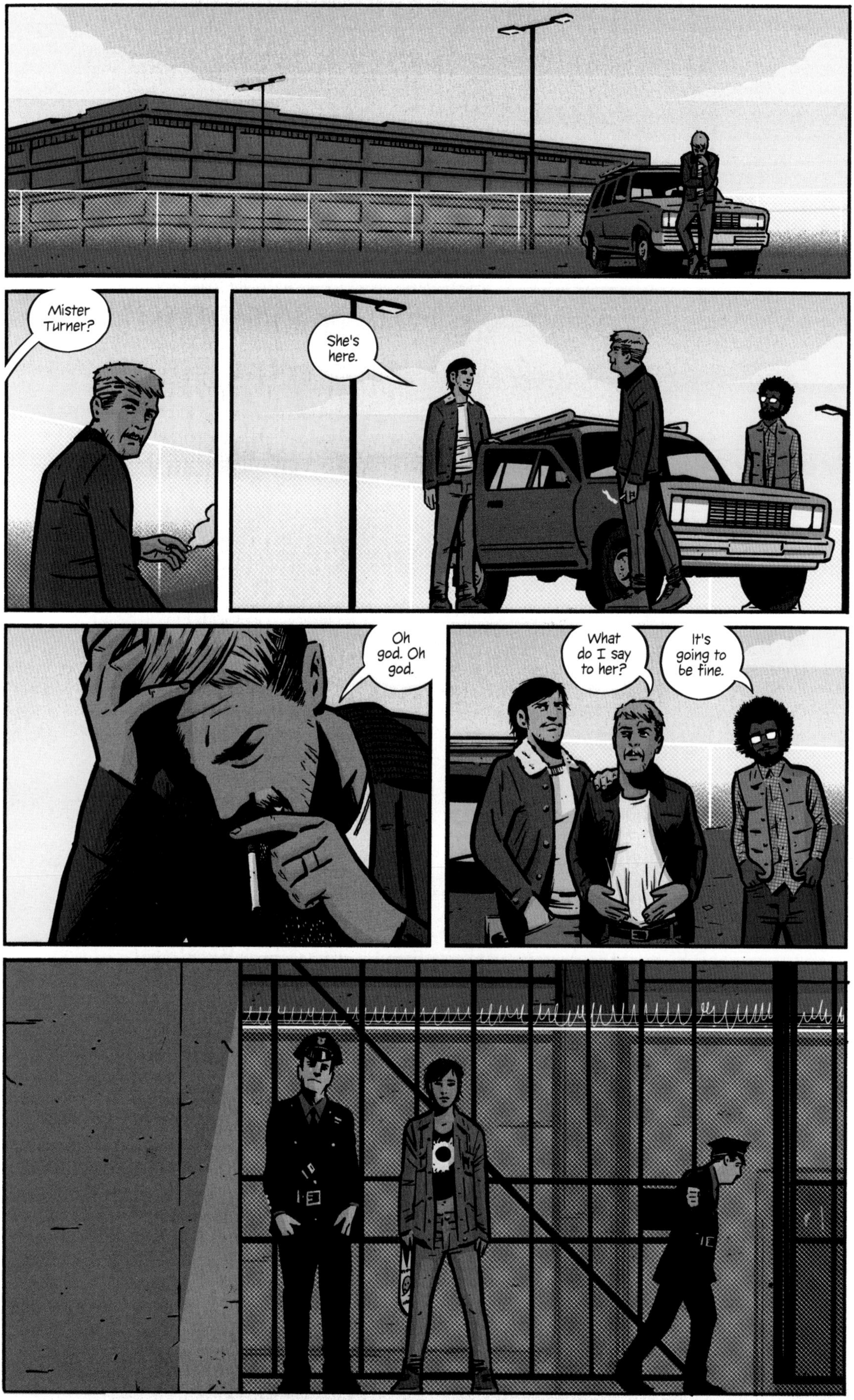
Mister Turner?
She's here.
Oh god. Oh god.
What do I say to her?
It's going to be fine.

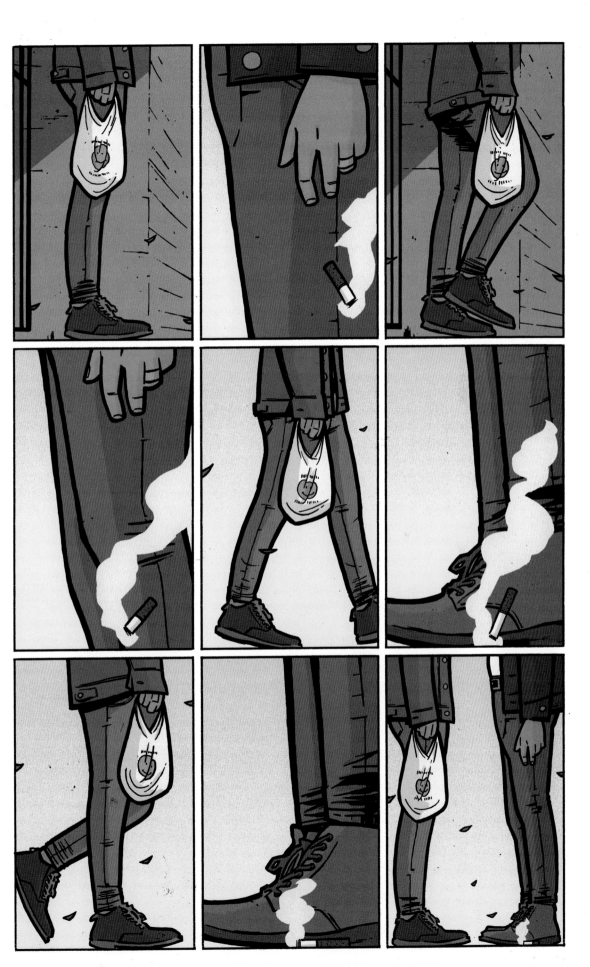

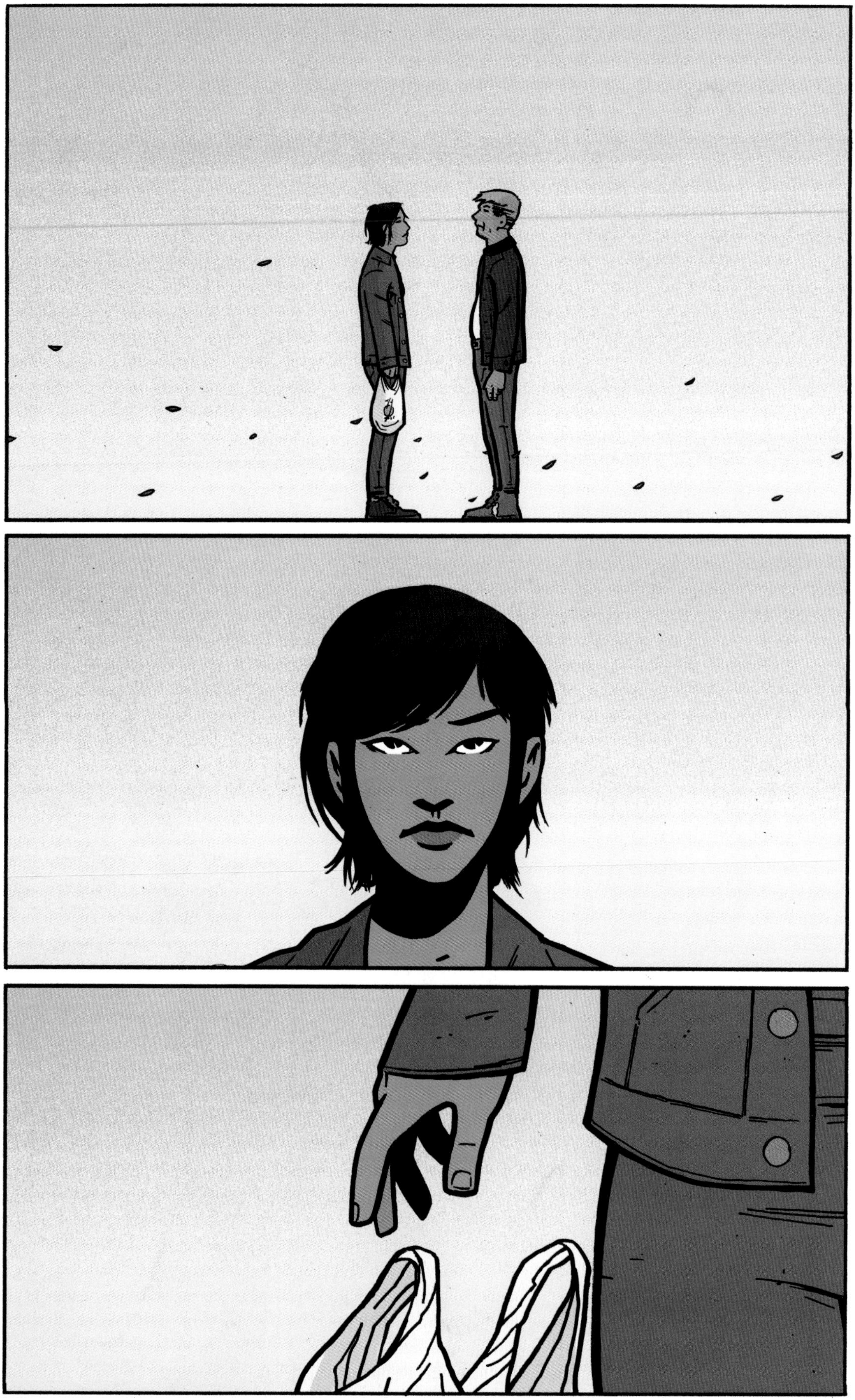

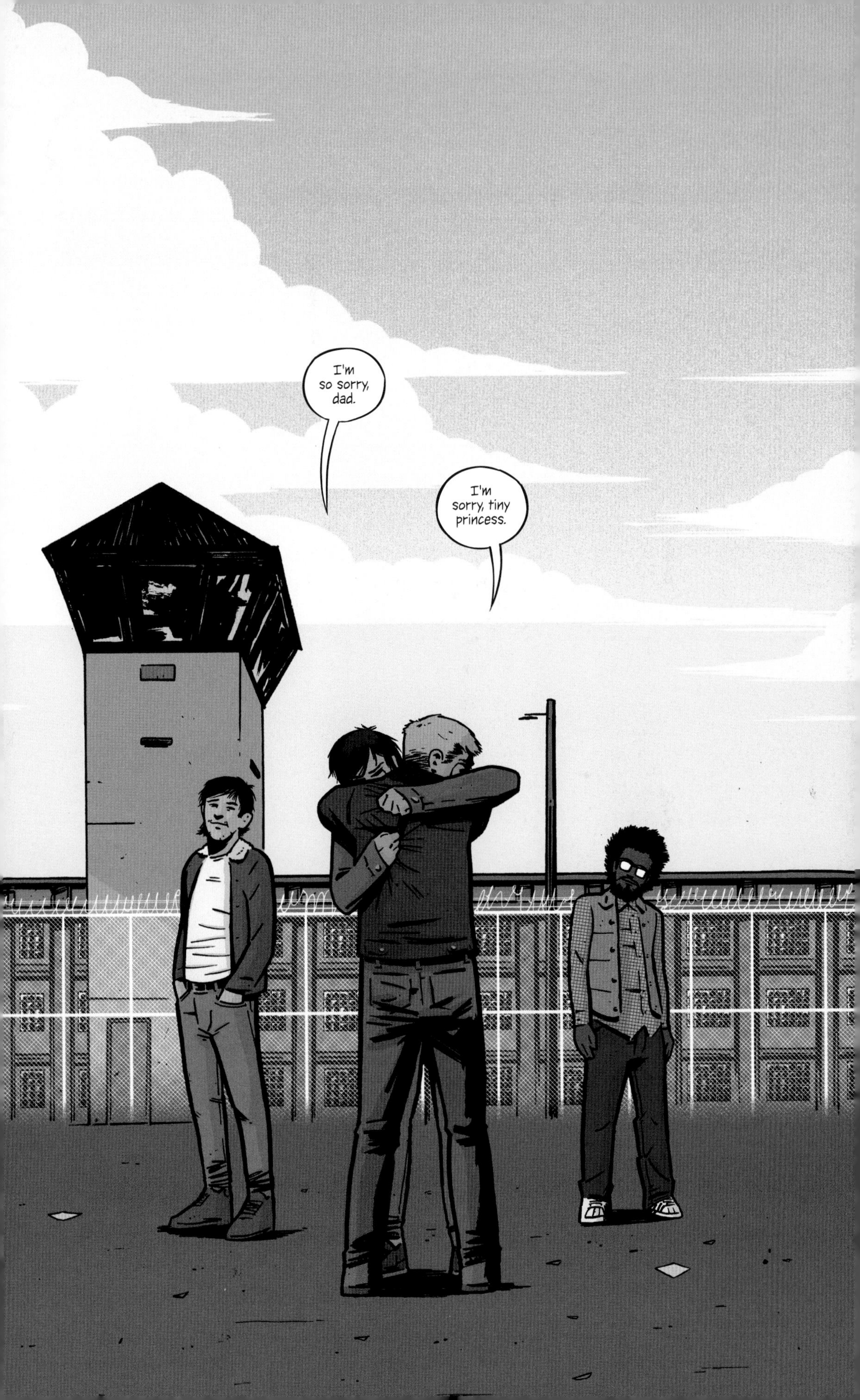
I'm so sorry, dad.
I'm sorry, tiny princess.

THE END

This is the part where we thank everybody who helped us make this book.

Thank you to Matt Pizzolo for agreeing to publish this and working with us on it every step of the way. And thank you to Steve Niles, Brett Gurewitz, and all at Black Mask. We're so proud to be a part of the Black Mask family and all the dysfunction that that entails. Thank you to the friends who let us crash at their houses and agreed to be seen in public with us. To the friends who didn't do those things, it's okay. We get it. Thank you to the squirrel who broke into Matt's apartment and woke him up for New York Comic Con, you're forever in our hearts. Thank you to all of the comic retailers who took a chance on us by suggesting, promoting, and even just carrying this book. Your support and encouragement really does mean the world to us. And sorry. You know why. Thank you to all the serial killers who didn't murder us at any of the sketchy hotels, motels, and airbnbs we stayed at. Thank you to all the comics journalists, podcasters, and bloggers for not making too much fun of us. Thank you to all the readers who picked this up in single issues as it came out on time, every time, for 5 months in a row just like we said it would. Thank you to Orlando Perez for the kick ass trailer. Thank you to the guy in Chicago who told us he loved the book but that the covers are "dog shit." Thank you to Rich Bendel and everyone lucky enough to work for him at The Pleasure Chest. Thank you to the car rental lady who said she was going to get Tyler a good car and then gave him a Jetta. Thank you to Veselka, obviously. Thank you to Robert for being such a sweet/kind person and proving there's still people like that in this world. Thank you to Dan, Matt, Dan, and Pat for not agreeing to be in this book. Thank you to Alex Rubens for the kind words. Thank you to the entire cast of The Sons of Anarchy and the city of Houston for the weirdest weekend of our lives. Thank you to all the writers and directors we brazenly stole things from.

And thank you to the countless comic creators and professionals who gave us nothing but encouragement and support, and we also stole things from. Especially Josh Hood, Amancay Nahuelpan, Josh Hixson, Dylan Magwood, Kristen Gudsnuk, Morgan Shay, Klaus Janson, David Mazzucchelli, Patrick Kindlon, Kieron Gillen, David Walker, Brian K. Vaughan, James Tynion IV, Frank Barbiere, Ed Brisson, Christopher Sebela, Greg Rucka, Scott Snyder, Brian Level, Josh Williamson, Vita Ayala, Ed Brubaker, Kyle Starks, Ryan Ferrier, Michael Walsh, Alex Paknadel, Ramon Villalobos, Gerry Duggan, Brandon Montclare, Steve Orlando, Tini Howard, Nick Spencer, Michael Moreci, Sam Johns, Ryan Cady, Charles Soule, Tony Patrick, James Asmus, Jim Zazzle, Eric Palicki, and our guardian angel- Curt Pires. Thank you for letting us be a part of this community.

Additionally Matt would like to thank Philip and Charlotte for teaching me how to do this thing I love, supporting me so that I could do it, and just generally making sure I didn't die, Mark and Steph for the constant support and encouragement, Claire for putting up with me. And Tyler.

Additionally additionally, Tyler would like to thank his parents for their love and belief in me, Josh for keeping a roof over my head and showing me how to make what seem like bold/illogical decisions, Courtney for literally everything. And Tyler. I mean Matt.

Additionally additionally additionally, Thomas would like to thank his wife for the music and providing initial design critiques, his kids for keeping things fun, and the Maker for always saving Threepio's metallic butt.

A very special thank you to Amanda Scurti for coloring, and Jim Campbell for lettering the first iteration of this book. Without your work this book would never have happened, so thank you from the bottom of our shallow hearts.

And most importantly, thank you to all the real child bank robbers out there for letting us tell your story. It's been an honor and a privilege.

COVER GALLERY

BLACK MASK

A TORRID TALE OF CHILD CRIME

4 KIDS WALK INTO A BANK

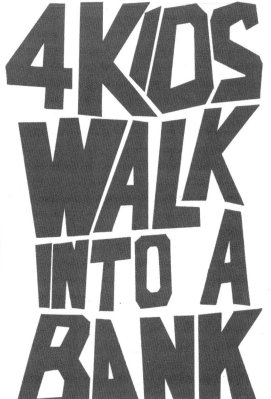

AS TOLD BY
BOSS & MAUER & ROSENBERG

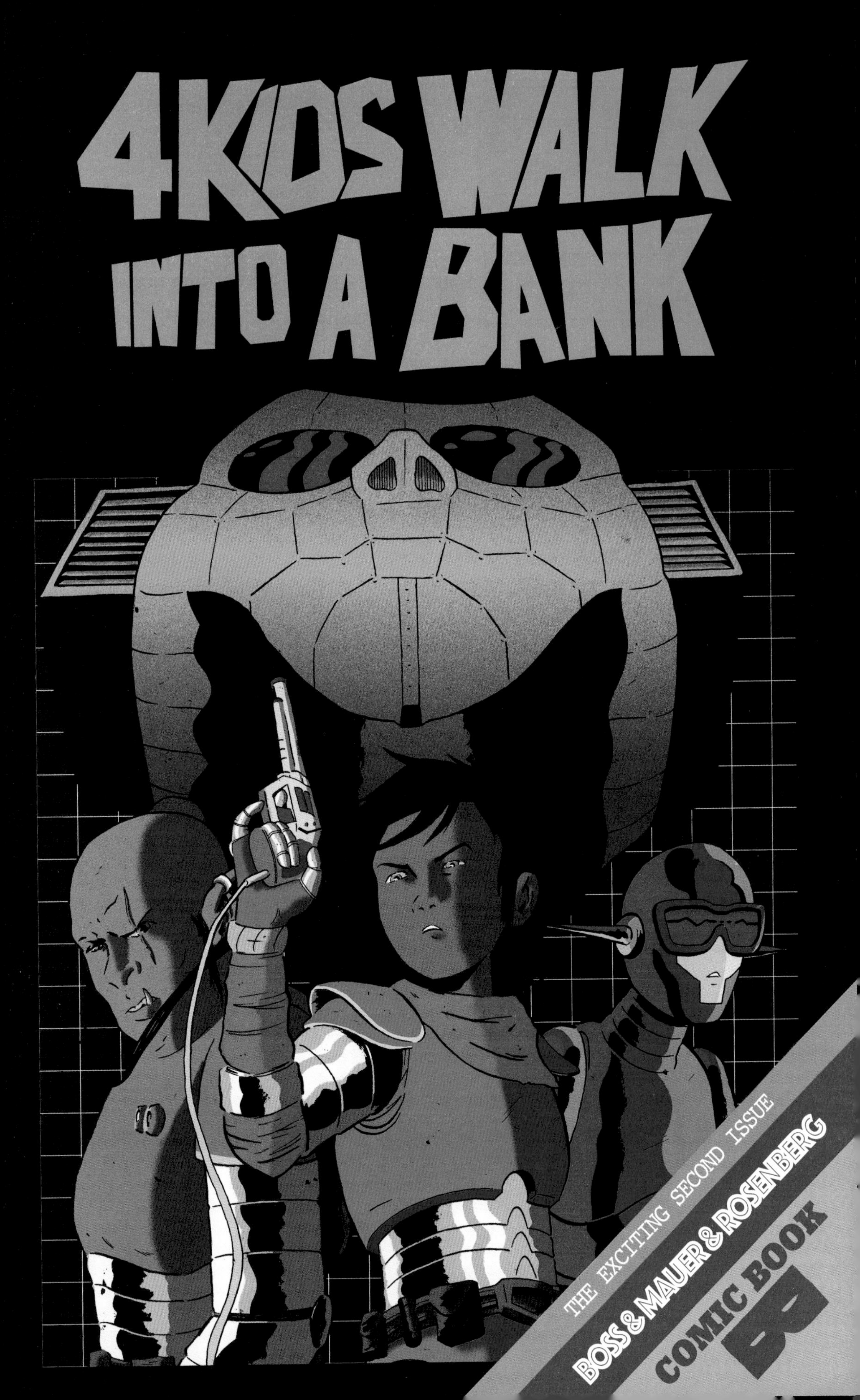
4 KIDS WALK
INTO A BANK
THE EXCITING SECOND ISSUE
BOSS & MAUER & ROSENBERG
COMIC BOOK

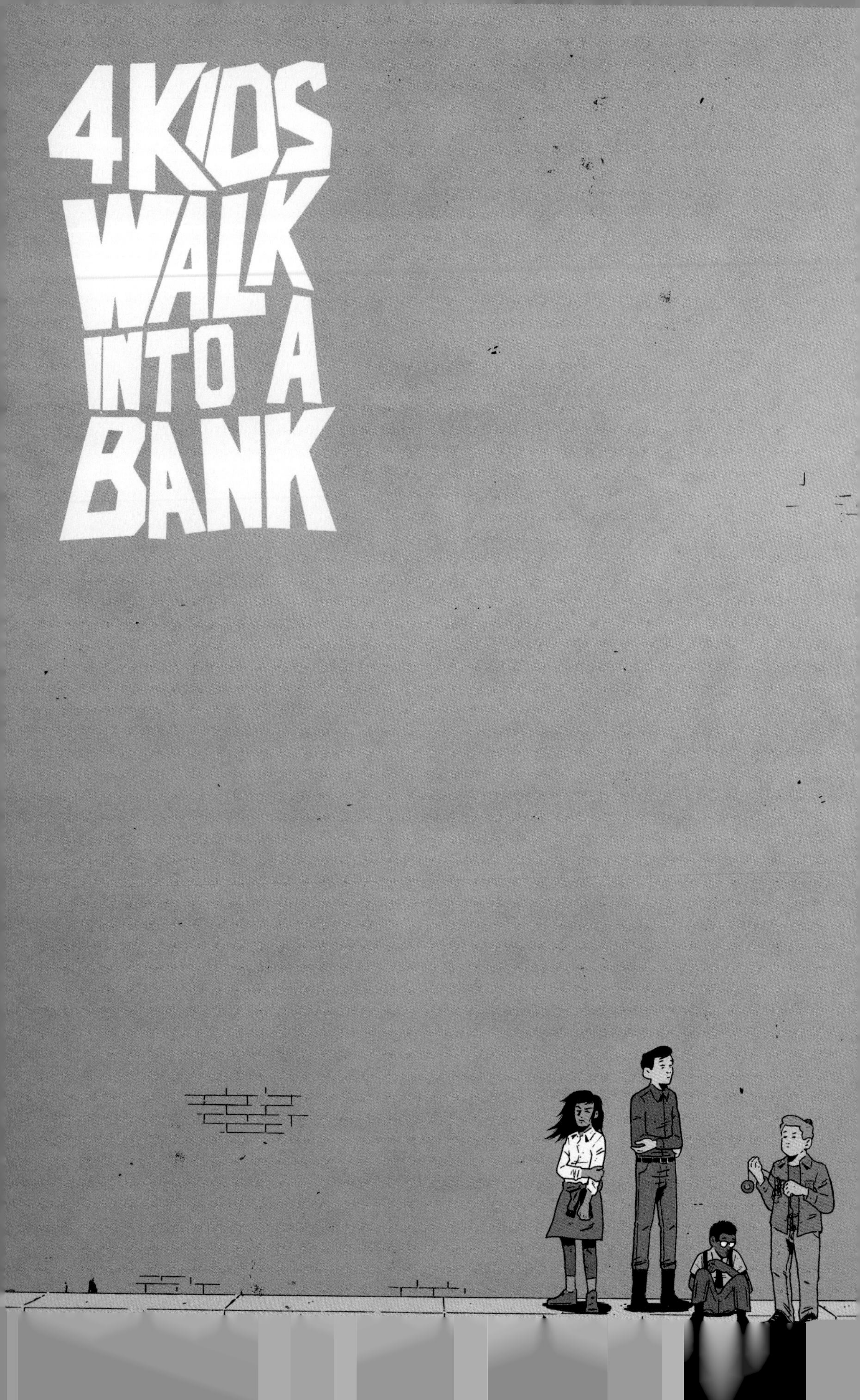
4 KIDS WALK INTO A BANK

BLACK MASK

$3.99

4 KIDS WALK INTO A BANK

BOSS & MAUER & ROSENBERG

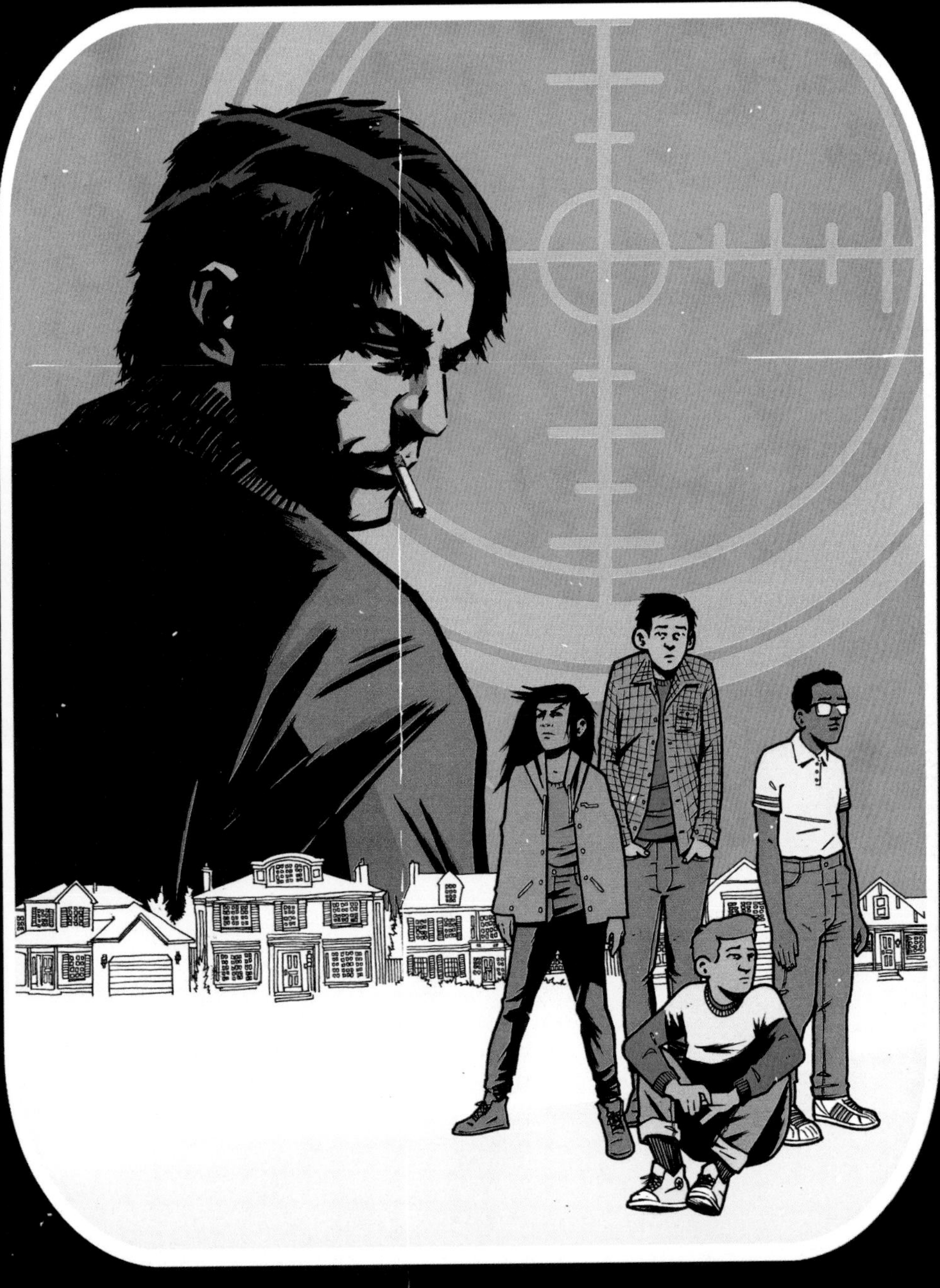

THE COMPLETE FOURTH ISSUE

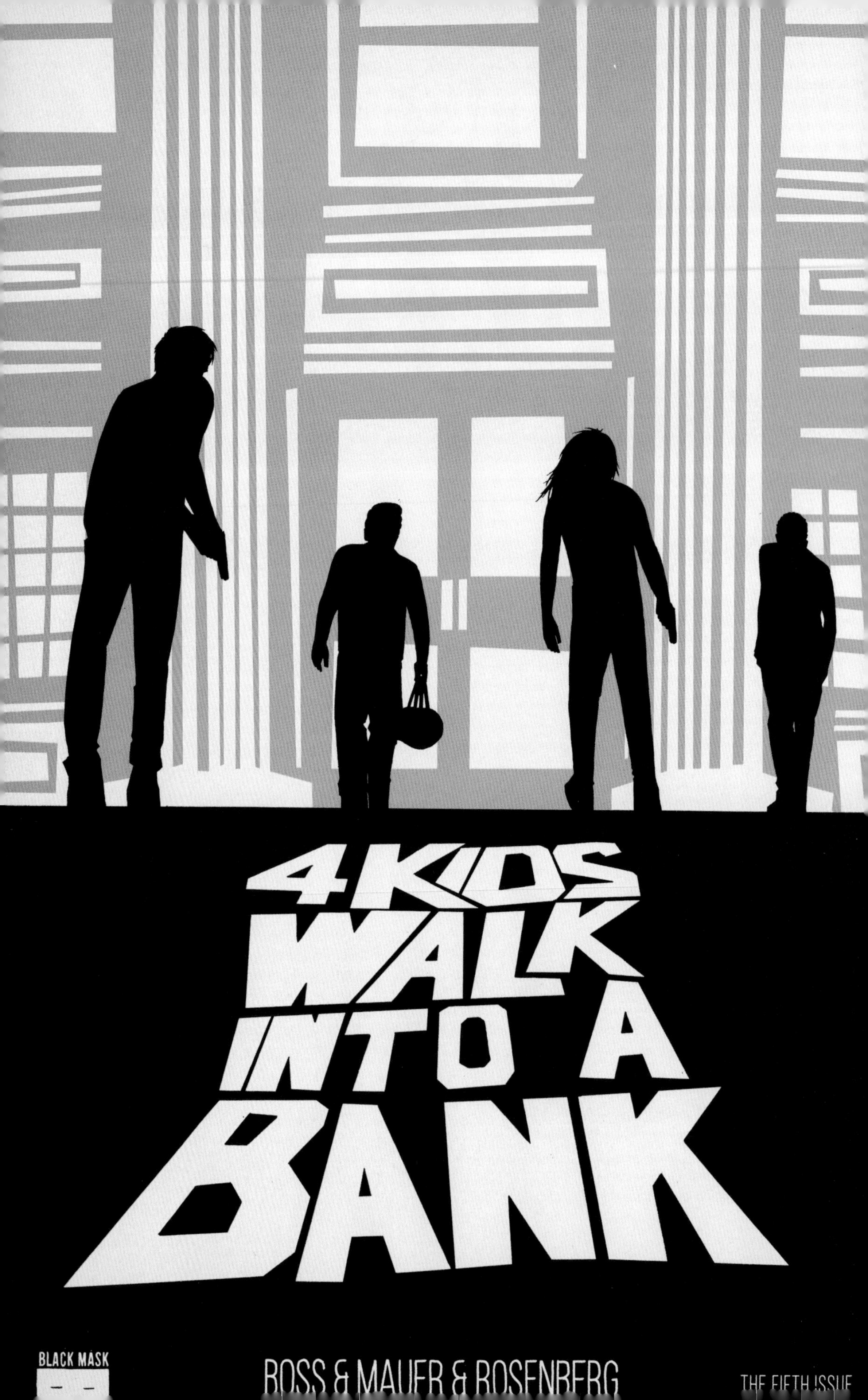
4 KIDS WALK INTO A BANK
BLACK MASK
ROSS & MAUER & ROSENBERG
THE FIFTH ISSUE

BLACK MASK

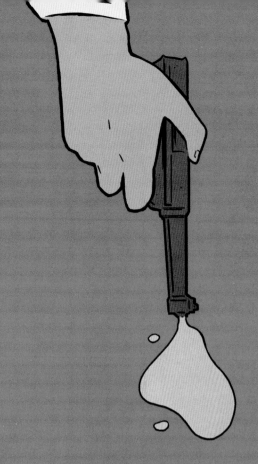

MATTHEW   ROSENBERG
TYLER   BOSS
THOMAS   MAUER

a comic from
Black Mask Studios

4 KIDS
WALK INTO
A BANK

BLACK MASK STUDIOS PRESENTS

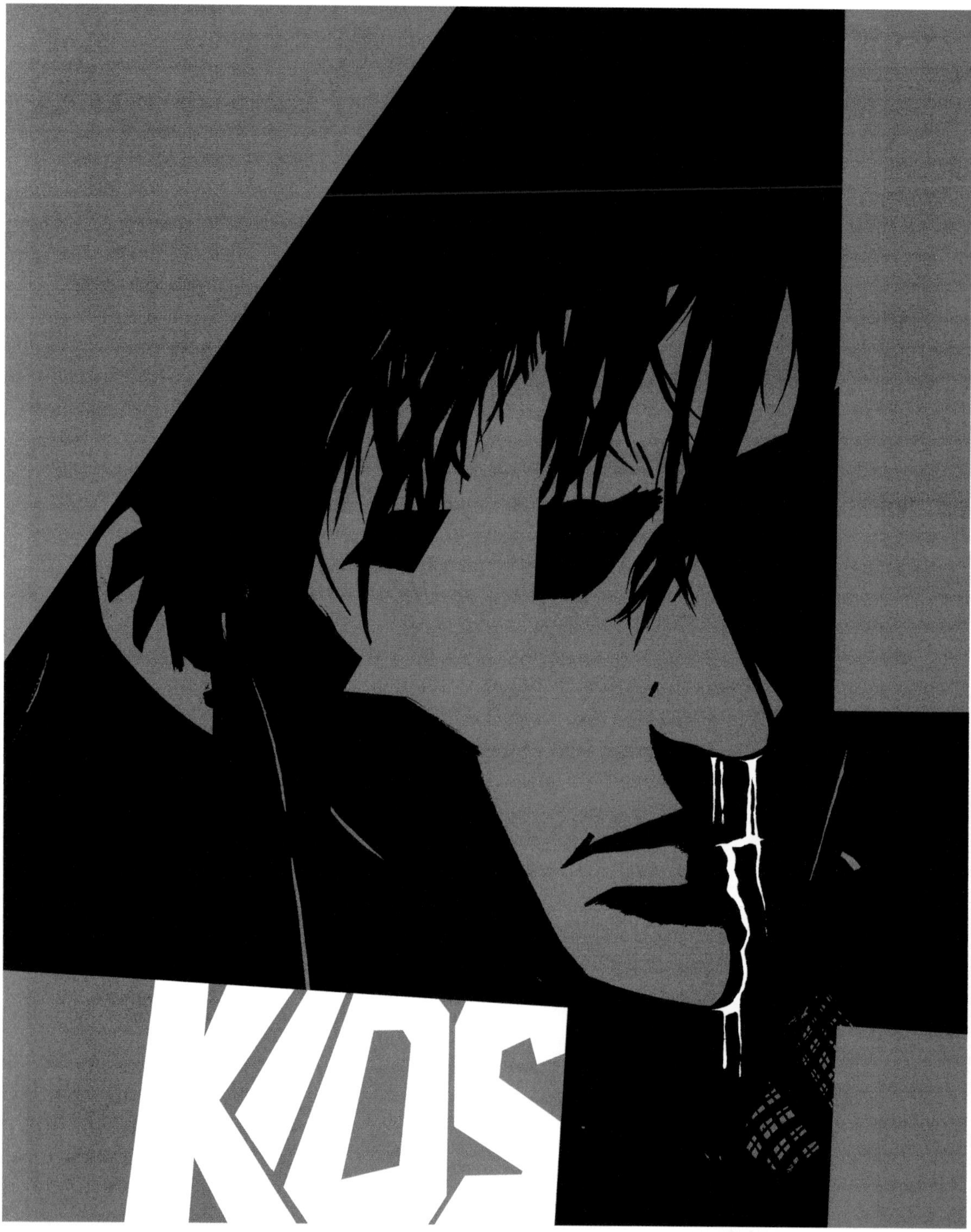
KIDS

WALK INTO A BANK

BLACK MASK

BOSS & MAUER & ROSENBERG

THE FIRST ISSUE

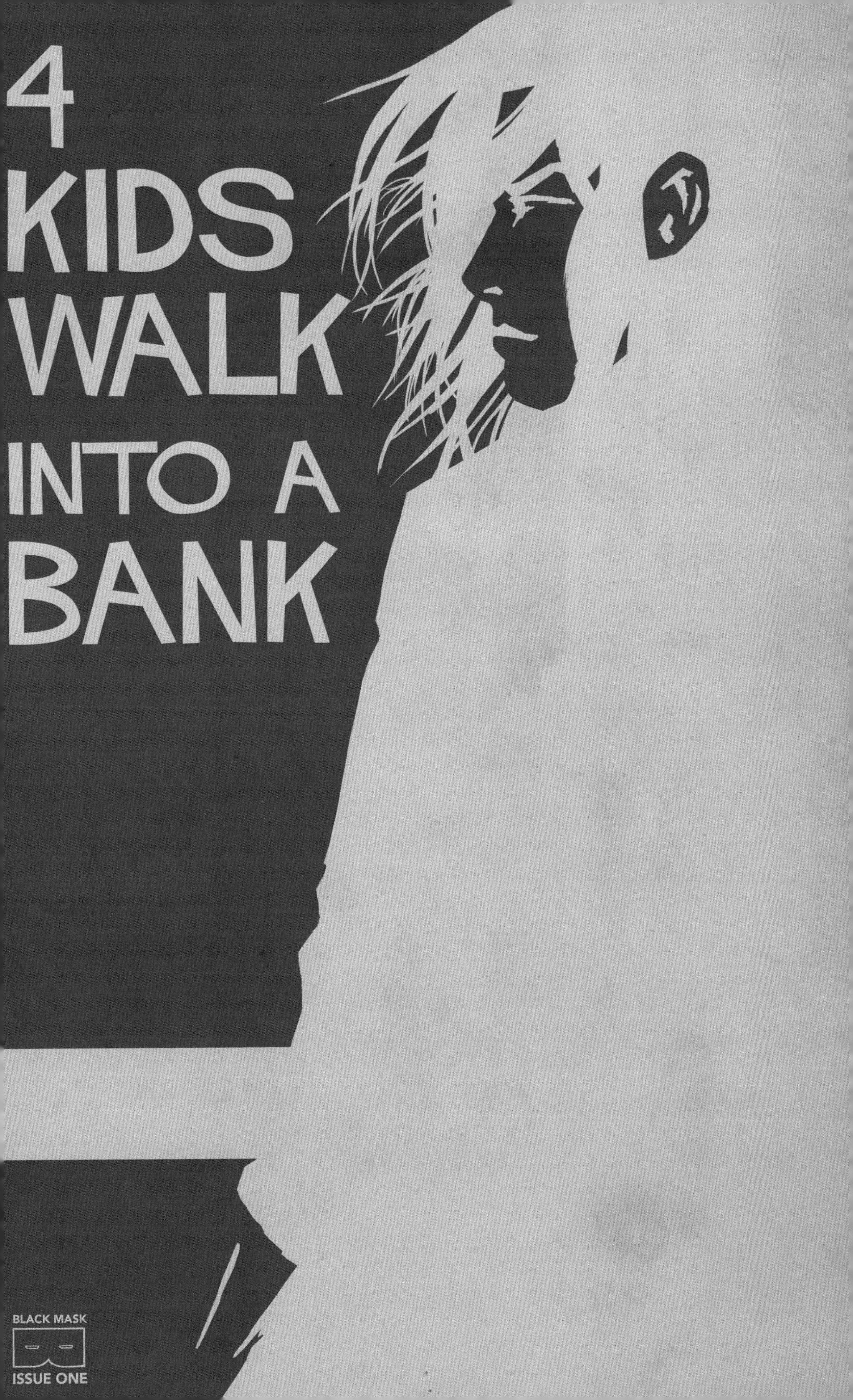
4 KIDS WALK INTO A BANK
BLACK MASK
ISSUE ONE

4 KIDS WALK INTO A BANK

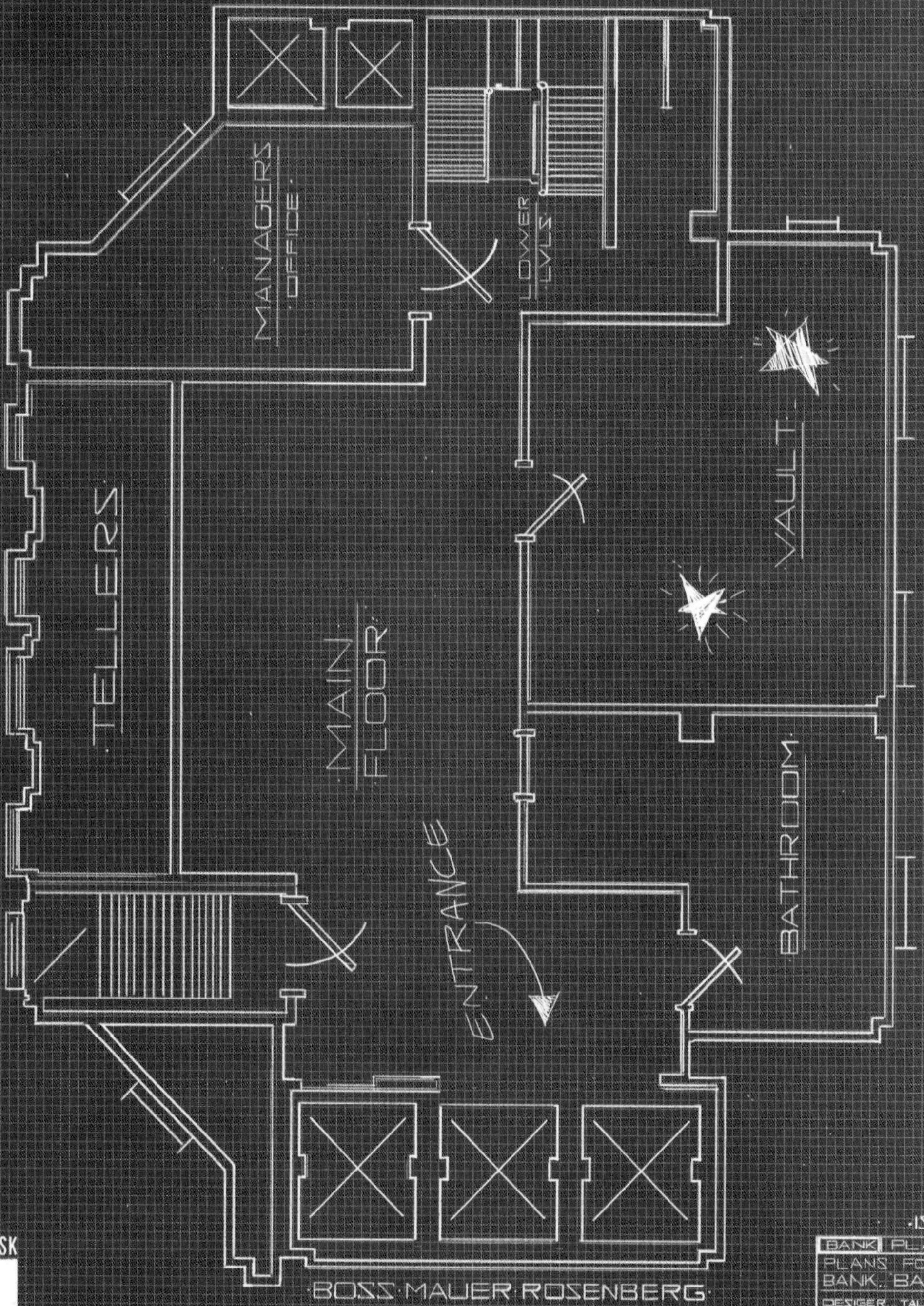
MANAGERS OFFICE
LOWER LVLS
TELLERS
MAIN FLOOR
VAULT
ENTRANCE
BATHROOM

·ISSUE 2·
BANK PLANS
PLANS FOR THE BANK. "BANK"
DESIGER... TAL BASS TB

BLACK MASK

·BOSS·MAUER·ROSENBERG·

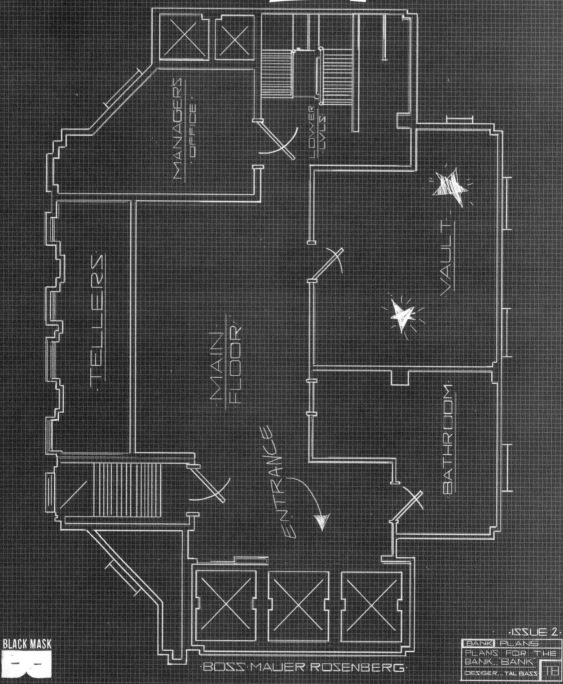

4 KIDS WALK INTO A BANK

BLACK MASK

BOSS & MAUER & ROSENBERG

ISSUE THREE

WHOA! FIRE!!!

Area Creep's House Burns the F Down

LOCAL MAN HATES CHILDREN

By CHASE MAGNETT

Comics readers walk into 4 Kids Walk Into A Bank with high expectations. The cover and title of this series are the best marketing campaign any comic book could ask for. It's an absolutely killer title that beautifully simple premise packed with opportunities for thrills, drama, humor, and fun. Those are six words that when strung together make you want to say, "Tell me more." The cover only enhances that very basic, but very compelling hook. Squirt guns, dice, a heater of a car give you pictures in your head that you want to confirm with this pamphlet. On top of all that, the very first few pages put artist Tyler Boss on display at the top of his form. He's someone whose style and storytelling exhibits a heavy influence from Aja, as well as other current greats like Lieber and Kindt. You know this is the kind of artist you want to start watching now before they explode, taking the lessons learned from those I just mentioned and leaving their own stamp on American comics.

All of that promise is what makes 4 Kids Walk Into A Bank not just disappointing, but downright frustrating. There's no excuse for this comic to be as bad as it is, but by the time that last page is turned it's very clear this is not simply different from the comic being promised at the start, but something that lacks the merits to promise much of anything.

The first half of the issue is a showcase for Boss. He displays a deft hand at panel layouts, regularly combining 7 to 13 in a single page without making it feel dense or overwhelming. There is a rhythm to these early pages as well, moving from a tightly packed string of action and humor panels to something wider, never stringing the most information-heavy pages together. The craftsmanship is clear in these early moments as the titular four kids play Dungeons & Dragons and break the game up over spilt Fanta.

Boss also exhibits a clear grasp of the most effective element in writer Matthew Rosenberg's script, the relationship between these four children. There's a smart alecky nature to them that only 11 and 12 year old possess in this certain way. They possess camaraderie based in geographic circumstance, but that forms into a much deeper loyalty. These are the only friends they have, so they will damn well stand by one another. It's these implied connections and jovial mish-mash of rivalries and affection that make these opening pages tick. Boss doesn't overplay emotions or moments, instead utilizing the fewest lines possible to convey each action and reaction effectively. It's crisp and it works.

At least, until it doesn't.

As the concept heightens and the criminals arrive, the cracks begin to appear. The use of humorous captions with D&D style stats to introduce the heroes of the story twice already are used again, and then again to introduce the villains. Words fill up the page and cover up a brief moment of action in an attempt for humor in what should be a very tense moment. Writing begins to cover up what was most effective about Boss'

AN ARTICLE

storytelling, while adding nothing of value to the story.

Rosenberg's script pushes itself to be more clever than it is. Three distinct elements add up to a slingshot to the eye in a funny sequence, but each element is overwritten with descriptions that are far too precious. Rather than allowing the story to be told sequentially, the script attempts to catch the reader in each moment of what is designed to function as a rapid fire joke. There's so much dialogue on these pages that small bits of style and nuance are lost in effectively moving through the exchange. A panel of three kids shouting "Cool!" while the fourth vomits is placed at the center of a page, but there is not enough space for Boss to effectively provide reactions outside of the speech bubbles or vomit.

This bit is troubled, but it isn't broken like the second half of 4 Kids Walk Into A Bank. All of the bad tendencies surfacing in this scene become a pace-breaking, plot-destroying,

art-wrecking whirlwind of disaster throughout the final 15 pages of the issue. There are no less than five pages that function as static shots of talking heads for anywhere between 9 and 24 panels. The amount of dialogue packed into the back half of 4 Kids Walk Into A Bank #1 weighs so heavily on the issue that it reads as though it were a vast majority of the 28-page comic book. What was once fun and fast becomes a slog to get through with none of the visual hooks to precede it.

Three of the densest page rely on a 24 panel grid that features only shots of different heads as they go back and forth (although one opens with six of the panels merged). These create an interminable reading experience. Two character use an entire page to sling single-word insults at one another in a joke that goes from unfunny to exasperating and never gets any better. Not only is it a waste of valuable page space, but it brings the comic to a sudden halt. The manner in which these insults are slung doesn't even bother to imitate

SEX AND VIOLENCE? SURE.

By PABLO ARRIAGA

Four nerds met some evil adults. Such adults won't leave them alone, it's time to make them. If they can (sort of) take on their stupid bullies, they can go against a convicted criminal or four. 4 Kids Walk Into A Bank #2 has the Paige, Berger, Stretch, and Walter orbiting back into the lives of horrible people they can't seem to get rid of by conventional means.

Tyler is in full command of his craft with this book, he seems to be aware of every corner of his panels and use them to fully express what happens page to page. His style allows me to stop on every one of the panels rather than having one immediately transition into the next one, with conventional layouts of paneling for the most part, this comic would run the risk of becoming stoic from page to page. Instead, Boss shows the quality of his craft and finds the perfect moment that can be depicted on each panel to make each stop most enjoyable. A kid trying to mess with Paige and 4 Kids Walk Into A Bank 2her gang gets exactly what he's been asking for and Boss' clear joy to depict that is transmitted through the page only to be accentuated by Rosenberg's clear understanding of the dialogs from each character.

Rosenberg's command of characters has been put to the test for two issues now. Reading issue #1, I was scared of the two pages filled with talking heads, fearing that he might just go into a full Bendis territory with a lot of words and little to say. Instead, it proved to be a delightful read resulting in audible laughter in public places. Every line serves the purpose to further the story or accentuate a character and grow the attachment to them. He charmed his way into my heart the same way watching The Sandlot or Stand By Me did in their time.

Boss' design chops are also showcased in this issue as well. The changes in layouts for some sequences that serve as a tell for a well studied person on the likes of Chris Ware and shifting for other into more cartoon-like influences for other. This is an artist who's shown up to serve the story.

4 Kids Walk Into A Bank #2 has a very unique charm that's uncommon in comics of recent, thus becoming another assured hit from Black Mask Studios as one of the best series this week, and one of the best series overall.

This review needed to be a paragraph longer to fill the space on this cover but it isn't so I will continue typing nonsense until it's filled. Are you enjoying this or isn't just super annoying? I'm sure it... I'm annoyed with

BOSS & MAUER & ROSENBERG

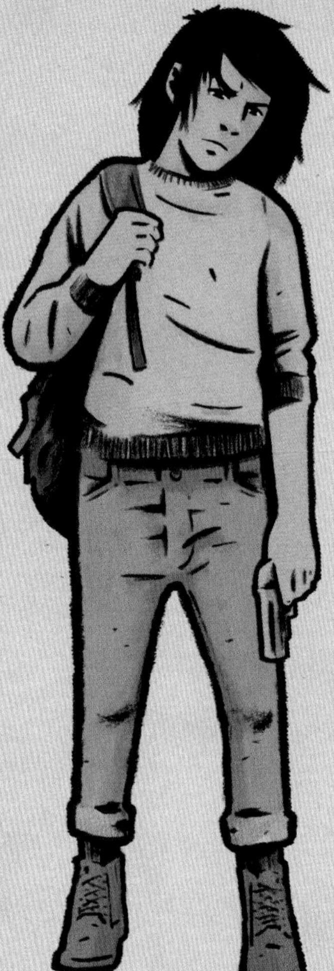

ISSUE

FOUR

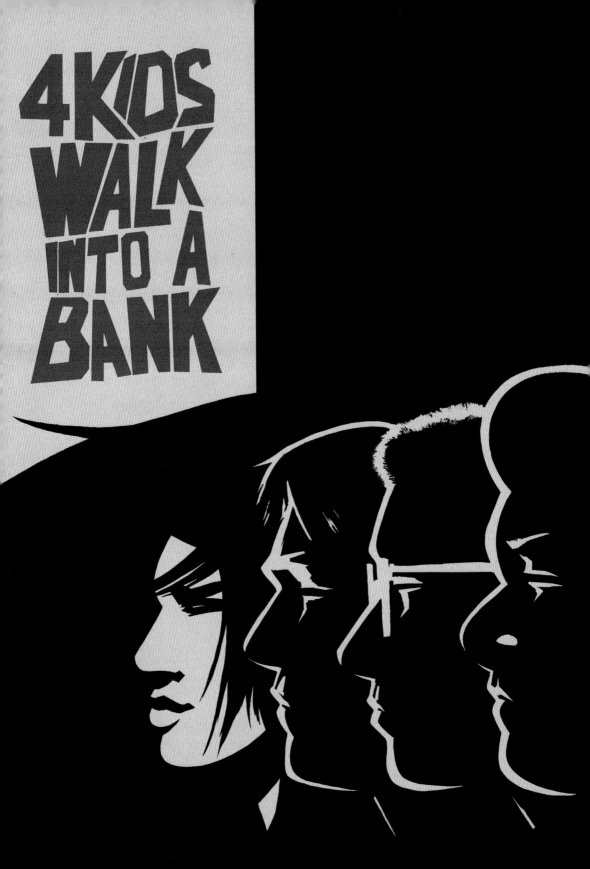

4 KIDS WALK INTO A BANK

BLACK MASK

BOSS & MAUER & ROSENBERG

THE FIFTH ISSUE

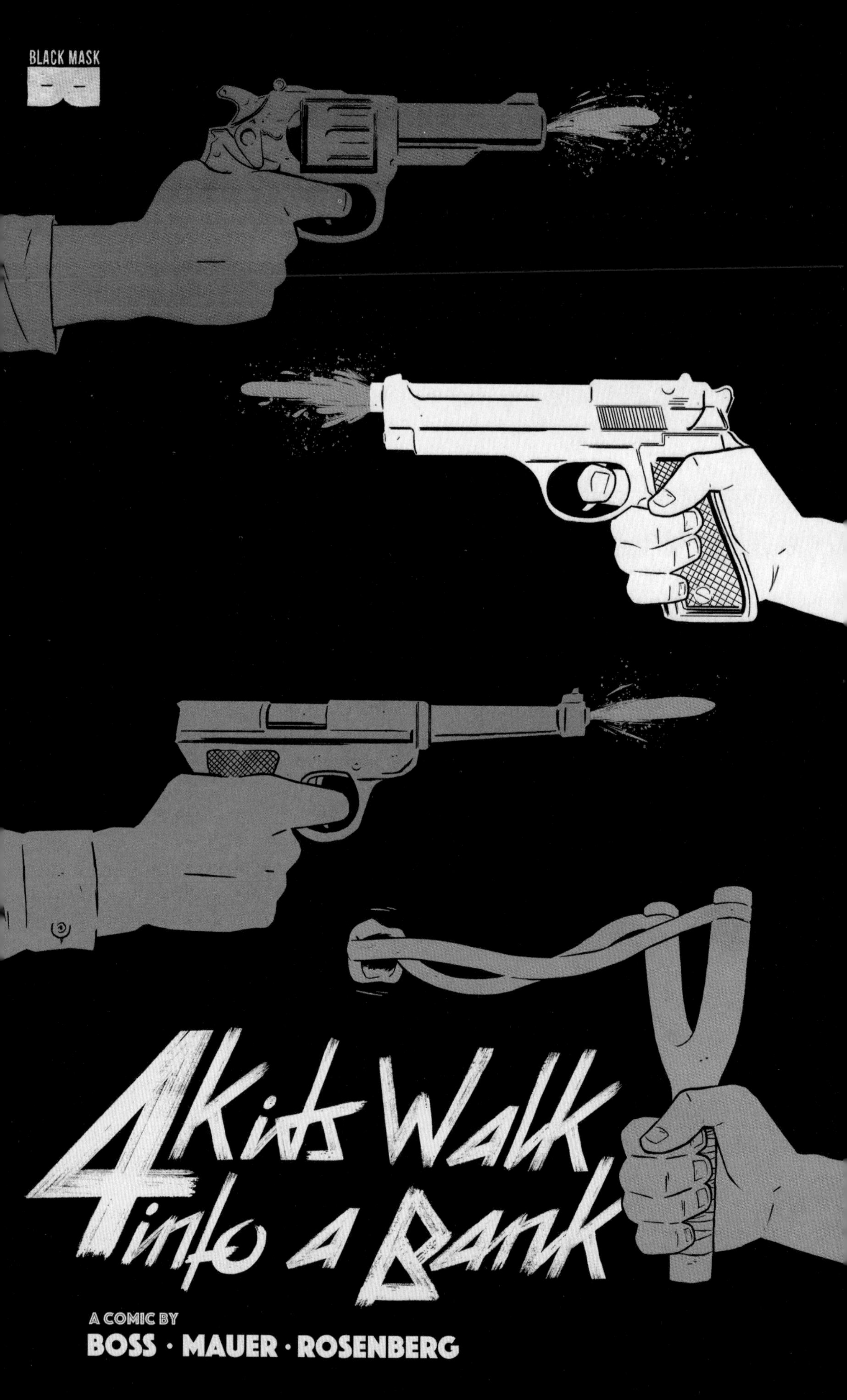
BLACK MASK
4 Kids Walk into a Bank
A COMIC BY
BOSS · MAUER · ROSENBERG

BY COURTNEY MENARD

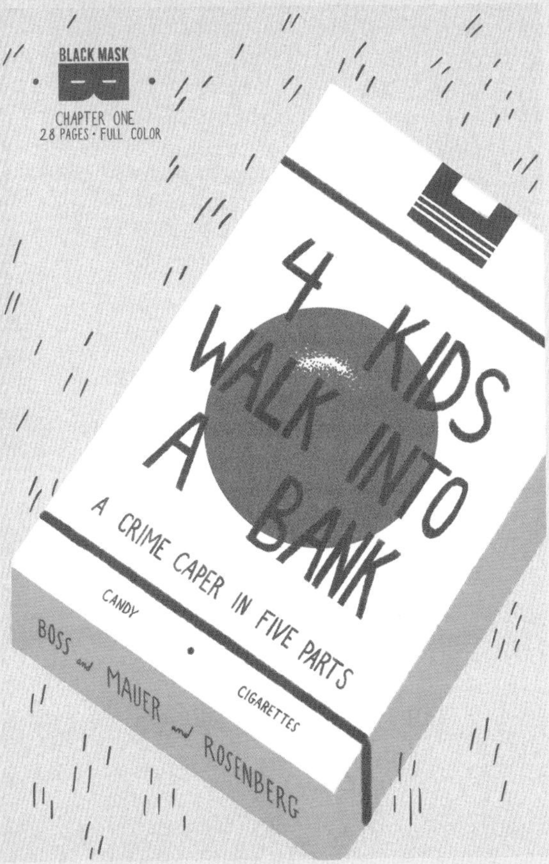
BLACK MASK
CHAPTER ONE
28 PAGES • FULL COLOR
4 KIDS WALK INTO A BANK
A CRIME CAPER IN FIVE PARTS
CANDY
CIGARETTES
BOSS and MAUER and ROSENBERG

BY COURTNEY MENARD

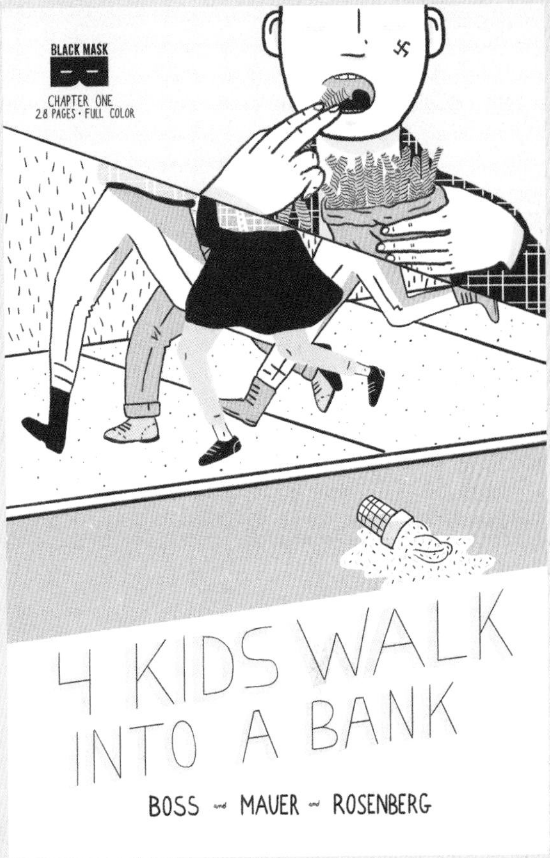
BLACK MASK
CHAPTER ONE
28 PAGES • FULL COLOR
4 KIDS WALK INTO A BANK
BOSS and MAUER and ROSENBERG

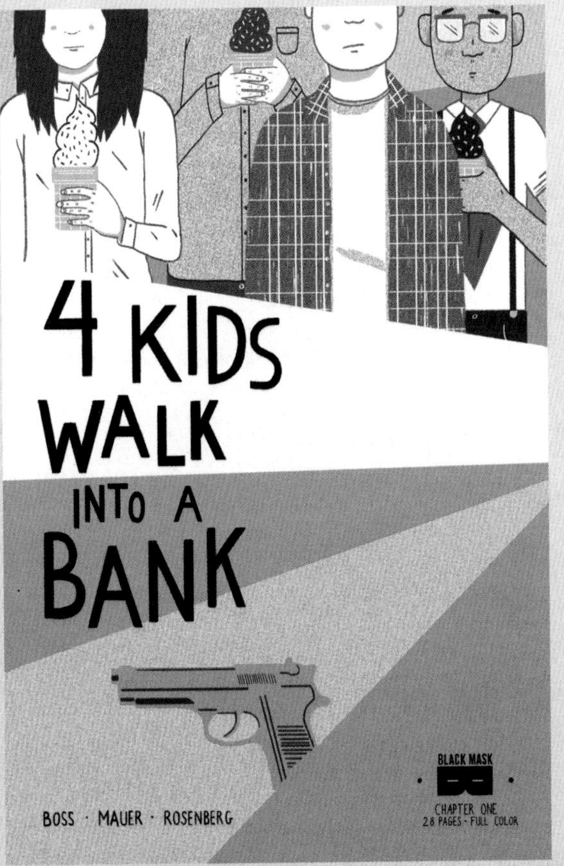
4 KIDS WALK INTO A BANK
BOSS · MAUER · ROSENBERG
BLACK MASK
CHAPTER ONE
28 PAGES • FULL COLOR

BY COURTNEY MENARD

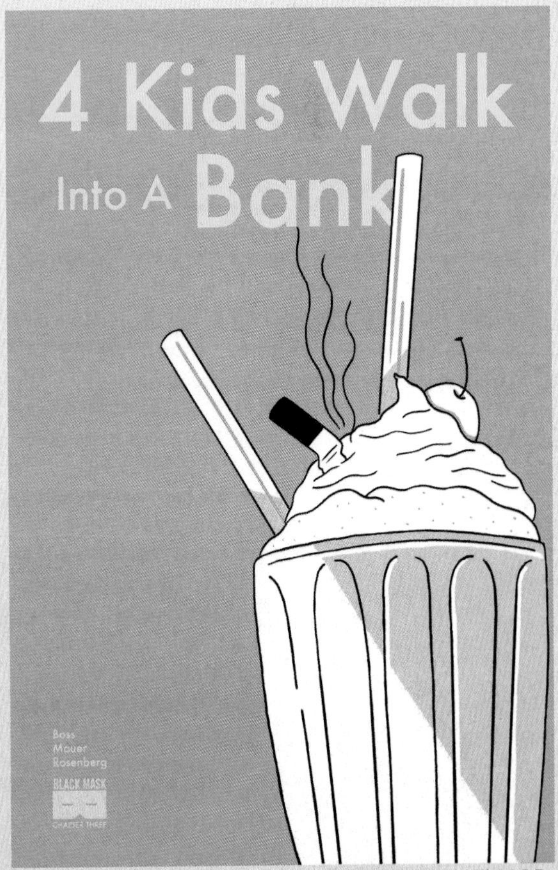
4 Kids Walk Into A Bank
Boss
Mauer
Rosenberg
BLACK MASK

BY COURTNEY MENARD

BY TYLER BOSS

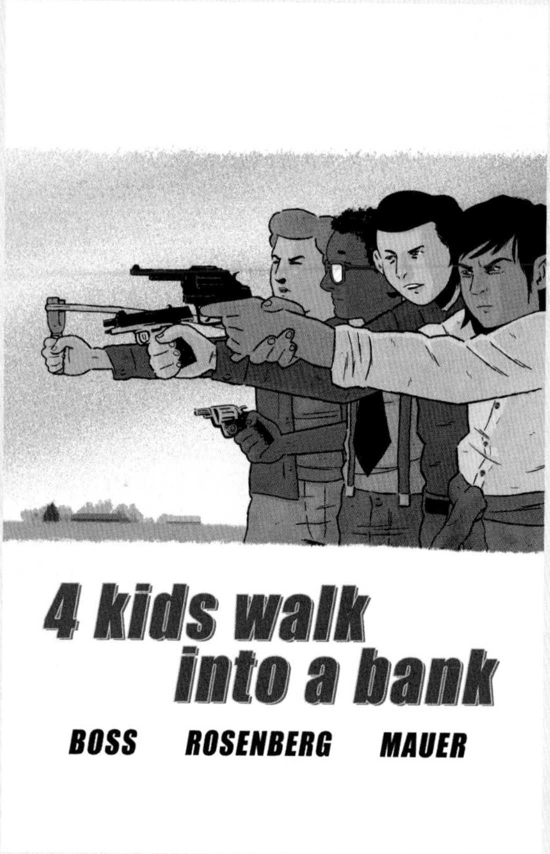

4 kids walk into a bank
BOSS
ROSENBERG
MAUER

BY TYLER BOSS

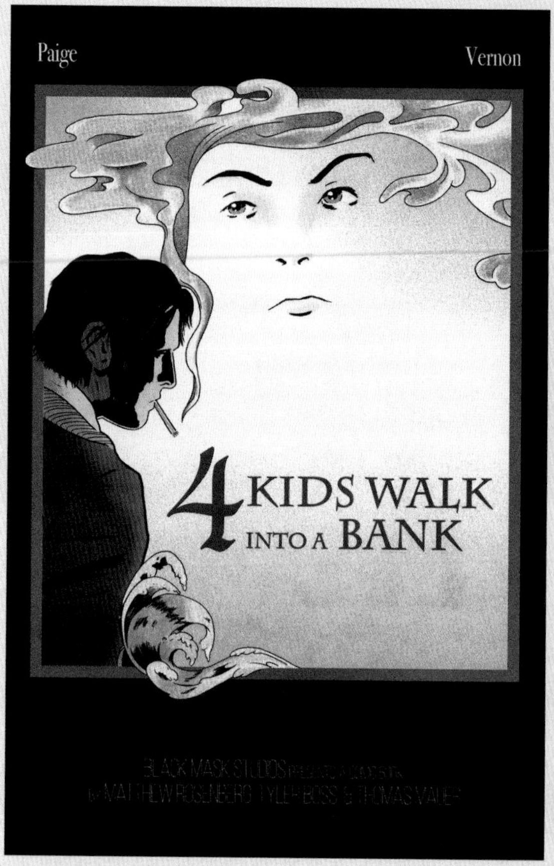

Paige
Vernon
4 KIDS WALK INTO A BANK
BLACK MASK STUDIOS
MATTHEW ROSENBERG TYLER BOSS & THOMAS MAUER

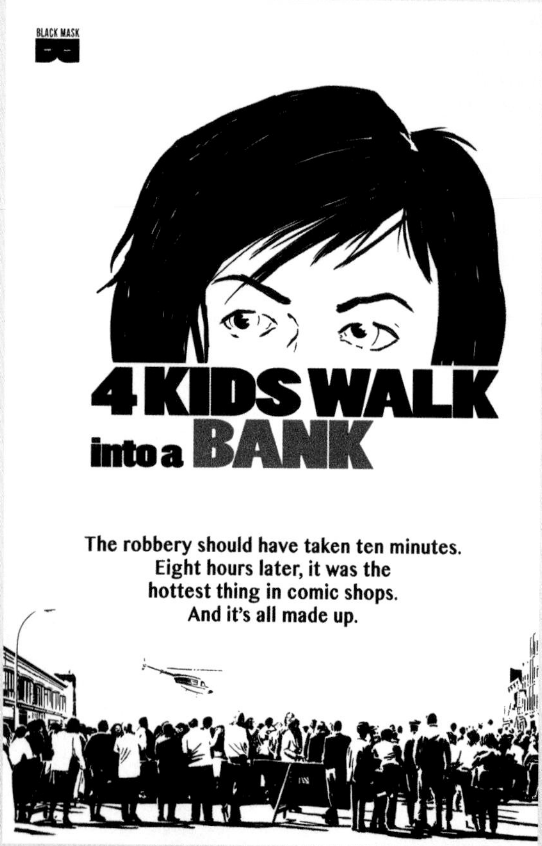

BLACK MASK
4 KIDS WALK into a BANK
The robbery should have taken ten minutes.
Eight hours later, it was the
hottest thing in comic shops.
And it's all made up.

BY TYLER BOSS

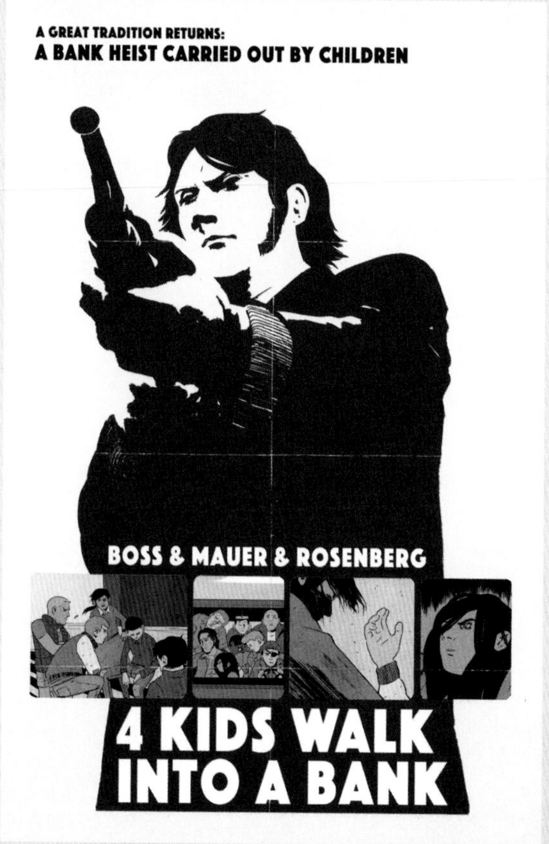

A GREAT TRADITION RETURNS:
A BANK HEIST CARRIED OUT BY CHILDREN
BOSS & MAUER & ROSENBERG
4 KIDS WALK INTO A BANK

BY TYLER BOSS

BY TYLER BOSS

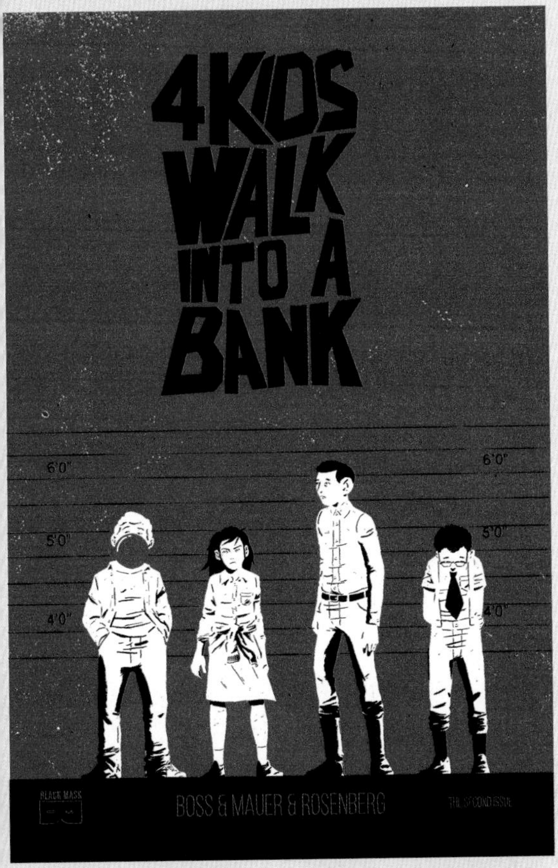
4 KIDS WALK INTO A BANK
6'0"
5'0"
4'0"
6'0"
5'0"
4'0"
BLACK MASK
BOSS & MAUER & ROSENBERG
THE SECOND ISSUE

BY TYLER BOSS

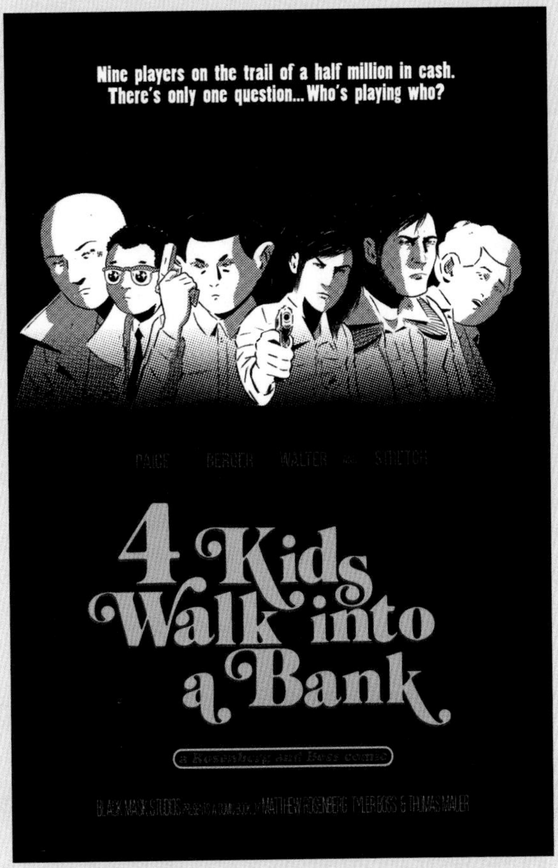
Nine players on the trail of a half million in cash.
There's only one question... Who's playing who?
PAIGE BERGER WALTER STRETCH
4 Kids Walk into a Bank

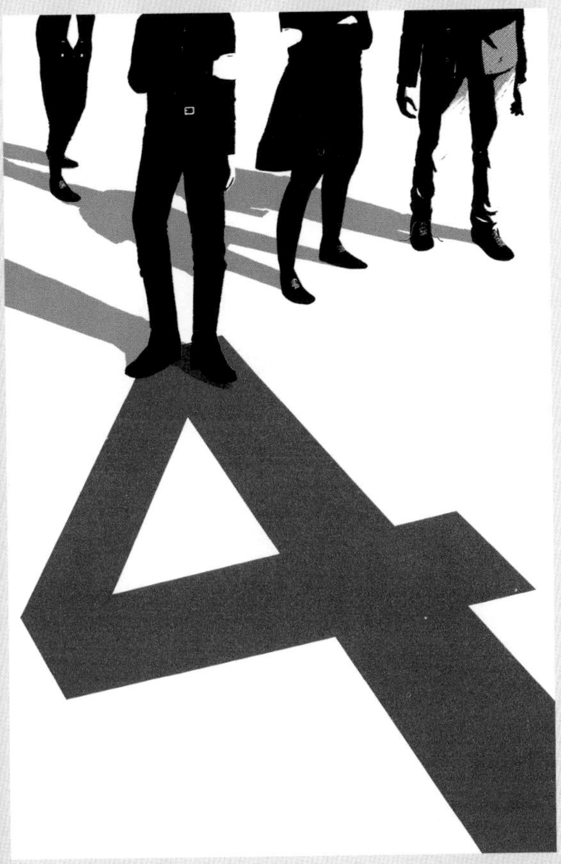

BY TYLER BOSS

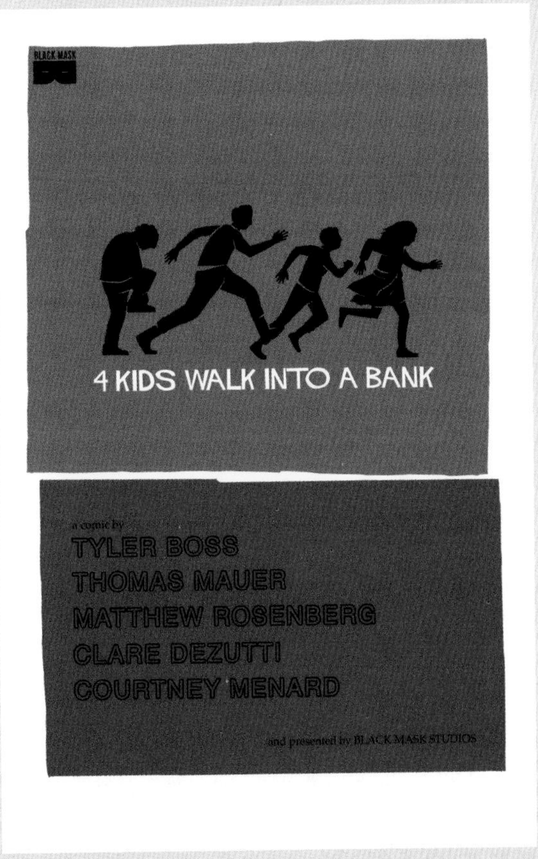
BLACK MASK
4 KIDS WALK INTO A BANK
a comic by
TYLER BOSS
THOMAS MAUER
MATTHEW ROSENBERG
CLARE DEZUTTI
COURTNEY MENARD
and presented by BLACK MASK STUDIOS

BY TYLER BOSS

BY TYLER BOSS

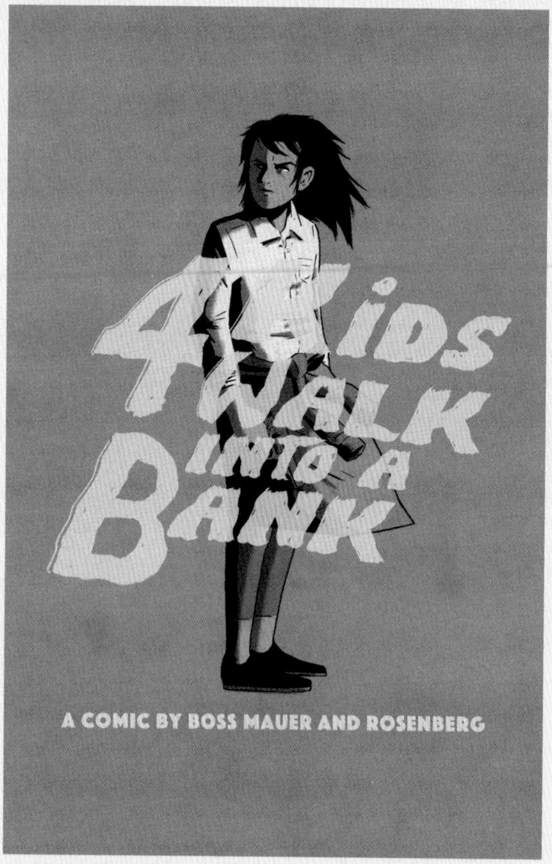
4 KIDS WALK INTO A BANK
A COMIC BY BOSS MAUER AND ROSENBERG

BY DYLAN MAGWOOD

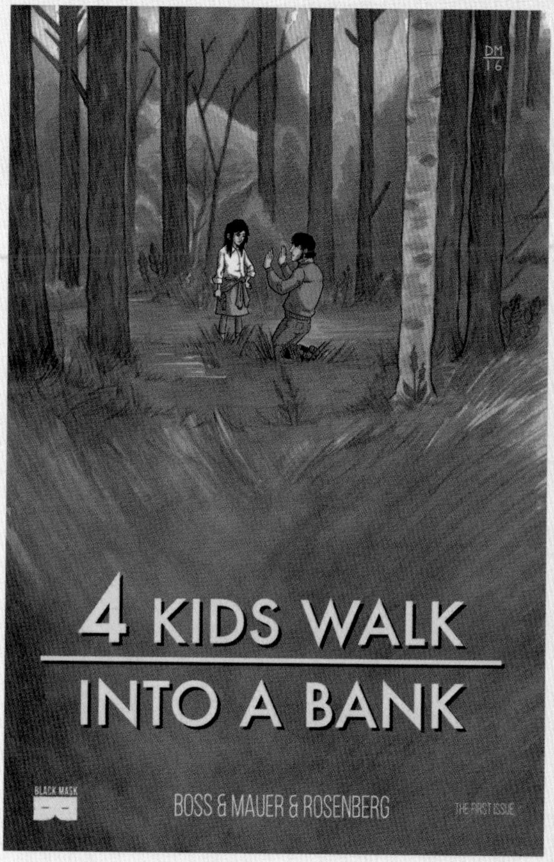
DM 16
4 KIDS WALK
INTO A BANK
BLACK MASK
BOSS & MAUER & ROSENBERG
THE FIRST ISSUE

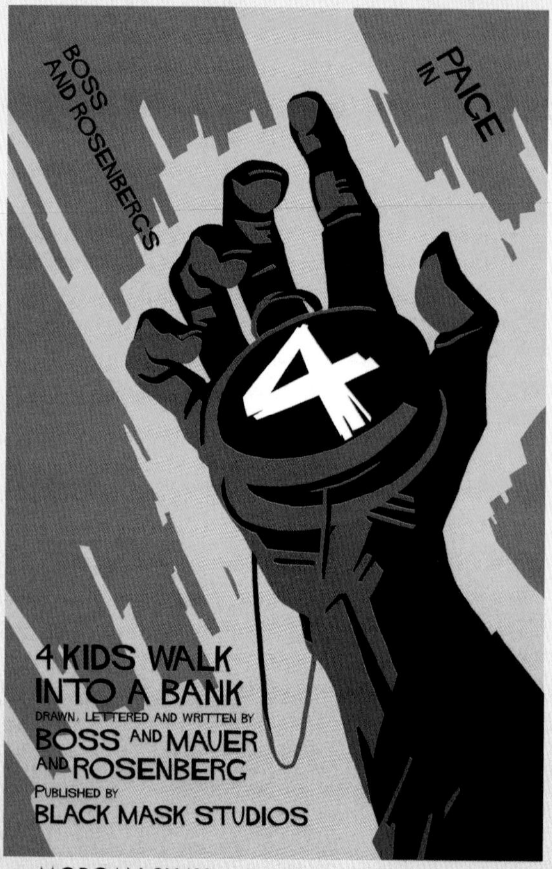
BOSS
AND ROSENBERGS
PAIGE
IN
4
4 KIDS WALK
INTO A BANK
DRAWN, LETTERED AND WRITTEN BY
BOSS AND MAUER
AND ROSENBERG
PUBLISHED BY
BLACK MASK STUDIOS

BY MORGAN SHAY

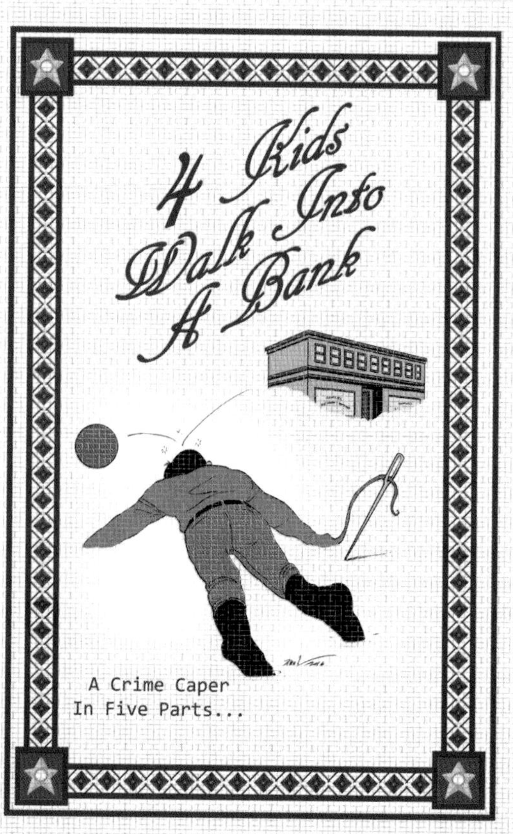
4 Kids
Walk Into
A Bank
A Crime Caper
In Five Parts...

BY AMANCAY NAHUELPAN

BY AMANCAY NAHUELPAN

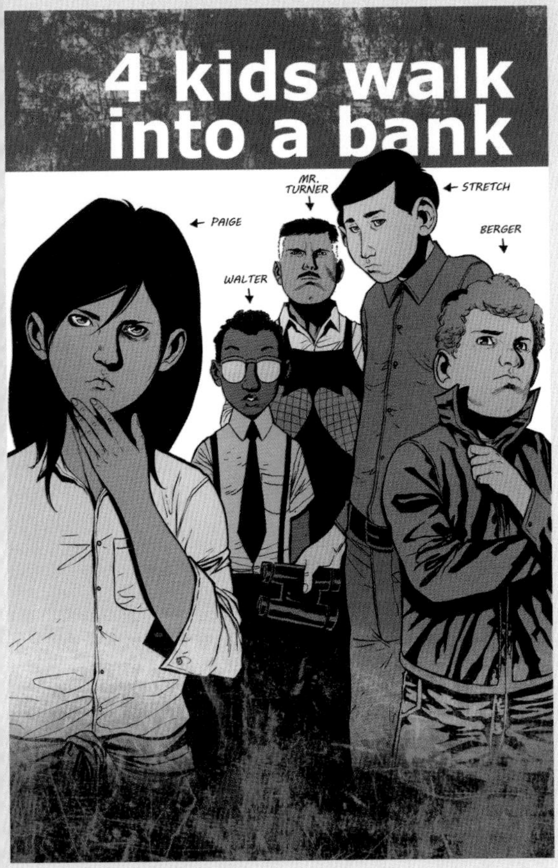
4 kids walk
into a bank
MR. TURNER
STRETCH
PAIGE
BERGER
WALTER

BY AMANCAY NAHUELPAN

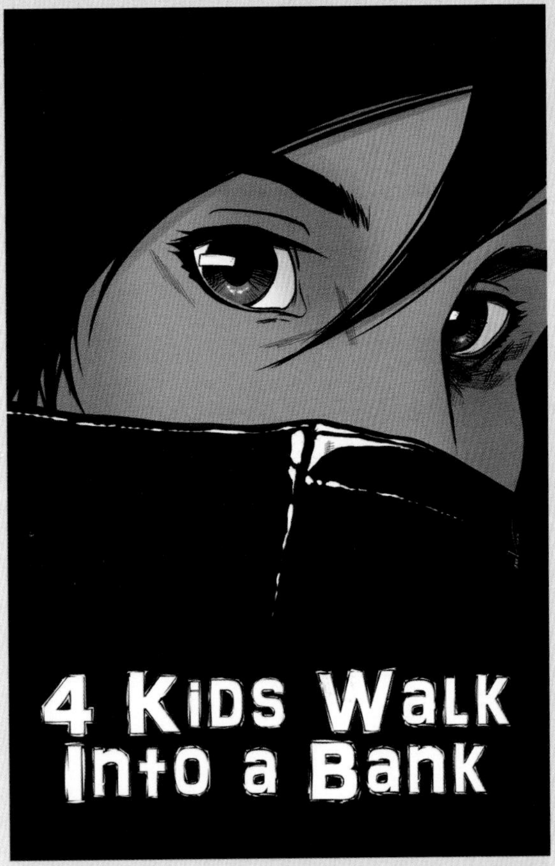
4 KIDS WALK
INTO A BANK

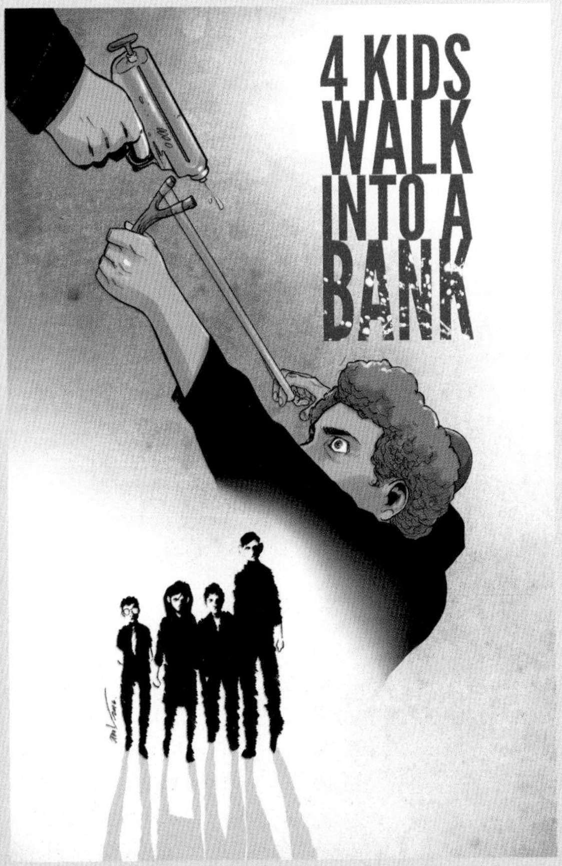
4 KIDS
WALK
INTO A
BANK

BY AMANCAY NAHUELPAN

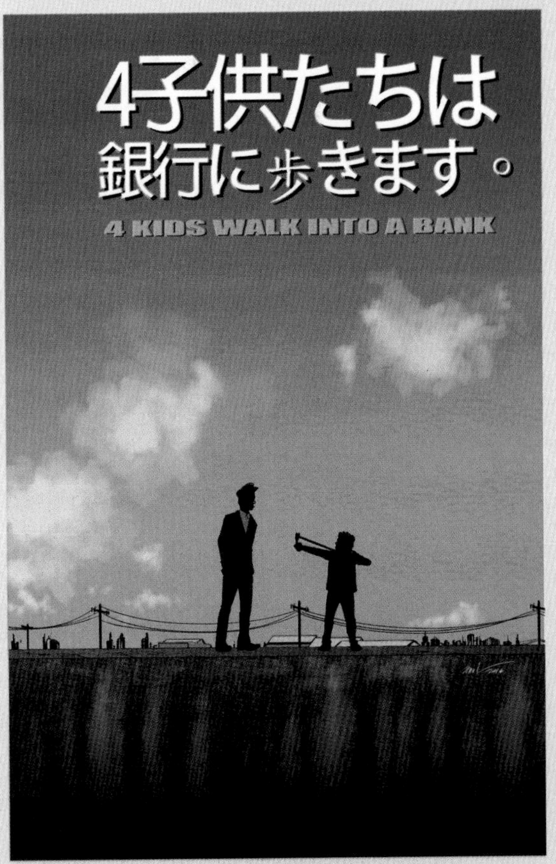
4子供たちは
銀行に歩きます。
4 KIDS WALK INTO A BANK

BY AMANCAY NAHUELPAN

BY AMANCAY NAHUELPAN

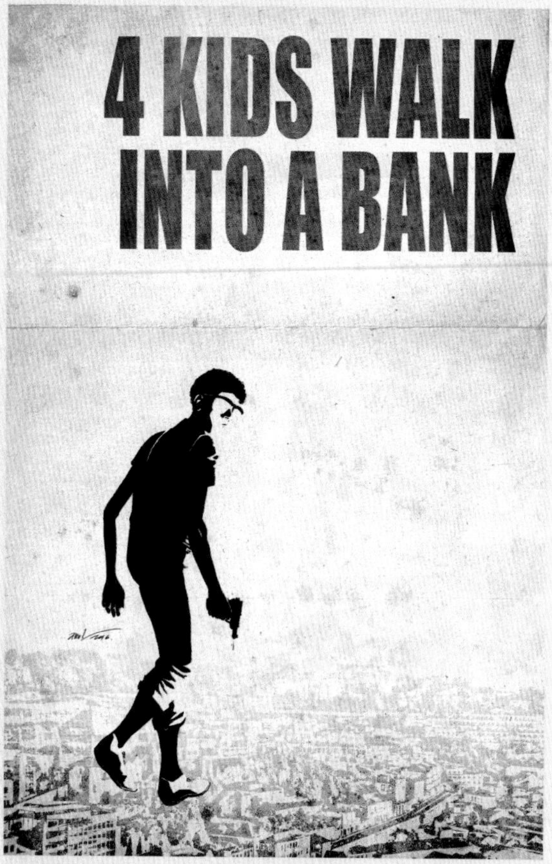
4 KIDS WALK
INTO A BANK

BY AMANCAY NAHUELPAN

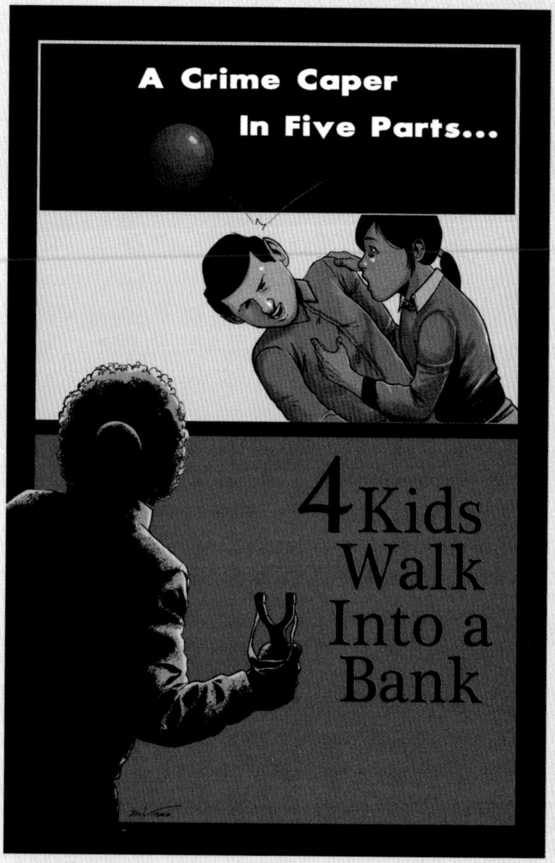
A Crime Caper
In Five Parts...
4 Kids Walk Into a Bank

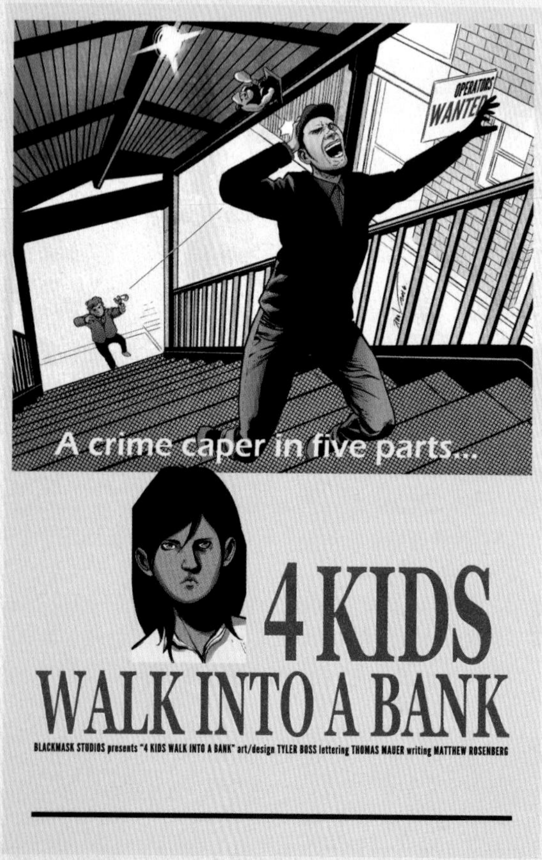
OPERATORS WANTED
A crime caper in five parts...
4 KIDS
WALK INTO A BANK
BLACKMASK STUDIOS presents "4 KIDS WALK INTO A BANK" art/design TYLER BOSS lettering THOMAS MAUER writing MATTHEW ROSENBERG

BY AMANCAY NAHUELPAN

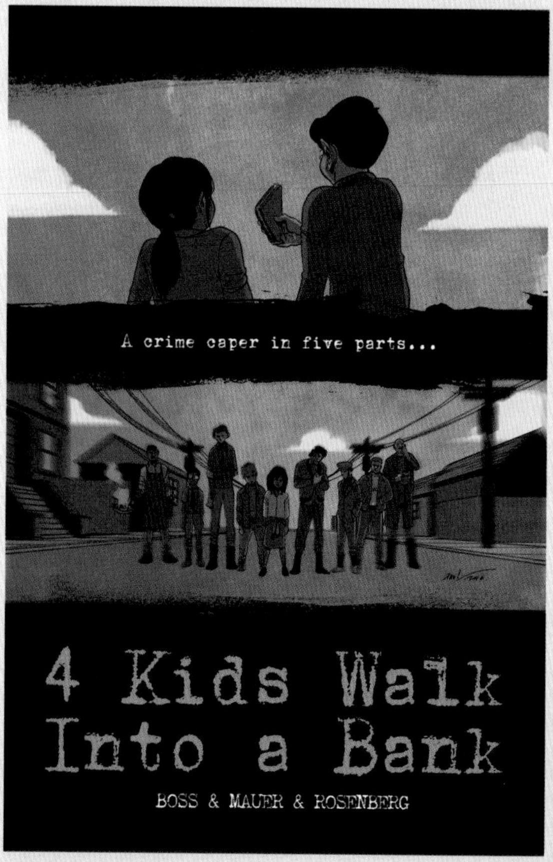
A crime caper in five parts...
4 Kids Walk
Into a Bank
BOSS & MAUER & ROSENBERG

BY AMANCAY NAHUELPAN

BY JOSH HOOD

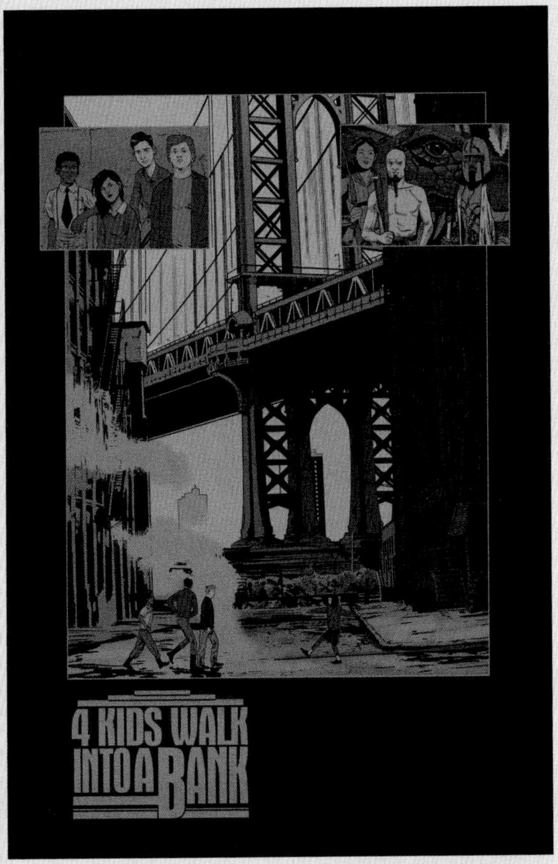
4 KIDS WALK INTO A BANK

BY JOSH HOOD

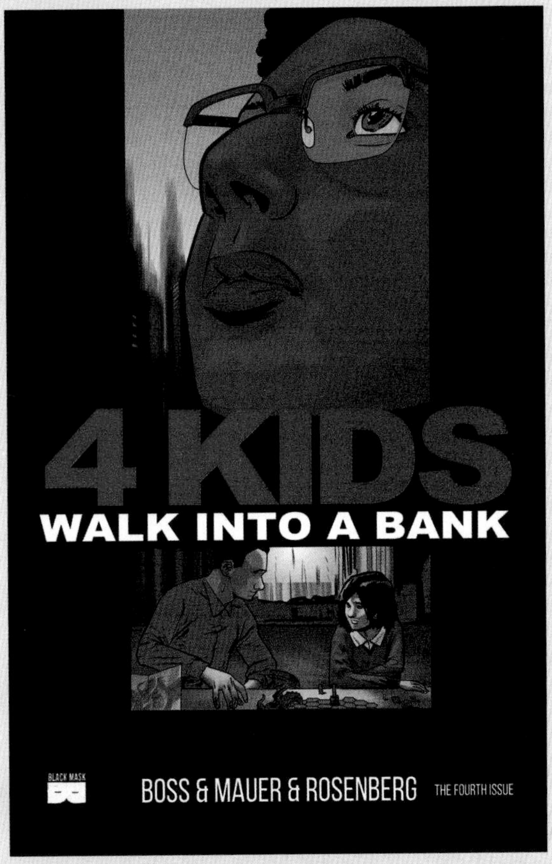
4 KIDS
WALK INTO A BANK
BLACK MASK
BOSS & MAUER & ROSENBERG
THE FOURTH ISSUE

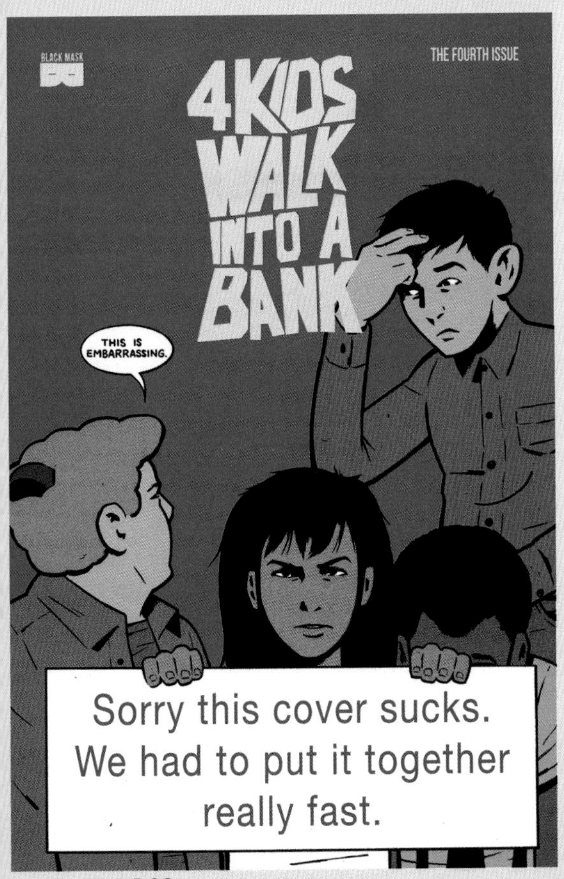
BLACK MASK
THE FOURTH ISSUE
4 KIDS WALK INTO A BANK
THIS IS EMBARRASSING.
Sorry this cover sucks. We had to put it together really fast.

BY TYLER BOSS

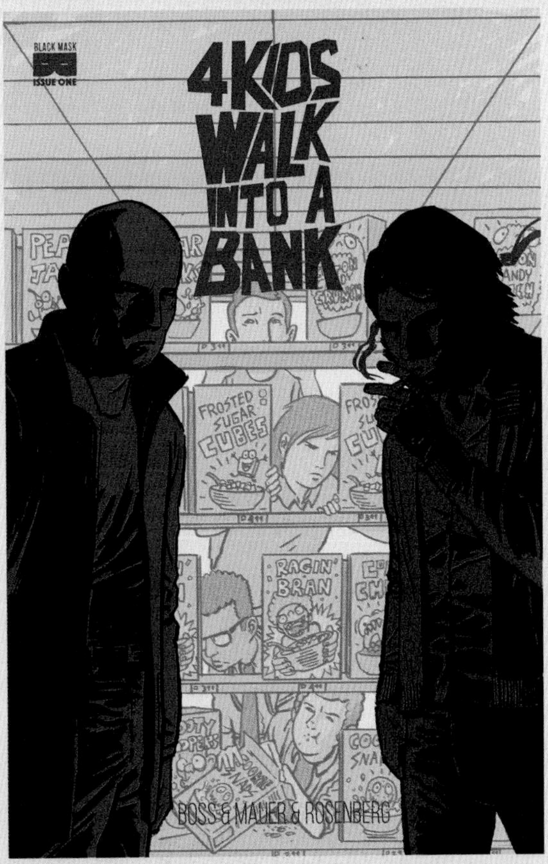
BLACK MASK
ISSUE ONE
4 KIDS WALK INTO A BANK
FROSTED SUGAR CUBES
RAGIN' BRAN
BOSS & MAUER & ROSENBERG

BY JOSH HIXSON

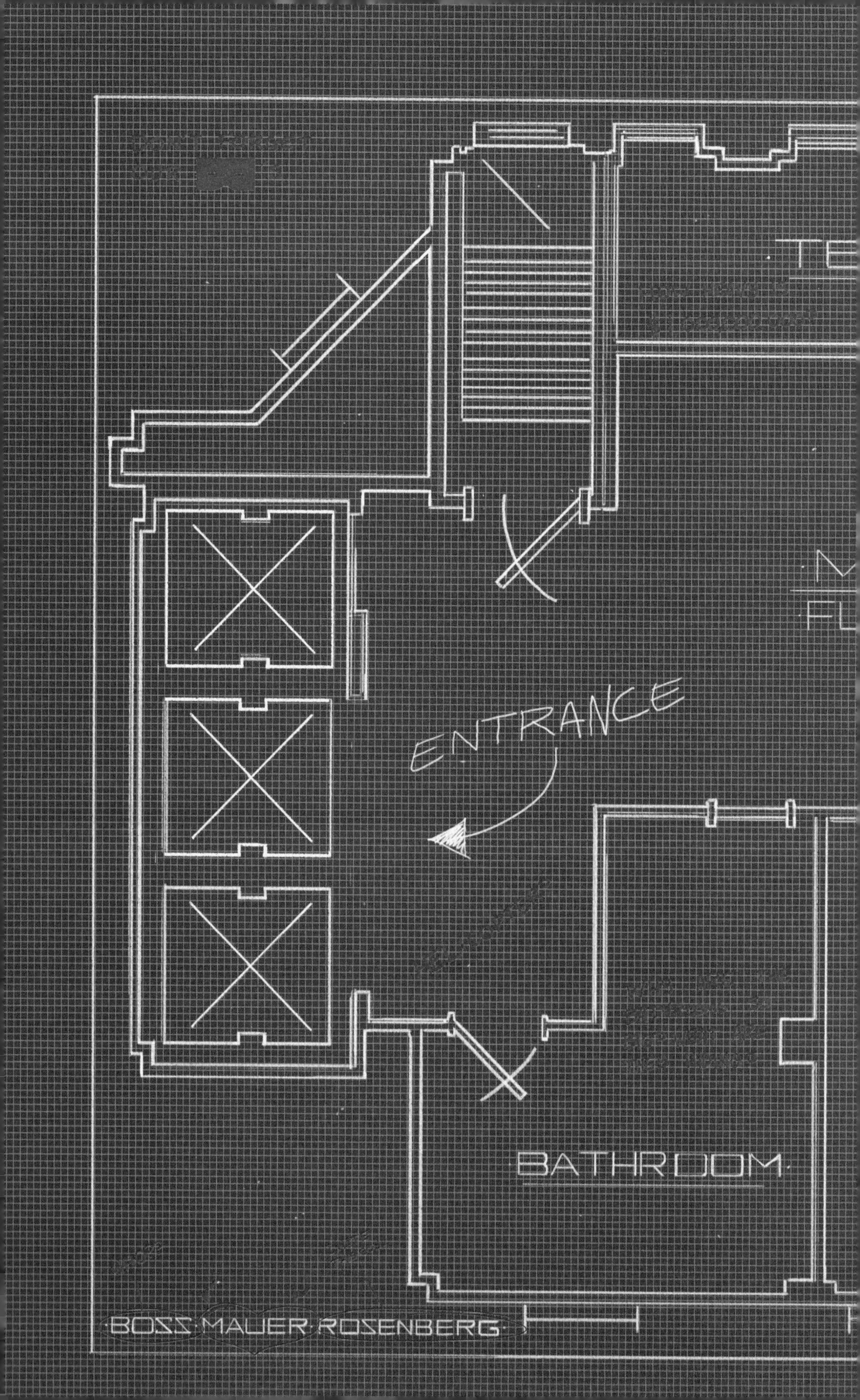
ENTRANCE
BATHROOM
BOSS·MAUER·ROSENBERG

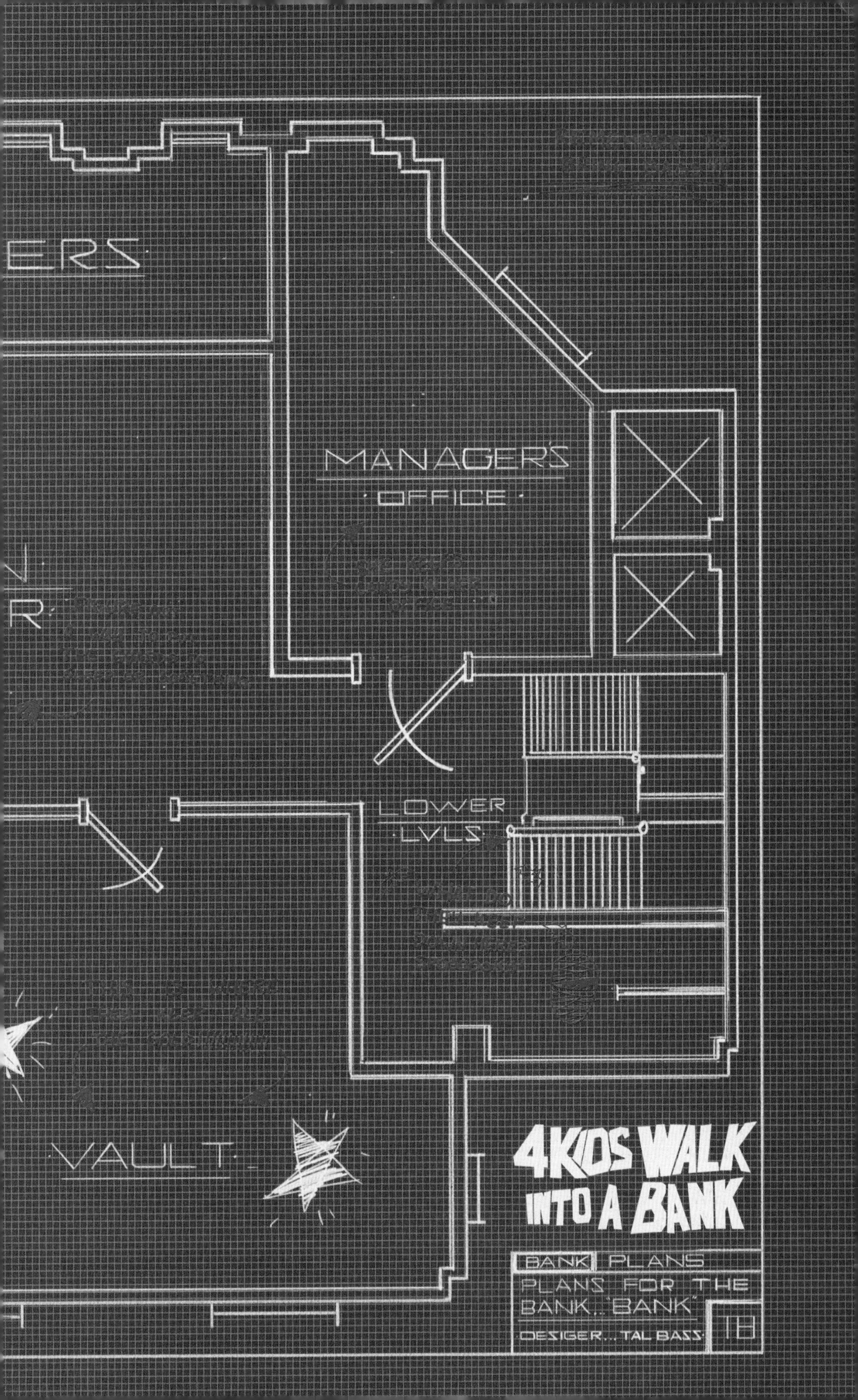
ERS
MANAGER'S
OFFICE
LOWER
LVLS
VAULT
4 KIDS WALK
INTO A BANK
BANK PLANS
PLANS FOR THE
BANK..."BANK"
DESIGER... TAL BASS

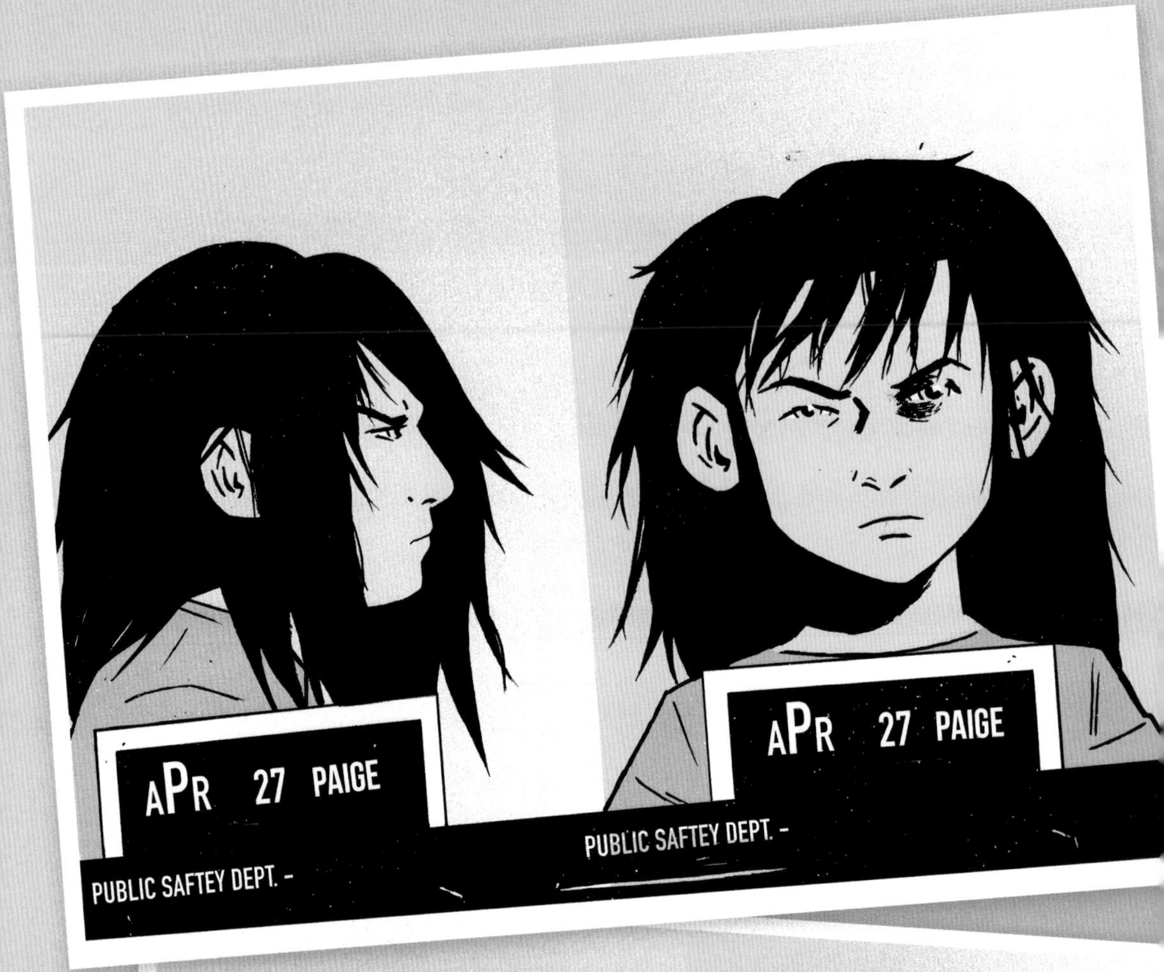
APR 27 PAIGE
PUBLIC SAFTEY DEPT. -
APR 27 PAIGE
PUBLIC SAFTEY DEPT. -

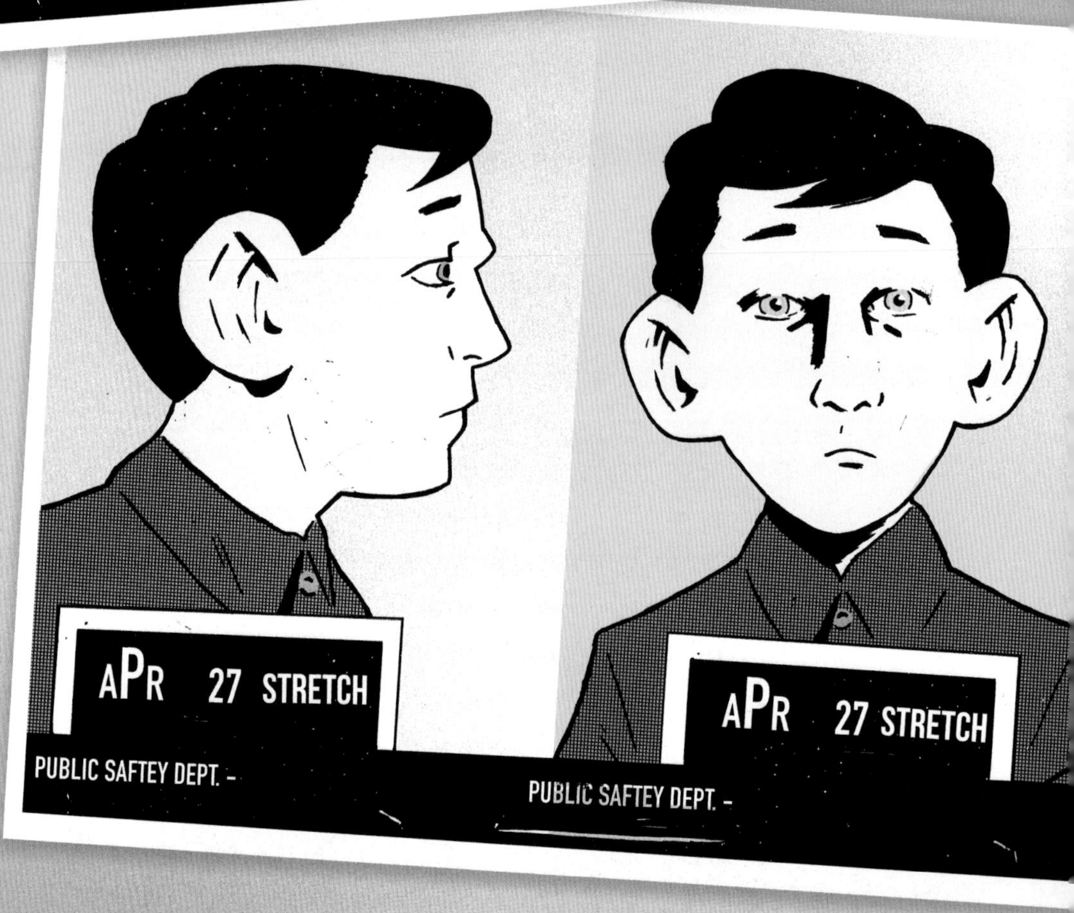
APR 27 STRETCH
PUBLIC SAFTEY DEPT. -
APR 27 STRETCH
PUBLIC SAFTEY DEPT. -

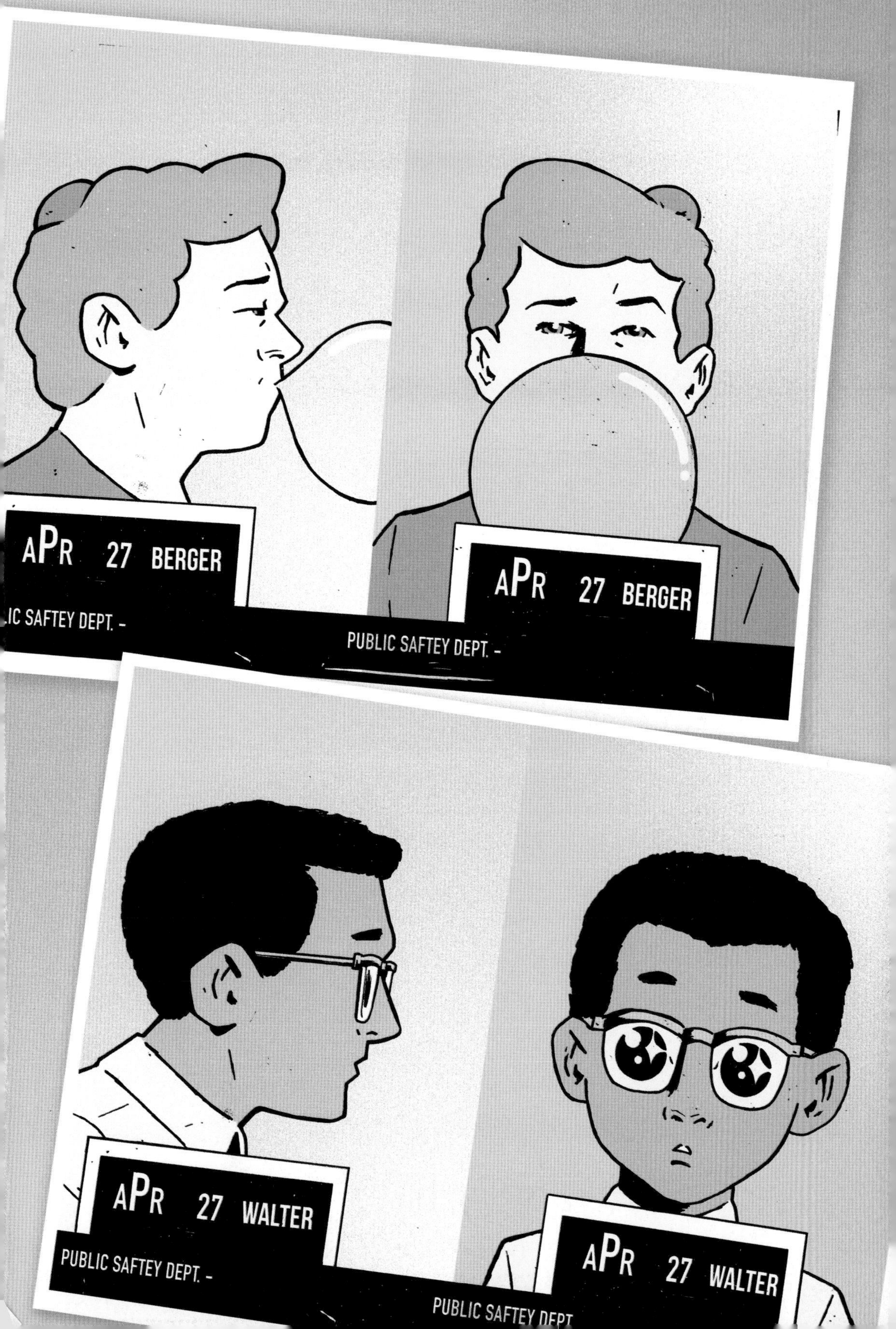
APR 27 BERGER
LIC SAFTEY DEPT. -
APR 27 BERGER
PUBLIC SAFTEY DEPT. -
APR 27 WALTER
PUBLIC SAFTEY DEPT. -
APR 27 WALTER
PUBLIC SAFTEY DEPT.

First Edition 2017 | Printed in Canada
10 9 8 7 6 5 4 3 2 1

For licensing information, contact: licensing@blackmaskstudios.com